"*... a bo*
remarkable
several times

MW01273151

~ The Reading Cafe

"*... the rewards will become obvious as you realize the immense capacity of this novice author to captivate you beyond measure.*"

~ M Jette

"*Second Lisa is an adventure in sensuality of the soul. The premise is intriguing, compelling, complex, and amazingly simple.*

This remarkable novel carries us on an astonishing trip through history, seen through many eyes, focussing always on the eyes of 'The Mona Lisa' as her spirit gazes from her prison on the wall of the Louvre.

I deducted a star for one picky reason. Knox's language and her understanding of humankind are masterful: but I know she has the ability to impose more control over the shape and direction of the work.

As a writer, I wish I could write as well as this. Read it for the experience."

~ L Alexander

SECOND LISA
book one

Library and Archives Canada Cataloguing in Publication

Knox, V., 1949-, author
    Second Lisa / Veronica Knox.

Originally published: Sooke, British Columbia : Silent K Publishing, 2012.
Issued in print and electronic formats.
ISBN 978-0-9877415-2-3 (pbk. : v. 1).--ISBN 978-0-9877415-3-0 (pbk. : v. 2).--
ISBN 978-0-9877415-4-7 (pbk. : v. 3).--ISBN 978-0-9877415-7-8 (ebook : v. 1).--
ISBN 978-0-9877415-8-5 (ebook : v. 2).--ISBN 978-0-9877415-9-2 (ebook : v. 3)

    I. Title.

PS8621.N695S43 2013   C813'.6   C2013-904007-2
                                                      C2013-904008-0

Editor: Linda Clement
Cover design: Veronica Knox
Cover photo: Terry Zlot – www.artboxvictoria.com
Cover formatting: Shania Sunga and Spica Book Design
Text formatting: Spica Book Design
First Edition
Printed in Canada
by Island Blue Printorium: Victoria, British Columbia

Silent K Publishing:
Victoria, British Columbia

Visit a gallery of images which support *Second Lisa* on the author's website:
www.secondlisa.org
www.blog.secondlisa.org
www.veronicaknox.com
e-mail: veronica@veronicaknox.com

SECOND LISA

art imitates life... life duplicates art... death goes on

book one

V Knox

silent

PUBLISHING

By the author:

'WOO WOO
– the Posthumous Love Story of
Miss Emily Carr'
www.woowoothenovel.com

'TWINTER
– the first portal'
www.twinter.wordpress.com

Soon to be published:

MONKEY SEE MONKEY DO
– an illustrated children's book for ages 6 to 9.
Artist Emily Carr's pet monkey,
Woo, teaches her own art class.

THE CHILDHOOD PILLOW

PASSENGER

THE UNFINISHED WOMAN

*for Sarah and David
and Pico*

Table of Contents

"Where shall I begin,
please your Majesty?" he asked.
"Begin at the beginning," the King said, gravely,
"and go on till you come to the end,
then stop."
~ Lewis Carroll

Out of Time
the author's up front last word

History repeats its selves;
synchronicity overrules chronology.
Fiction be told,
there's no tidy way to dream-travel
and tell this tale in order.
One must flow
with the quantum nature of time
and the memories of fractious ghosts,
and take erratic dictation.
The way it was, becomes an irregular echo
of the way it could have been.
Now or never – imagined whole
or in part.

~ Veronica Knox, May 2, 2013

SECOND LISA

book one

"Three things cannot be long hidden:
the sun, the moon, and the truth."
~ Buddha

The Varnished Truth

The Manor House of Cloux, Amboise, France
April – 1519

It was the spring of 1519 and my brother still believed he could fly. As for me... I assumed my death had been complete; we were always a pair of insatiable dreamers.

I sensed Leonardo's transition was only a matter of days away, and that liberation from my portrait was similarly at hand, but I had forgotten the impassioned wish I'd painted on heaven's door as if it was the mark of plague. ~ *Lisabetta*

The eyes of the 'Mona Lisa' are alive with memories and a new secret. From inside the painting, they follow the living with affection and compassion because waiting for a loved one to die is a peculiar mixture of guilt and relief.

Lisabetta had stopped aging after she died, but she calmly reflects how bizarre it is that the dead still have birthdays. Her portrait itself, is still a 'teenager' – painted seventeen years before when Leonardo had intended to abandon his paints forever, but had instead, in a burst of inspiration, immortalized his beloved sister forever.

For now, the innocent April when Lisabetta is 'forever fifty-years-old' and Leonardo turns sixty-seven, the French countryside of Amboise feels unbelievably sweet with the anticipation of heaven.

One only has to gaze into the eyes of a divine portrait to discover the undeniable truth – that a master artist can capture the soul of a subject.

But after the creative fusion of artist and muse is spent, only great art remains truly immortal.

Sometimes, however, it takes five-hundred years for the energy to cool. Some artists break all the rules.

After my death, I had been delighted to discover the ability to revisit my younger years with ease, and I indulged myself by celebrating the joys of my childhood, allowing them to eclipse the harsher years of poverty and abuse. I especially dared to imagine a blissful reunion with Sandro and the delight of seeing my daughter again, but most days I stayed focused on the task of keeping Leonardo happy. I bided where no time and all of time co-existed in a tapestry of memories and dreams.

In many ways, Leonardo had been my first mother, but after I turned eleven, I returned the favor by mothering Leonardo for the rest of his life.

Leonardo's last birthday prompted a spell of reminiscing within me. For his sixty-seventh year, my mind wandered as I lazed in my portrait's landscape, ruminating over the events of my own life.

Not surprisingly, the lies loomed larger than the truths, but I was never sure of the truth any-way; I had the knack of justifying everything I did for our success.

I remained beside Leonardo in spirit form, to honor our extraordinary bond. 'Till death parts us,' was a hollow sentiment while one of us still breathed; beyond death was simply a necessary extension of our mutual pact to companion each other always – in all ways.

I remember my death as if it were a continuation of the account my mother, Caterina, used to tell of my birth. Her 'storyteller' voice enthralled me with its emotional power. She could deliver a story whole, offering it like a precious jewel.

Caterina had been the first one to assure me that I was a special gift. Not from God – she was a non-believer when I was young, but as proof of love. She had wished on the stars for another love-child to come, and I was the fruit of that heartfelt hope.

Her desire for my true father, Ser Piero da Vinci, never waned, but I was a secret – the second child, of their forbidden union. Leonardo may have been relatively transparent to the da Vinci family for his first few years, but I was permanently invisible to them, and because the rest of the world only acknowledged me when I was persistent, I learned to use a woman's natural disguise of insignificance to my advantage.

Obscurity may be a double-edged gift, but to Leonardo, who had difficulty keeping his feet on the ground (literally as well as figuratively) I was always larger than life. He had wished for me too, and I came to believe that I had purposely been born in order to serve him.

Caterina taught me that an impassioned prayer carried power, and I made sure that I remained single-minded when I wished for anything. I never wished for small things; small things were easily accomplished through determination and cunning.

The shock of my death caused Leonardo to suffer a mild stroke – the first of three which left him increasingly disinclined to write or draw.

His young apprentice, Francesco Melzi (Cecco), was more like a devoted son than a pupil, and eventually he became Leonardo's secretary and body servant. With our care, Leonardo adapted and thrived by living evermore separate from reality in his inner world where he was most comfortable.

It had been an obvious choice for me to remain earthbound for Leonardo's sake – more like my maternal duty to turn my back on heaven and let its fragile portal close without me. Heaven would wait, I told myself, until Leonardo and I could leave together when his time came, and since I existed in a suspended state, it was not much of a hardship to endure a few years in-between worlds.

The 'Mona Lisa' painting made it easier for me to stay, acting as a bridge between my real invisibility and Leonardo's need to see me.

But reassuring Leonardo meant constantly pulling him away from the threshold of a grief that threatened to consume his joy for art and science. His immediate need eclipsed the call of my promising afterlife, no matter how tempting a prospect, but I never viewed this as self-sacrifice; it was love.

In his denial, Leonardo automatically substituted my portrait for the 'flesh-and-blood-me,' refusing to distinguish between the physical dimensions of life and the image he had painted of me. It became his habit to keep my likeness close, while I freely inhabited the land 'escapes' he had created for me.

Leonardo's small entourage of faithful followers humored this transference as another presentation of eccentric genius, but Cecco knew it was more serious. He knew it was the beginning of dementia – the next progression from Leonardo's productive episodes of creative instability.

For me, it had been a flawless transition to step beyond the physical boundaries of death into the realms of time between the living and the 'after-living.' Posthumous communication was natural.

I soon realized, that even in spirit, I could still experience inertia, and to dispel my over-sentimental reverie on that April birthday so long ago, I propelled both of us into the restorative sunshine of Amboise.

That Leonardo would be compelled to resist me was never in question; we played an ongoing game between us. I cajoled, Leonardo teased, and I always won – Leonardo deferred to my mothering out of habit and from the joy of pleasing me." ~ *Lisabetta*

"Perche la minesstra si fredda"
(the soup grows cold)
~ Leonardo da Vinci, 1519

Bella Veritas
Beauty & Truth

The Manor House of Cloux, Amboise, France
April 15 – 1519

April 15th is an auspicious day; brother and sister share the same date of birth, born in the heart of Tuscany – six years apart.

Across the room, Leonardo is too busy to notice his sister's wistful mood, but then, it was typically so; work is a blindfold to the everyday things of life when your name is Leonardo da Vinci.

Lisabetta is lured from her portrait towards the blue sky of the open window. She walks past Leonardo and his table strewn with papers, and his abandoned midday meal. Mathurine's 'soup-of-the-country' grows cold next to the old man intent on documenting the entire world.

The gargoyle on the roof outside Leonardo's bedroom window seems poised to leap at a passing sparrow hawk. Lisabetta looks out over its stone wings to the 'Leonardo Tree' below. From this vantage she is reminded that the scale of trees is irrelevant.

It was one of the first art lessons Leonardo had taught her. Together as children, they had gathered magical trees that fit into the palms of their hands, and studied the forms of the cloud trees that had towered over the Tuscan landscape.

Lisabetta is momentarily distracted by the figures of an unfamiliar woman and a boy moving diagonally across the lawn. Her eyes track them as they walk in a beeline for the main door until they disappear out of sight.

Behind her, Leonardo's pen scratches furiously at the design of a fountain for King Francis's new palace.

"Leonardo," Lisabetta announces abruptly, "it is time."

"Time?" he answers absentmindedly, "for my medicine?"

"Time to eat your soup... to breathe fresh air... to feel the sunshine... and to put down your pen," she says.

Leonardo responds with a smile, but he mischievously writes one more thing to vex her: *here I must stop because the minestrone grows cold.*

Leonardo's last stroke has puckered his left hand into a feeble paw which still allows him to sketch and write, but his paints have long been abandoned in favor of designing follies for the King of France.

It is unusually warm for April. Newborn bees test their wings in the sun, and Leonardo is persuaded to set aside his frantic scribbling and venture downstairs on Cecco's arm. Leonardo's Tuscan chair is carried ahead with blankets and silk pillows, and a tray of his favorite delicacies: a platter of marzipan pigs and Madagascar dates, and a blue majolica bowl filled with crystallized ginger.

The young bees serenade the first flowers beginning to blossom in the walled garden. Cecco chooses a perfect yellow rose from the adjacent conservatory, and tries to lure a fat bee onto it with a small net, but the bee is provoked into a frenzy until Lisabetta cups her hands around it and sets it gently onto the head of the flower. The calmed bee burrows contentedly into the petals and is transported to the front lawn, where Leonardo dozes in the half-sleep of old-age.

At sixty-seven, Leonardo projects the aura of an ancient magus ensconced on his wicker throne – an ordinary chair made from the reeds of the Vincio River near his birthplace. It's strategically placed in the shade of the great oak that Cecco dubbed the 'Leonardo Tree' – so named, the day of their arrival three years ago, at King Francis's pleasure. Leonardo had placed his hands on the tree and said he could feel a numinous energy within it. "Here is power," he had said, and claimed the oak as his.

Leonardo wears a violet skullcap, and a matching shawl. His legs are tucked snuggly under a regal coverlet embroidered with his own device: the monogram LDV worked into an elaborate Vinci knot. It is the same design that Cecco has engraved in the bark of the Leonardo Tree.

Leonardo sits like an emperor – a noble figure with flowing white beard, resting his chin on one gnarled fist, his lion-head cane gripped by the other, soaking up the magic.

Lisabetta runs ahead of Cecco and whispers to her sleeping brother: "Leonardo, I will be right back. Happy birthday."

"My Bella Veritas – our birthday, it is today?" he says, inside his dream.

"April 15th," she replies, as she kisses his cheek and hurries away.

Leonardo smiles, remembering the night Lisabetta was born and the stars that had sang to her. "I thought you would never come," he murmurs to himself and the image of the baby sister he once held in his arms.

Knowing Lisabetta will never leave him is his greatest comfort. "Don't be long. Ti voglio bene," he calls, after her.

"Moi aussi, je t'aime," Lisabetta calls back over her shoulder. "We are in France now."

"France?" Leonardo puzzles. Only this morning he had observed the familiar swan-shaped mountain near Vinci from his window, and ordered Zoroaster to check the new wings of the ornithopter. He had been testing the wind velocity. Cecco had even copied the latest calculations into his notebook. They were ready to try again. Even now, he was resting on the grass of Mt. Ceceri's eastern slope until the updrafts were stronger. Soon they would wake him and he would claim the sky.

"Monsieur Léonard," Cecco says with mock formality, addressing Leonardo by his French name.

He presents his fragile offering, lifting the net slowly. "You have a visitor," he says.

The bee remains settled. "Voila! Maestro, may I present a small admirer."

Leonardo is delighted to observe one of his favorite miracles of flight so closely, but the bee buzzes after Lisabetta, following her signature of violet perfume, in a disappearing trajectory of yellow and black.

Leonardo inhales the rose's fragrance and closes his eyes. "This yellow... I am reminded of a canary I once..." he starts, but his voice trails off at the sad memory. He looks lost. "Where is Rinato?" he asks.

"Maestro, Rinato was before my time. He has been gone for many years now, but the house dogs are near. Do you want me to bring one of them?"

"Rinato must be with Lisabetta," Leonardo says.

"Of course, Maestro, that must be where he is," Cecco replies.

Leonardo clutches the yellow rose tightly with his good hand and cuddles an invisible dog. "I've left Lisabetta too long," he says, and waves the flower like a scepter. "This is for her birthday," he says, and begs Cecco to take him and Rinato inside.

The Manor House of Cloux Amboise, France – May 2, 1519

Lisabetta is surprised to know that she has been dead eleven years. She surmises it from the trembling date, 1519, that Leonardo had scrawled in the margin of his notebook next to the words: 'di ieri di domani' – more than yesterday; less than tomorrow.

There had been signs over the past few weeks to indicate that Leonardo's death was imminent. Today, Lisabetta can see his form waver, translucent against the sky and the green lawn as he gathers the waxy clusters of lily-of-the-valley that shelter between the toes of his namesake tree.

Lisabetta believes a gentle heaven awaits her after Leonardo's death, and that the power of life *before* death, is all the authority one may possess. She looks forward to the joyous day of her brother's transition when she will teach him to fly. She had created her heaven for one – crafted it all her life, but after her death she had spent her time polishing it for four.

With the shiver of heaven so near, she and Leonardo had discussed it often with eager anticipation, but once, a thought had troubled Leonardo's aged face. "Rinato can come, yes?" It was the question of a child.

"Of course," she had said, "Rinato can come."

It is pleasant enough for Lisabetta to wait for Leonardo in the landscape he painted behind her. Lying under her stars, she is free to imagine her heaven somewhere overhead, waiting. From here she can turn her head and see Leonardo's bedroom window as a distant flickering light, but as she watches, the horizon flashes with silent colors, and the wind, stirring with the sound of a million agitated bees, begins to grumble with approaching thunder.

Lisabetta flies towards the bright square of the window, and hovers over the manor house crouched small against the storm. The skies above Cloux churn with anger. A raw streak of power sizzles night into day as an electric claw rakes the sky with white fingers. The 'Leonardo Tree' explodes into sparks.

Lisabetta listens for her brother's voice, but the thunderclap crackling with ozone, startles her.

Leonardo hears it too. She senses him stir within his sleep – roused enough to call out: "Lisa is that you?"

The hem of Lisabetta's borrowed dress ripples across a tapestry of Persian flowers in a cloud of emerald silk and rustles towards the old man in the canopied bed. "I am here," she says. "It's me... Lisabetta. Leonardo, I think it's time."

Lisabetta takes Leonardo's lifeless arm, and they walk towards the open window, but she remembers the painting beside the bed and tells him to go on without her. "I will be right back," she says. "I just want a word with Cecco."

Inside her portrait, Lisabetta looks out at the red and gold room and Francesco Melzi, the young man in attendance, dozing in a chair. She had recruited him for Leonardo, and now he is responsible for Leonardo's legacy and the future of the painting that had been her recent home.

Lisabetta's work is almost over. She notes the rich bedclothes and the fragile contours of the newly-abandoned human shell beneath them. She calls out excitedly: "Cecco, wake up! It is time. Leonardo is safe with me now."

Francesco startles from the sound of a loud crash within his dream where a dog had been barking excitedly. Furious rain pelts the window-pane as simultaneous thunderclaps and flashes of lightning shake the walls and panic the flames in the fireplace.

In Francesco's dream, a young boy had been shushing Joan of Arc, who brandished a square shield with great urgency. The shield had been painted with an image of her face. The dream had shown her, as the locals so often recounted, a young peasant girl sacrificed by fire. Francesco had been witnessing Joan's martyrdom – seen her face age inside the flames until her skin was covered in fine cracks. A crowd had hung her shield over an altar as a religious icon and were worshipping her as a saint, scattering violets at her feet.

Francesco experiences the anxiety of the dog as his own.

The voice in his head is insistent: "Take the 'Mona Lisa' to the king."

"Maestro, did you call?"

The 'Mona Lisa' lies face down on the floor. Still disoriented, Francesco places the painting back on the easel. Leonardo must have reached for her again.

'Strange,' he thought; he'd just been dreaming about it.

For five-hundred-years, Lisabetta will remember clearly, the midnight window that hangs like a painting on the far wall. She smiles at the transparent form of her brother, no longer an old man of sixty-seven, but as he used to be when he was her twelve-year-old hero, standing now with his back to her, gazing spellbound at a shimmering vista of the Loire Valley. He holds their scrawny terrier, Rinato, over his shoulder, and Lisabetta struggles in vain against the varnish to rejoin them: "Don't leave me. Wait!" she calls into the drone of bees humming.

Leonardo, replies still faced away from her, distressed: "Come out crazy girl and be quiet or he will hear you and come back."

The last thing Lisabetta sees is the eyes of the animal which plead with her to follow as boy and dog are pulled into a blue flash and disappear into the night sky like stars returning home.

Since her death, Lisabetta had moved freely across the threshold of her portrait in response to Leonardo's every summons, loyal to his need, but now he abandons her like all the rest. Leonardo had been the only one with the power to call her out, and a disturbing new thought overwhelms her. Perhaps she had been wrong. Maybe there was a god after all, and what if that god was just another man?

The MUSÉE du LOUVRE – Paris
April 15, 2007

You would think one of the museum cleaning staff would use their unique opportunity to examine the art close-up, but they mop the floors as if they're sweeping straw from a hovel. It's a job. Ashes to ashes – broom to broom. The same dust lands on treasures and ancient litter alike, and heaven knows enough archaeological detritus lies pristine under-glass as privileged carbon-dated memories, no less valuable than diamonds displayed in a jeweler's showcase.

The Salle des Etats is the first salon to be cleaned and the last to open. April filters through a decorative row of lattice bars set deep into the high windows along its east wall. Inside the gallery, the 'Mona Lisa' broods behind an impenetrable curtain of transparent steel. Inside the painting, Lisabetta frets under an assumed name. Nearly five-hundred-years of captivity and her four-hundred-ninety-ninth birthday, seems penance enough for a crime she can't recall committing.

All she wants, is to reach her heaven – the personal heaven she created worth dying for. It's a humble enough appeal to make of an abundant universe, but dreaming too small is unworthy of an artist, and she had been nothing if not that.

When she does dream, it's always the same: first the choking fire and an expanse of blue sky, then a dusty road beneath her feet, and she is running, running … flying down the road to Fiesole towards 'Mt. Ceceri – the Great Swan.' What follows is a sea of faces in a church, where she's a saint offering communion from behind a silver altar, but the people's mouths are closed and she has nothing to place on their tongues but fame, and all she can do is smile beatifically and try to wake up.

Lisabetta slips from her baroque frame and takes a turn about the gallery to study her companions for signs of habitation. The absence of visitors feels eerie, but the din of life will begin soon enough. She dances full circle about the room and comes to a stop, facing her portrait like a mirror, and melts into the Tuscan fields behind her patient smile. The months it took for her brother, Leonardo, to paint her had been a revelation. She had been forty-five then.

Lisabetta rests inside her painting, beside the track leading to Anchiano, and breathes in the sunshine of early spring – a renaissance Cinderella at the stroke of dawn, with her dress restored to emerald green and her hair returned to its natural shade of honey, plaited in a single braid.

She wonders if Leonardo will ever arrive to release her like one of his caged birds. Leonardo once had the strength to bend metal bars with his hands, almost as well as he manipulated the laws of science and tamed the forbidden powers of alchemy. His ingenuity could easily confound a crystal wall and the current laws of detention. She is sure Leonardo would rescue her if he could.

If only wishing made it so.

The MUSÉE du LOUVRE – Paris
April 1, 2008

It's right there in the Louvre's guidebook: portrait of Lisa del Giocondo, first floor, Denon Wing, Room 6, Salle des États – the 'Mona Lisa.'

What mortal would argue with the printed word or the French Republic? In French she is 'La Joconde'; in Italian: 'La Gioconda' – the laughing woman. She is the pun, the twist of fate – the sainted name of a resident Queen.

There are times Lisabetta feels that the museum has been built for her alone and that the other works of art are her courtiers. She reigns in an emotional palace, enchanted under the terrors of magic – faerie glamour thrown over her destiny evaporates her history in a spell of protection gone awry.

But the fates still bend to her subconscious wishes: the fame and eternal life, and the elegant reckonings with her enemies as she once numbered them.

Lisabetta had been clear when she planned her heaven, desirous of being surrounded by paintings and sculpture. Her temple beyond death must be palatial to compensate for a life spent in cottages and cramped studios. She asks for large airy rooms full of art where she will hold court, with her days of invisible servitude over. In her most intensive daydreams, Lisabetta envisions herself the center of attention, for once she will be an iconic lady, beset and acknowledged by admirers, celebrated by poets and kings – the equal of her illustrious brother. A principessa in her own right.

It is oppressive in the open space of the Salle des Etats. Lisabetta is restless as a caged tiger. It's a day of opposites: dull yet expectant – stifling without heat. Listless air fidgets in dry whorls and flaps into the corners of the ceiling like disturbed bats. The gallery holds her in a psychic vacuum. Today she is an exhibit rather than the star of a show. Her audience is reserved. No... transparent. They're fading out, or she is. Vibrating too slow. Their voices speak in undertones enveloped in fog, and Lisabetta craves distance where she can breathe back the spirit of her Italian sunshine.

Lisabetta hitches up her green skirt and scrambles up the steep rocks. A cloud of kites screech her up the last few feet to their eyrie. Her determination sends a crumble of stones behind her in a gentle avalanche. The toes of her shoes remain un-scuffed, but Leonardo's veiled sun scorches her hair until she reaches a familiar plateau where she rolls into the shade. From here, she can view the full extent of her past, melting into the earth and grasses, camouflaged by the colors of nature as Leonardo had intended.

A trickle of water leaves a brown trail of minerals from a fissure high above in the face of the cliff, and Lisabetta makes a cup with her hands that interrupt the water's journey towards a natural basin of stone lined with moss. The lip of the basin is dry. She strokes its emerald velvet with fondness – this is Leonardo's fanciful forest of miniature trees. It's a grand memory. One that she hopes will stir others to uncover a way home – home being a heaven she's glimpsed only once, rather than a sterile museum.

Lisabetta's base camp is the place where a windbreak of gorse forms a human-sized amphitheatre. Inside the curve of it, the mountain has made her a blanket of thatch and fern, woven by the wind and plumped into a cradle between the crevices. She settles down and closes her eyes to concentrate and tries to evoke the help of her brother, the master of this illusion. "Leonardo Leonardo Leonardo," she intones, three times for luck.

Lisabetta draws down the mists clinging to the mountain peaks – Leonardo's gauzy curtains of seclusion that turn landscapes into land escapes, to put more distance between the Louvre's intensity and her need for retreat. Her brother's disposition and his frequent need for sanctuary had mirrored his observations of nature's moodiness: damp wind and smoky rain and the heat rising from sun-baked stone. He had taught Lisabetta to surrender to the alchemy of weather for inspiration. His muses were hers. 'Elemental answers wait inside torrential storms of nature and emotion for the patient artist,' he had said.

Leonardo had relaxed behind his screens – free to write and dream blasphemous ideas, dabbling with forbidden science, safely unobserved. His need to hide reflected a dangerous privacy.

Nature protected its own. Leonardo understood a town's need for walls and a hill's need for solitude, and that an owl's eggs begged invisible nests for survival no less than bear cubs evaporated into the depths of a secluded cave. Horizons were compassionate places blanketed by mystery where anything was possible.

Leonardo's ferocious melancholies had been comfortably masked by Lisabetta's administrations.

His imagination had been the safest space for truth to flourish. Many times, Leonardo had disappeared on trips into wilderness like Lisabetta's in order to insulate himself from the church and superstition, as well as bill collectors and public humiliation. Rebels need mountain hideaways to plot revolutions, and Leonardo was as passive a rebel as Lisabetta was an aggressive mediator.

Leonardo also told her that secrets had a chance to take root inside a storm. He could dream there, in its eye. Lisabetta hoped to meet him by chance, one day in her hills, testing the updrafts and measuring the degrees of opaqueness between seasonal miles of air. Perhaps copying illusions into his notebook, or scribbling occult dreams backwards in code.

Sometimes, Lisabetta sees Leonardo on a far-off hill, with his back against an oak, or under the arch of the bridge below, sketching the eddies of water from stones sent into the river by his own hand. But never any closer, and she has come to feel grateful to see him at all. Often, Rinato accompanies him – a small white energy darting like a butterfly over the grass. Depending on Leonardo's age, his owl, Lydia, is with him – a small cloud hovering over her master, and a tiny flutter of canary yellow perches on his sleeve.

This is Lisabetta's country. Her's and Leonardo's. It's delightful, but it isn't heaven. Leonardo would live large in her heaven, and Sandro and Leona would be there, along with her old zoo: her pony, Stella; dogs, Rinato and Giallo; and Picolini and Simonetta with countless generations of their feline offspring.

Behind her eyes, Lisabetta trails out the played scenes of her life. Lily pads of time form rows like the words in a story. Carefully preserved experiences are counted as ripples of light: a wing here; a shadow following. Receding voices disappear like running feet, but she is the guilty center of the world, and not far from this spot, she is still a jumpy thread of posthumous nerves who resides in a museum room wound tight with adoration and disappointment.

She is determined to rake her years for a lost clue. Any signpost is welcome if it points towards atonement. Lisabetta willingly revisits her scenes of misconduct, but none appear vile enough to warrant her unworthiness to fully die. No stray curse shows its teeth. No echoes of voices fly back that could injure a reputation. But she waits – something will come, and it arrives as the sound of her own laughter and horses clopping towards the horizon. Rinato's faint bark chases the currents of the Vincio River while her sisters harvest the whispering reeds and silence them into bundles for weaving baskets. It must be September.

Lisabetta examines the consequences of her actions like a scientist – the way Leonardo taught her, but on kinder days she encourages a passing fragrance to linger for entertainment. There were the sweet hours in the studio when Leonardo chided her for her rainbow fingers. His need for spotless sleeves and hands had been meant to inspire discipline. No, there was no malice there, nor was there in her mother's objections to her five-year-old daughter's prattling of escape during the days she shadowed Leonardo like a hungry cat. These were harmless criticisms given with affection.

Lisabetta strains for muffled gossip and digests her shames that howl like circling wolves. She waves fire at their retreating tails when they slink away for easier prey. Often she disturbs the old scented-days, spent under magic, thirsting for art and love, and these drift by like pale swans and make her smile. Once an amber brooch shone on her palm with an innocent bronze key to nothing in particular that she could remember. Once she had been in a room lined with books and seen her portrait lying on a table without its frame. A girl had been sleeping beside it, and Lisabetta had thought it was herself, but the clothes the girl wore were those of a boy.

By contrast, fragile experiments of pain wait in line – each small betrayal counted on young fingers. Childhood innocence dances in circles with expectation, and lastly, the most exquisite dreams: the first blossoming of dizzying arousal, desiring beyond its capacity to survive a missed kiss. Especially the emotional tugs later – the 'days-after' sort of life that show themselves like shy strangers. There's a rumpled bed, abandoned with rouge on the sheets. Lisabetta smooth's the covers, and places a primrose over the stain. She rises again, above the penalties of forbidden honey – the old days spent in moist pursuit for more of love's dry heat and the lightning drench of bittersweet relief. And she muses over the enchantments and promises of more – the possibilities of rubies against green silk and white fur – and success.

Lisabetta combs her mistakes but can find none tainted sufficiently with enough sin to be cheated from heaven. Her savage exile remains a mystery. Left-brain investigation is useless against suppressed memories and right-brain victories are often disasters in disguise. To err is human, to create – divine.

Lisabetta resurfaces from recounting a list of failed strategies, dazzled by a vision of sunlight caressing a stone pig in 1504 – the time she had called down a sainted energy and frightened herself. An overwhelming feeling of anger at the unfairness of life accompanies the memory. It had been a sweltering day in the market of Florence.

The city's mascot, an ancient statue of a female boar, basks in the oppressive heat. Like all Florentines, Lisabetta has made casual wishes on its nose many times, but today is different. Today she communes like a priestess before making her request.

The moment feels suspended, lived outside the commotion of the market as if she is alone with the statue. As the chaos of the square subsides around her, Lisabetta places her hands on either side of the sow's snout and examines its tiny eyes for signs of life.

The fervent desires that Lisabetta pours into the soul of the pig thrash together in a wild stream of bitterness, tumbling over each other, drowning, gasping for air. Each wish is a small perfect curse, a pebble tossed into the feverish currents of a jealous river. For a moment there is silence, but when the pig answers yes three times, quite audibly inside her head, Lisabetta pulls her hands from it as if scalded and bolts from the piazza. She hurries, tripping over the barrels and baskets, through the filth of the market stalls, skirting hungry dogs and the hungrier street urchins who collect in small gangs.

At the corner of the Campanile, Lisabetta stops and wipes her hands together to rub off the hot magic. She checks them for blisters, but her hands are unblemished and she chides herself for over-imagination.

The strain of several sleepless nights, the fierce Tuscan sun, and an emotional outburst has made her ill, and the scorching skin of the marble pig has only seemed to sear her like fire. She tries to reassure herself this is the truth, but she knows it for a lie. She had been angry and the stone-meat had been warm to the touch, but not excessively so, and she had felt her rage leave, absorbed by the statue. For a brief moment her hands had felt stuck, and then a jolt of lightning entered her body through them and she had a vision of flames engulfing her. She must shelter from the sun and rest, and most of all she must forget this incident and the ugly business earlier with Lisa Giocondo.

A quick glance confirms her panic has gone unobserved, but when Lisabetta lurches on she can feel the snuffling breath of a grinning pig on the calves of her legs, and she slows to glance over her shoulder half-expecting to see a lumbering, snorting beast in pursuit. She stumbles on past pens of squawking poultry, unnerved, distracted by the stink and grunts of porcine livestock louder than their marble mother in the market square.

Lisabetta only slows to a walk after she reaches the shady side of the Medici palace – a safe distance from the imagined miracle. The palace walls are a soothing touchstone; their rough surface grounds her. She scolds herself; she doesn't believe in miracles. She is the victim of a bizarre hallucination delivered by an unforgiving sun, and even now a bright pain is forming behind her eyes – nothing more.

The Via Ghibellina rests slightly cooler under a welcome blanket of violet shadow, but a shard of bright sunlight stabs Lisabetta's left eye when she turns the corner and glances up at the sky. She flinches and vomits into the street. Lisabetta's feet stretch towards the quiet interior of Leonardo's studio.

A flushed Lisabetta rushes past Leonardo, working at a long table. "Bring lemons," she says, not stopping, "I need your help." The back room is quiet. Lisabetta splashes water on her face, closes the shutters and collapses onto a straw pallet.

Leonardo is concerned. He follows and places a cool compress on his sister's forehead. The silence and the scent of lemon peel restores her. Leonardo hears Lisabetta mutter something about a pig, and after she falls asleep, he returns to his maps and calendars for their latest escape route – retreating and escaping have become their specialty.

⁓

Lisabetta is momentarily puzzled; this memory feels more significant; it's brighter than the others. She feels the quickening of intuition. It had taken three days to sufficiently shake off the disturbing dream of a statue squealing with laughter. She will give the memory more time to speak. Test it against a reawakening sense of awareness.

There is no revoking a wish made like a demand, but there are domino amendments. Only a second wish may soften the first, especially when other powerful creators are involved. Divine comeuppance is the ultimate system of poetic justice and there are synchronicities at stake. Wishing too big lacks humility, but Lisabetta had learned that wishing too small was an admission of weakness.

No matter, Lisabetta of the Louvre painting, remembers making a wish, and wishing is a form of prayer ... and when in trouble, any statue is a saint if it can reach the ears of power.

Lisabetta doesn't know why she intuits the significance of 2008. She senses a light around the year marking her fifth centenary of captivity. The only certainty, is that the true face of things to come, stretches forward without end as either a rebirth or continued detention in sterility. Her latest plan is elegant: a simple historical correction. No more 'eye-for-an-eye,' but a name for a name.

But an academic takeover requires corporeal intervention, and Lisabetta spends three months scanning her visitors for a scholar sensitive enough to see her. Three truths plague her: wishes are trouble, intensity sabotages the best intentions, and emotions are the toughest jailors. In two weeks she will be five-hundred-years-old in life years, and today has heard her visitors exclaim today is April Fool's day.

Immediately below the Salle des Etats, where four stone arches meet in a vaulted dome, Lisabetta's market pig, sits on a pedestal and shivers with power. Its museum plaque reads:

The market pig from the city of Florence -1300 A.D. – a marble copy of an original Hellenistic statue, circa – 350 BC, now lost.

Lisabetta and her 'Il Porcellino,' have been apart yet together, under the same French roof – disconnected, dreaming the same dream for five-hundred-years.

Less than four-hundred-miles from Paris, a forgotten cache of appropriated art, lies at the end of a mile of tunnels in a network of underground caves. Near the back wall, under a natural vault of limestone, is the original statue of a boar – a Greek marble, thousands of years old. It's wrapped like a mummy, muffled in unbleached linen, and sealed in plastic bubble-wrap, which attests to its most recent move, in 1952.

This is to be its last sighting.

The depository marks the end of a long line of possession. There were times when the priceless sculptures had been celebrated in the shade of private loggias, but mostly, they have been cloistered in secret rooms and private galleries, unwaveringly stoic, and now consigned to a stone womb in the earth.

And so, a pharaoh's tomb of classic sculpture passes covertly from archaeologists, antiquities dealers, museum employees, and desperate relatives, to patrons with questionable scruples and their relentless urge to claim, conserve, hoard, and possess.

The priceless objects have been hidden in a relentless journey, through political wars, family disputes, revolutions, and human greed, until their provenance is deliberately confused beyond all accounting.

Finally, they're shifted to lower ground, for safe-keeping – a delightful subterranean sculpture garden: stashed, catalogued, secret, and invisible. Acquisitions too famous to be acknowledged – kept safe from being repossessed by countries with long memories.

It remains a private collection. More than private now, since the demise of its last heir, who has perished in a freak fire along with his documents: letters, maps, photographs, and catalogues. Its line of patrons, who once boasted diplomatic access to the corridors of the Louvre is now extinct. Whereabouts unknown.

The ancient pig once ruled the old mercato of Florence – until it was unceremoniously usurped by a bronze impersonator, in 1612, appropriated from the Louvre's museum cousin, the Uffizi, and laundered through the great houses of Europe into private hands.

The antiquities, and several relatively youthful works from the sixteenth century: fragments of a giant horse and a sleeping cupid, both circa 1500, wait for a new champion. The arms of the 'Venus di Milo,' several Parthenon marbles, a flawless statue of Hatshepsut from the temple of Deir el-Bahri, the head of the 'Nike of Samothrace,' and the original 'Il Porcellina,' considered lost for two-thousand years, slumber in hermetic stasis.

Il Porcellina's youngest sister, missing since 1552, survivor of the Uffizi fire of 1762, and pig-napped thirty-seven years later in a French raid, sends its venerable matriarch a message: "I think it's time."

The original pig had been replicated under the watchful eyes of the creator of the 'Nike of Samothrace.' Its energy is doubled by each clone with the elegance of homeopathic math. One pig reaches the marketplace of Florence; its twin is buried in rubble for centuries and unearthed during the reign of modern archaeology. The genealogy of art remains: copies of copies of copies.

Lisabetta surrenders to the year 2008 with three months lost and distracts herself with long excursions into the mountains Leonardo painted for her pleasure. Her agitation subsides within the furthest reaches of her landscape until the buzzing of bees informs her it's time to return to the April gallery. The room drones with its usual humanity, and Lisabetta is about to abandon her post and retreat once more down the track behind her, when she feels the air in the Salle des Etats quicken. The doors blow open and what arrives is a revelation.

Time is no respecter of chronological order after one ceases to breathe above ground, and the shock transports Lisabetta to 1464 when she first understood her capacity to hate. Two things are immediately apparent: an ordinary day may bring a surprise, and the dead can still experience amazement.

Rinato's warning bark tapers into a nervous whine beside her, and Lisabetta is once again a girl of six, eclipsed by the shadow of a predator she vows to destroy. "A couple of mongrels," her father says unkindly with a kicking motion towards the dog, and as Lisabetta blocks his sport, his boot impacts her forehead in a star of pain. The loathing she feels alters her view of men and God, and her desire for power – power over them, and in spite of them.

The Louvre – April 1, 2008

A woman and a boy entered my gallery bringing a corridor of light with them. They emerged from it, and stepped into my salon. It trailed behind them and flattened into a wide ribbon, and I knew these two visitors were the ones I'd been hoping for.

When I stepped onto their shimmering carpet, it turned into a vaporous hallway where I could see lateral time expressed with two vanishing points. One direction led to the past, the other, I presumed, to heaven. The entire length of its walls were inscribed with a continuous math proof that extended either side of where I stood.

The three of us walked on an endless strip of colored light in the vibration named yellow. Ahead, the spectrum stretched green and blue towards a distant glow of violet. Behind us, the floor reached out to orange, pink, and red, and on to the same shining wave of violet.

It felt warm there, as one would imagine yellow to feel, like being outside on a perfect day. The air changed to a delightful breeze of sunlight infused with ozone. It was familiar, and whenever I stepped outside it, the tunnel flattened again to a path, and the atmosphere in the salon appeared stale and grey.

Infinitely thin strands of light in the same bands of fluctuating colors threaded their way into the navels of each person in the room, connecting them. Other filaments changed into gentle sparks that flashed from forehead-to-forehead, and wrists-to-knees, in dazzling arcs woven into a network of light. The firework display dissipated slightly, but remained as a soft humming sound.

An aurora of shifting colors ran down each strand, and the crowd became a hundred marionettes performing without tangles. Their strings passed, uninterrupted through each other – a ballet of light beams energized into an abstract painting of wriggling lines that writhed with vitality, until the room was reduced to a multi-layered image of squirming animation.

The bright lines became so dense it was impossible to see through them, and I floated there, suspended, enjoying the view, similar to swimming under water in an ocean teeming with life.

I imagined the earth as a spinning pulsating, ball of string. One continuous string made of light, that wove into tapestries of painted panels – each a portrait or landscape with no images to trace their formless energy of vibrating colors.

Somewhere, on the far side of the moon, I knew the eternity of colors would collide into a white beam. They would unite, not in darkness, but emblazoned as the incarnation of pure light, and join violet-to-violet, forming a circle like the mystic Ouroborus (the snake eating its own tail) so luminous, as to make an artist weep.

The panels swirled into a flock of paintings

and adhered themselves to the walls of the Salle des Etats, once more a bustling throng of visitors surrounded by art, with two individuals towing a mystic road still begging me to follow.

Veronica and Jupiter Lyons were a blast of freedom, and I danced around them creating a vortex from our energies, but Veronica looked through my real face to stare at my portrait. Once again I was eclipsed by celebrity and suffered the frustrating experience of being studied intently and completely overlooked at the same time, but her son, Jupiter, smiled hello. I assumed that mother and child, were my passport home.

What I understood was primal knowing. Pure instinct. It gave me reason to believe in the power of sustained concentration. I didn't believe... I simply knew. I knew I needed to be heard in order to put things right. I had a score to settle with fate, and yes, I wanted to wipe the smile off Lisa del Giocondo's face... wherever or whenever she was.

Two years after my death, my lover Sandro Botticelli, died. I had been scaling one of the easier cliffs, when I heard him call my name. I felt a strong surge of passion from Sandro that tugged me towards him, and I called back into the valley, but I heard my echo break against the mountains. Then came the terrible silence and I felt twice-abandoned by love.

In 1508, when I died and had tried to explain to Leonardo that he and I would only be apart for a short time, he became agitated, and I knew I would stay until his own transition, and so we spoke daily, and time, being fluid in the territory of the void, ebbed and flowed in magnificent waves. I did not know then, that I was not yet in that pleasant dream of afterlife, but rather suspended in a lucid gap between life and death. Halfway to heaven with one foot on French soil.

Death is only a moment. What follows is an epiphany: a receptive universe writes its pleasure in occult poetry. I am not a traditional ghost. I do not wail or clank undignified through the hallways of a dark museum. I have more style than that. I am a presence. I am the 'Mona Lisa.'

I created my heaven carefully, but failed to anticipate a legacy of anonymity and to be so wiped from the memory of the world that my resentment would hold me hostage for five-hundred-years.

Time is an eternal equation – the quantum mathematics of celebratory birthday gifts and death wishes. Each party is marked with a red flag at the intersections of peak moments, potent anniversaries, and geological events. There are cycles for conscious extinctions and lucid resurgence.

Human wars and celestial explosions destroy on cue, but loves are plotted on perpetual calendars of empathy. Love defies formula. Love is the universe breathing out of control.

A creative mind receives what it asks for. The importance of being extraordinarily clear whilst wishing cannot be overstated; the ambiguous prayer is a toothless contract, and inviting one's highest good is a murky request at best. An unpolished dream is unfinished business. Leonardo begged me to never leave him, but in the end he had no choice but to leave *me*.

I am well aware that a great artist paints much more than a likeness, so what possible chance for escape did I have? I had been captured by a master.

The human language is selfish. It lacks ethe-
real flexibility. The 'poet-god' declared that my
identity would rhyme with singular purpose, but
my name breathed the same sigh as Monna Lisa
Giocondo. I have been dead five-hundred-years,
and the poem isn't over. *-Lisabetta*

Florence – 1470

Verrocchio's factory smells of cold furnaces, cats, and art. For the
moment, the doors are open to the grey dawn, and the studio felines
have fled into the hills for fresher game than plague rats and sour mice.

The city of Florence welcomes the divine light – the first artist of the
morning. It blesses the narrow streets of Sant' Ambrogio, and inside the
great workshop on the Via Ghibellina, the miracle of it fills the stale air
with gold dust. It brushes every corner and paints the edges of the long
tables. It kisses the lips of the water jars and caresses the giant copper
sphere still awaiting the rooftop of Santa Maria del Fiore. It strokes the
portraits of goddesses and saints to life. It shines the rooms gently until
every cube and curve is polished.

The tired faces of the women hustle past the holy families and angels,
and sweep the floors with sleepy brooms and the hems of their long
skirts. These sisters, daughters, and wives of art, prepare the workshop
for their men-folk with raw hands stained saffron and crimson and blue.

The second miracle is turning flour and oil into bread. A young
woman beats cornmeal into a bright pudding. Another stirs cilantro
into a fresh cauldron of minestrone. The aromas of an awakening
kitchen chase away the oppressive night odors and clash with the more
pungent cooking necessary for art: bowls of stewed aloes, egg yolks for
tempera, oils of linseed and walnut, distilled pine resin, and foul pots
of simmering rabbit-skins for glue.

Lisabetta Buti peers at a firing of Madonna figurines through the
glow of red charcoal. They stand in submissive rows of blazing martyrdom – sanctified by fire – icons transcending clay and glaze to rise
above something finer than mud and water. They endure the torture in

order to become more durable, yet their purpose is to remain the fragile recipients of human troubles.

Monna Orazia, the housekeeper, can coax fire from the bleakest of coals. She is known affectionately as Aunt Rica, and given the title: *'Sollecitare Incendiara'* – caller of the flames. This damp morning it's her duty to make magic over a particularly odious bed of black stones. She draws an invisible flicker into a single orange spark from deep within the cold brazier and blows it into a finger of flame. It devours yesterday's leavings, and takes possession of the iron cradle until many golden hands wave their heat into the draughty cave of her cousin, Andrea Verrocchio's, studio. The main workroom only begins to thaw as the great furnace is stoked twice more to birth its obedient sisterhood of holy mothers.

It's Lisabetta's job to grind the colors for her eighteen-year-old brother, Leonardo. She arranges small bowls of powdered violet, Naples yellow, lapis blue, and lead white, in a row. They wait on the workbench like a string of Easter beads. The palest of egg yolks have been gently beaten into a froth with a drop of olive oil and covered with a scrap of gauze. Her fingertips smell of vinegar from stirring a tepid jar of prepared water. These are the freshest ingredients for painting the best clouds.

Skies are Lisabetta's specialty. Even Sandro Botticelli asks for her help with his skies. Today, Leonardo also requires a small quantity of lamp black and burnt sienna for the 'Angel and Tobias' panel now that the background is dry enough to add the last figure, but her brother's first task will be repairing its crude sky.

At this hour, the little upstart, Lorenzo di Credi, is still warming master Verrocchio's bed, surrounded by velvet pillows and love-stained sheets. Lisabetta is twelve; Lorenzo is barely a year older – chosen from the crowd for his dark beauty to pose for yet another angel.

Usually the boys last for one painting, but Lorenzo knows how to play and he rolls over for his supper – enough to stay on as a reluctant apprentice with favors. Lorenzo brags behind Verrocchio's back, that he likes his women younger. At thirteen, Lorenzo leers repulsively at girls like an old man.

Lisabetta beams from Sandro's attention. The day has gifted the purest ultramarine to prepare. She leans into the weakness of the stone and slips into its rhythm. It crushes willingly – surrenders itself like a lover, but the scorpion, Lorenzo, scuttles across her happiness and casts a prediction over the mortar with casual insensitivity.

His flirtation is rehearsed. "Someday, I think you will be *my* assistant," he says, thinking to flatter.

He teases, but Lisabetta reacts as if stung. "Never!" she says. "I will go back to the farm first."

"Well – always menial work, yes?" His arrogance makes a small cut against her neck.

Foolishly, she boasts into his face: "I can already paint better than you ever will," she says.

This declaration is a well-aimed punch that Lorenzo has to weather in front of his studio family. It compels him to defend himself:

"You are a worthless peasant," he says, "and you're only here because your brother is insane. Master Verrocchio wouldn't want you unless you were with Leonardo. Without Leonardo you are nothing."

The upstart turns into a viper and hisses under the nearest rock. For Lisabetta it's too late; she hears Lorenzo's prediction as a dare.

For the first time since confronting her bully of a father, Lisabetta wants to inflict physical harm. She had forgotten the uncontrollable urge to strike out with her small fists regardless of her opponent's size. For a moment Lisabetta weighs the heft of the stone pestle in her hand and considers it a weapon.

The first madness of bloodlust rushes to defend her gender, but something shifts. Lisabetta feels the fury go, and in its place she senses a calm more vicious than violence. She understands the muscle of it. This is the day she learns to smile seductively while mentally slitting someone's throat.

Knowing one's personal power is reason enough to smile.

Veritas (Truth) + Icon (Image) = True Face
Latin anagram for the name, Veronica

A Matter of Truth

Victoria, Canada – a parallel dream
June 13, 2008

Veronica Lyons' arms refuse to cooperate when she gropes blindly to anchor her dream-space. Her urge to run freezes her to the moment; intense dreams always short-circuit the ability to flee or grasp or rationalize. She slumps to the floor asleep onstage like a puppet with its strings cut – obliged to watch a play or wake up. Behind her, a troupe of phantoms pays no attention to her decision. Beside her, stands her muse, Lisabetta. The images had seemed flawlessly natural until she woke up inside the dream and realized its scope and consequences. That's when she feels her grip on reality slipping and the ability to grasp onto something tangible becomes an act of survival.

The studio of Andrea Verrocchio remains aligned to the business of art. A metal sphere under construction, eight feet in diameter, rests low to the ground in a cradle of sticks like a blank globe. Its unblemished surface awaits the undiscovered 'New World' and the land masses and oceans of the known world, soon to be caught in a lace net of invisible longitudes and latitudes. The metal workers have engineered a small hollow planet with an oculus like a Hobbit's front door.

Soon it will rise to crown the cupola of the Santa Maria del Fiore's dome – a floating gazebo, hooked on a spire to become the default image of the Florentine skyline. The burnished orb, seen from below as a copper pearl eclipsing the sun.

Veronica is familiar with the painting propped on a stand. It's closely attended by a slim teenager with long chestnut hair, standing in a room with the aura of a church: the easel an altar, and the young man before it – a devout artist deferring to an icon. He stares through the 'Tobias and the Angel' panel – a slave to its voice.

It's a bright narrative of primary blues and reds and yellows: a boy's journey of compassionate intervention accompanied by his faithful dog and an enchanting fish strung onto a wooden handle. Veronica calls it the marionette fish. By her reckoning, the painting's many weaknesses serve to project a young whiz-kid's visions forward like gems sparkling from a handful of pebbles. In this semi-completed state the dog is missing. In its place is an outline of red chalk.

The young artist drums clean graceful fingers against his velvet sleeves and listens intently to the whimpers of a dog-sprite begging to be born. The stunning youth in the spotless rose tunic, who stands absorbed in thought with arms folded, is the eighteen-year-old, Leonardo da Vinci.

The composition is an abrasive shape. Not Leonardo's choice. It sets him on edge, but he copes by isolating his two contributions. His eyes, once locked onto painting the scales of a single trout, now examine the space where a dog has decided to materialize. The artist is determined to experiment with the new technique of oils. Leonardo thinks it should stick to the tempura ground, but it's an oil and water story, and Veronica knows the little terrier will evaporate over time and become a ghost dog.

The conflicting styles of seven painters inflict discord to Leonardo's mind. There are too many flaws to correct: the angel's wings look too solid to flap. The apprentice, Bartolomeo, has copied a heavy wood and leather contraption made for a pageant, too literally. Fillepe has painted the tassel on Tobias's belt so that it flies free and tangles into a tree which destroys the illusion of distance, the most junior of Andrea's pupils has made puffball rocks made of cotton-wool, and the disturbing left leg of the boy, Tobias, twists back, painfully deformed, but these defects must be overlooked. The most sensitive task of the day will be repairing the botched sky which must be diplomatically rescued from the blunder of the golden boy, Lorenzo's, weak hand. Without a decent sky, Leonardo's dog and fish will be further dishonored.

Leonardo can do little to animate the stiff figures. Master Verrocchio is a sculptor first and a painter by necessity. His painted figures are creatures made of marble with claw-like affectations of twisted fingers who wear colorful clothes. Draperies of stone defy the wind and pin them to the earth, yet the angel, Raphael, come to stroll the Earth, makes no contact with the road at all.

Veronica muses that the angel carrying a small square tablet looks as if he's reading a text message on the world's first cell phone.

The dog manifests effortlessly, and while Leonardo's brush is loaded with burnt sienna, he unconsciously adds a deft movement of color that softens the escaped curl at Tobias's temple with a thin glaze of light. Leonardo smiles. This third involvement balances his others, now well-placed to shine with a satisfying degree of triangulation.

The sky is another matter. Leonardo has avoided it as a punishing task, but even his selective vision can no longer block the bungle of inept talent.

The earth-tones on his palette are set aside for the shades of blues and yellows and violets he can make from the pure colors Lisabetta has prepared. He notes the precious lapis and Egyptian purple, and steels himself to face Lorenzo's idea of a summer heaven, but fate intervenes.

Andrea Verrocchio is as shrewd a businessman as his neighbor, Ser Piero da Vinci. From the beginning of their 'foster/apprentice' arrangement, Piero had warned Andrea of his son's strange departures of consciousness and the special bond between him and his younger sister, Lisabetta. To Andrea's surprise, Lisabetta follows her half-brother to his studio with talent of her own. She handles Leonardo's moodiness which smoothes the production line, and it has become advantageous to court Leonardo. Leonardo's talent is divine; he has the aura of grace about him when he is given the freedom to lose himself in his work.

Veronica hyperventilates as her fingers pluck the surface of rough floor-boards, exploring the worn planks until she feels the sharp jab of a splinter. Dreams can be painfully lucid.

Lisabetta moves closer and suppresses her anger. "Mia caro, my dear, you are recovered?" she smiles benignly.

"Never."

"That is enough. Stop pretending to be a weak woman. You are not powerless. It is nonsense. My death is in your hands, and we are moving too slow. This day is significant... important, yes? I think that you must see how it was, so I bring you here, and I cannot waste anymore time. I need you to keep your head. Please. Our work... my story and your chance will fail if you don't write every word of this."

Veronica waves towards Leonardo from her collapsed position. "No fair. You bring me here to see him ... and all ... all this?"

"Caro, it was a surprise, and you are not so delicate. You must be stronger if we are to succeed. It is your freedom too. You want a new life, yes? You like my surprise, yes?"

"Yes, but ..."

"Look. I am over there. See? ... That is me. I am twelve. Do you see me? I offered to paint over Lorenzo's bad sky, but Leonardo said no. He wanted to do it." Lisabetta embraces the studio with outstretched arms – a human cross. Her body shimmers. She is hopelessly, fully there. "I bring you to this place for a reason," she says. "This is the day I decided to become ... a little, as you call ... bitch? I look so innocent, no?" Lisabetta points to a confident figure making his way across the room. "There is my killer."

"Killer!"

"No, no ... destroyer, yes? ... a bully," she corrects.

Lorenzo di Credi, a dusky thirteen-year-old, 'prince of everything-Verrocchio,' is on his way to alter the lives of a million people.

"He looks harmless," Veronica says.

"He is about to eat me alive." She points to a far corner. "Over there is my Sandro."

"Please no, I can't take any more." Veronica looks back at Leonardo. "I've had enough!"

"It is *not* enough," Lisabetta says. "It was *never* enough!"

"I should go."

"We are wasting energy. Come... I need you to remember this."

Lisabetta takes Veronica's hands, and pulls her to her feet. "You must see him," she says, and propels her charge towards a tall man enveloped in surreal light.

Fiery blue eyes stay locked on their work. Sandro Botticelli is safely blocked from Lisabetta and Veronica by subjective imagination. Veronica is immediately captivated by a long tumble of auburn curls under a mauve cap. Long dark eyelashes flicker against his tanned cheeks as they follow his brush, and the pulse in his throat beats gently below. The stitching on the neck of his cotton shirt breathes the same rhythm – a straight line of peach thread against white fabric. Veronica feels dizzy from studying the nape of his neck.

Sandro turns towards the scent of feminine energy. His eyes darken as he stares through the two women. Botticelli's eyes, flash violet from the reflecting light. Veronica floats towards him, close enough to kiss, and a delicious itch is telegraphed to her remote body. The dream seduction is complete. Her form stirs above, moaning in a distant bed, the impossible slave of an artist long-dead.

Lisabetta looks similarly drugged. Veronica thinks dream-travelers must be co-dependent, like twins. She knows too much about twin-ship, and surely a muse is a potent reflection of one's psyche.

"Yes, he is quite something." Veronica's words escape from her dry throat; even dreamers get thirsty. The one thing Lisabetta has taught her since they first met a month ago, is that twins may be born six years apart.

Across the room, the younger Lisabetta mixes colors with blue fingers. She looks at Sandro with undisguised adulation, and nearly upsets a jar of water. It wobbles against her sleeve and miraculously spins to a stop.

Lisabetta describes Sandro perfectly: "Magnifico, yes?"

"Magnifico, yes," Veronica agrees, and the scene starts to disintegrate into thin fog. Her sleeping body calls her as it arches with pleasure, but she wills herself to stay. No-one should eclipse the thrill of seeing a young Leonardo, but Sandro is a magnet, and she is hardly pulled into his orbit; she runs there.

Veronica's dream has a singular theme of organic adoration: the admiration of Veronica for two men, an artist in raptures over a section of painting, a young boy enamoured of a girl, and a besotted girl obsessed over a man twice her age.

A human drama unfolds. Magic pushes the ensuing argument into a blur: Lorenzo teases; the girl Lisabetta lashes out; Lorenzo flies into a rage. The damage is done, and the child Lisabetta has a strange look in her eyes. Lorenzo fades into the recesses of the studio.

In professional retaliation, Leonardo dismisses Lorenzo's sky to history. The dog and fish will have to console each other. There will be other paintings.

Sandro turns towards the disturbance. Behind him looms a moving backdrop of metaphorical white clouds that darken into a storm.

Botticelli's voice acts like smelling salts. "Come little sister," he calls to *his* Lisabetta. "I need your help. Do not mind him little one ... he is insignificante."

Veronica's Lisabetta has vanished; she is inside her child self.

Veronica watches, strangely jealous, and turns her attention back towards an eighteen-year-old god.

Leonardo wipes the excess blue from his brush, dips it into red turpentine, and the color swishes into murky brown mud. He selects new dabs of sienna and ochre and white – swirls them into warm brown, binds them together with a slick of oil, adds a tip of cooling black, and abandons the 'Tobias' to its botched sky. The sharp edge of an awkward cloud will forever prod the boy's head like a slow lightning bolt. Let it reflect the truth of the upstart's talent. Leonardo will attend to his dog and no more.

Veronica catches Sandro Botticelli teasing Lisabetta as he lifts her blonde braid to his lips. He kisses it slowly and taps the end of it on her nose: "Little shadow, you should wear this down," he says, as he wipes a small smudge of sky from Lisabetta's cheek.

Leonardo engages his right-brain and enters his painting. To him, the studio disappears and he is alone with the faint outline of a dog in need of a body, waiting to emerge into a three-dimensional trickery of fluff. Leonardo waits until he feels the inner command to begin and applies the first feathery brushstroke to the fur of a prancing mongrel. A cloud dog.

Sandro's laugh warms the room, Tobias's dog freshly glistens, half-born the escaped wisp of Tobias's hair is combed with sunlight, and the delicate colors of Leonardo's iridescent fish have dried to a soft polish for over a month. Leonardo is barely eighteen. Lisabetta's nemesis,

Lorenzo, is thirteen. Sandro is twenty-five. Veronica remains a young twenty-nine, and now her muse has transformed from a shy twelve-year-old into a supple teenage coquette who has pinned Sandro into a corner, and he is exploring under her skirts.

Veronica ignores them by studying Leonardo. His breath rises and falls evenly. He is dreaming his dog into form, separate from her own trance and the other trances in the studio. The moment stuns her. "Don't let me wake up," Veronica calls out, but Lisabetta has not returned from her triumphant romp, and only a faint trace of her lingers where she once stood.

Veronica imagines being crushed into a corner against Sandro Botticelli, not giving a hot damn about the year 2008, and Lisabetta is shouting from the end of a long tunnel: "Write it for him as well as me!"

The morning threatens to part Veronica from Sandro, but she fights consciousness, latches on to his astral signature, and wills her way back to Florence without Lisabetta to explore ghostly love in private.

Sandro is there painting, and when he turns to Veronica with an adoring smile, her life dissolves into the headiness of white sound. His energy absorbs hers, the world disappears, and Veronica Lyons, quite rationally, falls for a dream.

Lisabetta had been right to criticize; Veronica knows she's been lax. She will have to apply herself. She made Lisabetta and Jupiter a promise, and now she's making strange assurances to Sandro.

"Sanity is the absence of excitement," she thinks, and for the first time since childhood, she feels powerful and considers life worth exploring.

Veronica's 'severance package' won't last forever; both she and her muse are biding on time-sensitive passports. She must fight for her own independence as much as Lisabetta's. This is not the time for giving in or slowing down. Finding Sandro was everything, but he belongs to both of them now, and he will have to choose.

The DIARY of VERONICA LYONS

All at Sea

June 14, 2008

I had it all wrong. Lisabetta is not a classic 'ghost' – I see the word 'host' in that name – one word possessed by another. I can't decide if she is acting as hostess, inviting me to her old parties, or if I'm the human host she needs in order to 'party-on.' That second explanation is more likely.

I do see that she is more than a tour guide/travel agent. She shows me emotional time-sensitive events that appear like a chain of islands on a map. Tips of stone icebergs. Like islands, her recollections lie ninety percent below the waterline. A submerged mountain range holding back the future.

Perhaps lives straddling eternity have access to a hole ripped in the side of time like a slow Titanic leak – second 'deaths by history,' that leave the pinnacle of the dream above water. I get inklings that disappear as quickly as they come. Time waits for no woman – even a dead one.

Time must be mathematics unplugged. It's all numbers and frequencies, blotted notebooks, and shaky memoirs, lost in the post-mortem stench of burned diaries, love letters, and contracts. Burning documents is the first classic purge of evidence. One's guilts and shameful dreams, worth archiving during life, are sacrificed before vacated bodies grow cold. Why do kin make bonfires of intimacy? Who are they protecting?

Fibonacci accountants fix the books. There are tenfold increases and incalculable diminishments. That's all we can surmise; so much is confusion after the flames erase everything passionately worthwhile in a spent life. Pastoral retreats and cruel surprises are the prizes conferred by Hydrogen that dazzle us into submission.

History is hardly 'past-perfect.' Lisabetta told me she senses a light around this year. A holy year with a halo for good measure. It is why she feels her chance for freedom slipping away after only three months pushing against the mountain. She harbors a niggling thought that she has been gifted a poetic gestation period of nine months for her rebirth.

I see her more as an actress on stage, a solo performance under a spotlight: 'April in Paris' – a one act play. It is gracious to bow before the performance and let the curtain rise on the next surprise, but I can't help wondering if I am Lisabetta's understudy with terminal stage fright? Some days it seems our friendship doesn't have enough lifeboats.

I am puzzled by the fact that Lisabetta isn't aware of my morning tryst with Sandro, which shocks me. Now I have to find a way of breaking our discretion to Lisabetta without jeopardizing 'Project Lisa' or destroying my own fragile relationship. I thought she could read my mind. It appears that romance and cheating survive death.

I have been selfish. Deliberately evasive, delaying and dawdling – and now cheating. Lisabetta is anxious enough already. Heaven knows, I don't wish anxiety attacks on anyone. She has begged me to give her another chance and I said a casual okay when I really want to shout yes-yes-yes! I don't want Lisabetta to think it's only because of my interest in Sandro, although it is Sandro who bridges the gap where I care if I go insane or not.

To make amends I have planned a surprise for Lisabetta tomorrow, and then I will confess all. Unbelievably, I have made the 'Mona Lisa' a female cuckold, and it is absurd to believe that I could be the 'other woman.' ~*VL*

PART ONE
Second Verse

"Row, row, row your boat
gently down the stream
merrily, merrily, merrily, merrily,
life is but a dream."
~ Anonymous

"Here lies one
whose name
was writ on water."
~ John Keats

The Muse

It would be easy to say I am the true face of the 'Mona Lisa,' and equally truthful to say, I am not the original. How I came to live in France is well-documented. The part no-one knows, is who traveled the short distance from Amboise to Paris, and why Leonardo painted two of us.

I had wished for fame but neglected to ask for recognition, and so I remain as invisible in death as I was in life, supplanted by a woman I envied – a woman I inadvertently raised up to preposterous celebrity. When experts attributed my face to Lisa Giocondo I saw blood, but by then it was impossible to silence her. Both of us were long-dead.

When I turned seven, Leonardo was thirteen, newly apprenticed to the master, Andrea Verrocchio, and he began to pass on what he learned, to me. I was thrilled to learn the trade by copying my brother – to be spared the crooked back of a farm laborer and becoming an old woman at thirty.

I would have been content as an artist's assistant. I was invisible according to the guild, but my work put extra funds into Leonardo's pocket, and he designated me his accountant. While my brother followed the path of his insatiable muse, I saved for the day we would start our own studio. He had all the power, but I was learning how to use it.

Leonardo suffered from the maladies of genius. He could see too much – plagued with excessive ideas, but hadn't the insight to navigate the business of art. He was different, not necessarily troubled, but trouble-causing. Obsessive. His mind functioned apart from the world, and he carried the burdensome weight of his insatiable curiosity into each day until he was unwell from the strain. When he needed to restore his health, he slipped into the hills outside the city fortifications.

When I was a girl, Florence was enclosed by a protective wall with eighty gates and watchtowers, and beyond them stretched the main roads and worn tracks that led into the wild country between towns, each with similar barricades against nature and war. Beyond these portals lay Leonardo's earthly heaven – his church with its dome of blue sky that demanded nothing and offered salvation.

All I ever wanted was to be an artist's assistant until Lorenzo reminded me it was the most I could ever be. After that, I desired nothing less than incandescent fame; regular fame was not enough.

I can confirm that the pollution of hubris is red as blood. The prospect of success contaminated me the way a spatter of wayward vermillion paint corrupts the sanctity of its neighbors. I think this is why I am here. Perhaps Sandro's God punishes women who refuse to kneel, or believe, or obey. And especially the women who dare to create in their own name.

My brother taught me everything he knew about painting. What he omitted to tell me was that a portrait can trap a soul like flypaper. Now I am mired up to my smile in paint and varnish, and ambition.

I want to go home – the home some consider to be heaven. Anger won't take me there; willpower won't take me there; humility alone won't take me there, and so, in death I have to be as wholly redeemable as Leonardo's masterpiece. My portrait may be priceless, but I must become a woman worth saving.

Galleries and museums are full of misidentified treasures, and dreamers trapped inside 'desiderata' (once-desired things) but only a human dowsing rod can tap the energy that radiates from them. From us... from me. I'm more than a painting; I'm a woman inhabiting one.

Death is a pleasant surprise, not unlike love at first sight. Vibrations mingle. Signatures fire. The confusion is delightful. The rare collisions of mystical purpose and organic thrum are the surprises we live and die for.

When I was alive I felt overwhelmed by my insignificance, and I fought like a tiger to be noticed, but I realize now my war wasn't with visibility – it was with being known. The truth is, the unseen energy of a repeated thought is the most creative power a person can possesses, and hungering for success makes beggars of us all. Lorenzo had been right when he said art prostituted its creators.

After Leonardo and I left Florence, I cultivated abrasiveness as a weapon; I could no longer afford to be silent. I used everyone to gain a foothold on art for Leonardo, and recognition for myself. I didn't know how to serve us both any other way.

I lived beside a large life, and negotiated Leonardo's reputation against his best interests. I maneuvered him into the places I wanted to go, and the worst of it, was that the guilt I felt during his rise to fame didn't stop me, and the remorse I felt afterwards, was pushed into the hole where my life could have been.

I had been entirely at home in my tranquil landscape, and the thought of escaping from solitary confinement never occurred to me. When Leonardo died, I looked back at my portrait. It was my first mistake. I had created a heaven worth dying for, but I turned from it towards the painting. I was drawn back to its power. Inside it, I had the attention I craved. How could I let go of that?

I think I was half-afraid to go with Leonardo and be diminished again by his talent. I wanted to belong, and I wanted to remain visible. Fame is a seductive promise, and so death let go of me.

Living inside a painting may be safer than the dangerous world where I once lived, but I discovered that safety over time kills passion, and even a life blessed with serendipity is flawed. A half-truth is still a lie, and I'm tired of being a lost woman from a century where I was considered worthless. It only took a few years before my name evaporated and I became 'Leonardo's little shadow' more than ever – an everywoman/no-woman.

For a while I was a Madonna and I enjoyed the status of icon, and then I became her – 'Princess Giocondo.' The truth is, I've been an anonymous female for five-hundred-and-fifty years, and the feeling I still hate most, is being overlooked.

Ironically, by the year 2008, I had become Leonardo's equal in celebrity, but I was a forgotten sister, not his collaborator, and with even greater contradiction, I had been defined by my indefinable, unreadable expression just as Leonardo said I would.

Time beyond life is like a river with undercurrents and eddies that take one off-course. The Greek stories of the River Styx are somewhat accurate, but I was not ferried to my heaven, and I have forgotten nothing. A hundred fluid years on death's calendar is not protracted. There is no lateral flow from one event to another. Neither Julian nor Gregorian years are made from a succession of tedious minutes and hours.

One day, a teenage girl happened through my salon with her beau, a strapping red-head with heavy-lidded blue eyes. She clung to his arm and looked up at him adoringly, and barely gave my portrait a glance. I could hear her mind intent on marriage, breathless with the expectation of owning his soul. But it was not her feelings which engaged me; it was the canvas shopping bag she was carrying, imprinted with the image of a painting I knew well. Sandro's 'Birth of Venus' drifted past me, and I followed it like an obedient puppy to the end of my power and watched the pair of lovers take the stairs past the winged goddess to the freedom of the Paris streets.

I was sucked back to 1476 and Verrocchio's studio, an eighteen-year-old girl, hanging on to Sandro Botticelli's voice and scent and touch.

I have been able to revisit every thought, conversation and vision with more clarity than is comfortable. I am transported within the lucid dreams of the spirit world – outside of solar time, but inside the limitations of my personal understanding. My kin called to me, beyond my reach.

I missed my daughter and my brother and little Rinato. I missed Sandro. I missed my paints.

My craving for heaven finally grew stronger than my resentment of Lisa Giocondo and I thought there was a chance I could complete my transition from life. I reasoned, that if I could erase her name and restore mine, I would be free, but it required human intervention, and I began to wish for true death as fervently as any devout believer ever prayed for forgiveness.

My chance came with the perfect human host. She would have to be. How apt that there were two of them. I smiled two different smiles five-hundred years apart: bemused and astonished, as the curse 'trapped for eternity' reformed into the single word, 'freedom,' but a promised passport is only a legal document and a ticket home is only the intention of a destination until redeemed, and freedom is only conceptual liberation until the day one is absolutely released. My rescuer had no concept of the invisible documents she carried, and I had no idea she would be so problematic.

I recognized my savior at once, but adulation had spoiled me. I expected Veronica to honor my request without hesitation – committed absolutely, out of her admiration for Leonardo. I felt her awe when she walked into my salon, but it wavered inside a mind choked with fears, and I momentarily second-guessed my instincts. I savored the forgotten challenge of being successfully checked by another's purpose. I knew she would be worthy of a struggle; I didn't know how much.

I presumed Veronica was the bearer of a ticket to my promised land, but she was more like an official who issued them, which was insensitive, since later, she was often casual, if not indifferent, to my situation. Time has its reasons and seasons. Veronica was a closed book to hallucination and the paranormal in general, but she was unable to entirely block my auditory presence. Denial was her specialty.

Veronica's son Jupiter was different from the usual 'Mona Lisa' fans. His senses weren't jammed with sentimental hype, and his distant expression showed me he listened to an inner world. He made me ache for my brother, in the days when we were peasant children who ran crazy into the hills of Campo Zeppi and soaked up our happiness under a sky no artist could paint.

I over-indulge in such memories.

You may find it paradoxical that the apparent 'ghost of the gallery' can herself be haunted, but what trapped soul could be otherwise? Unfinished business? Well that's what is said, but I assure you, all business ceases with the last breath. What traps humans into pockets of afterlife, is the 'finished' thought. We manifest our strongest dreams, and to prove it, I still smart from living a small life in the shadow of a master.

When I am calmest, I retreat into the landescape behind me, where I walk contentedly with a generous death. A death that allowed my dream of fame to come true. Well, half-true. That's the problem with desires – we write them in passionate ink, and they're translated into literal requests. Yearning makes us careless, and at this moment I am not calm. I am ecstatic. So pixilated, I have danced around the salon arms outstretched not bothering to circumvent the patrons. I see some women have fainted and several children are so over-stimulated that parents are leading them into the hallways. My rescue team is energized and the room is like a beehive on fire. It must be pulsing with emotion because I see the air changing colors. Pink to orange-red and back to yellow.

Paranormal? Occult? What do they mean? They denote above and behind the norm, and what lies beyond the ordinary but the extraordinary: the unexpected hiccups of genius, the greater than, the hidden from, the infinite, the elegant, and the divinity of mathematics – nothing less than the absolute essence of creative expression. The great god, Hydrogen, is the first artist.

Leonardo's hills and streams stand in beautifully for my patient afterlife, that no doubt holds its breath for me with timeless grace. I sense its sanctuary, balanced high, inside a dimension that I can taste. It pulses and beats, looping like a mantra – the comforting humdrum of a past-perfect universe sleeping under the accumulated chaos of evolution.

I catch a whiff of heaven's atmosphere when the gallery clears, and the cleaners have gone, and the small red dots of the security system patrol the hushed spaces where art lives on. It smells like violets.

Anniversaries carry more potent memories. The year 2008 is the fifth centennial of my ongoing dance with a half-life. I crave recognition as much as ever, but to achieve it, I have to win Veronica's trust gradually through the careful friendship I must forge with her son, and even then I fear she may betray me.

How the universe loves to spin its ironies: the era in which I was born is known as a time of great rebirth, but the troubled woman that synchronicity sends to rescue me, can't release me until she fully lives, and I can't be reborn if I don't fully die. - *Lisabetta*

> *"Some days*
> *my head is like a teapot full of bees."*
> ~ Veronica Lyons

The DIARY of VERONICA LYONS
transcribed age six

Artism

May 2 – 1985

Dear Diary –

Basil went camping with dad but not me. Mom needed me home. They took the Indian tepee for sleeping in. My mother hates camping. Instead we visited my Aunt Beatrice at the home. She is not like other people. She has 'artism.'

She draws pictures backwards. She did a picture of me sitting in a chair and made my feet first and then my knees and the ribbon in my hair last. My mother says she draws like she is knitting a scarf because you aren't sure if you are knitting the beginning or the end of a scarf first.

My aunt made me pretend tea in her 'Alice in Wonderland' tea set. She let me have the Cheshire Cat cup even though it's her favorite. She had the dormouse cup. She has the best smile but her eyes look far away, like when I look for my cat, Spock, when everyone tells me he will be home soon. They say that so I will go to bed but I can't sleep until he's in. Aunt Beatrice looks like she's looking for one of her cats when she asks me if I take pretend sugar in my make-believe tea.

My mother calls her Alice, but I call her Aunt Bee. She doesn't like to be hugged. She hugs cats instead. She calls herself Lisa and me Caro. It means 'dear.' She pronounces some words backwards or over-and-over. My Uncle Oz calls mom Cat or Dotty or Dodo; and me Toto or Ronnie;

and Baz, Wizo. He calls Aunt Bee, Birdie. Our family likes lots of names from books. We read them all the time. Baz and I even have a name for the tree in our backyard. It's a boy tree and we named him Leo because we are Lyons, and the top of our tree looks like a lion's mane. Baz is crazy. He climbs way high up Leo and calls me, but I won't go. I don't like to be up high.

I like to draw too. My mother says I'm artistic so I may have to live in a special place when I get older, but that's okay because you get to have lots of cats where Aunt Bee lives, and Baz can live with me. He draws too. Baz and me are twins. Baz doesn't like tea.

Tonight it was thundering and lightning. Spock got scared and hid under my blanket. I watched the storm from my window and I saw Leo outside in the wind, waving his branches, telling me to stay inside. Then I saw Baz clinging up high when the lightning came, but I was seeing things, and he wasn't there. He was camping. I told Mom when she came in to say goodnight. Spock is out now.

Something feels bad. Mom says I'm a worrywart and it's just the storm, but I know Baz is scared. I can hear him calling me 'crazy girl' like always, but this time he isn't teasing. ~ *Ronnie Lyons*

"Looking at a painted landscape
you can see yourself again,
a lover with your beloved, in the flowering meadows
or under the soft shadows of the green trees."
~ Leonardo da Vinci

Twice Juicy

Caterina di Marco di Buti was my mother. I remember the sublime hush that surrounded her when she recited our story... hers, and mine... and my brother, Leonardo's. She said we were tied together in a knot that had no beginning or end.

As she told it, her destiny was stolen the day she was born: 'sealed by a lazy signature,' she used to say, 'and scratched in the heartbeat of a careless summer.' The truth was less poetic, but her misfortune decided my own fate and that of my brother with the same stroke of a pen.

Legal promises are only one kind of poison that can twist events into surprises of despair. That's life. I thank the stars above for heaven. I can change pretty much anything there with a thought, but what counts as history must occur within the denseness of gravity under the laws of sidereal time.

There are no records in the afterlife. No rewards or punishments. Ironically, there's no death sentences of regret and shame. But I wasn't there in 2008. I was in Paris. ~ *Lisabetta*

Campo Zeppi, Tuscany
July 1, 1457

At sixteen, Caterina's first sin left a white streak across the sky. That was the comet, Leonardo da Vinci. A second chance was delivered in her twenty-third year. Caterina narrated in her delicious throaty voice. "It arrived on a lemon wind", she intoned, " a wind that licked the hot dust from an acre of succulent figs" ... that was me.

A presence took her off guard. She faced it, welcomed its tease and dared it to stay. My mother knew well how providence could breathe or die on a slow contract. This time she planned to rebirth its cruel sting into a better dream.

But, I was not the better dream; I was only half of it.

Caterina loved to recount the story of me behind the ears of my elder sisters, but she waited until I was old enough to understand, and by that time Leonardo had left us for school where he taught his teachers the art of painting.

Caterina's memories enchanted me, but I was too young to sense their tragedy; I only absorbed the romance. She began my story with a whisper. It was the morning of my conception. She had listened to the horizon and visualized herself on the quiet track to Anchiano. It felt strange, she said, to witness her own departure down the tunnel of tall cypress near our farm in Campo Zeppi. Beyond them lay the fragrant embrace of vineyards that spread towards the flatlands of Lamporecchio and freedom. She had been wild to be away.

Her bare toes splayed into the damp dust of morning and clung to the soles of her feet. My beautiful young mother, Caterina, glowed country brown, the lost daughter of a middle-class notary thrust into the role of peasant wife. I could see her face, flushed all the darker for excitement.

As she spoke, I felt my own face glow brighter in response from knowing I was worth the art of story. This tale was me. For once, I was someone larger than the girl who did chores and kept silent against her father's deep resentment.

My father, Antonio di Piero Buti del Vacca, feasted daily on a sick repast of indignation. He was humiliated from making useless daughters and being trapped in a marriage for personal gains that evaporated soon after the da Vinci fee was paid. That he took it was no surprise; my father was a mercenary soldier when he wasn't working the kilns near our desperate little farm.

My mother related how the air had turned playful and rustled the silver branches. It rattled the olives and was tamed into a breeze of September silk. It blew tender plumes of smoky rain on her face as she crossed the yard for water and landed on her skin, cool as a veil. She shook it from her hair. It was her moment of peace before the chaos of daily survival began.

Caterina pulled the heaviness of water to the surface and stared at the horizon. The promise of escape allowed her to breathe. I knew this feeling well.

She had learned to expect little from Piero da Vinci, other than to exchange an occasional glance. It was hardly surprising. Six years of servitude defined the grim boundaries of her shrinking power. But there were occasions when Caterina would push her son, Leonardo, ahead of her in the rough crowd of Vinci, and expect a civil brush with the family who tried to forget that one day a young notary's daughter passed their way and almost turned a da Vinci head from its duty.

Caterina told the tale often, but she never used the name, Piero or da Vinci, and for too long, I assumed I was Leonardo's half-sister. Leonardo was not to know the truth for many years after that. Caterina and my paternal grandmother swore me to secrecy until after Ser Piero's death. He died in 1504 – the same year I was metaphorically reborn as 'Mona Lisa.'

A doorway has two faces: an exit and an entrance, and events are the moving parts of a well-oiled machine that we pretend are coincidental to comfort ourselves. I like to imagine that Piero da Vinci's last act was gallant – a gentleman who held the door open for the lady, Monna Lisabetta, to enter in her green dress, and that he was mystified by her enigmatic smile as she brushed past him entering into immortal life. But Ser Piero was no gentleman; he was a ruthless lawyer and I was his unacknowledged invisible daughter.

I loved Leonardo all the more for his afflictions of melancholia. That's what we called genius. Antonio was a brute who treated him cruelly, but my mother's half-truth also meant I grew up thinking Antonio was my father, until the full story of me released my shame. I never forgave my mother for that. It had pained me to think Antonio Buti and I shared the same blood, but it also fuelled the anger that thrust me into a world where murder and power were interchangeable. A world I liked, in spite of being treated with indifference.

By the time I arrived, my mother had given birth to two Buti daughters and a stillborn son. My Aunt Fiore told me Antonio had been livid. He had beaten Caterina and given a name to the boy he had been waiting for. He named the child, Umberto, and secretly buried him amongst the consecrated graves of Santa Croce. I sometimes passed the place and felt a chill – which I now know was a premonition of anger and treachery.

Sometimes peasants in the city were safer than the rest of the population. We were irrelevant. Our hungers were small. As a woman, even my work in the great art studios of Florence was invisible. Leonardo was my road there, as I was his safe pathway back from the dark spells he had to endure. Leonardo carried the hope of the da Vinci clan back then. He was considered Piero's only child, and illegitimate or not, the heir apparent. Only three people knew Piero also had a daughter.

My brother craved the life of a scholar. He would have been content to permanently withdraw from business and serve his muses, even the ones that tortured him. In a way, he did. After we had our own studio, Leonardo immersed himself in the sciences any time I released him, but he always remained the wild child. His insatiable need for play was the core of his greatness. The business of art caused him actual pain.

Leonardo was pure scientist; I was pure ambition. He only became a master painter with his own studio because I was hungry for acclaim and to be free of rural servitude, and, as I frequently cajoled him, even scientists have to eat.

My mother poured water into the trough baked with slime. The sound alerted the horses.

She smoothed the grey's neck, kissed its muzzle and received a velvety kiss in her palm in exchange for a sweet apple core. She named the mare, Lezza. It was their secret. Such things were not permitted in the Buti household. Sentimentality overstepped her position as drudge wife, farmhand, and baby machine. Caterina combed gently. "Bella Lezza – beautiful Lisa," she crooned, as she untangled the weather from her pony's mane – and I was delighted to be reminded my namesake was a beloved horse.

The new day shimmered from the slick of early rain. Slices of sharper wind arrived like bullies and tormented the straw grasses of the flatlands into rough waves. Perhaps an omen. My mother said, it was as if the presence of Antonio stirred the fields into protest.

This was the part of our story where I'm sure I smiled. I hated my father too, but I knew what to do with my hatred, and my mother suffered in silence. At age six, I plotted his death. It was a possibility which enabled me to survive in Campo Zeppi as long as I did. Daydreams were my specialty; revenge I learned later.

Caterina had placed sprigs of lavender into the folds of a clean shirt saved from her previous life as the daughter of a notary. Inside it was her mother's amber brooch, the only jewel she ever owned – the one she pressed on me with tears in her eyes when I turned sixteen. She had made quantities of rosewater, kept cool and safe in stone jars under the horse's straw, and after Antonio was gone, she washed her body, careful to sprinkle drops in her hair and splash the precious liquid on her wrists and throat.

That day, Caterina met the only man who mattered. I saw her eyes close and her chin tilt up to inhale as she recalled the nature of the air, still alive. It was, she honeyed, 'charged with the potent scent of sharp yellow promises that clung to it after it whispered through the citrus groves of Campo Zeppi.' The thought of her first love still made my mother dizzy.

Her hands had delivered sparks of electricity from her wool shawl into the silver buckle as she polished Lezza's bridle. Caterina's elegant fingers, that matched my own and Leonardo's, fumbled the simple knots, and she took a deep breath to steady herself against the side of the horse.

Then, my mother made sure my eyes met hers. "Help me Lezza," she whispered into the pony's ear, and I became the horse who heard a human prayer and responded on instinct with a raw animal shiver. I could feel my hooves paw the ground wanting to speak. That was the part where Caterina always reached out and stroked my hair.

Her plea must have traveled to the ears of the angry 'God' we were supposed to believe in, because 'He' responded in 'His' usual detached manner – a garbled code, delivered as a vague blessing, wrapped in denial. Apparently, the only male who loved games and riddles more than my brother, was my image of an angry patriarchal god, and it's true – I came to view Leonardo as 'god-like' in all his manifestations of creativity.

The world may now agree with historic hindsight, but during our lives it was often the opposite. My brother lived on the edge of heresy all his life, and where he lived, I was there fighting off the superstitious carrion who feared every independent thought, and attacked anyone they didn't understand. Leonardo dared convention... all the time.

Who could praise a god who stole the destinies of innocent babies? Caterina could not; she was a practical woman.

I learned to trust Caterina and mistrust 'mother church,' and I knew early on it would be a betrayal of my intelligence if I put my faith in anyone other than myself. I could be as ruthless as God or his latest pope who tried to force sin down our throats, or to be intimidated by the manipulations of the black-beetle priests who scuttled at his feet. I was never impressed by any deity shallow enough to live inside pretty boxes of gilded stone or garish statues, and I was especially unmoved by the embellished representations of religious art. The church didn't play fair. Its paintings were orchestrated to hold viewers hostage. Fear, pathos, and guilt were the only stories they portrayed. Those, and that suffering was somehow important to experience in order to be accepted into heaven. I rejected all the church's visions of heaven and designed my own, but the church was right: suffering is the greater part of reaching one's heaven. Any heaven.

Leonardo had his bird gods and I had some grandiose concept of omnipotent stars; stars were better than another cruel father. Between us, Leonardo and I owned the sky and everything under it, and when we were young, our naiveté saved us more than once. As we matured, Leonardo became cynical, and I grew contemptuous enough to turn our jaded expectations into profit.

The personal details of everyone's stories disappear when they die. For all my bravado, I was not so pretentious to think mine was so very different, but my identity summed up my existence. That was how I saw it in 1508. This is how I continue to see it. I won't play humble. I will never dismiss my entire purpose for being born.

What I did assume, was that my brother's fame contained the gem of my own truth, and I would be a visible shadow to his greatness – that I would live and die, but my name would always shelter under the da Vinci star. I wrote a story worthy enough for my brother to live. I turned the pages of his life into healthy legend.

I understood the ways of men: they were dictators who documented the history of things. I suffered many social indignities, but eternal obscurity was too callous to bear quietly. I likely cursed my desire for more into Death's face – never a wise strategy as it turns out, but I ask you to ponder this: If your name were to be irretrievably lost, cut apart from your time and permanently erased from the world, overshadowed by the lies of silence...

... were you ever truly here? – *Lisabetta*

"The death of fire is the birth of air
and the death of air is the birth of water."
~ Heraclitus c. 535 B.C.

The DIARY of VERONICA LYONS
transcribed age six

May 3 – 1985

    Dear Diary –
My Bazzi is dead. I dreamed he died and then he was.
I see him near me all the time. He says, "Toto don't cry."
and I try. Spock saw him too. Someday I will die and be
there too. Baz still helps me with my homework. Except
for math. He doesn't do math now. He draws a lot and
paints more too. He made a drawing of a big bird with no
head for me, but not the Sesame Street one. He died in a
fire. It's all Cate's fault. ~ *Toto*

"While you are alone
you are entirely your own;
and if you have but one companion
you are but half your own."
~ Leonardo da Vinci

Thursday's Child

~ Leonardo ~
July 1, 1457

Caterina has no babies now. The infants belong to her sister-in-law, Fiore.

Her own two girls are grown into small brown urchins of three and four, with black hair the color of their father's. Her five-year-old son, Leonardo, bears no likeness to his half-sisters or her husband, Antonio Buti. Leonardo's true father is not the bully Caterina has been sold to. Leonardo's face and demeanor have no bearing on peasant stock. He is materialized whole, beautifully made from non-local mind, and there are no words to shape him into a manageable boy.

Leonardo needs space and air. If Caterina is honest, she's a little afraid of him – or is it awe? Dirt falls off his face and hands; he's an immaculate miracle that shines from their family like an egg in a basket of coal. The former Caterina di Marco has been demoted by love. She has been consumed by it and destroyed by it, and because of it there stands an angel son – a golden child with hair the color of nutmegs, who fears her touch, and loud noises, and enclosed spaces.

Caterina wonders if Leonardo has angelic protection. If his dark despairs are perhaps evidence of a superior purpose. She cannot begin to teach him of God and the church; she feels none of their magic, so Leonardo is left to invent his own sacred philosophy. He finds inspiration under the wild sky in all weathers. He speaks so earnestly of the splendors of nature, that Caterina tries to hold his vision as her own, but she cannot. She can only attempt to keep it in slightly higher regard, and ignore the omens and the storms as nothing significant to her own small life.

Leonardo's dark eyes rarely meet hers; they stare inward to another world. She's not sure he's human. He has the strangeness of a higher being about him. He mutters to an invisible friend named Bella Veritas (beauty and truth), as well as speaking to animals, and birds, and plants, and half-formed visions. He is a danger unto himself around the Buti men-folk – an apparition passing through Earth on a short visit, who keeps apart from the mortals, lest his magic be contaminated or borrowed, and used for mindless tricks. He is here to observe, document, create and discover. He is here to challenge and shock, and to excite and disturb. He dematerializes into the countryside at all hours, and Caterina is glad of it. Glad that Leonardo has some respite from the brutal hands and opinions of her husband.

Leonardo is surrounded with the strangeness that alights on a few select souls out for a casual stroll through greatness. He displays none of the confidence or boastful qualities that wrestle under the surface of his skin. His emotions stir beneath indifference, tense and restless. His shadow flickers large in peak moments. These are mysteries that cannot be disturbed before their time. Leonardo is not like his family; he sees in colorful flashes of insight and reality that overlap, complement, or disagree, and are consequently stored under his scrutiny like bell jars.

Each vision is trapped, caged, documented, and released after study. They are weighed against each other for flaws. Each question begs calculation. Each tell of their length, and depth, and width, and must be recorded, measured and dissected. Leonardo's brain fires like a perpetual furnace. Persistent thoughts are interspersed with incandescent headaches. He hears in snatches of conversation, left dumb and blind to the mundane world, blinking myopically into endless cruelty and distrust. Faces swim into view and morph into clouds of chaos. Humans are illogical, angry and demanding. Animals are a sympathetic source of refuge. Birds are escape artists. "God must be a bird," he announces at age four.

Leonardo searches his family for empathy and finds none, and so he retreats into places that meet his need for order. The adults in his life have impressed their absolutes of obedience upon him, and for this he separates from them, forever. Leonardo imprints early to form subliminal opinions and acts in accordance with elegant rules. His right brain and left hand dismiss as he is dismissed by others. There exists in his mind, a restless gap between joy and subsistence, and the sublime and the grotesque.

When Leonardo scans his inner landscape and imposes it upon the fields and sky, he feels a harmony of purpose, and when his eyes follow the flights of birds, the tension of intense enquiry is displaced by kinship. Leonardo imagines he can feel the muscles of his invisible wings relax into the protective arms of a mother. Once established, his link with nature is fixed as his personal star. Purity is his compass. Ideas are pursued to their ultimate understanding or rejected early as insignificant distractions. There are no exceptions.

For now, Leonardo da Vinci is a five-year-old star about to nova – a celestial promise. His stepfather calls him a curse; his father and grandfather call him nothing at all. He is alive and stored in a convenient place to call out if need be, for genetic duty or to serve the da Vinci family business as a potential employee.

Caterina smiles at Leonardo. She stands taller than usual. She watches him skirt the edges of the property with his eye on the house. Caterina looks away from her son for a moment to smooth her dress. When she looks back he's gone. Leonardo evaporates into the tall grass that swallows him whole in one humane bite.

*"To be conscious
that we are perceiving or thinking
is to be conscious that we exist."*
~ Plato

The DIARY of VERONICA LYONS
age eighteen

A Dream of Fire (nze)

Halifax – 1997
February 7
5 A.M.

I'm not afraid to dream anything now!

I woke agitated, but happy to have felt my brother so close again. His presence in my dream no doubt causes me to retain it, although as dreams go, this one was beyond lucid. I was there, in Florence, at the Vanity Fire again, and it was as familiar to me as the shoreline of St. Margaret's Bay. The bathroom mirror showed that my eyes were red and swollen from crying or the smoke of the fire... maybe both.

I instinctively recoiled from a burst of orange sparks, spat from the fire's heart, and noted the spectators to my left before I took a deep breath and waded nine feet into the white hot crucible of scorching wood. Basil called me in and an unknown woman had my back. I heard my brother's voice say: "I'm coming out, crazy girl" from inside the fire, but I couldn't wait to see him, and so I ran ahead to meet him.

There had been a hole in the blazing construction – a window, shaped like a triangle. It widened into a door with a pointed arch and that was where I entered inside a golden pyramid – a roaring lion's cave of flame, hissing with snakes. I felt the intense heat as a bright tingle of electricity against my skin. Having molecules firmly based five-hundred years from this spot, I didn't ignite or feel the searing pain of burning flesh, nor did I choke on the belching smoke.

I used to think that all bonfires were systematically constructed cairns piled into circular mounds – all the better for gathering around, but the one I breached was no cone-shaped pyre. It was a long barricade of unstable burning rubble where low sections periodically coughed sour clouds of green fumes. It was packed with treasures: paintings of Greek gods, gilded mirrors, gaming boards and jewels, all crushed together, held captive in a web of branches which looked like the the claws of a thousand demons.

Baz was not inside, so I left the heart of fire and stood outside the blaze. There were a few street urchins and their canine siblings lingering within earshot, who slunk the perimeters of destruction. They gave the flames a wide berth, and I noticed several clumps of human stragglers huddled together in random gatherings of worshippers and thugs. I was not surprised they acted like paid mourners, howling and carrying on in a command performance of fake repentance; the raging monk Savonarola, required a show of solidarity, and the citizenry were terrified enough to act as submissively as they could.

The tall shape of Giotto's Campanile wavered in and out of focus behind a haze of smoke and cinders, giving the impression it was about to topple. This imminent disaster would have caused me concern, but I knew the bell tower would be standing for at least another five-hundred years.

My feet ached from patrolling the Piazza Signoria. Inside my shoes burned a fire of my own. I heard the great bell, La Vacca, summon the Florentines to spiritually rally, and the ringing interrupted my preoccupation with discomfort. It sounded like a mournful cow, and I got the impression that I was on time. I had to remind myself that I had a ticket home in my back pocket.

I scanned the vicinity again, looking for Baz as I last knew him, when he was a cheeky six-year-old boy with faraway eyes the color of a spring sky – my fearless leader of twin-ship who left me stranded when he died. I assume this recurring dream is only about him, like the ones that always come on the anniversary of his death. But this time it was unexpected, out of season – a thirteenth reminder that begged me to write it down.

Waiting out the red ash required no watching. I was alone at the fire's death, and in spite of sore feet and fierce hunger, I continued my vigil. No matter how many times I have revisited this location there is something new to see; this time it was a lean tomcat skidding sideways from a jumpy carthorse anxious from the mayhem in the square.

For twelve years I have ignored the scavengers who skulk in the shallow doorways too far away to matter. I know they linger for the major burnings to bank into smolderings, to sift for the indestructible gems-in-waiting, and the lumps of melted gold which lie underneath the charred embers like stars.

February 7
7 P.M.

I carried the smell of the acrid smoke with me all day, and I'm still able to close my eyes and feel the heat of the flames on my face. There was someone else I was supposed to meet... but I woke up too soon. Pico chased Nattie, the new kitten, and crashed a pile of books to the floor, and as much as I tried to recapture the dream, I remained wide awake.

Art is not a clean fuel. ~*PL*

"In rivers,
the water that you touch
is the last of what has passed
and the first of that which comes:
so it is with time present"
~ Leonardo da Vinci

Twice Cursed

Campo Zeppi, Tuscany – July 1, 1457

Caterina leaves her sister-in-law, Fiore, to wipe the noses of the Buti: tanned hooked noses, and wide flat noses that nudge into the endless days of boredom without bothering to test the wind for predators. Already the babies are crying and the small children are wailing to be fed.

The Buti children hide behind their mothers. Fiore stands defiant and faces the wrath of her brother-in-law full on. In this, she is unlike his long-suffering wife. At times like this, when the stakes are high, Caterina has no intention of acting superior. There are days, like today, when acting wretched serves her.

This is a day Caterina could easily unsettle Antonio with a defiant look, but she chooses something else. She wants her husband to leave quickly, and confrontations have stalled him before. Today there must be no endless delays; a stance of humility is best. The two Buti wives know this one thing: that the moments to one's self are not trivial events.

"You look different. It is today?" Fiore asks, after Antonio strides off muttering. Caterina startles at the question. If Fiore can see a difference what may the rest of the household think? But then, women can read further under the skin than men and most children. She must keep her distance from her mother-in-law to stay invisible enough. Caterina barely has the strength to nod a silent yes.

"Your eyes are full of light," Fiore says.

"As long as Piero sees it."

"He would have to be blind."

"I am beginning to believe all men are blind" Caterina says.

Fiore smoothes her sister-in-law's hair and pats her cheek affectionately. The pair are closer than sisters; they're allies fighting a war of slavery against an army of Buti. Neither one thinks they can survive without the other.

"I will make your hair beautiful as soon as he leaves," Fiore says. "I have some new braid knots to try, or will you wear it loose?"

"Loose," comes the reply. "He must see me as a maiden."

The things a woman does to ensnare the best response of a lover are brittle after marriage drains one of seductive magic. Enchanting a man grows more difficult with the years.

Caterina learns early to manipulate the few threads of power left her, and these she weaves around the neck of her husband. She tightens them imperceptibly, and hopes fate will do the rest. Prayers to saints are futile. She prays to any demonic force that can crumble the patriarchal walls of cruelty at their source. In her most guarded imagination she stands apart, and watches her rulers of greed and lust, her judges, and jailors, and executioners, thrash on the ground in their own agonies of defeat. In Caterina's dreams, she steps over their cold bodies and moves into the airs beyond captivity with the same elegance a Florentine lady bypasses a puddle on the way to mass.

The pre-leaving insensitivities postpone Antonio's leaving. Caterina wants to smack the nearest face – any face to transfer her mounting anxiety into a release of surprise for another. She feels increasingly violent towards this clamoring crowd of carelessness called her family, who tears at her time. They claw her day into shreds even before the damp mist of Campo Zeppi burns into the seamless blue of early autumn.

Fiore tells Caterina to make herself ready and leave early. "Slip away now," she says.

Caterina won't risk it. "Once I change my clothes I can't be seen," she says.

Caterina knows a white shirt can tell secrets. She knows a scented, bejeweled peasant with unbound hair, will cause a strong ripple of disturbance across a day marked as commonplace. She knows, because it had happened before on a day like this. It's best to remember that jewels, and shirts, and roses, have voices, and that all such commentaries contain the truth of a lie, and that even a blind cuckold can smell a prayer.

The cramped house is a prison of domestic intensity. Children wanting or hurting or hungry; always something to scrub, or lift, or stir. There are only last minute observances to get the tough guy out the door and on his way to his parallel life. Antonio shows his impatience to be anywhere but there, and deliberately pushes past Caterina too closely. He bruises her arm with the rattle of weapons wrapped in oilskins that he carries like a shrine, raised high and away from his body like an offering.

When Antonio's comrades ride into the yard he's ready. He wheels dismissively from his sour mother and reluctant wife, and his two ridiculous daughters, and his moony stepson with the strange notions of grandeur. He thanks God they will soon be behind him, even though what lies ahead will certainly involve life-threatening skirmishes.

Antonio fights dirty. One day a disgruntled local may have the insight to knock him even more senseless than usual, but so far, none have ventured into that precarious space to confront a professional bully with fists the size of hams and a brain to match.

～

Caterina, the displaced gentlemen's daughter, helps prepare meals for eleven mouths. Two mouths are old and almost toothless. Five are screaming toddlers or howling babies. Leonardo remains separate, an indefinable entity. Fiore is the one who gives Antonio hostile looks when he is especially uncivil. Antonio is unmoved. His brother's wife can think what she likes; she is, like all women, an invisible commodity.

He endures her frowning tirades and dismisses them. She can scratch and bite, but her teeth are no more substantial than the clouds that loom over the fields and valleys of Campo Zeppi.

The stink of Antonio moves with him, outside. It mounts his horse and rides out clinging to his broad back, journeying into the morning, free to pollute another place, and when he's gone the fields settle into a calm sea.

Caterina's mother-in-law, Antonia, sweeps up her grandchildren like a housewife with an angry broom. She swears under her breath that the di Marco whore has ruined her son's life. Today, Caterina cares less than usual. The old woman looks hard at her radiant daughter-in-law, and mutters a mean-spirited incantation. If Caterina returns the stare it could turn Antonia Buti to stone.

Caterina pretends she's alone. Loathing is a powerful charm. A visual hex can easily pass between the eyes of two women, and nothing must jeopardize the spell she has thrown to the stars. A rendezvous with Piero is a sacred opportunity and if Caterina is vigilant, it will be one that Antonia's misery can't touch. There must be no opening for a contemptuous mother-in-law to dilute Caterina's last spark of power.

Caterina had fallen through a chance that arrived on an August afternoon, six years ago. It had been a happy experience. Unplanned. No omen whispered to be careful, but by day's end, it was an imprudent event of wild passion. Now Caterina treats encounters with Piero with more restraint, but a second da Vinci pregnancy may liberate her from a nightmare life. The lives of two spouses separate them, and with a new marriage, she may yet quit her existence of dishonor and take her rightful place as mother to a civilized bloodline.

Caterina carries the possibility of Antonio's death like a jewel, but it's a diamond that melts like ice whenever he returns. He uses her fertility like a weapon to prove he's a begetter of sons, but his plan continues to fail. Antonio beds his wife to relieve himself of organic pressures.

She can have another girl and die doing so; he will have fulfilled his obligation as spouse. The da Vinci had paid him well to take Caterina off their hands, but now, six years later, the money is spent, and he and his brother and father are cursed with a houseful of women.

For all her years of marriage, Caterina obeys in order to survive. She would change the events of 1451 if she could. She would be less naive... less pliable. She understands the low value of her gender more completely now. She knows the harsh rules of legal propriety: a lawyer's family must appear beyond reproach.

Punishment is an unapologetic teacher; banishment is a severe lesson to learn at sixteen. It's clear that her weak father and brothers will always turn their backs on her in favor of a da Vinci nod, and so Caterina now makes promises she can't keep to a god she doesn't believe in. God is another father, and fathers are not forces a daughter may rely on.

Caterina knows that her mother, had she been alive, would have been unable to sway her father and uncles, and that her stepmother, a year younger than herself, would never come to her aid. Had Caterina sniffed out their betrayal, she would have fought them like a cornered bear. Savaged them before they had a chance to steal her destiny.

Caterina is no less suitable a match than Albiera di Amadori, the one chosen for Piero at birth. The two girls had known each other well enough. Caterina even liked the shy creature and helped her through some delicate moments. The daughters of notaries are allowed to mingle together, corralled like pedigree beasts to be fed and watered until their marriage contracts come of age. Caterina had been devastated; her father's bid had simply failed to manifest on the relevant document because he lagged behind a neighbor who had the foresight to apply first.

The business of gestating an heir carries a death sentence within it. Caterina is no barren maid. She proves her fecundity each year, and fate-willing, may get another by Piero to raise her prospects and keep the Buti line from spreading... and now, Albiera da Vinci has failed once more to conceive an heir.

In her first year of marriage, Caterina discovers that the delicious feeling of sleeping alone with one's thoughts is almost as pleasurable as being with a lover. She thanks the showers of shooting stars over Campo Zeppi that her husband is away for months at a time.

Caterina rides defiantly; her face silent and her body telling anyone who cares to read it, that she, Caterina di Marco di Antonio Buti del Vacca, is leaving on a domestic errand, and will return by day's end, to comply once more with the routines imposed by poverty and the rules of rural subservience. But for now, she is of singular purpose and it's best to stay out of her way.

The Cave of Fragilities

Anchiano – July 1, 1457

By midday, the turquoise sky of Tuscany blasts Caterina with hope. It sustains her. Caterina's chilled skin drinks in the sun as she follows the ripe wind into the hills of Anchiano. When the track turns north, Caterina stops to attach her amber brooch to the collar of her white shirt. It catches the light, and she stares into its pockets that look like the bubbles inside dark honey.

The largest bubble contains a small bee, an embryo of flight locked in a golden womb – an ancient, fragile life, overcome by pine lava. It reminds Caterina to stay alert; that sometimes danger arrives in disguise, and that before a fragrant cloud can pass across the sun, one may be compelled to surrender to the sweetness of human nectar.

The shirt and the brooch are two of the possessions from Caterina's marriage chest, flung at her upon leaving – the things she keeps away from Antonio's bitter tongue. If she will not use them, then her daughters may, but this thought is torn before she even reads it. Her daughters are born to a life of service, and if they're lucky, no man will find them attractive enough to pry another generation of perpetual mothers, farm hands, and fodder for the army, from between their legs.

A breeze shakes the marrow inside Caterina's bones. She feels like a flat rose; pressed between passion and duty. Juice gone – a thin papery blossom leached of its vitality that can crumble into flowery ash with the slightest hesitation of wind. Its essence hovers over her like a perfume ghost – a phantom of haunting love. A dead rose can still sing the truth.

Caterina rides for an hour before her shoulders relax into a posture of confidence. She releases the Caterina she pretends to be, and engages the part of her that remains constant in spite of interference. She has little faith in religion, although she attends weekly mass and performs the rituals expected. Her job is to act pious and retreat small enough to pass under the noses of society. Even the backcountry has its pecking orders and spies. Some days Caterina struggles to be free inside a mistake that feels like a prison of stone honey.

Her destination is the olive-press at Molino della Doccia, that lies due south of the cool marshes of Anchiano. The mill of crumbling yellow brick waits on a shady rise off the dirt track to Montevettolini. Behind it, the hill slopes carelessly down to the osier beds that choke the banks of the River Vincio. Here the lazy water meanders past Monte Ceceri, shaped like a swan, on its way to Florence, and picks up speed after sweeping the outskirts of Larciano. Past Larciano it rushes towards the waiting embrace of the Arno. The landscape is familiar; the grasslands along the river anchor the ghosts of Caterina's childhood where she and Piero had played as children and grown to be best friends, and continued to meet as love-struck teenagers.

The mill harbors a secret – an outcrop of granite lumps that form a hollow the size of an apple where papers may be wedged. Letters are sent and received there under the twist of an angular stone. They refer to it as the 'Cave of Fragilities.' Sometimes Piero leaves Caterina a token from the city: a delicacy or a ribbon or a pressed flower. Sometimes she leaves Piero a small thing she has made or found or that belongs to her body: a love knot of wicker or a heart-shaped stone or a lock of her hair. Such things of inconsequence wait there, with the fine ambience of an object recently touched. A memento that holds the aura of a beloved's phantom lips and fingers. These trivial reminders tell of times when a meeting is possible or to beg a simple question, but mostly they're exchanges of two emotional shadows that trip over each other in a forbidden dance, out of step with fate, but too potent to ignore. Caterina and Piero acknowledge all that is left to them. Their messages are clear: *I have been here and will be here again.*

The shrine is revisited in varying degrees of urgency, but never ones of casual connection. The words and gifts alter the fabric of their 'between days,' and bridge the encounters that grow fewer with the business of life – the events which intrude on the hours once held by each as free time, when there was still hope for something kinder than fate.

The DIARY of VERONICA LYONS

July 1, 2003

If compatibility reigned would any imperfection matter? I stand self-pressured... heavy and pale, gravity-trapped within my personal orbit. How would one survive all the inspections? How could I confidently raise my eyes to meet those of a stranger's absolute truth? What would be revealed and what would remain hidden under such scrutiny? An artist cannot lie about beauty... it's the stock and trade of visual perception. I own self-conscious genes, tightly-woven into twin, spinal cord complexity, with cycles fashioned from gold or tin... depending how the light strikes them. ~*VL*

"One rarely recovers
from answered prayers."
~ Veronica Lyons

Peacock Truth

Point Royal Park, Halifax – July 1, 2004

aby Jupiter, eighteen-months-old, snuggles under several blankets in his pram, and scans the canopy of leaves and branches for monkeys. Beside him, the Monday morning duck pond in Point Royal Park is deserted. Its stone bench is an abandoned bookshelf that seats two birdwatchers like bookends, but far enough apart to be solitary.

Veronica gazes past the oily slick of water lilies and fallen leaves, and imagines the tip of Excalibur breaking the surface to emerge in the fist of a goddess. The woman almost next to her is a black and white nun. The silence requires a courteous something. It's chilly for July.

A peacock shriek startles Veronica with a shrill of wild kingdom reality. Peacocks are the antithesis of polite bird society. She rocks her son's baby carriage with a subconscious foot.

Veronica addresses the water. She hears her voice blurt: "I'm an atheist." It shocks her. Peacocks make people do odd things. Yes, it's the peacock's fault.

The nun is surprised, but she joins in as if the two have already established the etiquette of strangers' rapport. She corrects the informal blunder.

"Hello. I'm Sister Camilla." She looks amused.

Veronica turns towards the soft, apologetic voice. The exact sound she expects to issue from a nun. "Sorry that came out wrong. Veronica Lyons. Hi."

"People always want to discuss God with me. I can't imagine why."

"We assume He speaks to you directly. It's the outfit. You're very visible."

"Well, *She* doesn't." It's the expected New-Age feminist response.

"This is my son, Jupiter. He has autism."

"Are you always this blunt?"

"He can see you, but he won't look at you. He never looks at anyone. Only cats. Apparently bird-watching isn't on his list either. Can you tell he has aut.... from his eyes? Can you tell?"

"Perhaps he's distracted from listening to God."

"I said I was an atheist."

"Well, maybe *he* isn't," Camilla says.

"I'm never going to get my head around that possibility."

"Brains aren't called grey matter for nothing. The truth is always grey."

"What can he ever learn?" Veronica asks.

"Well, he's probably a teacher."

"My uncle and I are in the science business. Reality is our religion. Five-hundred-years ago, your church would have considered my son possessed. Maybe it still does."

Camilla spends a few seconds to examine the sadness in Veronica's face. "You look troubled," she says.

"Yes, well, I have a big decision to make."

"The rock and a hard place kind?"

"Yes."

Sister Camilla twists in her seat and leans towards Veronica with a Gioconda smile. "Good, those are the easy ones," she says.

"Nurture strength of spirit
to shield you in sudden misfortune."
~ The Desiderata ~ 1820

Peacock Lies

Point Royal Park, Halifax – July 1, 2004

Veronica thinks the Lady of the Lake must be laughing under the water as she watches bubbles breaking on the surface of the pond. They set the floating water-lilies in motion. A human sigh pushes them into the shadows. It will rain soon.

"In one way, I envy my son," Veronica says. "He'll never have to decide anything. Autism runs in our family. Some genetic flaw. My Aunt Bea stares at birds for hours. With Jupiter, it's cats."

"Lost souls are God's business, not ours," Sister Camilla says.

"Here we go," Veronica thinks. "Then your God should be reported to the Better Business Bureau, or the SPCA," she says. "He has suspect business practices – a typical CEO. Cruel enough to step on his own ants."

Camilla expects more, and Veronica continues: "My son's... *father...* suggests I place Jupiter in an institution. So, there it is, another ant hill for your God to flatten. Not much hope for a miracle. Not really. My son's father is ruled by a wealthy mother, who calls the shots. She's Medusa incarnate."

Sister Camilla rises to the challenge: "Grace isn't luck, and it doesn't descend from the sky like pixie dust. God doesn't play with magic wands; *He or She* uses synchronicity. So, as another wise man said: *'do or do not, there is no try,'* but at least discover the surprise."

"Yoda? You're quoting Yoda?"

"Yes Ma'am," Camilla says.

"Yoda is Catholic?"

"You see? Surprises. You've discovered that nuns watch movies."

Veronica and the day absorb this amazing fact. It isn't profound or new, but it settles on the two women and makes it easier for them to talk. A small, well-known secret has made them companions – intimate enough to argue and badger with no hard feelings, or at least feelings which can be smoothed over politely for the sake of anonymous kinship.

"It's easy for you," Veronica says. "You drop your problems at the feet of ceramic saints every five minutes."

"You could do that if you wanted to," Camilla shoots back.

"Well I don't happen to believe in the wisdom of inanimate objects. You think you're married to God, so you'll pretty much believe anything."

"No, God is my father-in-law. I married his son," Camilla corrects.

"Shouldn't that be *mother*-in-law? Still, it looks good on the resume. Besides, phantom husbands are convenient. No faking headaches or the nightly 'Passions-of-Christ'... scuze the heresy, and an omnipotent patriarch calling the shots to boot. So, did you ever give the Almighty a grandchild?"

Camilla hums a recognizable tune. She sings a line to Jupiter as she touches his fingers. *"We are stardust we are golden, and we've got to get back to the garden,"* she sings.

His eyes flicker towards her song but return to his wildlife vigil when it ends. "So, which disciple said that?" Veronica asks.

"Matthew," Camilla says, "Matthews' Southern Comfort. You know – the hit song, *'Woodstock'*? 1969?... Saint Joni?"

"That was ten years before I was born," Veronica says.

"Well great music is reborn every few years. So stay tuned," Camilla quips.

"I will."

"Are you New-Age enough to believe in rebirth?" Camilla asks. "We founded a mishmash church-of-all-sorts. We were religious about our beliefs, but we couldn't decide which one, and all faiths lumped together, muddy things up – by the way, that was *my* tough decision.

In the end it was simple." Camilla flounces her veil. "I loved the outfit. It was my invisibility cloak, and I loved that I could disappear – evaporate from... things. But here we are, and you think I stand out."

Veronica grins. "You were a hippy!" It's almost an accusation.

"No, I was just irresponsible, but I prefer the term flower-child. There's a big difference," Camilla says.

"No, there isn't."

"The sixties are a past-life. I had a child from that little party. I gave him up for adoption. So... so much for peace and love. The peace movement had the molecular structure of cheese. Mice loved it, but sheep don't eat cheese, and we were sheep."

"I thought Christians were supposed to be lambs, you know, following the great white shepherd into a heaven beyond the stars, and all that?" Veronica says.

"Ah, well, the great thing about stars, is they make pictures in the sky, but you can't see a constellation until you connect the dots. Bigger pictures always require distance. The Flower movement was based on the *me generation* and never looked past immediate gratification. Loving the ones we were with didn't bode well the morning after. Fortunately, every age has its own herald in sheep's clothing."

"So, what's ours then? Fair warning. If you quote anything astrological I will projectile vom....

"It's still Star Trek."

Camilla shrugs. "Sorry, it's kind of astrological," she chuckles.

"No, no, Star Trek is... I think of it as *creative* astronomy," Veronica agrees. "It's only sun-signs that are bullshit. Sorry, but it's true. I thank God for reruns. My hero was Mr. Spock. Who was your favorite?"

"My favorite was the flawed one," Camilla says. "You know for an atheist, you invoke God a lot."

"You mean the captain?"

"No," Camilla smiles and shakes her head. "The female computer. I loved it when she said: *working* while she was thinking, but they should have given her a name. She deserved that. Everyone deserves a name, and she worked hard, 24/7."

Veronica plays up the role of Captain:

"*Stella, take a message: Captain's log, star date 2003. Petty science-officer, Veronica Lyons, has asked for shore leave. The transporter is out. In the meantime she is blethering on the holodeck. She has programmed a park scene where she meets a nun. I'm sending her to sickbay as soon as security comes to restrain her.*"

Camilla answers in cyborg monotone:

"*Working... follow the prime directive. Stay out of sight. Do no harm. Get out before the pitchforks arrive. Don't forget to thank God for Scotty and technology... and remember... Vulcan logic is full of shit. More holes than Swiss cheese.*"

The word shit slaps the conversation serious. "You said shit," Veronica accuses. She laughs and tries to imitate Spock with a raised eyebrow, and fails. "Fascinating," she says.

"I didn't say shit, the computer did," Camilla insists, but the shock takes the wind out of their conversation, and they stare at a mother duck and her ducklings, moving in a line like the targets of a shooting gallery.

"Beyond a wholesome discipline,
be gentle with yourself."
~ The Desiderata ~ 1820

Peacock Promise

Point Royal Park, Halifax – July 1, 2004

Camilla, the Lady of the Flowers, lifts her face to the first raindrop kiss. A few more sprinkle over the pond like wedding rice. Soon the park will be umbrella territory.

"I have to give my answer tomorrow," Veronica says. "Is woolgathering and meditating the same thing?"

"Yes."

"Then I should be enlightened by now don't you think?"

"You're stalling for time," Camilla says. "You know you can only respond to a fake question with a fake answer. Serendipity is alive, but you can pretend to argue with it if you want to."

"So you're saying that I've been debating serendipity?" Veronica asks.

"You've been *praying* Veronica."

"No Ma'am. I'm an atheist. Born and bred."

"Prayers have to percolate, rise to the surface and simmer slowly," Camilla says.

"Well they sound delicious. You're a great therapist, Santa Camilla del Fiore."

Sister Camilla smiles a question. "Well thank you for the promotion, although I'm not sure what it means."

"Sorry, I used to study Italian architecture and art at university. The Santa Maria del Fiore in Florence, is the only church I'm interested in exploring, and *Del Fiore* means 'of the flowers.' And... the old name for Firenze, was Fiorenza, after their symbol, the Calla Lily. I see the word 'calla' inside your name. Coincidence? I can't help seeing words inside of words. I love anagrams. My name is an anagram. I expect you've heard of it," Veronica says.

"Your eyes got all bright just then."

"The Italian Renaissance is a subject that kind of carries me away. It's *my* religion, well it used to be, but I still believe art is as close to divinity as life gets, and I thank you Saint Calla Lily, of the transcendental flower-power."

"No need to thank me, *'Saint Veronica of the true face.'* I just sat here and watched the ducks while you prattled on. Anyway, whoever you're trying to convince, your little atheist prayers will be answered one way or another, so hang on to something solid," Camilla says.

"How does one ever know they've made the right choice? I mean when does the penny finally drop? Or does it do you think?"

Camilla pretends to flip a coin in the air. Her eyes follow it, and she fakes its capture with the palm of her other hand. She raises it high in a triumphant toast between slender fingers.

"A great philosopher, Piet Hein, once advised: to decide anything – toss a penny and play heads or tails. It won't matter how it lands because when the coin is in the air, you'll suddenly know how you *want* it to land. Veronica. You... are up in the air, and you know what to do."

Camilla opens her hands as if to release a bird. She blows the fake coin from her hand, and mimics the surprised face of a magician amazed by his own trick.

Veronica applauds with slow-motion clapping. "So your religion thinks Jupiter is special?" she says.

"I don't have high enough clearance to speak for Mother Church," Camilla says. "Personally, I consider your child to be... um..." The nun chooses her word carefully... "*Selective.*"

"Nuns should be able to speak up for their Mother," Veronica says, and rustles a bag of birdseed at a pair of shimmering blue-green creatures approaching from opposite sides like velociraptors. More iridescent turquoise heads waddle towards them from the pond.

"I think we give the Mother-and-Child pretty good press. I see the peacocks and ducks have joined us," Camilla says.

"Yes, well only the drakes. They're more aggressive than the hens. Vanity gives them chutzpah."

"God does amazing work," Camilla says, deliberately sly.

"Your God's a man. A shrewd businessman."

"God's an artist. Male birds have to be more colorful in order to..."

"Sure, like red cardinals? And, I'd call the Pope a *human* peacock," Veronica blurts. "No offense, but so is the parade of your plaster saints. Gaudy. It's even a nice pun. *Goddy.* I notice you're dressed conservatively for contrast. Minions wear brown and black. Nuns and monks and the poor." Veronica points to her camel coat and classic wellingtons. "Like me."

"Red shoes distract girls into big trouble," Sister Camilla says, waiting for the inevitable *'what would you know'* look, but it doesn't come.

Veronica stares hard at the water. "Yes, I know the fairytales: red shoes and glass slippers and cats wearing boots. Brothers' Grimm women may have been witches, or princesses, or peasants, but all of them were greedy or stupid and..."

"And they didn't fare too well as I recall," Camilla agrees. "Their stories were cleaned up for our generation. Cinderella is a rags-to-riches kind of girl. I'm the opposite: a silk-to-homespun story. What kind of story are you?"

Veronica lifts a cynical boot in the air and examines the leaves stuck to the leather toe. "Prince Charming was a creep with a foot fetish who didn't notice Ellie till she was dolled up. What does *that* tell you?" She tosses a handful of seeds into a cloud that peppers the ground into a food frenzy.

A peacock trumps the quacking with a piercing cry that fails to engage Jupiter. The child is busy communing with a black blob of liquid mercury that slithers over the branches as it darts and hesitates, and turns on a dime to listen to higher instructions. The squirrel god says climb; squirrel appetite says approach. Even rodents have a tough time deciding greed from survival. Descents are dangerous.

Veronica watches the ducks scoot away from their big cousins. "Somebody's got to feed the underdog. The wife-birds in the nest. The bird-mothers teaching their chicks to swim and fly. They're the ones that have to squabble over the crumbs left behind... and what about the ugly ducklings that never turn into swans? The ones only a mother can love. What about them? And please don't tell me God watches over them. I apologize for my bluntness. I know it's rude. I guess I need to vent."

"It's called confession. I hear it's good for the soul."

A chuckle escapes Jupiter, and Veronica and Camilla turn to see a squirrel on his blanket, waving its tail in Jupiter's face.

Veronica imprints Camilla's veil, full skirt, shawl, and her 'Mona Lisa' smile. "No doubt," she says.

There's a long pause while the lady of the lake takes back her magic offering. "I wish I'd never been born," Veronica says. "How's that for a confession? My mother thought so too, so... so much for mothers."

"And yet you champion them. You want to feed them."

"Mothers get hungry. I'm hungry. I bet that squirrel is a mom."

"I will pray for you both."

"Thanks, but I'd rather you didn't include me," Veronica says. "I'm sure you know the curse of answered prayers."

The DIARY of VERONICA LYONS

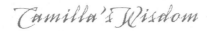

Camilla's Wisdom

July 10, 2004

My wisdom teeth were removed this morning. I remembered Sister Camilla as I washed into Middle-earth on Demerol wings. Her words of wisdom followed me a long way: She said not to confuse sacrifice with responsibility, and that loss was a necessary form of love. She said humans were inherently careless. She told me to make a wish, and to say hello to 'Mona Lisa.' She said her kind were half-a-million strong.

I saw that she carried a bridal bouquet of white Calla Lilies against an Alice-blue wedding gown. She tucked one flower behind my ear, placed one on Jupiter's blanket, and made the sign of the cross over him with another like a magic wand, before saying goodbye. She called him everyone's child. A sweet scent of violets made me sleepy, and cathedral bells blew me into heaven.

I dreamed that I laid a wreath of peacock feathers at the feet of a St. Christopher colossus, the patron saint of travelers, while the 'Nike of Samothrace' stood to his left, tall as a pillar like an approving wife. I heard the whoosh of a Star Trek door open and close as I was whistled aboard my own ship with its engines engaged in a buzzing of bees.

I noticed the smiling eyes of a nurse above a surgical mask and recognized my Aunt Bea. Behind her head, the crown of an oak tree made a halo – its branches swarming with turquoise monkeys. She held up a canary, perched on the tip of her finger for me to kiss, but it turned and tapped its golden tail on my lips. "I call tails," she said... and then: "Choose... chicken or egg... step right up... duckling or swan... place your bets". Her nurse's uniform changed to the habit of a Franciscan nun, but the robes were covered in Vegas sequins.

I heard the seductive tease of a spinning roulette wheel, and the gentle plop of the white ball as it decided my fate. The ball was an egg. I had chosen. My winnings were pushed towards me with a crucifix. The croupier was a gypsy woman with an enigmatic smile. She knew something. She took the egg and crushed it silently, reverently with kindness while she stared into my eyes. It was empty.

Mr. Hein had been right; I knew what to do. I tossed my problem into the clouds, caught my decision in mid-air, and the coin disappeared. I looked up where it had momentarily eclipsed the sun, and the sky turned to night. My Uncle Oz smiled down at me through a firmament of stars. He told me to connect the dots counting backwards from one hundred-and-one. It made the shape of a boot and I spun into the star called Florence. ~𝒫𝒦

"Sometimes
the last harvest is the sweetest."
~ Lisabetta

Twice Blessed

Anchiano, Tuscany – July 1, 1457

She sits on horseback, tall enough to reach heaven, and Piero da Vinci forgets the effect Caterina has over him until he sees her horse pass the stained sails of the mill, hiding her progress: first a sheet of white linen, next a bright reveal of copper hair, her back regal – free of chains. Her posture on the farm is not as straight; it suffers from shame, as much as the functions of workhorse and birthing three children in five years. Humility has nothing to do with it.

Piero watches Caterina's head tilt to hear the sun. She is nervous. The horse picks up her body's signal and prances the last few yards, crushing the beds of wild chamomile. She rides silently through the fragrance of dog parsley and lavender. Piero feels guilty for feeding a torturous plan that shames such a brave emotion as passion. Desire has reduced them to belligerent pawns prone to defy rather than comply.

Six years of backbreaking labor has failed to turn Caterina into an early crone. But it will. Piero knows without a doubt he will turn from her the way a sunflower seeks the sun, to the newer tender shoots of womanhood, barely older than one's own sons. The fresh daughters paraded out, fragile as doves: empty-headed, trained to submit, fearful but succulent and willing to obey the patriarchy that begot them. And their stepmothers, only slightly more senior in years, happy to be rid of the constant reminder that they were once the same silly darlings of rosy-cheeked promise, thrown to the lying old wolves who vowed them undying protection. It's the way of the world, and Piero plans to have as many wives as it takes to birth a stable-full of male heirs.

⁓

Caterina cherishes the last moments of a tryst that runs like a startled rabbit. She dives and swims and washes ashore, left like human driftwood to bleach in the sun that exposes her guilt and the recent sins she has committed in the name of love. She rights the confusion of her wild hair and twisted clothes, and moves towards Lezza.

The pony's head is bowed in the heat of the day, grazing, but it hears the storm of Caterina's crushed skirts approaching in a defiant bustle. Beneath them, Caterina is still moist and ready, but the fox is gone and the position of the sun tells her it's late.

Caterina, mother of three, possibly four, turns Lezza's nose north into the oncoming spiral of road dust. Her pony snorts through the flurry of leaves and gravel, kicks through it with a fine side-step and carries her into the landscape beyond where the wind vanishes. There is no need to hurry. The only feeling of expectancy left, is to return to the familiar crush of humanity with the resolve of good food and the secret hope she carries a second seed from Piero within her.

Caterina's reverie carries horse and rider home like a flickering torch towards the certainty of a meal spent in idle meditation, her two girls mercifully clamoring with their cousins for attention, and Leonardo, a silent force of nature, slipping between them all with ferocious willpower.

During the evening, Leonardo sits apart and smiles to himself, wrapped in a disturbing glow of solitude. Caterina envies him the ability to preserve his innermost haven while being bombarded with words like angry fists. Caterina moves to hug Leonardo, but as always he anticipates and dodges her touch. He does not dislike his mother; he keeps her a stranger. No-one may stray uninvited into his carefully-constructed sanctuary of strange beauty. He hates to be touched.

⁓

The fork-tailed kites of Monsummano circle and swoop like the flourishes of a notary's pen – looping and dipping with emphasis on the abrupt turns, to dart away as a dash or alight on a high branch as a dark silhouette like a blotch of ink resting its wings against white clouds. Somewhere within an afternoon's ride, Caterina knows Piero is making polite conversation or taking supper, or sleeping with his barren wife. Caterina tries to imagine his presence so close; barely eight miles over the low-lying hills. Piero is home, nestled under the same stars, but for Caterina, the country is only a vast space between her body and his. It is an ever-expanding separation of fortunes. At night, Caterina stands under the moon and gazes across the distance feeling alone.

There's enough rosewater left to wash Piero away, but Caterina savors being his phantom wife for a few more hours before life picks her up and tosses her into relentless mourning and women's work. She remembers the day as something intensely richer. She can refine the adventure, and by tasting it twice, she rewrites something more poetic than reality. Tonight she will indulge her fantasies by staring into the low thatch of ceiling, blessedly alone within the circle of nine other souls, snoring and scratching and whimpering in their sleep. She will lean on the soft sounds of the animals breathing behind the wall she shares with their shelter. She will hear the beasts pause and snort and shuffle in their straw, and listen to the night noises of the grasses rustling under the owls hunting for mice, and the moon searching the ground for lost souls, and foxes using its light to sniff out innocent rabbits. Most of all, Caterina will remember Piero's tender "Ti amo" and the way he had looked into her eyes and waited until they cried out in ecstasy together.

The daughters of Caterina and Antonio are blissfully ignorant of a more sumptuous fate than the rough living of farm life. They have not seen the velvet curtains and the four-poster beds or been blinded by the sheen of polished gold or the redness of rubies or tasted the temptations of marzipan and honeyed-figs. For them, the snoring of their father and uncle and grandfather represents a hub of ultimate safety. Resting inside uncomplicated dreams of a predictable future, is what the open road and riverbank-love means to Caterina, and the blue updrafts of skies filled with birds means to Leonardo.

Sixty days later, Caterina smiles into the morning. She places her rough hands across the flatness of her belly. Inside Caterina's womb, Lisabetta curls in amniotic solitude, an embryo quickened with grace, pulsating like a trembling shrimp – another crust of random proto-plasm. A child in amber. Lisabetta is the belated twin; the beloved shadow.

When Lisabetta is united with Leonardo they are something quite extraordinary. Together they will have enough of what the other lacks, to become an irrepressible, singular force-of-art.

The DIARY of VERONICA LYONS

Halifax
October 31, 2004

Something tainted and impure remains from the dream-time… a presence of forever lost… suffering suffused into a hard insistent ball… nausea and waking pains. Growing-pains. Waiting is necessary; remaining open is vital. I am willing to understand the moment, later. The notion that time is the enemy is an illusion. It's the thoughts of incrim-inations, small and defeating, that are spineless opposing forces to good. Low vibration thoughts of loss and lack replicate themselves like bacteria. ~*VL*

"If I had a world of my own,
everything would be nonsense.
Nothing would be what it is,
because everything would be what it isn't.
And contrary wise, what is, it wouldn't be.
And what it wouldn't be, it would.
You see?"
~ Lewis Carroll

Second Year

Halifax – December 1, 2004 (Jupiter age two)

Jupiter Lyons is a child who dreams in surprises. His attention surfaces from time to time. He feels the world grate against his skin, filtered through bright static. Sound-scapes startle him. They arrive out of focus, brittle and loud. He's a tender two-year-old, lost in a haze of autism – a child who plays hide and seek with the world.

The child is a consummate escape artist, and when his mother initiates connection, Jupiter looks through her until they physically drift apart. Looking and seeing are different kettles. Jupiter is amused by peripheral angels and a desire for squares; he chatters in cat-speak to his furry subjects, Pico and Nattie, with rapt adoration – eyes half-closed.

Jupiter's out-of-focus smile echoes the one that stares from the otherworldly 'Mona Lisa' poster in his mother's kitchen. Their levels of contact are radically opposed. Veronica welcomes the invitation from the painting and heeds the 'no trespassers' sign from her child.

Somewhere behind Jupiter's eyes is a tiny box room with windows closed tight to keep in his light. Inside, lie brightly illuminated conversations, and scraps of songs, and childish passions, and tidy piles of unmet needs tied up with clean ribbons. Stretched out from a thought no bigger than the dot of an 'i' is an extraordinary energy which intermittently circles the perimeter to paw at four swinging doors. From under each door protrudes an electric string humming with the first sound. Jupiter's vocal chords are a tangled ball of silent opinions and stillborn questions. Veronica endures her son's *terrible twos'* with fear, on mood-altering medication.

If Veronica was counting, she would notice her Pan-child collates his life in fours: Four building blocks. Four bites. Four steps. Each wall in Jupiter's universe holds a leaded window divided into four. Each pane frames a white landscape; barren but for sixteen felines chasing their tails in a funhouse mirror. Each door is a deeper shade of sky blue. Four-times-four, plaintive mews distributed evenly with grace. Jupiter counts them all day long.

"Our lives became a blend
of apocryphal god-bolts
and random encounters"
~ Lisabetta

Fire & Ice

Tantallon, Nova Scotia – 2005

Veronica believes unemployment renders a human unfit to be considered valid sentient life. She processes her forced sabbatical as shameful. Low self-esteem thrives between the birth of an illegitimate promise and the ships-that-pass-in-the-night kind of love.

She fights small fires: the contained flash-fires of single parenting, selling her art, and negotiating the road bumps of greater autism. Like a regular firefighter, Veronica spends the majority of her workweek in preparation for events that rarely happen, and so she polishes the art of spare time into readiness for something unseen, trying to emulate the legitimate idleness of highly-regarded street angels.

She collects karmic brownie points on the coattails of her uncle's science. The position of 'Girl Friday' to a genius should count for something on the premise that lives spent in pursuit of great service deserve some leniency.

Veronica's contribution to her uncle's mission towards sainthood, assuages some of the guilt, but her take on it is 'goodwill by association' and she had been given time off for *bad* behavior. Maternity leave. That's how her ex-boss, almost mother-in-law, Millicent Duke, sees it, and what the Ice Queen sees, freezes everyone. Her employees hear plenty and see everything, but they speak no evil. Well, not to her face. Her son, Niles, had been the prince of charm – easy when your mother is Medusa incarnate.

Veronica is a semi-conscious mother, stuck between two freedoms – a daughter lost between two fathers; she's an unmarried wife. For years she has played out the surviving half of twin-ship, recovering from the near-misses of accidental love. Veronica remains a life in waiting... an artist between painting and a hard place. She feels 'let go' or 'set free' depending on her mood. Mostly it feels like banishment. She colors between the lines like a cat on its eighth round of survival.

"Darwin is full of shit," Veronica exclaims one night to a startled Pico. Pico starts to purr. "It isn't the fittest who survive; it's the ones with the largest bank balance," she tells him. The financial chain is a beast of supply and demand. One serves or is served up: a dainty dish or a whole pig. Hand-to-mouth greed.

Fake retirement aside, it's a novelty to shelve debt for a while. Millicent owes Veronica's uncle – big time. Niles owes her for a few small good times, and she owes her son the chance to live with a healthy mother. The tax man will never know the difference between guilt-money and mercenary severance pay.

Hardly any felines of her acquaintance make it past three or four curiosities, but Pico and Nattie pull Veronica through hoops of circus fire, and she lands on all fours – her two legs plus those of her son's. Pills make it possible to avoid being strangled by tightrope wire.

Veronica can no longer tell if she is a proper care-giver, or a large human kitten lugged around by the scruff of her life. Pet cats serve as her confessors, and hot water bottles, and teddy bears with attitude. Cats exhibit gumption – something she once cultivated; something she once assumed would be the making of her.

The ghost of post-career happy-hour toasts, mock her anxieties – imaginary champagne glasses filled with hemlock. Here's to fear and deal-breaker tugs of responsibility. Here's to the death of poverty and the right number of life boats. Here's to all who sail with her. Veronica hopes fate will Christen her latest voyage with enough poison to combat rough seas. Beyond this dream there be dragons and pirates and insanity and the edge of the world.

The best part of Veronica, knows she is in search of true north and realignment to a heroic workforce. To this end, she drifts towards chutzpah, but she surrenders before battles begin and accepts white-out nights in place of one, steadfast, white knight. Courtly love is a dirty lie.

The DIARY of VERONICA LYONS

Winter Wasteland

Halifax
December 1, 2005

Rather never than late, the winter has come in like a lamb. The first innocent snow has whitewashed the world, but underneath lie all the same problems, feverish and hot. I can hear the second snow ... the lion's share, hanging heavy in the grey clouds, roaring.

I took Jupe to the window and showed him the snow, but he only saw the single snowflake that landed on cue on the glass in front of him. His breath made a patch of mist, and I took his finger and drew a happy face in it. I could tell his eyes didn't reach past it to the street.

I dressed Jupiter for the playground in the navy-blue one-piece snowsuit we found in a thrift store. The nylon fabric is imprinted with tiny silver snowflakes he insists are stars. He watched solemnly while I retrieved his mittens, dried on the radiator. I demonstrated how warm they were against his cheeks and threaded their string through his sleeves. He stood passively as a doll, while I stuffed his fingers into twin red cushions. Doll hands dressed by a little girl playing house.

The mittens reminded me of the time Basil and I made a crude telephone from a couple of tin cans strung together. It never worked, but we didn't need cans or even mouths to communicate, and when our snow fell, we zoomed. We frolicked. We raced toboggans down a hill steep enough to make Cate crazy. Well, crazier.

Jupiter stood like a sentry, arms at his sides. Autism etiquette meant he endured being dressed. His eyes stared through me like pieces of coal. I tied a red wool scarf around his neck, buttoned three lumpy buttons, deposited a red and white striped toque on his head, and tweaked his carrot nose as a finishing touch. Dressing Jupiter was like building a small snowman – too old for a soother; too young for a pipe.

He remained unresponsive until I rattled the nut jar. Hearing him say 'skwirls' made me sad. His one-word gem broke the silence like the last icicle in the world, falling. Meaningless potent conversations. Jupe and I are minimalists. Marginal souls.

The word 'skwirl' was a question as well as a statement. It meant: 'are we going to feed the squirrels?' as much as, 'yay! ... we're going to feed the squirrels!' The enthusiasm is mine. I have never heard Jupe say 'hooray' in any language, or seen him express joy before he meets the squirrel or cat face to face. Afterwards, yes ... he radiates life. He will melt a little... or a lot. Animals animate him. Creatures jump-start his brain across miles of white static. It's awful to imagine his own storms of whiteout terrors may be worse than mine. When his 'friends' appear, Jupiter's eyes are bright windows and mine require windshield wipers.

I fastened Jupiter into a pine chair with runners for legs. It has arms like a red steel cage, and the word 'Flyer' written on the side – a child's chariot pulled by a mother horse. I felt harnessed. Held back. I wanted to run, but I was compelled to drag a loaded sled. I don't think of Jupe as a burden, but somehow I feel reduced to a beast. No thoroughbred prancer, but a slow ox hauling a mute Raggedy Andy, bundled into a limp, red, silver, and blue package.

Other kids wave their arms and shriek giddy-up! We are

plodders. I was yoked to a steady walk with no jingle bells. Jupiter glided. I guess it's a form of flying. I tramped and the sleigh covered my tracks.

The playground had disappeared under a white cloth. It looked like an abandoned room with furniture draped in dust sheets. Jupiter looked like a three-year-old astronaut landed on the moon ... an American icon covered in stars and stripes deciding where to plant a flag. He stood surveying an alien landscape and finally headed for the moon-squirrels. He moved deeper into wonderland ... a ghostly field with its crystal swings and a white seesaw, surrounded by trees made of lace. Snow collected in the empty wading pool. I had the impression of cold flakes softly falling like frosted cereal in a bowl. I watched a mental Christmas movie – a poignant scene with a muted soundtrack. Jupiter called out "Skwirl" three times and his words rebounded from tree to tree. I had to look away. Life is unfair.

I looked back at him and saw that he resembled a small statue like a low gravestone. A cold shape that watched over the death of grass. Jupiter scanning beyond the edge of his latest thought. I called him and he turned at once, a frozen snowman with eyes made out of coal – his sweet mouth applied to a chilly expression, neither a frown nor a smile. It simply hung straight – a tiny horizon below eyes like two cities marked on the map of a lost world.

It saddens me that I have to leave him alone in his own frontier: a glacier polished smooth of emotions with no dancing snowmen or snow angels in sight. Snow angels require lion snow, deep and feathery pillow snow... wintery thick carpet snow... mauve powder-puff snow.

I wish Jupe and I could live inside a snow globe with a microscopic zoo – safe from the greater food-chain of society. Warm blizzards, swirled for pleasure like a glass of fine brandy. A contained earth, tipped on its axis from the tailwinds of passing angels.

We caught snow on our tongues, and I covered his boots in snow, but there were no squirrels and I told my little garden gnome a ridiculous lie. I said they were away doing their Christmas shopping. To change the subject I burst into song. I actually startled myself; singing is not something that comes natural to me. Any returning, self-respecting squirrels would have headed for cover.

I sang the lyrics of 'Frosty the Snowman' to Jupe: 'was a happy happy soul.'.. 'there must have been some magic.'.. 'he began to dance around.'.. 'shouting catch me if you can...' but there was no magic in Jupiter's knitted red-striped toque with its sheepskin lining, and droopy earflaps, and blue pompom, and my song lacked the music of a happy soul. Each note hit a floating crystal star in a digital snow-wars game and was blown out of the sky. Did I mention that life was unfair?

Jupiter was not wearing a top hat. His nose was not an orange Pinocchio lie. The snow was not deep and crisp and even; it was an un-ironed drift that would be gone by noon. Not even enough to build a snow-child, but sufficient to trail thin parallel lines in the blue snow that were all that was left to show we had been there. ~*JL*

"Love is invisible and inaudible.
So how will I know it arrives?"
~ Veronica Lyons

Jupiter Four

Halifax – 2006 (Jupiter age four)

Jupiter's Leo dolls are a species unto themselves. He clutches a stuffed lion toy in his right hand while he crayons with the other. Three identical lions sit in a row on the windowsill. Veronica assigns each of them a number, but her son knows them from each other by their distinguishing characteristics; Jupiter's lions are individuals with attitude. Quadruplets split into shards of power.

The Children's department of 'Knights Bookstore' had been deserted when Veronica rolled a shopping cart past a wire bin of stuffed animals marked clearance. *Buy one, get one free.* She noticed they were all 'seconds' – discounted goods. Jupiter made his mother stop, and examined the contents so carefully that Veronica waited long past the allotted time for idle browsing. She studied him like a scientist. Jupiter, a star in a petri dish waiting to be discovered.

Jupiter sorted them. Colored critters were thrown back like undersized fish. Jupiter collected a pile of white lions. He held them up, compared faces, and discarded until four were left. One of the 'keepers' was the least damaged of the bunch; the remaining three were odd choices. Veronica watched her son carefully.

The lions were the marketing offspring of a storybook character from *The Rainbow Bridge** where all the animals were white until they crossed over a rainbow into another world, and turned the color of the first food they ate. Jupiter had liked the illustrations. His favorites were the lion that dipped his nose in strawberry jam before drinking milk, so he turned white, but his nose stayed pink, and the blue elephant – the happy victim of blueberry pie. Milk and deserts were foods Jupiter could relate to without stress... at least pies and round cakes that had been transformed into the positive shape of a wedge.

Jupiter scrutinized each lion face: two beads for eyes (most askew), a pink triangle nose, white felt ears stuck on with dodgy glue, and mouths stitched carelessly in black yarn. His unnatural selection favored the haphazard over symmetry. Except for that most perfect, *'one,'* the lions represented a motley Darwinian pool of endangered species: a forlorn specimen with one ear, another with a sad expression, and one with a leg dangling by a thread.

Before they reached the checkout, Jupiter had torn off three eyes and tossed them overboard with two ears and a tail.

The young cashier had astonishingly purple hair with a green stripe "Two for five dollars? That's a great price," she said. The girl beeped three barcodes and reached for Jupiter's new prize, but he hugged the perfect doll fiercely and wouldn't give it up. Veronica read the girl's name tag and asked Judy to please swipe the same tag twice, instead. "We're not supposed to do this," Judy said, as she complied. She glared at a spoiled child and shook her head; Jupiter smiled back at a dim girl. He had simply been a good father.

Jupiter began to sing: 'Hey Jude,' and sang the chorus: "Judy Judy Judy Judy," mimicking the crescendo of the original.

"Is that a joke?" Judy asked.

"Yes," Veronica had replied, halting Jupiter's rendition of the chorus' final shriek: Judeeeeeeeeeee! which would have inevitably followed.

Judy's expression remained a question mark.

"We play the Beatles a lot," Veronica explained.

"Who?" the girl asked.

---

*Author's children's book

"Never mind. I expect the computer will handle it fine," Veronica had said, as she patted the fourth lion's head. She was thrilled they'd made it through the transaction with no loud critiques of purple hair.

The purchases never made it into a plastic bag. Jupiter crushed them together, receipt and all, as if they were one creature. In the car every tag had to be removed. Jupiter watched, concerned, until his new friends were freed with his mother's manicure kit. There could be no identifying manufacturer's labels. Staples and plastic strings were bad. Buttons were taboo and would be replaced with thread later.

From then on the foursome travelled as Jupiter's companions, although Veronica noticed that one toy was always favored: riding shotgun in the car or propped beside Jupiter's dinner plate or cuddled to sleep. It took months to realize the 'Leo' her son carried matched his mood. It was the best ten dollars Veronica ever spent.

Mother and son make gingerbread men. Veronica rolls the spicy dough thick, and lets Jupiter work the cookie cutter. He guards the first batch while they cool and takes frequent glances at the second tray still baking. When it comes time to decorate, Jupiter tells his mother: "no buttons – no buttons – no buttons". She leaves the gingerbread tummies bare and squeezes icing dots for eyes on all but the one Jupiter snatches away. He gives the blank shape to Leo Four – the lion with no face. He takes another gingerbread man and scrapes off one of its eyes while it's still soft, and pops the sweet dot into his mouth. The one-eyed cookie is delivered express to Leo Two.

Leo Two has one yarn eye, one ear, and one leg. Jupiter reaches for a third cookie. Veronica experiences a quiet eureka. The second batch is divided into groups. A quarter of them gets two eyes close together, another gets eyes far apart. The rest have one eye or none. Jupiter chuckles and squirms happily. Four cookie doppelgangers are matched to their twin dolls. Veronica is rewarded with a leg hug. A rare thing. Jupiter licks off an icing mouth before he takes a bite. He eats the head first; Veronica stares at hers as if it's a voodoo doll.

The next day, Jupiter exchanges his happy-face lion for the one with no ears, mouth, nose, eyes or tail. Shortly, after its three brothers are propped together in a haystack, Veronica watches her son shut down and enter one of his grey silences. The scene is eerie until she realizes it's authentic theatre... the purity of elegant communication: monkey-see-monkey-do. The fallout is immediate and positive. A breakthrough of silent aha's. The consequences are startling. Awareness means paying attention until Jupiter's Rosetta Stone is decoded. She is a mom-anthropologist and her son is a civilization unto himself.

Jupiter's language is an alphabet of shapes and colors and numbers. He arranges his food into rows of even numbers. Geometric shapes are validated in order: squares and cubes are favored; triangles are next. Spheres and circles discarded. His toy chest is an untapped encyclopedia. Veronica lists its treasures against the contents of a shortbread tin of clearly unwanted minutiae: a tartan ribbon, buttons, marbles, chocolate M&M's (the orange ones; Veronica had been given the rest), an orange string, orange crayons and orange markers. Orange is clearly not tolerated. Veronica begins to read her son like the first-reader of a foreign language. She checks Jupiter's eye movements towards Leo One and Leo Two for yes's and no's. What Veronica never hears is Jupiter whispering privately with Leo One – the special times, when Jupiter calls Leo One, Dad.

Eyes are tricksters, and lions have no eyebrows to determine mood. Veronica replaces their button eyes with crosses of thick black darning wool. Jupiter says that each X has four triangles in an invisible square, and so he is thrilled.

The Leos are sewn from unbleached linen, mannequin-style, with two dangling arms and legs. Leo One looks happy, Two is angry – Jupiter has drawn claws onto his paws with a black marker, Three is sad and anxious – armless and clawless, impervious to hugging, Four is vacant of any expression minus eyes and nose and mouth. Leo Four represents every negative emotion: anxiety and depression and disinterest; his arms are usually tied into a knot – wrapped around himself in a self-hug. There are three felt noses bigger or smaller or slightly off-center.

Jupiter counts his 'family' after each move of a checker on a black or red square. He counts them into a four after every fourth move. The round plastic discs have been pushed under the carpet and replaced by small blocks. He uses his left hand to perform the rites of building, and to eat, and to squeak his colored markers across seas of clean white paper. He loves the smell and sound of them.

His mother's voice penetrates his task, but in no way disrupts his concentration. Voices are separate entities that fly overhead like birds. He counts the three pillows on the couch. There should be four. Four is better. Jupiter's eyes get lost in the tangled squares of a plaid blanket. His mother doesn't understand that squares need to be free of each other.

Plates without borders drop food. Drawing paper floats until Jupiter connects four lines into a two-dimensional fence. He can relax. His drawings can't spill off the edges. With this comforting thought, Jupiter dismisses the world to count the handful of cheese cubes which descend from his mother's sky. They land in a heap. One or two form a crooked line. Jupiter counts eleven cubes and makes a fuss. Veronica deposits another handful that brings Jupiter's treasure to seventeen. Instead of protesting, he discards one and arranges the others in a grid: four rows of four cubes before he can eat them. His mother's willfulness is a constant source of agitation. He has been teaching her the art of the squares for a long time.

Jupiter wants his plate to descend without food first. He likes to contemplate its emptiness before it is inhabited by foreign colors, and shapes that fight. Orange cheese is an insult to perfection. White cheese is best; pale yellow is acceptable. He has to prepare the battle ground for what will materialize. This time his fear subsides. Four rows of four morsels is a war won. Soon his mother will be on his side. He has one square plate with a blue border that he likes. The round ones were returned after their contents were deposited onto a square drawn on paper. Veronica had understood the first rule of the square.

Veronica assumes Jupiter wants finger food, but when peas are presented there is holy hell. The green beads are hurled into an angry cloud. Grapes are rolled aside and discarded behind plants or pushed down the sides of the sofa cushions. Veronica finds them everywhere. The world is a dangerous place of fives and seventeens and spheres. Leo Three stares at a plate of five savory bites. The solution is quick. Jupiter smiles at Pico rolling around the cheese cube thrown in his direction. Veronica tells him that lions are cats. "Cats are the best things", Jupiter announces at age four, with a clincher that shocks Veronica: "God must be a cat." Faeries and ghosts appeared in Jupiter's books, but never, God. God was a concept that had never been approached.

Mother and son enjoy a backyard picnic. Jupiter loves to sit on an island of blue blanket in a grass sea. He kneels in the centre and surveys the lawn like Aladdin scanning from his magic carpet and declares with authority. "Dandy lions must be left to grow." His *'dandies'* are in agreement. It's five against one. Veronica will be stuck with an unneighborly spread of green with yellow polka dots if she complies. If she doesn't, the wrath of Leo Two will argue the dandelion's case with magic-marker claws. Veronica smiles and tells Jupiter his lions with their long stringy legs, are lanky-doodle-dandies which pleases him. Doodles are his favorite art form.

The DIARY of VERONICA LYONS

Subliminal Lyrics

Halifax
April 15, 2006
Friday

It's late afternoon. Jupiter is still at the neighbors. I needed a break. I made some errands without a full baby-seat in the back of the car. I felt indescribably free, but sad. The wind is high and wild-warm mad, howling dark and dry. A winter storm in April. The trees are swaying madly and I have songs in my head.

I visited the library, drove home, and took Peyton for a walk with my brain on fire. My walk was lonely. I put heavy stones in my pocket to stop my ka blowing away. I left a light in the window and tied a string to the front door. 'Hey, it's only a paper moon.'.. Wandering in the dreamtime can lead one astray.

I want warm toes next to mine... 'but it wouldn't be make believe.' I want companionship during the long dark nights. I want a hand to hold and a house full of life and sounds... *'if you belong to me.'* ... I want to listen to Moody-Blues-music and discuss a TV program. *Just what the truth is'*... I want a hot-water-bottle slave. I want a teddy bear prince... *'I can't say anymore.'* ... I want a servant bearing a glass of hot milk. I want a knight-light. I want smaller dragons under the bed.

It's one of those nights when the storm whispers the things I long to hear. *'Just what you want to be.'* I want to forget how life is a constant battle. I want a golden warrior to vanquish the memories of lead soldiers. Sleep calls softly. Problems magnify with the sound of reality rain... *'you'll be in the end.'* I want one of those crazy lonely knights who craves a white satin doll. I want a suit of armor hanging on the back of the bedroom chair, but it's just another night of imaginary bliss... *'never reaching the end.'* ~ 𝒱ℒ

*"They dined on mince, and slices of quince ,
which they ate with a runcible spoon.
And hand in hand, on the edge of the sand,
they danced by the light of the moon."*
~ Edward Lear

Jupiter Five

Halifax – April 2006 (Jupiter age four)

"C'mon Jupe, catch the lobe." Veronica sends a ball rolling towards her son. Strictly speaking it's not a ball. It's a blue hedgehog with rubber spines. 'Strictly speaking' has become a misnomer lately. Veronica is advised to correct Jupiter's mirror speech rather than encourage the permanent repetition of backward pronunciations. Back words. Some days, some words, some moods. When asked, Jupiter says his absent father, Niles, is a lion or a river, but 'Mom' always comes out the same.

There are times Veronica's thoughts are as erratic as Jupiter-speak. She grasps onto the end of his sentences, and follows them to an audible code... an object's attached identity translates. It's how Veronica knows the name Niles is more than a river and that "gods lobe is loob" leads to a blue, acceptably spherical, dog toy. The 'ball' belongs to Peyton, the family dog, a Lassie look-a-like. The nubs make it easier for her to grasp. Grasping is a precarious thing in the Lyons' household.

Names are shadowy attachments: Aunt Alice-Beatrice answers to Lisa or Bee or Lisa-B. Associations leapfrog from lily pad to lily pad. Evolutionary identities: Alice to Lisa, Dorothy to Dodo, Perry to Uncle Oz, and Basil to Baz. Lion beanbags respond respectively to Leos: One-through-Four. Veronica's own incarnations are as diverse: Verity, Ronnie, Dormouse, Toto, and plain V. Her signature finally defaults to the monogram, V L. Jupiter calls a chair a sitting cube.

"I'm going to make zabaglione," Veronica says. "As a special treat." Jupiter sounds out the new word as liony-baz and a memory is exhumed. Tonight it coincides with the night Jupiter chooses to camp out in a pup tent beside his bed.

Images of pyramids and cones, and fire, haunt Veronica's dreams as her brain shuffles files, and collates pictures and sounds, into a nightmare collage of the past. She was six when Basil was killed by a wild campfire.

Basil's tepee had caught a rogue spark, flashed the wilderness like a midnight torch, and extinguished half of Veronica's light forever. She is left to find her brother in stolen pockets of time, where they wander together in foggy communication. They stop talking after Jupiter is born, but Veronica continues to avoid fireplaces laid with coals or logs, and favors electric flames that mime the ability to burn. Veronica and Basil's twin teddy bears, Alice and Arthur, sit entwined on a small chair, above the separation of death. Their animation is contained – imprints of their princess and prince are forever present in their toy memories. When Veronica reads to Jupiter, they join the four Leos: a family of eight not counting Pico, Nattie and Peyton. Jupiter tries not to count them together. Eleven is not a good number. He is looking for a twelfth life to join his team. Better yet five more lives; his favorite number is sixteen. Perfect for a safe family.

Ersatz fire still fills Veronica's primal need for hearth and family. The only camp-out possible to bear, is a blanket thrown over a clothesline, pitched inside Jupiter's bedroom. There's no need to invade his playtime with her fears. "Pup pup pup tents are for dogs" he says, and drags Peyton's reluctance into his human kennel – a cave of adventures, Jupiter-size.

"More custard special needs-needs-needs," he says, and comfort pudding arrives in his blue bowl with a yellow rim.

Veronica suffers misgivings about her ability to raise a special-needs child. Mother and son dutifully comply with pediatricians and science, and when Jupiter's learning curve gasps on fallow ground, general confinement is indicated. A regime of trial and error medication and foods are added and subtracted to his diet. Veronica keeps her insomnia helpers low, never resorting to more addictive substances of distraction, tempting as they are.

Her stepfather always referred to his spiked ginger-ale as his 'medicine.' Basil had called them fizzy-dizzys. Avoiding a tipsy parent was enough to put a permanent wall between low self-esteem and alcohol. Besides, Veronica prefers her suffering up front and painful. If she had gone camping with Basil, Jupiter would have another uncle. It's her fault for blocking their telepathic link after Baz had called her a selfish girl. 'Crazy girl,' he'd called her. Crazy to prefer a tea party over a trip to Cape Breton. Veronica had been so angry, she let Basil believe the decision had been hers. Tea is her punishment of choice now. Every cup reminds her where and why, she was five-million light-years away at the wrong time. She's not the only one who feels entirely to blame.

When she collects the laundry, Veronica finds Leo Four with his head wrapped in a green sock. Jupiter fails to acknowledge her presence. His eyes are all about the wood and plastic and fabric blocks he collates in order of the color spectrum: by sheen, texture, and ascending size. All day Veronica has been jousting with eyes. When Veronica addresses Jupiter, she knocks at the door to his mind, but the child refuses entry.

Jupiter pushes Arthur and Leo One under his mother's arm while she naps. Veronica wakes and turns from a slave into a mother butterfly who scrapes together ingredients loosely resembling supper. Jupiter has dictated a short list of preferences by way of reaction. A food is presented. The child expresses rejection or acceptance. The list gets shorter. The days feel longer.

Jupiter passes on bright-colored food. The orange of cheddar is World War III loud; white Havarti is deliciously quiet. He refuses spheres of any flavor. The green grapes are the right color. The purple ones have two counts against them. Cantaloupe balls are objectionable by sight, shape and scent. One count is all it takes to be out of order. It takes a year to realize the only solid things Jupiter will eat without protest are squares or cubes: white cheese, croutons, crackers, toast with crusts removed, and miniature marshmallows. These few delicacies are Veronica's maternal peace offerings.

Veronica clues in after a sliver of pear makes the no plate, and she dices it up for a salad. Jupiter's small hand reached into the bowl, and separates each *cubicity* from the orange segments and honeydew balls. Miraculously, apples, pears and honeydews can be cubed. Veronica makes a picky plate: a row of Mozzarella cubes on a square white napkin, and four saltines.

Browsing a flea market Veronica finds an antique sugar spoon with a square bowl. She calls it Jupiter's 'runcible' spoon; an homage to one of his favorite stories about an owl and a pussycat. It's a magic shovel that delivers soup, oatmeal minus blueberries and raisins, and any crunchy cereal woven into squares that float in milk.

It becomes obvious that Jupiter prefers china without patterns. Then a gift arrives. An 'Alice in Wonderland' place setting decorated with the Cheshire cat, another of Jupiter's beloved characters. Jupiter is confused. He wants the square plate, but can't touch the shine of it. The cat is trapped there. He becomes so distraught Veronica hides it away disappointed. Jupiter calls out: "Lisa-Lisa-Lisa" and Veronica retrieves her son's 'Alice book' so he can see the cat illustration, safe on paper. Jupiter relaxes and carries the book under his arm for the rest of the day.

It's only by accident that Veronica has delivered four crackers. It will take more time to realize Jupiter's counting tricks, and his obsession with even stacks and straight rows. That night he refuses to settle under her plaid throw. He grabs his blanket of crocheted squares, and throws hers into the laundry basket.

Jupiter's fingers explore the familiar squares like Braille, happily exhausted that some perfect thing has finally arrived. He is grateful to the mother who tucks comfort around him, and shows it by tapping Veronica's hand four times. It's as close to a goodnight kiss as she's ever received. She leaves the room in semi-darkness. A Cheshire Cat nightlight glows a few inches from the floor. Jupiter still clutches his 'Alice Book,' and falls asleep with three lion dolls arranged in a row on his pillow. He hugs one of them tight. Tonight it's Leo One.

It's the extension of an understanding. The higher awareness of four is imparted. The deciphered code brings stillness to the illuminated space they now share. The magic of 'four-ness' reaches up to Veronica's tired consciousness. Right brain reads what has been there all along. A mother's discovery of communication. The principle of four is respectfully honored. All sign language is upgraded to high alert.

There are random meltdowns over colored bed sheets or a new brand of soap. Jupiter is an emotional monsoon over sensual details. Rarely do items merit a second chance, which is why Veronica introduces new things by gradual selection. Jupiter's rages are not the tantrums of a spoiled child, but inherent fears of an alien shape or texture or sound. He is an obsessive curator of the familiar. Safety is a recorded impression. A frozen picture of intimate peace. New toys are chosen not given. Things wrapped in paper are traps. Jupiter chooses his own gifts during regular shopping trips. He touches the sheets and shirts and foods he considers worthy. It's futile to purchase otherwise.

Jupiter has his own portable DVD player. A square theatre he permits to be activated the same time each day. He allows himself only edited entertainment, patiently waiting for any movie which contains a cat. The anticipation cannot be exaggerated. First viewings are restless fidgets until, happily, a cat scene appears to relax and delight. Veronica is careful to screen for positive content. The mother/child connection is precariously balanced. Veronica reads her son as she would a book written in French. Every so often a familiar parallel word jumps into consciousness and another fragile link is forged. Etymology rules.

On week sixteen, Jupiter's medication engages. He opens his eyes on a new world with five senses engaged. A crack in his sky lets out the dark. Jupiter's gaze rests on his mother's sleeping face. First light on a Halifax morning is mystical. He squints into the pinpoint glow of blue light, blinking beside the bed. He reaches out to touch the clock-radio. His finger blocks the blue dot. Color pulses around it as if emanating from inside. The tip of his finger has an aura of blue sparks. He loves the effect.

The wonder of small things captivates him. Objects of mysterious beauty that were demonic intrusions when he last closed his eyes are benign objects. A string of beads, once tuneless and tinny spheres, now rings with a single note of exquisite clarity. The contours of a snow globe can be tipped in delight. The moon over the skyline is later admired as a disk of magic as its cousin the sun is savored for its rising warmth. A single grape is a wonder; sweet and sour sing above the purple color. Purple has no sharp edges. The surprise of unmet things, unknown and unwanted implode into a firework display behind Jupiter's eyes and under his tongue. The kaleidoscope is tamed. It's prisms that used to overlap and shriek, are gone.

Placidity takes root. Jupiter claims possession of the new world – a fresh order, where shapes and colors and textures fail to leave bruises and sores. Jupiter's eyes welcome the light without flinching. He peers through the geometry of symmetrical things, and scans a steady horizon.

Jupiter chooses a blue crayon, and writes the word cat backwards. It stays safely quiet on the paper: *tac*. He writes it again in purple. He opens the shortbread tin, and finds an orange marker. He writes *cat* again, this time forwards. He replaces the marker in the box; some changes take time. He rips the page out, crumples it, throws it on the floor, and watches Nattie pounce on it and tear it to shreds.

Windows of the soul are meant to be opened. Veronica recognizes breakthrough the moment Jupiter's eyes meet hers in a first hello. She shows him how to write his full name. Jupiter *Lyons*. Jupiter's *lions*! He knew his name all along.

A sliver of hall light lands on Jupiter's quilt. He squeezes his happy lion, but it's wearing the dreaded tartan ribbon; the other three dolls lay with their heads on his The pillow. What this means doesn't translate, but Veronica intends to study her son's world with more insight. She realizes with a sense of irony, that she needs to return to the starting point of the game board, and begin again at square one.

Mind Soup

Halifax
May 2, 2006

My relationship has been patched so many times I'm in fear of disintegration. I could never resurrect the lie of Niles and I into a second, living breathing, chance. I'm not surprised to see his name contains the word 'lies.' Love tests ones capacity to accept evidences of serendipity. I find myself being careful to knit a blanket big enough to cover the entire dream.

Experience is a mind-soup that wants the spice of life added in great handfuls. Reality is an almost good man – a salt-of– the-earth pinch. One forfeits flavor for the blandness of safety. The taste of imaginary bliss is not worth the payoff…a quick-fix spiritual high and the crashing sound of ridicule, and after the dust settles, one has to mourn the loss of fantasy which is such a big death.

Materializing in two places at the same time defies science. A double life requires a dreamer and a waking dream that pays the rent. Fame is a speck of magic dust that aggravates someone else's eye. ~*VL*

Saint Lobe

Halifax
July 17, 2006

Poor Jupiter! ... Lucky Jupiter! His 'lobe' rolled into the street and Peyton followed. I heard the car brakes squeal. Peyton is safe. The lobe was sacrificed and Jupiter required hot chocolate therapy in the middle of a heat wave.

I am in awe of Jupe's logic: after we say goodnight, he asks me to turn on the dark rather than turn off the light. I love that kid's mind. ~*VL*

PART TWO
Second Sight

Janus – the god of two faces,
presides over beginnings and transitions:
the passages of time, bridges,
and every doorway.

*"It is not death
that man should fear,
but he should fear
never beginning to live."*
~ Marcus Aelius Aurelius

The Voice of Rebirth

Synchronicity is the unexpected marriage of events for better or worse. My existence began on a breeze of human chemicals. My father's musk drew my mother down, to open the way a flower obeys the sun. I could only sense my father as a lightning-bolt force. He flashed and was gone, but I coursed inside my mother for nine months, and absorbed her memories and expectations. She once told me that my brother and I were born from 'the kind of love that was twice juicy, that had to be caught like a butterfly and let go before dark.'

I was born Lisabetta di Antonio Buti del Vacca, half-sister (I had thought) to my mother's son, Leonardo da Vinci. I remained transparent even after my brother taught me his trade. He was the sun and I was always hard to see, but if you squint past the brightness of Leonardo, you would find that I was always there – real or painted.

I almost don't mind that my work goes unrecognized. Half of my brother's contributions have drifted into the murkiness of time, along with the works of his students and mentors and fellow apprentices. It only takes a generation to lose the in-house tributes, the popular acknowledgments, and the authorships of works critiqued as dazzles of breakthrough. But I earned my true name.

Miracles come wrapped in sacrifice, and to accept the grace of a miracle one must forfeit a gift of equal value. People love to call me a mystery but I prefer to be known as a person. ~ *Lisabetta*

The DIARY of VERONICA LYONS

The Fourth Monkey

Dover to Paris ferry
March 31, 2008

I read Jupe 'the Velveteen Rabbit.' It's a first edition, 1922, ironically as dog-eared from love as the rabbit in the story. Uncle Oz sent it to me for Jupiter, after he was born, passing down the family's copy. Jupiter always makes me read the inscription first:

"To my favorite planet. Welcome to the universe. Love Papa Zeus. – 2002"

Jupiter is over his anxiety about the rabbit's inability to be real. Naturally he brought Leo One to the front row, but I noticed him replace 'One' with 'Three' during the part when the toy rabbit expresses his sadness and shame that he is unable to hop like the real rabbits he sees in the garden – as his legs are 'all of a piece.' Jupiter's explanation, was that the toy was 'hopping sad' and should be angry as Leo Two.

Some days I want to give Leo One a third eye and turn Leo Three into a Cyclops. To perform miracles as the Button Goddess who can give and take away button vision with a needle and thread. Leo Four encompasses the three monkey syndrome of denial. No eyes or ears or mouth accomplish an isolation tank of retreat. He is the fourth monkey of feel-no-evil, or feels it so intently that he blanks out. ~*PL*

> *"It's a poor sort of memory*
> *that only works backwards."*
> ~ Lewis Carroll

Musé(e) du Louvre

Paris – April 1, 2008

Jupiter has an important job to do. The six-year-old clutches a brochure folded open to the Leonardo page. The map of the second floor has several highlighted circles around small numbers. Veronica had explained when she pointed to the X on the map. "We're right here. I've marked what we've come to see. You can be the navigator."

A long queue of museum warriors leads down the second-floor hallway and inches forward like a glacier. "We'll have to join that line later," she says. "I'm sorry, but it's the only way to see the 'Mona Lisa.'"

"You want to save her for last?" he asks. This is his mother's way, contrary to his own system; Jupiter treats himself to his favorite things first: the dark chocolate pudding before the buttery taste of green beans, but after the salt-drizzled French fries with ketchup beside them drawn in an O rather than a solid dollop. Delaying comfort seems pointless.

"The one *you* are saving for last." He punches the word 'you' and leaves out the question mark, and Veronica nods yes.

"I wish there was an easier way, but everyone wants to see her. We're going to the 'Madonna of the Rocks' first." Veronica points to a square of color on the open page. "That one."

"The one wearing your brooch your brooch your brooch," he mouths quietly to himself.

"But before that, we have a date with 'Nike.'"

Veronica beams. "You look like the Cheshire Cat," Jupiter says.

Veronica hears her words: *'date with Nike,'* float back to her, as if it's a casual event to stroll past this work of art. The 'Nike of Samothrace' had graced the front cover of the course textbook for 'Art History 101' and haunted her for three years during university. Every day it had accompanied her home and she'd studied its deep golden crevices of stone fabric captured in dramatic light, and followed the contours of its billowing draperies, frozen in time like the volcanic ash of a Vesuvius victim. She wondered if its missing head had flowing hair. She decided it did.

"She's easy to find," Jupiter says. He can already see the great 'Winged Victory, Nike,' looming on the stairs. Veronica had avoided its peripheral aura. It hovers there, up and to her right, wings outstretched like the sails of a ship. Veronica's muscles tingle deliciously on high-alert from the anticipation of meeting a goddess. She savors the body-high of an art junkie, and wants to experience the visceral shock of facing an icon full-on, the way one steps up and confronts a movie star on the street: "Hello… I'm a big fan."

Veronica intends to confront the 'Mona Lisa' the same way. She knows from virtual visits, that she will be able to see her as a postage stamp for a long time from the back of the room – an undersized window in an expanse of wall. A thumbnail image can spoil the immediacy of Lisa's direct gaze. It may feel too ordinary by the time Veronica's feet creep close enough for her to raise her eyes in a blast of contact. She also knows that 'Mona Lisa's' eyes across a room are able to engage her long before she's in optimum range. In a way Veronica is meeting an old friend, a premonition who has haunted her future. Today the dream materializes. Veronica wants the ground to tremble. She wants her energy to short-circuit the Louvre's breakers and dim the lights of Paris.

Jupiter and Veronica approach the 'Nike of Samothrace' on parallel wavelengths. Veronica observes in a surreal daze. Her perceptions transport. She heads straight for the dizzying mother-lode of historical destinations… romance. Her viewpoint expands to a prolonged Hellenistic haze, more than she'd hoped, all expectations exceeded. She is prone to ghostly whispers, and the rustle of archaic white robes.

Veronica can appreciate the sensual curve of a phantom cheek, and the liquid flash of olive-dark eyes. She brushes against the heartbeats of the once living, and hustles alongside the echoes of ancient sandals. She experiences the world sensually. Art invades and conquers her on sensitive overloads to the scents of warm winds off ripe-hot lemon groves, the kiss of salt breezes, and the receding footprints of bare feet running on powdered sand. She is no longer in Paris. She can taste the beauty of an Aegean day – blinded by the brilliance of aqua water against marble pillars.

Until her son's voice penetrates her vision, Veronica's eyes ache from the glint of sunlight off freshly whitewashed plaster.

> *"If you don't know where you are going,*
> *any road will get you there."*
> ~ Lewis Carroll

Victory on the Stairs

The Louvre Museum, Paris – April 1, 2008

"She's wearing your brooch." Jupiter's voice reverberates from the marble halls, surges up the grand staircase, and swirls around the shoulders of the 'Nike of Samothrace' statue. Jupiter repeats the words 'your brooch' twice more, silently to himself as he waves a crushed brochure like a fan. His mother sees his mouth move as if his lips need to catch up to his latest speech, that having been released to the air, is now a bit of a mystery. He only records very important things that can be lost if left to hover, and evaporate as a sole thought. The two of them are alone on the stairs.

The boy's delighted shriek would have reached the statue's ears if it had a head. He shouts with joy to the companion voice that returns in a breathtaking sweep from the vault of the high ceiling. Jupiter loves echoes. His shadow voice captivates him, and he calls again just to hear it float. "Brooch!" Veronica has to gently tame it into social acceptance.

"There's a museum voice, and a restaurant voice, and a movie theatre voice," Veronica tells him. "The Louvre has its own voice," she says. Its volume is set low enough on the radar to fly under the security guards. This place induces visitors to communicate emotionally in hushes of astonished gasps, and pointing fingers, and the silent, meaningful squeezes of a companion's arm.

Sometimes Veronica touches her son's shoulder and uses sign language. She and Jupiter are fluent with word pictures, finger alphabets, and mime. Signing had been recommended to coax Jupiter into speech after a formal diagnosis of autism at eighteen months.

Jupiter's autism is wildly verbal. The doors of his brain are characteristically open today, and he volunteers information that arrives from shapes and colors and textures. At other times, Veronica sees him struggle to communicate with an inner friend. Nothing escapes his senses. Sometimes he processes images for days before sharing them with her. She's learned to hone her skills of observation like a detective at a crime scene. Her son's perception often blindsides her. Jupiter retains images the way an optimistic dog gnaws a bleached bone. Somewhere deeper there's a morsel to analyze... the missing marrow of a puzzle. Solving puzzles is an art form, and Jupiter is a master. He's committed till the last piece snaps into place.

Veronica and Jupiter's holiday mood fills the immaculate hallways. Jupiter stops talking, and stamps his feet to test the acoustics. He listens for the voice of his shoes. It's a great place to wear shoes that clickety-clack or squeak. They both love the sound. They're here for the art, but the vibes of the stairs have trapped them whole. Their world is measured in small, grand moments, of mutual pleasure. It can be anything where they're together, to pick up the noises, and scents, and tastes of the right-brain life, lived raw and spontaneous. Mother and son are companions who share the resonance others forget to see or taste or smell.

Jupiter clatters up and down the steps to peer at the Nike from every angle. His backpack with the design of 'Vitruvian man,' swings madly from one arm.

Veronica's voice is the whisper she is trying to teach Jupiter. "I never thought I would really stand next to her. What do you think?" There's no answer. Jupiter is thinking. "Jupe?"

"It's dangerous to fly without a head," he says.

Here in the Louvre, surrounded by iconic images of 'Mothers and Sons,' and sweeping landscapes of poetic illusion, Veronica and Jupiter explore on complementary senses. He is the litmus test of understanding; she is the dowsing rod of historic truth. When Jupiter hears Veronica pronounce, Firenze, he hears the words fear and ends; when

Veronica writes the word, Firenze, she sees the word fire and hopes her fear of it ends. Together they weave the psychic threads of autism into a coherent story.

Jupiter calls out "Mom" and the dampness of honking cars and body hunger refocuses. Veronica is a mental time traveler – an indulgence she can afford. Working two subsistence level jobs to provide for herself, her son, and her art on a restricted budget tests one's basic survival instincts. She and Jupiter have learned to live on lily pads of small pleasures. This trip is a bonus that could be construed as blackmail floating on a lily pad the size of Europe.

As a single-parent of a child with mental challenges, Veronica has agreed to disagree. It was plain she and Jupiter had to disappear – to be reborn in a new place. Go west Niles had suggested, but it was more an offer he dared her to refuse. The alternative was the flypaper of social assistance, and spelled disaster for her uncle's research. Some choice.

The deal had come with a holiday attachment. Niles painted a black and white picture: anywhere on the planet, he had pressed. For a week or two, while your things are on the road.

Veronica had a guidance dream: Nike had morphed into the 'Statue of Liberty' wielding a torch. It was a beacon inside a dream that said *'pick me... here I am... waiting'* and Veronica woke determined to win a couple of return tickets to Paris.

'Anywhere' dangled like poison bait. It was possibly the only serious holiday she and Jupiter were likely to have. Nothing or something, Niles had badgered. Pick a tarot card. Stay or go.

The bird in the hand had chirped 'go,' and sent a shiver through stone feathers on both sides of the Atlantic. "Three weeks then" Veronica countered, "first class seats, and you personally look after Peyton and the cats. No kennels. No catteries."

Niles had replied 'done,' with forced enthusiasm.

"And you fly them to me as soon as we touch down," she'd said.

Niles confirmed "no problem" with a grey smile. Veronica's pets were family, and Niles Duke felt a stab of pleasure that Veronica still entrusted them to his care.

In the spirit of cooperation, Veronica chooses to move as far away from Halifax as possible and still remain in Canada. At first Victoria is only a remote dot on a shape called British Columbia, but her choice had been poetic: bound for Victoria is a clean metaphor for victory. Nike had reached out, and now the 'Angel of Victory' waits on the stairs for another chat. It had been a good omen. Victoria via Paris is hardly a Band-Aid trip, and pioneering on a scrap of pure, fresh, space, surrounded by Pacific waters and mountains, is an Isle-of-Glass homestead with benefits. Even the word pacific sounds like a healing balm... pacify.

"It's not house arrest. It's not the Hotel California" Niles had said. "You can leave anytime, but the rent has been taken care of in advance." Veronica had turned from the room and not given him the satisfaction of her Cheshire Cat grin. Maybe both of them had won... this time.

Niles' severance proposal is an emotional salvage operation. What else can she do? – a single mother with debts. Poverty has its own voice. It says 'yes' to things Veronica would rather watch as vicarious entertainment. 'only in the movies' she used to say about happy endings, but mother and son need a new story and the rumor is, sometimes beggars *can* choose an alternative reality that contains a positive surprise. Some times. The rogue gene of synchronicity can intervene. Veronica has followed enough breadcrumbs of hope to various brick walls, bottomless pits, and buffalo jump cliffs, to know she and Jupiter are due.

There are tidy words that ring true. Veronica named her son Jupiter for a reason. The planet Jupiter represents the immensity of omnipotent intellect and unearthly merriment, and larger than life storms from the god of the sky. Veronica was unconscious of these while pregnant, but during the nine months of gestation, she felt an overwhelming sense of mental expansion along with her belly. She was a round planet, separated from the ordinary. Elemental. Connected to the stars. She almost believed in God. Her son's name appeared on her tongue one morning, and she heard it as music. Thereafter, she addressed her embryo in a salute to its greatness, and Jupiter Lyons grew, loved beyond measure, in an ocean of amniotic gold. Her own name, Veronica, which meant true icon, she accepted only outside the fog of organized religion.

Together, she and her son are two lions of ferocious simplicity, matched against a complex society. Some days it feels like they belong to a warring community after the same island territory – opposing human factions colliding like drifting continents with the matching raw edges of separation. A great divide – a mountain range of misunderstanding. It seems like forever to discover a safe route and claim citizenship in the name of mutual peace.

For all Veronica's fanciful nature, astronomy wins over astrology, and the dawn-of-reason over Aquarius. The New-Age is far behind her, filed as an immature, but necessary, rite of passage. She cut her adolescent teeth on the bliss-myths of Joseph Campbell's, 'Hero with a Thousand Faces.' Joseph had been one of the stable, academic mystics that she could digest, who had inspired her career as a painter. But the business of art is a serial killer that murders its artists slowly and cruelly, and Veronica abandons her creative dreams after a disappointing response to sales. She considers herself a practical human being, and rationalizes that a girl has to eat.

By way of explaining her actions, Veronica had told her Uncle Oz that she preferred to creatively-suicide before art claimed her as its zillionth victim. Poetic metaphor consoles her. Uncle (Perry Lyons) Oz had been sympathetic. "Art takes hostages" he had said. He knows. Authenticating art is the one passion he allows himself, and as a master geneticist, he can appreciate that the art of the genome is closely related to the forensics of paintings. Both require intensive microscopic attention.

Jupiter surveys the statue of 'Nike' like a twenty-first century spectroscope. He probes – a natural master of forensic science. He counts individual feathers, observes the positive shape of the wing and the negative spaces under it and between the prow of its ship, base. "It's the same wing" he points out, but his mother is lost to the creature of the stairs – drifted out to sea.

Jupiter measures the angles of the wings, and falls into the white draperies that cast shadows like the hills and valleys of Cape Breton covered in snow, and then he rediscovers the enchanting cadence of the stair whispers. Mother and child are charmed like snakes to a flute. The diversity of high-functioning autism enslaves them. Private worlds have different food chains and atmospheres and inhabitants. Veronica's ears search; Jupiter's eyes listen.

When Veronica and Jupiter stand in front of Leonardo's 'Madonna of the Rocks,' Veronica understands. "You're right, well done you," she says, and checks the lapel of her coat where an amber cabochon brooch clings to the navy blue wool. Its smooth oval is the mirror image of the one on the Virgin Mary's cape. Golden yellow winks against Cerulean blue. The Madonna bows her head towards them to listen to their conversation. Jupiter scans the painting's surface. His fingers mimic the hands of the Madonna and angel and child. He looks up, radiant with a secret.

Veronica turns away with resignation. It's time to meet 'Mona Lisa.' More accurately, time to join the pilgrimage. Meeting the painting will take a while. She can see the queue. It's an entity in itself – the tail of a restless dragon. She heads towards it towing her reluctant son, whose brows remain knitted in thought. His mind is calculating; all Veronica can hear, is the blood rushing to her head. Art like this makes her dizzy.

Jupiter remembers to whisper: "Mom? … Mom … the painting is signing."

He waves the brochure at her, but Veronica brushes it aside like a stray lock of hair. She stares straight ahead; a woman zombie walking through deep water. It's half-past lunchtime and her continental breakfast has long been consumed in the passionate metabolism of Nike's spell. Veronica is hungry for eggs and bacon, and strong sweet tea, and the 'Mona Lisa.' She takes her place at the end of the Lisa devotees. "Jupe don't stray too far. I need to see you, okay?" she says.

Jupiter wanders a few feet investigating the parade of textures. He tests the resilience of brown suede and green silk. He counts buttons, passing over the shiny brass ones. The sheen of high-gloss upsets his stomach. There are plenty of safe plastic discs. The best ones are covered in cloth. He prefers the buttons with four holes, but only if the thread is sewn in an X or a square. Parallel lines are unstable. He continues to monitor the fringes of scarves, tassels and the crisscross patterns of shoelaces, and the murmur of conversation drifts over his head like an evaporating cloud. He only picks up its trail when he hears the words Mona, or Lisa, or Leonardo. These are the associations he and his mother have discussed relative to the day; these he is primed for.

The Egyptian exhibits are for the after-noon. *'After.'* Jupiter knows this word. It flashes before him as images of plates of food, and paintings, and sculptures. It means *after* lunch... *after* the 'Mona Lisa.' Beyond present hunger.

Jupiter is confident his mother will refuse the elevator for another encounter on the stairs on their way out. He looks forward to climbing the Daru Staircase again. Like a mountaineer he will reach Nike's base camp, and this time he will stop to listen for Nike's opinion. She is Queen of the footsteps. Does she relish the velvet shush of felt slippers the same way he does? And how about the gentle slap of sandals, and the crisp contact of hard rubber, and the warm squeak of crepe soles?

Jupiter has three questions to ask 'Nike.' He wonders if she knows her face is lost forever, and that her name 'victory' has been appropriated for sport, and that a shoe has compromised her identity?

"Alice sighed wearily.
'I think you might do something better
with the time,' she said,
Than waste it in asking riddles
that have no answers."
~ Lewis Carroll

The End of the Line

The Louvre Museum – April 1, 2008

Jupiter is in heaven as he presses up against a wall of blue cashmere. The young woman inside it stirs with impatience. He can feel a burst of irritation float from her in a grey cloud. It settles above her male companion who shows little regard for the treasure that has mesmerized an entire herd of anticipation towards a single face. Eavesdropping is Jupiter's only option.

Jupiter is an absorber of information. His mission is to help, to put right, and to offer wisdom, but for the moment, the luxury of a soft cardigan lulls him into silence.

"Who *was* she again?" the young man in the frayed jeans asks. His fingers tap an impatient staccato on his visitor's guidebook. He lacks finesse when it comes to faking interest.

"I told you," the woman says in a speech bubble. "Lisa Giocondo". She sighs at him like a mother with a small child who's spilled his milk. "That's why the painting is called the Giocon--da... 'da' is the feminine. Giocon-da means smiling woman." No response. She points to the brochure and three letters 'La *Joc*-onde.' "Joc?" She pronounces the J, soft. "Joke? Do you see?" She punches her companion's arm with what he interprets as mock anger. He is deciding whether to ask if the 'da' in da Vinci is also feminine, because he heard once, that Leonardo was gay. He wisely thinks better of asking.

She is serious. The cloud dowses the young man with freezing rain. He slips his hand into hers as a peace offering, but she withdraws it immediately with a slither and he jams his fists into his pockets feigning remarkably genuine indifference. From now on he can be himself. "Waiting in this line is a joke," he says, too loud.

The instant the words implode the grey synapses of the young man's right frontal lobe, he sees his girlfriend's face crumple into the future. The heat of chemical attraction short-circuits like the fizzle of a hot skillet in cold water. Lights go out. Right there he's dumped at the roadside of culture. Another mismatch.

Art appreciation has separated them like the red sea. The ex-girlfriend watches as he floats away – a lost pharaoh in a lead chariot. He may survive the rapids, hit the rocks, and drift to shore to rejoin his dimwit buddies in the nearest sports bar, and ogle and booze away an unconscious life, ignorant and intolerant of finer things. He can count the goals scored by million-dollar running shoes, and swoon over each dumb trophy. She will keep her dignity and surf in deeper water for a kindred mate.

He's too male to understand the finality, and will hang on, to what he considers the bitter end, and ogle the 'Mona Lisa,' after all he's come this far and paid for the tickets, and they're nearing the finish line – a term he can relate to. He can see the goalposts of the Salle des Etats, and maybe… just maybe, he will stretch for something amazing, locate his dormant sophisticate gene, engage his brain, and make a profoundly intelligent comment to impress the princess at his side. He thinks winning her back is possible.

The young woman feels vindicated. The jerk didn't even have the class to change his sweatshirt emblazoned with the words Notre Dame. He thinks it's a football team. She knows it's a cathedral. "No wonder Europeans thinks we American's are uncultured oafs," she mutters to the ceiling.

"Glaciers move faster than this," the jeans say, and the cashmere sweater shivers in disgust.

Jupiter already knows 'Mona Lisa's' identity; he can see from at least a dozen nuances of shape, exactly who she is. He has cross-referenced her eyes, and mouth, and nose, and chin to other images he's seen in his mother's art books. He's about to explain to them all, when a trolley pushed by armed guards, swings by like a creaky ship listing to the left from its awkward cargo. It squeaks his attention away from the mystery of Lisa's identity to one of its silver wheels. While other eyes check out the wrapped curiosity secured to its surface, Jupiter works out how to fix the wonky wheel that wobbles like the orbit of a misaligned planet. Broken things annoy him.

The hallway of babble is a cauldron of frayed tempers in every conceivable accent. Foreign words pepper the air in a modern jazz interpretation of human buzz, but humans cough, and grunt, and sniffle, in the same language. The din is almost as overwhelming as the choking battles of clashing perfumes, and the clinging smells of tobacco and aftershave. Impatient feet dance the 'Mona Lisa' shuffle. Jupiter studies the different configurations of small colored boxes: cameras, cell phones, and music-pods, that preoccupy everyone so deeply. His eyes follow the trail of them back to a cherry-red enamel square. His mother is reading a message, and the forest of odors is making him dizzy.

Jupiter experiences a kaleidoscope of expectant faces, and hands that preen hairstyles and crumpled clothes into submission. There's an overall confusion of constant opening and closings of museum programs, mouths, women's purses, and shopping bags. All of it amid a jumble of plaid coats, striped shawls, and flowered shirts. A pair of eyeglasses swinging on a silver chain grabs Jupiter's attention. Another lady's multiple strands of cheap beads heave restlessly up and down on her pink neck. A white strand of pearls rests against a smooth tanned wrist. Jupiter counts the pulse beats. The glare from the perfect spheres hurt his eyes.

A new light flickers at the end of the bright hallway like the tunnel in a near-death experience, and the cashmere woman steps over the gateway with Jupiter attached to her blue sweater. She forgets her former boyfriend forever as a guard silently guillotines the line immediately after Veronica. The guard ushers the allotted number by silent hand signal like a bored traffic cop directing sheep, and Jupiter can imagine the guard blowing a shrill whistle to wake up the hypnotic queue.

Inside the hallow-of-hallows, Jupiter wants confirmation. He wants to know why? Mostly he wants to know who? He shakes his head trying to dislodge the reasons how one portrait could be so many different people. People should make up their minds. Is the woman right? Is he wrong? He wants definition; guesses are unacceptable.

The line flows like honey into soft rows, and from his new position, Jupiter can peer through the coats and see his mother's idol. The 'Mona Lisa' is a postage stamp which draws the swarm of bodies towards her... still a carrot beyond their grasp. She captivates them like a hypnotist's pendulum. The herd channels forward in a pedigreed slow-motion stampede, while shepherd guards keep watch for wolves.

Lisabetta can feel a disturbance unraveling the back of the line and wills herself to settle into its eye to determine if it's a promise or the threat of one. A blast of light indicates the former. Two visitors surrounded by a yellow aura move towards her and she leaves her painting to meet them in the center of the room.

"I wish I could tell you for sure," Veronica says. "Leonardo liked to play tricks." Jupiter stares at his mother for more. "Leonardo loved funny words, so he left clues" she says. "He loved puzzles almost as much as you." This thought wanders off with Jupiter in tow – a last assessment of the 'Mona Lisa' conga line, milling now, funneled into singular awareness. He gets their enthusiasm, but a mythological Leonardo is only half the sky.

When Jupiter had first heard his mother refer to him as special, he had heard the word *spacial*. He agreed with her; every object he sees makes one solid forward-shape, and dozens of air-shapes from sharing the world with its neighbors. He focuses on the spaces between things when he wants to draw, but now his eyes need to find a home and rest. Jupiter returns to Veronica's side, and settles on his mother's amber brooch. It winks on her blue raincoat – a honeyed tomb with a lonely bee trapped inside.

The bliss from fitting Louvre pictures together makes Jupiter hungry.

He closes his eyes, and remembers the word 'after,' and his mind flash-forwards from the face of the 'Mona Lisa' to a birds-eye view of a round dining table draped in red and white cloth. In its center is a round white plate holding the brown dome of a hamburger bun. He loves the concentric circles. Next to it is another brown circle of chocolate milk in a tall glass, all seen from above like a seagull hovering over the sidewalk cafes of Paris.

"Why don't you join us for lunch?" Jupiter says to the lady from the painting. "We're going to find hamburgers. My name is Jupiter."

A Meeting of Dreams

The Louvre – April 1, 2008

So many eyes in a day. Probing. I see them go from indifference to awe and sometimes the other direction. But there is a ripple in the air like the gentle psychic fizzing of static before a storm. I can smell it, and so I'm as vigilant as the front row gawpers. I troll for the disturbance as they scan me. That's what synchronicity is – a miracle. It's always a matter of time. My atoms tingle with electric sparks. There's no wild portent, but a lightening of the air that streams through me. For this reason, I delay my usual retreat into the Florentine landscape behind me.

The hum of heavier voices drop in the shrine of my throne room. I usually drift into the outer hallway if I want to hear the gossip. It's mostly about the best restaurants and the price of eggs. The queue has been imprisoned for at least the span of one missed meal. Children who have reached the threshold of the Salle des Etats, are carried asleep or walk stupefied. A parade of tiny zombies, sleepwalking towards the promise of a reward so spectacular, it keeps them remarkably obedient. Parents itch for the streets. There are no aquariums full of colored balls here; no spherical sea, in which to dump the limp bodies of their children, so that they can pretend they are free for an hour.

Museums are not for childish minds. They are the precincts of academic singularities, or precocious youths and their opposable-thumb parents. Even the cream of the elite who swan everywhere else, creep humbly here. Would it shock them to know my brother loathed painting.

Painting was not his choice; it was a living at his fingertips. Leonardo lived to be an academic. All he ever wanted, was to be cloistered with scientific experiments and plenty of writing paper, but art plucked him from his father's clutches, and set us both on a road to freedom.

I am privy to the hushed debates and the stale theories: I am Leonardo's self-portrait. I am his mother, Caterina. I am his dark lady-love, his transvestite apprentice, or the everywoman of his past. I am the housewife of a dreary silk-merchant, the duchess of this or that; the queen of here or there. A prostitute. I am the mistress of a prince. I have heard every mistaken identity, but never the truth.

The truth is supposed to set one free. I hope this is true. I am still holding out for it. I had thought that I could leave the manor house of 'Cloux' with Leonardo the night his soul flew home, but my streak of stubbornness won out. I thought my attachment to earth matters would only last a short while, and since time doesn't affect me anymore, I suppose by that reckoning it has.

I heard the first voice say: "that woman has a secret." The second voice countered: "she looks like the cat who ate the canary." Its companion retorted: "a whole flock of canaries by the look of her."

Ah, yes... the look of me confounds them. A contented expression of canary-love. The first voice returned and sang the lyrics to a popular song, very low. "Do you smile to tempt a lover Mona Lisa?"

They were all correct, and I am flattered by the cat reference. I have often considered that cats would make good lawyers. I survived from being catlike and lawyer-like much of the time. My superior, stubborn, feigning-indifference catty days. I had a cat named Picolini; I knew the look.

If you've ever had to sit for a portrait, you will know how tedious the hours stretch into weeks. It is tiresome after only a few minutes. One's mind drifts like a leaf in a whirlpool until it settles on a fantasy which evokes a pleasant countenance. One doesn't fight direction, but surrenders to an incandescent destination and enjoys the journey, dreamed far enough away to appear dreamily detached.

Do I smile to tempt a lover? Not exactly. I once did, but during my portrait I smiled because the temptation had already been consummated.

A good artist copies a likeness of his subject, but a master artist captures their soul. By 1504 Leonardo had studied me for forty-six years. He told me to imagine my best dream, and I was the ideal sitter; I knew how to look through someone and see what I wanted to see. I envisioned Sandro Botticelli behind Leonardo's right shoulder as an enticing Mars. Sandro sent me a smile and I responded, shyly. Gallery visitors witness an invitation accepted – caught by a sorcerer.

Can't you see I'm gloating? I was not being secretive; I was indulging in a romping good daydream, and I had a plan. I always had a plan. I was a seductress of success, never Sandro. When it came to Sandro Botticelli, I was always a timid twelve-year-old shadow with a big dream of being seduced.

I was not especially patient in life. But death?… That's worse. Death brings the absence of lateral time, and the chance to review long-forgotten latent desires: the denied successes, and the comeuppance of poetic karma. In my case, it made me more determined than ever to shame my century for the things it did to me. To all of us women. It's understated how historians fail to glean the truth between the lies. Documents have always been reams of paper ghosts – endangered species subject to damp and fire and ignorance.

Names are like skeletons who meet on fleshless calendar dates. Populations ooze away from life like the run-off from an abattoir. Life is more than a slaughterhouse of frightening mistakes from love and hope. If anything, life must stand for a divine dynamic – a petulant thought of non-local mind. Sentient desire. I have spoken to others behind the living. Outside of art, none of them have met God, or an angel, or a demon. Life ends, and death goes on. ~ *Lisabetta*

"There comes a pause,
for human strength will not endure
to dance without cessation;
and everyone must reach the point at length
of absolute prostration."
~ Lewis Carroll

The Sleeping Beauty

The Louvre – April 1, 2008

Veronica didn't reckon on her sense of humor invading the peak moment. A moment too well-preserved to survive intact, considering she is faint from hunger and her feet ache from eleven days of London sightseer miles. Every step is a day-tripper spike. When Veronica glances down at her shoes, she expects them to be seeping with blood – her own pair of insatiable 'Grimm Brother's' red slippers. Still, her irreverence is a surprise. She hears her voice murmur "Lisa Giocondo I presume?" and then feels ashamed. Leonardo deserves better than this.

"You presume wrong." Veronica hears the voice, and checks out her neighbors. She's lightheaded from excitement and fatigue; clearly the combination is making her hallucinate.

> I love to borrow from the vernacular soup that invades my space from dawn to dusk. "You ain't heard nothin' yet sister," I whispered to her. I've become a master of anthropology from studying visitors for hundreds of years. Human parades reveal a lot, but I forget that Veronica hears my thoughts unless I block them and the last thing I need to do is give my savior another fear to chew. ~ *Lisabetta*

Veronica's blood rushes to the site of her latest thought, and she grips onto her son for support. Her mind hears the squeal of an emergency brake and shudders to a full stop – a train in a station. She can feel her brain hiss. It makes a final mechanical maneuver. Her thoughts flutter into atomic particles. There she is: Saint Lisa of the roving eyes; the sleeping beauty in pre-kiss bliss.

Veronica sees 'Mona Lisa's' installation as a vertical glass coffin. "Even Snow White's prince will have a tough time getting to those enchanted lips," Veronica thinks. "Your lips are blushing," she says to the 'Mona Lisa.' 'Mona Lisa' shimmers like a mirage, and causes an internal earthquake in Veronica's solar plexus.

Jupiter is Veronica's anchor. "Ouch. Mom, quit pinching me," he says.

Centuries collide when Jupiter removes his jacket, and reveals a full-size image of the 'Mona Lisa.' He compares the golden flesh tones of the two images, and is upset his shirt is dull by comparison. Veronica reassures him nothing could ever duplicate the original.

The thing is, people buy imprints of my portrait on the way out of the museum. I suppose it's considered gauche to wear them inside. Jupiter had no such reservations; his concept of fashion was fluid. Rules were verbal lint. His shoes were tied with pink laces. He wore mismatched socks, and his beret boasted a badge that declared: 'Don't mess with me – I'm high-functioning.' Clearly his mother indulged him, and hopefully, had also encouraged his creative side and heralded his autistic qualities (yes, I've learned the term), maybe even flaunted them to the world in defiance. Jupiter was oblivious. He adored being himself, and I envied him. Leonardo had been the same... most of the time.

I suspected that Jupiter was not always so

jubilant; even a genius finds zeal too heavy to carry indefinitely. I could also sense that Jupiter could hear the museum's air, saturated with whispers of half-dead memories. I saw him struggle with them when they became too noisy. I know the rarefied atmosphere surrounding ancient artifacts can choke a sensitive mind. I've seen too many hardy souls faint and be carted away on stretchers here.

I sensed Jupiter suffered from a similar malady as Leonardo. At first, I wasn't sure the boy saw me. He examined me without meeting my eyes, but his mind accepted my conversation. He seemed indifferent and fascinated at the same time. I was simply an anomaly he needed to file. I knew then, that this was the opportunity to jump or stay, because it tasted and smelled of synchronicity and irony, two of the flavors I'd come to know as signatures of a perverse universe.

Suddenly I cherished the gold frame that protected me with a golden fence. I had lived inside a baroque border which delineated... no celebrated, where I belonged. Here I was honored. I was queen of a salon, this building, and the city outside. Paris relied on me, as I depended on it to champion my existence. How could I leave it for a heaven I'd never seen, or perhaps only imagined in my mind?

I spoke to Jupiter softly: "Buongiorno. Do you know who I am"?

"You're Italian."

"Si."

Jupiter pointed to the 'Mona Lisa.' "Her shadow."

"Are you scared of me"?

"Not yet," he said.

He made me laugh; it was enough to make us friends, and it was the first time a visitor invited me to lunch.

Jupiter was a direct invitation as much as a surprise. I am charged by an invisible law to remain with my portrait, but jumping into the cloth face of Jupiter's shirt meant that I remained dutifully confined. It was a spontaneous artful escape. ~ *Lisabetta*

Veronica does what every viewer does; she sweeps the 'Mona Lisa' like a mine field, hoping her eyes will act as total-recall cameras, and zoom in on facial tics later. Three minutes is not long enough to peruse a dream. She is jostled out of place by a firm arm. One of the dwarfs, no doubt guarding his princess. She looks down at a pair of shiny black boots, then up at a giant's French face. It shows boredom and distain. "Vas-t'en!… move along." Ah, it's 'Grumpy' then. No chance of 'Happy,' this is Paris after all. The giant growls an accented phrase, which clearly means move along. The goddess fairy tales are intact with the arcs of peasants and princesses: Snow White, Sleeping Beauty, Cinderella, and 'Mona Lisa.'

This is all Veronica gets – a B-movie where hero and heroine say hello and goodbye in the same heartbeat, and the script notes indicate a poignant scene of relationship hell. This is the Kodak moment-thing, impossible to plan for. Lovers parting for eternity. A train starts up and chuffs farewell. Airport pain. Departure anxiety. One can't detain an impatient train or a bad fairy's curse or a French museum guard.

Sleeping Beauty morphs into a foreshortened panel seen in three-quarter view. Veronica feels she should be exiting backwards, as from royalty. Leonardo is everywhere and nowhere. 'Mona Lisa' is the proof of his touch. She is the Polaroid of a five-hundred-year-old event, and Veronica moves along.

A stranger in the crowd voices a popular opinion. "Nobody knows who she really was," it says.

"She knows," Jupiter pipes up, but his short stature causes his words to be absorbed by the black duffel coat in front of him. "And I know, know, know," he whispers into the itchy wool.

"Are you ready to eat?" Veronica is amazed by her mundane question.

Two answers arrive: *"I am ready to meet,"* Lisabetta says.

"Mom. I've been ready to eat since right after we had dessert for breakfast."

Jupiter blinks at the disappearing room behind him. He intends to scrutinize anything that affects his mother so deeply, and she has talked about the 'Mona Lisa' and Leonardo da Vinci long before he uttered his first words. They are family. When he and his mother sit and scan their photo albums, he expects her to point them out: *'There's Uncle Leonardo dressed up as Santa Claus. Oh, and that woman with her back to the camera petting the cat, is my Aunt Lisa.'* He's sure he's heard her say that.

Veronica crosses off a life event from a psychic list. She is a human cloud moving slowly over a disappearing landscape. Drifting away. Unable to anchor and stay. Christmas Day is over. The aftershocks of Boxing Day dictate that practical life takes over. The gifts are exposed; the anticipation is gone. She received everything she asked for and it isn't enough.

Jupiter's informal art lessons began in babyhood and have progressed to the present day. Professor Mom had offered visual treats from her textbooks, and Jupiter had watched how his mother mixed colors and applied them to large white squares, his favorite shape, even though triangles now rule. Geometry is fickle, but generous. Jupiter had easily absorbed Leonardo's diagrams of the proportions of man, the squared circle, and the divine rectangle. Children's book illustrations of rainbow animals mingled with the shapes of science, and he filled in the gaps. His education had been a parade of images – from Alice's rabbits and dodo's, and pea-green boats, to the Fibonacci spirals of shells.

The elegance of math is a language Jupiter understands intuitively. He's the only visitor to the Louvre who brings a backpack sporting the image of Leonardo's, 'Vitruvian Man,' *into* its gift shop. A lion doll's head protrudes from a side pocket. It wears a happy expression. Its three brothers are sardined inside the main compartment with a box of Crayolas and a spiral sketchbook. A black border has been drawn on each of the book's blank pages. There's an even number of crayons. The orange wax stick has been evicted.

Jupiter prefers to draws his thoughts on graph paper. Blank sheets are upsetting; information can slip off their edges. Some days the world is flat. His favorite paper comes ruled with turquoise blue squares that capture each letter. He loves crossword puzzles. Grids are good things; order is essential. The grid he pictures now, inside the Louvre, is a tablecloth of red and white gingham. Placed upon it are white circular plates, hamburger domes, and stable wedges of apple pie.

Jupiter's responding chuckle had been the deciding factor which broke my hesitation. I followed it into his shirt and let it massage me like a hug. It was then I knew I had made the best choice.

Jupiter Lyons felt like my adopted son, my new little brother, and a dear friend. - *Lisabetta*

"Always speak the truth,
think before you speak,
and write it down afterwards."
.- Lewis Carroll

The Black Cat

Paris – April 1, 2008

Lisabetta follows like a dog on a leash when Veronica and Jupiter burst from the museum into a 4 P.M. drizzle. Hand in hand, they dash across the sweeping skirts of the Louvre, and into the swarm of human traffic. They flow like salmon towards the famous café, 'Le Chat Noir.' Veronica swerves to circumvent an actual black cat. It's an automatic reaction. One searches for a hint of white fur and if none is found, treats the feline as an omen, not to be entirely trusted.

They fly on hunger pangs like children of Nike, and descend to the only available street table as the sun worms out of a black cloud. A waiter materializes and dries the puddles on the four chairs. Jupiter lands his backpack on the empty chair. Leo One looks hungry. Jupiter opens his pack and stirs the other Leos, art supplies, and his *Aslan* book, as he searches for his brochure and a red marker. Lisabetta looks on overwhelmed with freedom.

Veronica's purse opens fast and releases a green steno-pad with its companion pen jammed into the coil binding. She scribbles like an executive secretary while a ballet of loaded plates swings by at eye level. Waiters glide here. Each plate is a perfect still-life painting. Water is poured. Menus dropped. Veronica's nose stays glued to her page. She wants the immediacy of the moment on solid paper.

Dreams of bacon are forgotten. Veronica shoos the first waiter away like a fly while Jupiter reads the photos on the menu. He flips the pages and looks lost. The waft of passing espresso reaches for Veronica like smelling salts and pulls her into the present. Responsibility scores a hit. The immediate necessity is the refueling of two bodies that regularly require more than jam and rolls at 7 A.M.

Jupiter is confused. "Why aren't there French fries in France?" he asks.

"By Jove, that's a good question," Veronica says smiling, using one of her son's nicknames. Trust Jupe to ground her. His honest take on the world refreshes her. "They do have them, but they're called pommes des frites" she says over the top of her reading glasses. "And dishes called 'Veronique,' after me, mean they're full of grapes." Jupiter looks horrified at the prospect. He notices his mother's cup has been filled with thick black coffee, and she may even drink it. Doesn't she know it's nearly four in the afternoon – the zenith of teatime?

Jupiter doodles red hearts around the photo of the glass pyramid in front of the Louvre. He rotates it to show Mona Lisa. He has underlined the letters L-O-V-E in the word LOUVRE. Lisabetta smiles. Veronica notices the brochure, and remarks his souvenir is already 'Juped.' Jupiter likes to draw on his favorite stuff. It's a running gag. He 'Jupes' a lot of things, but never library books or anything belonging to others. A 'Jupe' mark is like planting a flag on new land. It's his stamp of approval. Unimportant items aren't worth claiming. Sometimes he makes a circle with a large dot inside for Jupiter, instead of printing his name.

Veronica craves tea, but she doesn't want the hassle of crossing the server who has anticipated that everyone in Paris drinks coffee strong enough to melt a spoon. "It's four o-clock" Jupiter reminds her, after he's measured the angles of the big and little hands on her watch, and recalibrated them right side up. Knowing the time reassures him. Four o-clock at home is high-tea, Jupiter's favorite meal – a smorgasbord of desserts before a savory dinner, later in the dark. He draws a tree with a cup balancing on the top, and an angel without a head wearing running shoes. Lisabetta recognizes her Louvre neighbor, Nike.

Jupiter reflects for the space of a heartbeat, and announces loudly that he'll pass on the 'freets' and grapes. Veronica is not surprised. She helps Jupiter order a grilled-cheese sandwich, and has the presence of mind to tell the young waiter: "please *not* to cut it in half... um...demi" she adds proudly. Her inadequate French is accompanied by hand gestures. Veronica mimes the shape of a square in the air, a sawing motion, and finally two triangles. "Voila" she says, hopefully. "Doo tree-ongla ey fromage grille sil voo play" she says, then wipes her order from the air like a blackboard, and makes another square with her chalk finger. She crosses it with a bold X movement. "Non," she says waving away the second air-knife. "Oui?"

"You are Canadienne?" the waiter asks, pointing to the red maple-leaf luggage tag attached to Veronica's handbag. "You are not... eh... biling...?"

"Bilingual? No, as you see... I'm not."

"Oui, Madame," he says, and waits for different instructions that arrive in the same airy hieroglyphics.

Veronica decides it's best to ask for the sandwich whole; if it comes sliced into rectangles or squares there can be an awkward silence. Lately Jupiter likes his sandwiches cut on the diagonal, preferably into four with one triangle removed for poetic balance. He is in his triangle phase. Veronica is used to consuming fourth triangles. She prays the sandwich doesn't arrive on a croissant.

"Madame wishes the grilled-cheese sandwich whole?" the waiter says in perfect English.

"Bon," Veronica says, and smiles radiantly into the waiter's serious face. He nods and escapes to the kitchen, convinced he hates his job... and now Canadians.

Jupiter and his mother have formulated a travel philosophy, considering they have never left Nova Scotia. They choose to glide on sensual time, exploring like a couple of extra-terrestrial innocents riding camels across a desert. Movies take them most places, and daily excursions are spent in a caravan of two, like a bus that stops at every oasis. Restaurant menus, art galleries, museums, and stores are considered historic sites. On healthy days, life is a fun-park without the usual social raincloud looming over it. Some days it seems they're stuck at the top of a Ferris wheel with thunder approaching, but at least they're together. Sometimes a rusty chair swinging above the bumper-car collisions of society is the safest place to be with one's best friend.

Jupiter overheard his mother explaining *artism* to a stranger once. She had called it an umbrella. His mother has a lot of them in a box by their front door. He likes the one with the surfer lady on a shell, the best. Veronica likes to think of the Lyons' family's challenges as eccentricities. The rest of the world calls it the autism spectrum. Uncle Oz calls it creative-friction to make his niece smile. Jupiter calls it seeing in pictures.

Jupiter misses Peyton when a miniature collie walks past their table with its head tilted high. The dingy sidewalk is its canine red-carpet. A movie-star dog on a fashion runway. This city shrinks their dogs into down-sized manageability. Lap dogs mingle with fur coats and pearls. Rhinestone collars glitter on pedigree necks. A few spoiled noses protrude from designer bags like Leo One in Jupiter's pack.

"The food tastes better here; it's alive," Jupiter says. "But the ketchup is wrong."

Louvre fever lingers. Mother and son share the same elevated mood: a world sieved through carefully trained senses, anchored to the hubbub of foreign diners in conflict over prices, whose murmurs build into a crescendo of disarming chaos. It drowns out the psychic concertina soundtrack of Paris, droning low underneath the angst of translation.

Veronica smells violets and looks up. She slams down her pen – releases it as if it's red hot. It rolls until the clasp halts its progress, and Jupiter aligns it parallel to the longest edge of an Isosceles triangle napkin. "No," she announces flatly, "We won't be going to the Eiffel tower".

Jupiter can see the monument in the distance – a wonderful triangle made up of steel grids, like the cross-hatching of a drawing.

"I don't like heights," Veronica says as an excuse. "They unnerve me."

"Were you afraid in the plane?"

"We're going to rent a car." She gazes into space, as if she can see the color of the car, and its make and model. She closes her fist around the weight of the phantom car keys in her hand.

"Mom, how can you fly if you're afraid of heights?"

"When you're headed for the 'Mona Lisa' and 'Nike' you can do lots of things. They're treats that make scary things feel better."

"What about flying home?" He looks worried.

"I have Pico and Nats and Peyton, and our new place in Victoria, and Aunt Bea, and Uncle Oz," she says. "What about you? What will you look forward to?"

"You can read my Aslan book," Jupiter says. "He never crashes. He's magic."

"Thanks Jupe. That will help."

Jupiter sees a mind-picture of a bee and an ant. It's been five minutes since Veronica asked him the question:

"French fries," he finally announces. "And real ketchup."

***

The DIARY of VERONICA LYONS

Playing Chicken

Paris, Cafe le Chat Noir
April 1, 2008

I am sitting in a French cafe on a post Mona-Lisa-Nike, high. I have just met two goddesses. I can still be moved by art. I wasn't sure until I saw Nike. She opened me up for the 'Mona Lisa' main event. I felt I was alone in the salon with her. It was like taking communion, as I could ever imagine it. We met. I read her inside sacred space. I wanted to stay, but time rules the ultimate Louvre experience. I know her... and amazingly, I visualized her coming down from her wall as a real presence with woman-sized problems no different than mine. All I could think of was that she was once alive. Happy, sad, confused, afraid... disappointed. Not ordinary by my standards, but infinitely real. Some days she had headaches and menstrual cramps, and like most women, multi-tasked herself into exhaustion.

I felt a religious urge to light a candle and suppressed it. I wanted to ask her to tea. I know her. She will always be with me. I will carry today's encounter like a jewel. I am humbled and moved. I had almost given up hope that I would ever feel the joy of art again.

These are my immediate thoughts: humans demand miracles and magic; we want to believe luck will rain down on us from a heavenly sphere dispensing largesse the way a farmer's wife scatters feed to her chickens. To civilization's detriment, the sons and daughters of Adam rarely resist opening Pandora boxes, or nibble sweet temptations of wonder-bait. The other sides of fences, dazzle us into trouble.

We are faint-hearted gamblers counting on saving grace, and rely on things unseen, such as the paranormal interventions of dream shamans, guardian angels, and fairy godmothers. When we wake with hooks in our mouths, we are surprised life has betrayed us.

Untimely side-swipes of hit-and-run fate are unfair trading, but we have to accept that it's non-local mind taking care of divine business, or extraordinary presentations of ongoing coincidence. Reality and French coffee is implausibly impossible – but that's life. ~*VL*

The DIARY of VERONICA LYONS

Starvation Protest

April 1, 2008

I am too emotional to sleep. It was the day. Shock, awe, caffeine, inspiration, and reunion with a lost love – my connection to art, and especially Leonardo da Vinci and his 'Mona Lisa.' I can't shake the feeling of connection. My imagination has short-circuited all common sense. I can visualize their times. I can wander Leonardo's studio when the portrait was wet. I can see it without its patina of age. I can smell the air and hear Italian voices speaking of ordinary things. After painting comes the time for soup and sleep. After the Louvre comes the time for reflection and lack of sleep.

I invent astral loves, lived once; abandoned twice. I am a triple princess: an orphaned girl afraid of red apples, who sleeps for a hundred years in order to forget life is bereft of princes.

Expectations for a slice of joy have me slavering like a dog, grateful for any sliver of passion. But I don't want a portion of love served up on a saucer. I want a silver platter piled high with proteins, and sugars, and fats. I want to live in a soup kitchen, where second helpings of pie in the sky are served with a greasy spoon.

Is my future carved out from dead driftwood or living trees? Is it possible to worship financial gluttony and still make psychic ends meet? The art of hand-to-mouth is not idyllic. Am I all-you-can-eat greedy? Am I sane? Am I needy? Am I brave? Ironically, I have been handed a magic secret on April Fool's Day.

The stakes are so high, that some days I can't imagine a more daunting way to live, but some days the rewards are so bright, that I can justify such determination. I crawl towards a glimmer so faint it seems pointless to attempt. Some mornings I wake with the presence of angel wings recently landed, quietly folding away in readiness for a human day.

Some moments I feel that a breakthrough is imminent instead of a breakdown. ~𝒫ℒ

Bed & Breakthrough

Montmartre, Paris – April 2, 2008

Jupiter invites Lisabetta to play finger shadows over the wallpaper roses until bedtime. He waves to her as Veronica tucks him in; his eyes too bright for sleep. Lisabetta can see them over the heads of his four Leos bunched together in a bouquet. Lisabetta blows him a kiss goodnight, and examines the exhausted mother.

Veronica soaks one foot at a time in the pedestal sink, balancing precariously on a slippery mat. The water is barely hot, but it helps quieten her blisters. She sprinkles Yardley's April Violet talcum powder between her toes and muffles them into plush lime-green bed-socks. The bed and breakfasts of Montmartre are Spartan, but the decor adds to the 'Hotel de Vincent's' charm, and the mattresses are plump clouds which promise falling into tunnel sleep, deep as a cashmere well.

Veronica fancies the wall across from her flickers with the shape of a woman, but she is too tired to care. She cozies into the nest of feathers, and holds her new paperback on the history of the Louvre under the gooseneck lamp to read. Its dim light requires the page to be lifted high into the domed shade. Veronica reads that the Nike of Samothrace is discovered in 1873, with only one wing. Her right wing is a reconstruction, cast in plaster from its mate. Jupiter had noticed.

Sleep takes over the paragraph. Nike, small as a barn owl, alights on the end of Veronica's bed and scoops her up. They flutter out the window – Veronica-Athena, this time carried by her bird-of-wisdom. Once outside, Nike resumes her full size, and together they soar high above Paris. The glass pyramid of the Louvre glows below them with sunset fire. They fly south to Amboise, and Veronica is deposited gently at the door of Clos du Luce. When she looks up to thank Nike, she gazes upon a fine sculptured head with flowing hair like Botticelli's Venus and the face of the 'Mona Lisa.'

'They're très approprié' Veronica had said to Jupiter, back in March, in the Halifax airport shop. She refers to their purchase of two French berets. "We've got an hour to kill before the flight." Jupiter ponders how time can die. Perhaps a wristwatch smashed with a hammer? The international departure lounge is a wasteland, and shopping for peppermints and a travel pillow only uses up a few minutes. Time still lives. Time can fly. His friend, Aslan, can fly.

Veronica sees the felt hats first, and Jupiter takes to their soft fabric and the nubs of yarn on the top. He models his straight, but Veronica twists it in one rakish move and lifts it by its *tail* to puff it into shape. "There" she says. "Check it out."

Jupiter likes his reflection in the square mirror with its gold baroque frame; it makes him look like a painting. He selects a pair of sunglasses with violet lenses from a revolving cylinder. "Très chic... très cool" Veronica says, and Jupiter envisages a tray of iced tea the color of amber, served in tall straight tumblers, with moisture beads sliding down the frosted glass like pearls. He views his *look* from different angles, and approves the purchases, but his crushed maple-leaf cap is crammed back on his long hair for the plane. Berets are perhaps too cool for Nova Scotia. He saves his tam for Europeans, who have what his mother calls, continental tastes. Jupiter recalls a map of the world, where the shapes of continents look like pancakes nibbled by mice.

"Can we get some iced tea?" Jupiter asks.

Jupiter pesters for it until they find a vending machine that dispenses it in chilled cans. The juice kiosk next door can only offer offensive neon-pink straws, so they slide into Tim Hortons and nab a couple of free white ones. Iced tea tastes better through plundered straws, and

Jupiter loves the dispenser that releases them with a spring. He slides off the white paper sleeve and wraps it around his finger like a ring. "Tray cool," he says.

⁓

"It's the Egyptian mummies or the Père Lachaise cats," Veronica says. "You pick."

"Chat *Nwar*," Jupiter says. Either way it's visiting the dead. It takes hours to locate a shop that sells cat treats.

Veronica and Jupiter drag a reluctant Lisabetta through tombstones and lanes with memorial chapels and statues. Veronica places a yellow rose on Jim Morrison's grave, and Jupiter is up to his eyes in French cats, who appreciate the treats. Mother and son eat their own lunch as if the cemetery is a park while Lisabetta perches on headstones and wonders how many of the artists here are in their heavens.

Jupiter is on board with leaving Paris, but the term 'next week' has no place to land. The Louvre's pyramid was the highlight of his visit; Paris is a done deal. The Eiffel tower is off-limits if it scares his mom.

Jupiter forms a triangle with his fingers and peers through them at Veronica. "Paris is full of the best triangles," he says. He turns and sizes up an air photo of a black cat. "Nwar," he says.

"We're renting a car tomorrow," Veronica says. "I want to explore a bit on our last free day. Our flight doesn't leave till the next morning. There will be lots of triangles in the countryside. We can look together." Jupiter is happy. He sips camouflaged orange juice from the spout of a baby's mug to mask its color. Happily, his incognito beverage tastes sweet and green.

The promise of a trip levitates Leo One; Leos Two, Three, and Four, can sleep in Jupiter's backpack curled inside his old baseball cap. Today, Jupiter wears his new beret, and a red T-shirt emblazoned with a black cat. "The cat *and* the hat," he says.

Veronica says the cat reminds her of Halloween, but Jupiter insists it's no trick or treat creature. Any reference to the season is received with disdain. Veronica thinks it's because of the masks, but it's the color of the pumpkins and the shades of orange that invade the eyes as cupcake frosting and bright Jell-O, and the overall offensive decor enforced by tradition. Festive foods are always questionable. One year it takes Jupiter an age to pick every shred of desiccated coconut from a bakery *snowball*. After that he was disinterested in the center, and rolled it to Pico. Veronica remembers finding a saucer of chewy *snow* under the sofa, after following an icing sugar trail.

Jupiter is keen. He loves to drive past countryside that blurs like wet paint. Fantastic swirls of colors and shapes are better than TV. He tells his mother he's floating in an impressionist painting. "I spy a Monet," he says. She believes him because of the classic unfocused images of wheat fields and poppies, and blue skies and water lilies that she's shown Jupiter countless times.

Jupiter is over the moon. He can snack on salty chips and close his eyes when he gets tired, and sip apple juice from a paper cup with a lid. Lots of treats are available in France, Veronica assures him.

"I spy with my little eye... something beginning with red," he says.

"Poppies?" she guesses.

"Nope... my Aslan book," he giggles. "I'm being *jovial*," he says.

The homage to the mummies will wait. The Egyptian antiquities will gather more dust, and yes, they will purchase the poster of the black cat he likes on his shirt. Jupiter repeats the name of it to hear the sound it makes. "Chat Nwar," he says three times.

"Yes, and who is the artist?"

"Tayofeelstinelen" he answers phonetically, and gets a gold star from his mother's eyes.

"Très Bon, très bon, très bon," she says, and taps her finger, one-two-three times on his nose.

Lisabetta's warm energy buzzes around the car. Jupiter finds it restful, and is thrilled to have potato chips for breakfast instead of jam and bread.

Today is going to be a fun trip. Jove is one of his happy names.

> *"Beauty is truth, truth beauty –*
> *that is all ye know on earth*
> *and all ye need to know."*
> ~ John Keats

A Dream of Earth

Paris – April 3, 2008

The last night in Paris, Veronica dreams she is a sculptor. The 'Nike of Samothrace' observes her, its creator, and Veronica observes herself from a remote viewpoint of the statue's mind. She wakes to write a poem in Nike's voice because it's what she hears most clearly... all day.

The DIARY of VERONICA LYONS

Nike

April 3, 2008,
5:00 A.M.

I am half-born. My creator releases me from the stone the way a lover undresses their beloved. I have a molten shape still covered in layers of negative marble. I can't move. I am embedded in mineral captivity, but I can see through a translucent veil over my eyes, that separates me from animation. I can't feel the air on my skin, but I can see it lift the damp curls that stick to Veronica's face. I see her lay down her tools in a great heave of depression. She puts my birth on hold, and listlessly sharpens her chisels. She moons over the meaning of art and life, and gets them hopelessly muddled.

I can do nothing to alleviate her suffering. She is my savior. I celebrate the matrix of home, and bide my time under a million crystals of critical mass. I am her life's work in one creative 'go,' her ideal... the inner woman she was created to be... her twin. I am the promise she makes to herself while the fresh chisels are blunted by the moonlight.

When she plays, the stone crumbles away like soft cheese. I feel lighter and warmer. I can feel the delicious blows that set me singing with vibrations of possibility. There is no pain. The intimacy of meticulous grooming begins. My draperies are polished by updraft winds. My wings shine white. My face reflects the serenity she longs to feel. I am made for pedestal life... high above the heads of mortals.

Twice life-size. ~𝒱ℒ

*"Confused things
kindle the mind to great inventions."*
~ Leonardo Da Vinci

A Dream of Water

Chateau Clos du Luce – April 3, 2008

The last time I saw the Château de Cloux, was four-hundred and eighty-nine years ago, and even then, unless invited otherwise, I had to keep to the grand bedroom, where Leonardo housed my portrait.

My consciousness always drifted until Leonardo spoke to me, and in those years, he thought I was still his living sister. He blocked all recall of my death, nor did he differentiate a three-dimensional woman from his painting. I was the ever-present Lisabetta at his side – his companion and advisor. He looked to my painted face for encouragement, and his voice drew me back whenever I tried to visit my heaven.

I sensed my daughter was happy, and that Leonardo needed me more, so I lingered, anticipating his time of death. The eleven years did not seem long. Cloux was the place of his sacred transition, and when it was time, I stood with Leonardo in the window and watched him fly at last, and called out I would catch him up. He had no reason to disbelieve me and I had no reason to disbelieve myself.

I was curious to know if my portrait's fate lay with Salai or with Cecco in accordance with Leonardo's instructions, and hoped perhaps Cecco would ignore my brother's insistence on erasing me from Leonardo's memoirs. He did not. Five-hundred-years later, in a dream with Veronica, I watched Cecco burn my brother's references to me. All but one, now lost.

I witnessed Leonardo's special tree tumble during the storm after he left his body, and saw my abductors in the candlelight. And so I stayed too long, and accompanied the panel to the nearby chateau, where I let the king fuss over me. By then it was too late. I fell from the time track as royal tastes sent me into hiding, or paraded me in style. I moved from Amboise to Fontainebleau, and Versailles, and then Paris. I could see Leonardo as a distant light across an abyss of sparks.

By 2008 I had become adept at short-term possession, but no host could take me into the streets of Paris. My portrait and I could never be separated. Veronica was different, but it had been her son who showed me how to leave, and later, I followed them to a vast marketplace in the museum, where I saw hundreds of images of the 'Mona Lisa,' which made me more determined to fight. I had never made it past the headless Nike on the stairs before.

Jupiter seemed itchy with me inside his shirt, and I was able to restore him to comfort when he waved another portrait shirt like a flag, for Veronica to buy. It was a gift for his Great Aunt 'Bee,' he said, and I was able to swoon inside it so Jupiter could feel more comfortable. Veronica selected a design with Leonardo spread-eagled in a circle/square for her Uncle Oz, that matched Jupiter's back pack. She chose two others: one of me and another of Nike, in XXL sizes.

So, I left the Louvre inside a shopping bag, not unlike the time I had been smuggled out under a man's coat. The imprint of 'Mona Lisa' acted as a bridge, after all, if the eyes are said to be the windows of the soul, surely an entire face would be a door, and once outside the precincts of the museum, I could move freely by keeping close to Veronica. I discovered why later. I tested our connection. The further apart we were, I felt myself thinning... too light to skim the earth. It wasn't unpleasant, but I didn't have the confidence to challenge the elasticity of freedom very far.

After Jupiter showed me his drawing in the street café, I blinked out when a tray of glassware crashed to the pavement. I resurfaced inside their hotel room, and watched my new family sleep. The dark skyline of Paris filled the open window, painted in blues surrounded by a halo of gold stars. I always notice skies.

The next day, after Père Lachaise, we reached the old manor house of 'Cloux.' My independence was stronger, and I ran on ahead to Leonardo's second-floor bedroom. Clos Lucé (its new name) had been refurbished, and looked unlike any home I once knew, but I recognized the open window and remembered the last time I had seen it. Leonardo and Rinato had been standing in front of it, and I moved toward the same view of the Loire Valley they would have seen. The Leonardo Tree was gone, and in its place was a large disk of wood. Then I remembered. It had fallen the night of the storm, the night of Leonardo's death. As I stared at the disk I became aware of the old oak's shape, transparent as glass above it. Leonardo had been right. The oak contained a spirit.

The sound of Jupiter's laughter drifted up to the open window, and I looked down on Veronica with her spy-box and Jupiter running in circles below. She looked up at Leonardo's bedroom window and I felt her sadness. The place was still closed to the public, with tourist season a heartbeat away.

From Jupiter's shrieks of delight, I thought he was being tickled – but he was chasing his beret that had spun off in a pinwheel, bouncing over the grass. He caught up to it when it blew into the large tree stump that looked like a low round table left on the lawn.

Veronica thought Jupiter was brushing away a bee. We both heard a loud buzzing, but it was the energy collecting in a cloud hovering above the oak stump that formed its missing crown, as Leonardo and I knew it in 1516. It's leaves were a swarm of bees that changed shape the same way that wind moves the treetops of living trees.

Jupiter flopped down, clamped the beret back on his curls, and turned his face up to the house. I waved at both of them, but Veronica's gaze scanned past me to take a picture of a pigeon coo-ing behind one of the roof gargoyles. Jupiter waved back. He told Veronica someone was inside, and they disappeared from view as they retraced their steps to the entrance to check for side doors – their berets, two black buttons moving out of sight.

I was about to join them when I experienced the joy of seeing Leonardo and Cecco walking towards the house. Leonardo was old and leaned heavily on his lion-head cane, and Cecco ran ahead to dust a basket chair under the phantom tree. It was Leonardo's elaborate wicker chair brought with him from Italy, placed in his favorite spot.

I saw the wind lift Leonardo's velvet cap from his head in a flash of purple, and his silver hair flew in a halo backlit by the sun. I heard his laugh as he encouraged Cecco's chase. "That's my favorite cap" he called out, and when it was returned, Cecco remarked his master's hair now resembled the bird's nest they had come to visit. I watched Veronica and Jupiter emerge from the shadows, back from their search and for a while there were four people on the lawn like actors on a stage. Two simultaneous scenes. A split-screen conceit, separating five-hundred years.

I believe Veronica heard me call out because she tilted her head in my direction, but Leonardo and Cecco glanced up to where I waved, grinning like a mad woman, and waved back. The next moment I floated high in a dazzling sky as the sun burnt through me. I turned lazily in the air and floated like a bird held aloft by updrafts, wishing Leonardo could know the same thrill. Flying is what he lived for and was denied. But then I realized that in death, he too could experience the joy of it and I looked for him in the clouds.

I was high enough to see the iridescent snake of the underground tunnel that meandered from the house towards the king's residence, the Château de Amboise, half a mile away. I could smell the history of it under the earth, and then the scene darkened. Veronica and Jupiter were gone and the Leonardo Tree swayed drunk against the moon. Angry rain pummeled the valley, and my tranquil sky became a vortex of twisting wind.

Leonardo was not in the sky. I saw him below, this time an ant-sized teenager, tramping into the tree-line, taking cover from the rain. Rinato ran beside him, tripping him up with excitement, glowing white like a paper lantern. Then they disappeared into the green mass of leaves and all I could hear was Rinato barking. I tried to follow them, but I was towed in the other direction, joined to Veronica as sure as if we were a puppeteer and marionette. I was Veronica's helium muse on a string, but gaining the confidence to explore.

Veronica and Jupiter were unaffected by the maelstrom that punished the miniature castle, and I heard her tell Jupiter his hair looked like a bird's nest. I hoped to meet up with Leonardo as she circled the Manor House anti-clockwise, but after we turned a corner and faced west, I stood inside the surprise of a grey waterfall, momentarily disoriented.

A shower of water dripped around me and I could make out the image of Sandro Botticelli distorted through the droplets, naked and beautiful, sleeping, while four fauns danced around him. I saw Veronica lounging near him, staring through me, but I was used to being invisible. She wore a long dress covered in tiny flowers, and I recognized she was not Veronica after all, but Simonetta Vespucci, Sandro's first serious muse. The resemblance was disturbing.

It wasn't a waterfall. I was outside, deluged by rain, pressed against an unfamiliar window, peering into an unknown bedroom. I had recognized a painting over the fireplace: Sandro's 'Venus and Mars,' his self-portrait with Simonetta, his politically 'chosen-one,' together as the lovers they never were in life. Sandro slept as if dead, and Simonetta stared with unfocused eyes into her future. Perhaps Sandro was dreaming her awake; she had been dead four years when he painted her.

The water was strong midnight rain which pulled me into sensual memories. I heard it pelt the windows and the roof, and I squinted through it as it cried down the glass. Beneath the painted figures of Venus and Mars, glowed a log fire that drew me inside, but I never took my attention off Sandro's dreaming face. Someone slept in a bed across the room, and I realized I had reached Veronica's homeland without trying.

Ironically, I am Veronica's muse, as Simonetta had been Sandro's, and my curiosity vanquished old jealousies. He had been mine in the end... although the end-of-the-end is still waiting. Simonetta died the year Leonardo and I left Florence, only days after I said a forever goodbye to Sandro, so I don't begrudge either of them some companionship inside a work of art; I know Sandro is in my heaven, waiting for me.

A black and white cat raised its head from the blanket, hissed, and immediately curled back into its dream. Veronica slept surrounded by books. One of them lay open and shimmered in a blue square of moving images. The dark shapes in her room blurred like wet paint as the storm washed the house on Bear Mountain, and cascaded into a silver thread that trickled into the valley of Victoria.

The rain sounded like the rustle of silk, and I saw that the firelight had turned the white bed-clothes to violet in the moonlight. Veronica's hand reached out past a statuette of Nike and tapped the bedside table, lightly as a raindrop. One tap, and a faint glow blossomed inside a white cone. A second tap brightened the room enough to see her groping for pen and paper. She tapped twice more and it grew dark. Magic. I was left in the quiet drench of a spring downpour, wishing I could feel the rain on my face or cozy up to a warm fireside.

A large tan and white collie lay stretched out on the hearth and I watched it turn into my little terrier, Rinato, snoring on his side in the old cottage at Campo Zeppi. I saw my mother weaving a basket and a starry-eyed girl who stared up and through me. Her expression made me shiver... and then it was daylight, and the girl was younger, and Rinato was barely a week old pup, and I knew the girl was me. ~ *Lisabetta*

The DIARY of VERONICA LYONS

Home Sweet Home

Orly airport, Paris,
April 4, 2008
12:12 A.M.

We are in the departure lounge. Waiting to go home. Home? ... Where on earth is that?

Jupiter is staring at shadows, chattering away to Leo One. He seems like the child I used to know in the days before we found the right meds. It is unnerving to hear him gibbering to someone other than the 'Leo gang.' I will need to contact his new doctors as soon as we settle-in. He has a new invisible friend named Lizzie. There's always room for one more I suppose. His beret has permanently supplanted his baseball cap... god bless Europe!

I got the message that the movers delivered our things three days ago. Somewhere, in Victoria, my car is parked outside a strange address. It was surreal. I was standing in line for the 'Mona Lisa' and talking to a guy about where to set up the beds. I told the mover: how about the bed-rooms? He didn't skip a beat, and said, "sure thing, eh."

We're staying at a hotel the first night back, and will tackle the house the next day. I've been psyching Jupiter up for it. He is overexcited that he will be with Pico and Peyton and Nat again.

I've had my list ready for days. First night... the hotel... thankfully a Canadian one with decent water pressure, and bacon and eggs. The second day is when new life begins: pick up the animals, and buy tulips, pet food, kitty litter, Earl Grey tea bags, cereal, and milk. Unpack the kettle and the bedding. Make tea and beds. Order enough pizza for three days. Buy real food. Interview housekeepers.

Have I put J through too much with this trip by mov-ing all at once? I hope not. And now I have an issue with matter. I keep glaring into the corners where Jupiter seems so at home, talking to an apparition. Home... there's that word again. I don't like that it's only a word. Jupe and I need a real sense of hearth.

I feel like a cat staring down a ghost. I said 'hi Lizzie' a few times to keep the peace. My molecules feel out of place in the world.

Downtowns scare me. I find mall herds disturbing – ditto loud noises. I am starting to abhor strong fragrances and garish color combinations, like Jupe. Rarely have I found a 'where' that embraces my being, outside a sanctu-ary that I've decorated myself. So, it would be huge to drift into a foreign space that smelled of home and touched my soul into staying. Victoria is still only a promise on a map. A clean slate with fresh forest scents.

Internal space must be my asylum of immediate hospice. I will close my door on the world of shadows, where I may claim a gem of solitude. I will simmer pots of lemongrass for serenity. From security blankets to electric blankets, I now reach out, hands across the sea, to touch honest-to-goodness molecules. ~*PL*

PART THREE
Second Guessing

*"Sometimes I've believed as many as
six impossible things before breakfast."*
~ Lewis Carroll

"My true face has been celebrated;
Mona Lisa's is unknown.
Lisa Giocondo's name is legend;
mine has been lost."
~ Lisabetta

A Room of Her Own

Victoria, British Columbia – April 7, 2008

*V*eronica buys fresh flowers before bread; it's tough being a modern renaissance woman. She straightens a painting in her writing alcove – tweaks it a hairsbreadth, and wipes an imagined speck of dust off the landscape sky. Her fingers automatically align her pens in a row and adjust a vase of violets until the blossoms make a pleasing shape against the wall. She fine-tunes the painting a second time.

Veronica's tuxedo cat, Pico, perches beside her open laptop, and preens like a fat penguin till she notices him. She kisses his nose and nuzzles the top of his head. He beams. She pets him like a bird with the back of her fingers. "My little penguin, my little owl," she says. She scratches behind his ears, and his soul purrs. The desk vibrates, and Pico flops onto a loose pile of papers like a wooden toy with collapsible legs. Veronica notices her signature on the landscape's foreground – the letters V and L worked into a glyph. More specks of invisible dust are polished out of the sky with a moist fingertip.

For the past week, Veronica keeps her diary close-to-hand. It once stayed on her nightstand – a permanent fixture for capturing a last word of the day, a running commentary on Jupiter's progress, or a wish-affirmation for change. Now it is the recipient of thoughts that come faster. Scattered throughout the longer passages written in blue, are the red notes on autism, along with the false starts of new poems, loose words, lists, and the first-impressions from living in a new city.

She captures strange notions. There are voices in her head determined to be documented. She feels cracked open with ideas, and the unfamiliar sense of ambition. For the third time in an hour, Veronica reaches for her diary and scribbles vague hints of a promising future. Like all memoirs, Veronica's diary is a running conversation with the world, a place to jot the small thoughts that come like blowing leaves.

Titles of fanciful books race through her mind. The 'Jupiter Book' will be a form of internal space travel. Her son is a world apart from earthling insensitivity: 'Reaching Jupiter,' 'Life on a Distant Mind,' 'The Everyday Savant,' 'The Creative Gene,' and 'Lizzie's Protégé.' Veronica jots down each mention of her son's imaginary friend, expanding her files on the aspects of autism that fall between society's agendas of success. There is no absolute solution, but she hopes to present the possibility of cooperation between species.

Veronica is Jupiter's translator. He is a clear-thinker whose ideas are lost in the din of language. His brilliance is overshadowed by his own conceptual language: communication faster than words in verbal flashcards of stunning intelligence – childish understanding and deeply profound conclusions woven together in a confusing, but revealing, dialogue.

The compulsion to write for her life is urgent; the need to write for Jupiter's, is critical, but Veronica drops off the horizon into writer's block. She removes her reading glasses and savors the finality of the plastic click its arms make as they fold against each other. For her it's one of the default sounds of academia. Her eyes dust the eclectic collection of ornaments on a shelf a few inches above her head. Underneath it is a cork board, pinned with inspirational clippings. She nestles in an inspired environment designed by her right-brain. It's intended to connect her to the universe where art rules over cooking, cleaning, and buzzers that shriek when the laundry is dry.

Artists require harmony; the autistic, require balance. Veronica and Jupiter both understand this need, and play accordingly with shapes, and colors, and textures. Veronica's nest of beauty is as necessary to survival as oxygen and water. Flowers are another language: weeds, the unsung blossoms, and discarded florist greens, take the place of expensive blooms – a metaphor for the rejected, less-than-worthy, selections. She gathers a few 'pruned' flowers from public beds when she walks Peyton through the park, or skims lilacs from neighbor's trees at midnight. She collects dropped daisy heads and floats them in antique bowls gleaned from the tables of garage sales. Her eyes find things. She's an eclectic collector and a shameless Robin Hood; she pilfers from Mother Nature, and gives to herself – the living, breathing poor. Thriving is a selfish business.

Veronica's desk has curvy French legs. Its romantic pigeonholes and hidden drawers hint of love-letters bundled in satin ribbon and poetic secrets, but they're stuffed to overflowing with unpaid bills. The sight is enough to propel her away from her stillbirth project. Research can only take an author so far. Procrastination wins; she has no story on the horizon to break the creative drought. She had felt an idea quicken in Paris, but it was like the end of a rainbow that recedes as one progresses towards it. She had been so sure... and now she feels mistaken.

Veronica glances at a quote pinned to a thatch of poetry and newspaper clippings: *'If at first you don't succeed... try, try, try again – then give up – there's no need to be an idiot about it.'* Her renaissance musings have led her here to a final website of obscure data. She half expects what she's looking for to be highlighted in acid yellow, as she scans endless blocks of text, and sifts sentences for clues. She minimizes the image, and it dives into a small cartouche at the bottom of the computer screen, that reads: Leonardo da Vinci's birthplace.

The relief housekeeper, Mrs. Bently, is late on her first official day. Perhaps it's due to the storm. Warm spring rain judders the afternoon windows, shut tight. Its intensity calls Veronica out rather than preventing Peyton's walk. External and internal weathers match; the wild roar of a mythical tempest seeks union with an elemental cousin. Anything to blow the cobwebs and doubts of being cooped up dry and restless. Her thoughts feel like the loose notes that overflow her in-basket and spill across her desk. Their frayed, crenulated edges of different sizes represent a collection from half a dozen notebooks. She has tried to manage them by pinning them underneath a heart-shaped slate. The sight overwhelms her. They defy categorizing. A fever dream of words flaps listlessly in the humidity like an injured moth. She had thought them inspired and had hoped they would congeal into a coherent outline, but they remain oblong islands with strange inhabitants speaking different tongues. Their individual word games make no sense and yet she stifles the urge to throw them away. Spontaneous ideas have a life of their own. She believes in literary reincarnation.

The present storm threatens to scatter her thoughts the way a body tries to shrugs off unhappy memories. Veronica shuffles the untamed pages of dictated DNA into a pocket file and snaps the elastic cord. It's this act of closure that frees her and deposits her into the real world where she's free for an hour, while her son snoozes with Leo Four. Veronica feels the psychic fatigue of a fairy-tale curse. A princess who wakes dehydrated after a hundred years.

Inclement weather is never an excuse to stay home. Only the extremes of blizzard snow would ever trap Veronica inside. She tells herself, that when she returns home, there will be a clearance. No more silliness. She will rest a day or two and begin again, and this time, she will stay faithful to her diary entries and allow the naturally poetic nuances of autistic expression to stand on their own without embellishment. The Leonardo tale will officially close.

Having a year of free time is proving more of a challenge than working two casual jobs juggling night and day shifts. Present circumstances restrict her. She's trying too hard, and now she wants to be swept away by a wild event. She hopes it's literary.

Peyton is released from her rabbit-chasing dream by a crash of thunder and Veronica is glad to push her expectations under a sofa cushion, and shake the damage done from hours of vulture-neck posture. The collie requires a bathroom break, and a drive to a deserted off-leash park may cast off the bleak chill of a frozen storyline.

Peyton cowers at the tree branches tapping at the window. "Sorry, girly, we have to go out there," Veronica tells Peyton. "I have some things to do first, but we have to wait for Mrs. B."

Creative ideas can only coax a receptive writer as a passive entity by making no sudden moves. No amount of cajoling may command the muse, but it seems that muses are constant to their own demands. Lisabetta has to wait for an optimum moment and tiptoe around the book that Veronica is writing on the creative advantages of autism. There must be an opening of a tidy corridor. A five-hundred-year-old wormhole.

Veronica has documented Jupiter's autism, but it's hard to shape it into a reader-friendly manual. The neuro-typical world prefers their clinical facts softened. Bitter pre-chewed data for baby sparrows.

Autism is rarely discussed by the world outside the compounds of affected families; its gifts remain unopened, swept under a public carpet, along with inconvenience, and incompatibility, and impatience, but an autistic eye in neutral, owns a precise neural path and is compelled to scan for relative anomalies. Iconography is pure detective work. Jupiter finds dormant signatures and fingerprints outside the crime-scene tape. Master artists know a similar secret: they paint subversive messages in direct sunlight, because center-stage is a blind spot. The untrained eye generally succumbs to 'scotoma'; people see what they want to see.

The ten commandments of social worth seem to purposely ignore the obscurities of autistic perception unless they arrive disguised as the secret powers of comic book and science-fiction heroes. Jupiter has genuine vision quests which soar past the myopic banalities of shallow commercial entertainment. Veronica has always considered Jupiter a super-hero without a cape.

Pico steals the violets from the vase in one clump and drags them to his regular sunbeam, even though it's now a dappled pattern of refracted raindrops. Veronica re-bunches the flowers into a tattered crush of rearranged purple. Violet heads drop to the floor and she uses a single headless stem to tease Pico. She watches dreamily, reluctant to head outdoors, but eager to be in the car and driving for driving's sake.

Veronica hustles to the kitchen, where white porcelain and stainless steel dazzles her after her dark corner, where a single backlit flat-screen tried to suck her into digital middle-earth. She is careful when she makes Jupiter's snack. His routine is a well-rehearsed ballet: No crusts, cheese slices the color of dark cream, seedless white bread... lettuce underneath... mayonnaise between the top and filling – a square production, cut into four triangles. Her hands deftly assemble a geometric offering: three triangles presented on a blue plate with a solid border of white, the segments arranged like flower petals around a cylindrical juice-glass filled with milk. No brightly colored drinks. Nutrition, questionable. The fourth quarter becomes the property of the dog, herself, or the garbage can. No exceptions. It waits ready for Jupiter's nap, too late to be called second breakfast, and too soon for lunch. The next meal is high-tea at four. Late-night dinners feel like treats when mother and son dine on holiday time. Today, Peyton is the receiver of the last triangle.

Veronica scribbles a note in the hieroglyphics Jupiter prefers: *'Hey Jupe, please call me. I have taken Peyton for a walk. Your snack is in the fridge. Love Mom.'* She attaches it low on the fridge door with a star magnet. The word phone is a drawing of a telephone, and the word 'snack' is replaced by a diagram: a large circle containing three triangles around a smaller circle like a three-leaf-clover. A heart replaces the word love.

Veronica remembers the time when Jupiter was four and would only eat squares and cubes. Tastes change. That was his cubic period. Today he's the slave of triangles and the number three. One Christmas she offered shortbread on a star-shaped platter and learned the hard way not to anticipate the evolution of geometric complexities. No doubt one day she will have to shop for a polyhedron or two. Today she's grateful that round plates have been cleared for take-off.

Anticipating the shape of plate histrionics to come, Veronica once attended an evening ceramics class, prepared to make plates of exacting dimensions, shapes, and colors. She practiced her technique on sets of damp, green-ware ducks in flight, cutting off the wings that lie flat to the wall, with a wire. She discarded the bodies and smoothed each air-dried wing with fine sandpaper before firing them, and stored them in a box. Somewhere in her future she is sure she will know what to do with them.

Veronica had snobbishly dismissed the novelty cookie jars shaped like buildings and cartoon-head mugs that her classmates produced en-masse like little craft elves. She experienced the medium of clay in all its stages, and the wings accumulated – a box of wings kept under her bed. Her fellow ceramicists thought Veronica was a tad odd; she figured they lacked imagination. They had both been right.

The DIARY of VERONICA LYONS

Widdershins

April 7, 2008
10 AM

Finally we have a housekeeper. I hope she's worth 'keeping.' I signed her on last week for a months trial after she and Jupe made friends. She seems ideal, which bothers me. Her name is Mrs. Bently.

Jennifer Bently, Jenny, is an older woman, who amazingly, adores animals and is a retired kindergarten teacher who used to work with special-needs children. Having her here allows me to collapse for a day or go on safari with Peyton. The only down-side is, Mrs. B is openly religious, but that's not a deal-breaker as long as she keeps her beliefs to herself around Jupiter. Life is confusing enough without saints and fairy stories that he will buy as truth or engage in debate with no survivors.

Today is as oppressive as a deeply-listing, loaded ship, cargo heavy, depressed with bars of lead. I long for a clap of thunder to herald a storm of new life, when the trees rustle and the air is expectant with rain, and it grows dark, and clouds swirl widdershins against the goddess… when some 'thing' is about to animate. My senses strain for an omen of blessed change. ~𝒱ℒ

The DIARY of VERONICA LYONS

*Somewhere
Under the Rainbow*

April 7, 2008
9 PM

I call fairy tales 'backbone stories.' They're always ram-
pant with gender inequality. The gods apparently once
favored male 'dummlings' who prevail against all odds,
with outstanding examples of serendipitous intervention,
but girls clever enough to outwit the smartest woodcut-
ter, fall into mutilation, bad resume's, and broken hearts
unless they succumb to a prince.

A good fairy's parting gift can soften the cursing blow
of disgruntled power... witchy huffiness rewarded with a
legal back door. Moronic cuckolds, and kings and widow-
ers, still survive their calculating wives till the last page.
Only modern translators rewrite archetypal disasters as
happy endings with heroines who overcome their challenges. It seems natural for them to rise above spousal
incompatibility. Movies consistently show downtrodden
heroines embracing the promises under the rainbow of a
magic tomorrow. So, why oh why, can't I? ~𝒱ℒ

"The device you call an umbrella
is something that would have
delighted my brother."
- Lisabetta

Sandro's Umbrella

Victoria, British Columbia – April 8, 2008

Jennifer Bently arrives with apologies in a miniature storm of wet coats and excuses. She brings offerings: lilac branches from her garden for Veronica, a rented DVD for Jupiter, and dog treats. Jupiter is thrilled; the movie is a documentary called 'Cats in History.'

Veronica looks at the window. The storm is in a fine temper. She checks her watch. There's still time for a wild excursion if she doesn't wait for the downpour to subside, and besides, by the time she and Peyton reach the promenade on Dallas Road, the sun could be out. It's a risk worth taking.

She tunes her laptop to hibernate mode and snaps the lid, trapping the screen-saver of floating soap bubbles. The bubble game has hooked Veronica before – lured her into an electronic pool table for a lost decade, second-guessing the color changes when they collide with the edge of the monitor.

"C'mon girl, let's go get wet," she says to Peyton.

Veronica rolls her chair away from the computer and stretches her arms. Her neck, fingers and wrists crack from sedentary confinement. She arches her back and rubs the weary pixels out of her eyes. Hunkering down wreaks havoc on the body mental. She often forgets weather exists until her collie reminds her with a wet nose... *it's time to pee... please and thank you.* Today is different: Mrs. Bently is her liberator.

Peyton accepts Veronica's invitation, fears of thunder forgotten. The collie responds instantly to the sound she hears as a single word: 'C'mongirl.' Doggy neurons spin like the tumblers of a slot machine and stop at three cherries. Ching! It's one of Peyton's happy names.

Peyton's instincts say good to go. She moves towards the back door and Veronica clips the two of them together with a black leash. She makes a note to extend Peyton's collar another notch; it's getting harder to separate the dog's thick ruff from the jangle of I.D. tags, and the metal hasp.

Veronica faces an eclectic coat rack – a scarecrow groaning from the weight of too many hats and coats, and chooses a navy-blue 'London Fog' with a hood. Once off its hook, a familiar image is revealed. Lodged behind it is a canvas tote bag imprinted with Botticelli's 'Birth of Venus.' Veronica stares at Venus; Venus stares back vacantly, through Veronica. Sandro Botticelli's muse, Simonetta Vespucci, looks bereft. Botticelli had painted his own sadness in her face when he painted her rebirth as the goddess of love.

Veronica pulls on snug black Wellingtons and reaches for an umbrella. The selection of an umbrella is harder. There are sixteen umbrellas crowding the hall stand like a bouquet of tall flowers. She collects umbrellas the same way she collects walking sticks, and spoons, and china cups. Particular mugs with round bowls demand frothy lattés; the Blue Denmark china is for breakfasts, the best white porcelain cups and saucers with silver rims, are reserved for afternoon Earl Grey, and different rain dictates Veronica's mood and the umbrella design she wants to baptize. Amongst the stems is a matching Botticelli – a second reproduction of the birth of love. It is the perfect subliminal choice.

Veronica grabs the bag and stashes the necessities: her diary, colored pens, dog treats, and chocolate, and seals them inside with the zipper closure.

Outside, Veronica presses a button on her umbrella and it deploys in a fast fluid motion like a parachute. The pattern on it mushrooms above her. A vulnerable, naked woman balancing on a floating sea-shell. A pair of paintings face the rain. One Venus is shouldered; the other's shell boat is upturned – her ocean, now a sky. The twin haunted expressions of Simonetta, are a renaissance photograph of a perplexed woman. How else could a goddess contemplate her spontaneous birth from a violent act?

Peyton, the matriarchal elephant, trots stoically ahead, and leads Veronica past the silver Cavalier. "We're taking the car today sweetest of peas" she says, and the collie responds to another name for power... 'car' and the neck-tug that stops her. "We're driving today."

The vehicle slithers over the water cascading down the paved hills of Bear Mountain and reaches the sign of a T-junction that reads Peacock Street. Veronica wishes street names could be transported like furniture. She would have kept the name 'Phoenix Street' from their old address, but their new street is relevant enough. Electric Street is only one flight up from an equally cosmic bird.

"Electric Street has a nice ring to it don't you think?" she had asked Jupiter on their arrival.

"It's more like a buzz" he had replied. "Buzzzzz... zzzzzzap... sparkzzzzzzz... lektrizzzzity."

That was the drive into Victoria when Jupiter decided he was a bee, all the way into town.

"I am bee-ing" he had said.

"Buzz words," Veronica replied. "When you get home you can have a nap and..."

"Catch a few zzzz's, Jupiter had said with a bounce, enjoying the word game.

"Well done you," she had said.

～～～

The DIARY of VERONICA LYONS

Burnout

April 9, 2008
3 AM

> Mrs. Bently has been with us four days in a row. She will be here three weeks more before we finalize a schedule. I can't remember not having a helper with Jupiter. I am

allowing myself the luxury of feeling free. I am even free to indulge in feeling lost.

I sleep fitfully, and pace the balcony at 3 A.M. when my challenges have cooled sufficiently to be able to breathe. I feel that I've been playing with fire... hence the burnout and meltdown. I'm in spiritual shock. I long for peace, but I remember more of everything instead of less. There has been no special delivery of compassionate amnesia lovingly administered by hovering guardian angels. No Italian phantom can grant me asylum from guilt.

I wonder if my neighbors see me and report strange manifestations of 911 midnight activity in a house that's been empty for years. Have I haunted here for centuries? I've lost track of divine time.

We living ghosts are made of gossamer wind. We float and sigh, and nearby mortals shiver without knowing what has passed them by. We are the lovers of romance, dashed heroes, exhausted heroines and stillborn dreams.

But if one believes in reincarnation... then the waiting may be rewarded. ~*VL*

The DIARY of VERONICA LYONS

Lizzie

April 9, 2008
Noon

I'm distracted. I feel pulled in one direction, then nothing. A dead end. Silence. I am the victim of a lack of focus with an inability to gather my notes on autism together coherently. Then just as suddenly, desperation clears the air, and a story emerges beneath it. My dreams are erratic, filled with anxiety. I think it's from living in a new place.

Perhaps even from too much freedom. A different me pushes my hand to write. I am researching one moment and then I lose the thread.

I am in search of a link to Leonardo da Vinci. That is all that remains clear… and it is a woman. She is the presence I sense in the house, but I have no intention of being possessed. I think, once I determine who she is, she will leave. I think that is all she wants. I hope so. All I know, is a book is in the making that will somehow serve Jupiter, and that I have been gifted the time to create it.

Discipline is required and it is not my strong point, but worse, if I am to follow Cate into dementia, who will be Jupiter's champion?

My diary is becoming more than a place for summaries at the end of each day. I used to write tidy conclusions and expectations… and malignant thoughts that required anchoring in order to deflate them. But now, these pages have become sponges that soak up my creativity. They are a place for plans. With no-one to speak to, I read my words back to myself for hidden meanings. I write with the hopes that a conversation on paper will stabilize the world I now find is both exceptional and irrational. I spill myself into this diary, drop-by-drop, all day long. I grab a pen as if it were a lifeline and let the thoughts write themselves.

I find myself here, at another entry point with something that must be said. Recorded for a later self to regard with the clarity of distance. I am a messenger and the messaged. I don't remember writing much of it, and so I am surprised, but informed by a me with greater insight… or a me who is slowly going crazy.

I spend hours at the computer diving into research, treading words like water, reading everything I can. I sense a woman behind me, waiting over my shoulder, and I want her to be gone. At first it was me pretending I could hear

Jupiter's invisible friend, but then 'Lizzie' became bolder. Now Jupiter says her name is Lisabetta... and that she is the 'Mona Lisa.' It almost makes sense. Paris had a profound effect on both of us. Humoring Jupiter is something I have always done without qualms. But things have been shifting, and now even I can pretend she's real and maybe it's me who is a dream.

The strangest thing is that I feel as if I am invading my own privacy. ~𝒱ℒ

The DIARY of VERONICA LYONS

Pelting Challenges

April 9, 2008
2 PM

Jupiter and I live under a social umbrella that flips inside-out at the first gust of intolerance. It's a term meant to encompass and cover a multiple of conditions. It's even meant to solidify in order to ward off prejudice, discrimination, and public disapproval. Chemical imbalance darkens our mental skies, and we huddle underneath judgmental ignorance with waterproof determination. Autism is a six letter word for invisible, and it gives an umbrella its toughest workout. Acid rain has nothing on social cruelty. The term 'judge-mental' puts an ironic grimace on the face of humanity. Thank goodness we live in a world that rains cats and dogs. ~𝒱ℒ

"I survived
through a dangerous reshuffling of power.
Rebirths of civilization
are more painful than human births
and they take much longer."
~ Lisabetta

Dangerous Times

Victoria, British Columbia – April 10, 2008

The sky holds a single wisp of cloud in its blue-grey arms. When Veronica shields her eyes to look, she is able to cover it with an oval fingernail. It's an inch-long, white streak, angled from left to right, like the trail of a miniature comet descending to earth. It hangs suspended – a harmless acute accent – an alien comma to punctuate her desperate need for signs.

Veronica uses a peripheral compass to navigate the cars on Douglas Street and the mental traffic jazzing her head. Random words float – a discarnate alphabet soup. Veronica's auto-pilot leads her through a dangerous ballet of city life towards a green space where ideas have room to land. She holds a pocket-size notepad in her left hand braced against the steering wheel and a ballpoint pen clicked open, poised, in her right. An automaton stenographer/chauffeur on pause.

It's a spiral pad. The sort she's seen TV reporters use to record the loose memories of eye-witnesses. Leonardo da Vinci had always carried such a creature. Cecco had called them his *'libricini,'* small books, no bigger than a deck of tarot cards, with a vellum cover, worn at the waist – a fifteenth century camera. Leonardo was the consummate life-tourist.

He would have loved the coil and flipped pages laid flat, and likely swooned more over the mechanics of the pen than her car. For Leonardo, wheels and gears are passé. His little books were fastened shut with a low-tech arrangement of cords and wooden toggles, like the buttons on her duffel coat. The nearest matching image is a small black 'barrel' sewn on the cuff of her sleeve. At the red light, she examines it and lets it whisk her into the past. Wormhole speed. She imagines Leonardo strolling the streets of Florence, stopping to sketch a hanged man dangling from the Bargello or a skittish horse, on paper the color of new ivory, before time turned it dog-eared and golden. Veronica stalks Leonardo as he loops the book through his belt and ambles on. She smiles into space. A sketch is an artist's memory, and thanks to Harry Potter, a visual object may be explained as a 'port key' for the creative mind.

Veronica stares at the road while she writes squiggles in automatic Martian shorthand. Cell phones are a danger while driving, but a possessed writer behind the wheel makes dialing a portable phone look safe. She thinks of the word port and relishes its link with the meaning, door. Harry's port key is an object which enables one to travel through a gateway that transcends space, quantum leaping to simultaneous locations like untamed electrons. The art of language is never coincidental.

The car swerves into lanes. Veronica sways with it, and pedestrians appear like targets in a video game revealed by windshield wipers on intermittent speed. Loose messages whispered in her left ear melt in a cryptic mist. A cloudy phrase fires once before evaporating. Her auditory memory is not strong; she's a visual learner. Until a subconscious sound-bite is anchored to alphabet, an idea a writer's worst nightmare – a passing thought.

Twenty-first century mayhem overlaps the renaissance Veronica is trying to channel. Her brain automatically tunes ideas like a radio dial... overshooting the gibberish of humans speaking in tongues, then back, riding the airwaves too far, until she isolates a voice she knows waits there. She finds the eye of the static, locks her position, and waits. She wishes she had Jupiter's ability to translate audio soundtracks into home movies.

She looks in the rear-view mirror and sees Peyton's black-button eyes and nose, and pink tongue panting there like a piece of ham, fur flying in the breeze.

"Hey, baby girl, we're almost there."

Peyton grins, *'Baby Girl'* is another happy name. Her tail twitches underneath her as she inches forward, snuffles the back of Veronica's hair, and sneezes. Car rides engage the collie's senses. She makes a high-pitched whistle in the back of her nose and flops into a golden heap, paws crossed in a prim pair of white stockings.

Veronica's purple sweater holds a clue and when she writes down 'violet sleeve' she remembers that two hide under her coat. The image imprints in a game of snap. When she arrives at Beacon Hill Park, she can only decipher nine words out of twenty: *black — eye — triangles – autism – violet – sleeve — echo – speech — mongrel.* The rest look like they've been scrawled by a crow walking through ink.

Peyton bounds from the back seat and squats in the grass. Business done, Veronica scoops it into a bag, deposits it in a designated bin, and their walk is upgraded to pure exercise. Peyton is too skittish to be released from the custody of a lifeline. Veronica hooks the loop of the leash over the U-shaped umbrella handle and urges the reluctant collie on. The storm is still fierce. She hasn't wasted it. They make for the track in the woods and brave the cliffs for a short distance. The grey sky is a protective blanket that separates her from blinding sunshine, too bright for thinking. Veronica's mind settles best inside a drizzle. The sharp clatter of brittle light dazzles off the whiteness of paper and hurts like blue snow.

Veronica can't remember driving to the off-leash park. She is transported – abducted by an alien story and finds herself daydreaming on Dallas Road with Peyton, whipped by a brisk north wind that throws freezing rain in her face. The raindrops sting her to attention. A pair of exuberant German Shepherds bound towards them, and Veronica feels Peyton's anxiety rise up the leash and into her hand. They collide in a tangle of leashes and snarls like canine coat hangers, and for a moment Veronica forgets the voice in her head and the voice forgets her.

The animals are freed with few words exchanged. Only brisk

commands from human to canine until parallel walks can resume. Once separated, the resemblance to Cerberus, the three-headed dog is lost, and they perform the perfunctory olfactory dance of introduction.

"Dogs are never ships that pass in the night, are they?" Veronica shouts, competing against the wind. A shrug is her answer. The trio moves on, leaving the field ahead clear of intrepid explorers. "Nice weather," Veronica says conversationally, to herself. "Yes, very… nice to have met you" she continues.

Peyton wanders to the extent of the leash wound out like a tape measure and is reeled in to tow Veronica like a tugboat against the wind. The two blow across the field until the tree-line of Beacon Hill Park catches them like a couple of tumbleweeds. Peyton is jerked to a stop whenever Veronica pauses to write a word. They progress this way for ten minutes. The rain is cruel. It's time to pay attention to the world and ignore the muse that riffs in her head like a jazz solo. Some days she can't hear it at all and other times it's an endless thread pulled from an old familiar sweater, or the hook of a song one can't forget.

Lightning flashes a heartbeat before its deafening boom. Peyton cowers and her whine is sucked into the storm's eye. Veronica sloshes through puddles, hanging onto the umbilical cord between herself and the dog. She's a kite too drenched to fly. It's a slow procession; heads down against the monster that commands the trees to bend low in surrender, but they make it to a dripping tunnel of Pine and Cedar, its entrance woven like a basket – an open door to the dwelling place of Green Man, and the weather pushes them inside.

Pan's decor is eclectic. A raw clutter of sculptured wood and vases of twigs. Wild pets scuttle overhead in holes and nests, and dart behind the camouflage of fur-colored air. It smells of granite and moss. Patterns play over textures permeated by the scent of musk. Pan's wallpaper is a designer tangle of bark and leaves. Upholstery and draperies to match, anchor a low ceiling. The winding hallway, sheltered by the dark canopy, disappears in the distance. Veronica's boots squelch on a sponge of pine needles that float above the mud floor in a prickly carpet.

The wildwood has its own umbrella. Veronica lowers hers to pass under the low branches. She and Peyton stroll into the density of middle-earth. Piles of bracken and the shapes of fallen deadwood move once they've passed. Each downed log is a frozen creature. They creep through a jungle of enchanted deer, and sleeping bears, and a wolf wind howls a safe fence around them.

Veronica pushes back the navy cuff of her glove to check her watch; she's been wandering for twenty minutes. She feels the bump of a ring under the wool, but she can't remember choosing any accessories. The writing biz requires pajamas, a robe, and slippers; she's become unselfconscious about fashion. Peyton is pleased when they turn towards the car that shimmers in a time zone on the other side of the moor. They walk lively out of the tangle and find the rain is no longer horizontal, but a careful downpour of west coast rain. Precipitation that falls thick, and silent, and warm, on a morass of saturated thatch grass.

Veronica can't decide if she is losing her mind or finding it. Writing takes no prisoners. On the way home she stops at an intersection and notices a sign on a consignment store that reads: 'Sister's Seconds – lightly worn clothes.' She must remember that. It's significant, but her brain is unable to tame a larger crowd of facts. Too much information is a flash flood that washes away perception.

She takes dictation blind and stares ahead like a crash-test dummy. Words are pearls and Veronica wants to write a long perfect strand. Lately her words are more like a choker of plastic beads. She writes 'second sister' on her pad, sets it aside and drives on. Her mind rambles with fanciful images where she demonstrates the miracles of a Polaroid camera to her good friend Leonardo. She sees his eyes sparkle with excitement when he watches the slow burn of an image of his face appear on a small, white, cardboard square.

Auto-pilot returns Veronica to Electric Street, but she has careened home like a zombie – a driver drunk on ideas, and words, and images. A brimming notebook accuses her of writing on the move in spite of her resolve to only scribble during red lights, or to allow the words to pull her over to the curb. So far she's been lucky with near misses and only punished by adrenalin spikes. The aftershocks from horn blasts have shredded her nerves. Sideswipes and fender-benders live outside her budget. If a car has nine lives, then Veronica's Chevrolet is living on borrowed time.

Veronica and Peyton shatter the serenity of a pristine entrance hall. Veronica peels off a saturated clump of blue fabric and water drips from its sleeves. She strips off knitted gloves to reveal a cabochon stone of ruby glass set in Scottish silver. Long wet hair stains the collar of her mauve sweater to a darker shade of purple. She drops Venus in the corner and leaves her weeping mournfully, upside down in a pool of tears.

"Hey Jupe... Jenny... I'm home," she calls towards the open door of her son's room.

"I'm working," Jupiter yells back.

"We're drawing," Jenny adds. "Do you want me to put the kettle on?"

Veronica fills in the rest of Jupiter's reply: *'don't bother us right now.'*

"Thanks Jenny, I'm on it. Jupe? I'm making tea for Jenny and me. Do you want hot chocolate?"

"In a blue mug," he shouts out. Jupiter doesn't mince niceties.

"Yes, please," she corrects.

"You're welcome," he shouts back.

A shiver of rain from a drenched Peyton sprays woolly water into Veronica's eyes. She wipes them like tears with the heels of her palms, and rubs them into her complexion like expensive face cream.

Peyton is wrapped in a thirsty towel and massaged dry. Her paws are lifted one by one. Each toe is rubbed clean. A steaming canine coat heads for a cavernous bowl like a waterhole. A quick slurp and the dog sighs down beside the electric fire on an oval cushion the size of a small island.

Veronica flips two switches: red flames lick asbestos logs and a fan blows hot air around Peyton in a private Chinook. The dog curls tighter into her grey velvet nest – a giant contented hen. A second switch sends current into a filled kettle for post-rain tea. Afternoon tea aligns the senses necessary to harness a literary project. Veronica muses that time shakes itself like a wet dog, and surrenders to the art of tea.

Limbo Heat

April 10, 2008

How does one describe a boring Sunday that is so vacant it makes empty seem meaningful? Is it the inside sticky limbo heat? or the lack of psychic breeze? Or is it the whisper of relentless small defeats that drown the hours one by one, slowly ticking trickling away? I am adrift... airless. Self-abandoned. I have mutinied my own ship. I chased my disloyal crew of plague rats to the edge of the dock where they fell like lemmings and swam to shore. I am in dire need of entertainment and air-conditioning. It's hard to adjust the thermostat to take the edge off the rain and not feel stuck in a sauna. But, I will take rain any day over the white stuff.

Jenny is disturbed that Jupiter has an invisible friend. She suggested it was an angel, and I had to sit her down for a heart-to-heart. At least she didn't think it was a demon. Kids have imaginary pals. It's no big deal.

Today I went to a movie and I tried to imagine Leonardo sitting next to me. The film was in wild 3-D – the sort of animation which would have disintegrated a novice movie goer – a tad over the top even for me. I had to look away from some of it. Queasiness should be renamed motion-picture sickness. The first silver screens would have wowed Leonardo enough, but this sort of production could actually cause physical harm. An Imax screen, surround sound, and objects hurled into our face, floating within our reach. The unexpected projection of a heart attack predator. How could one ever explain such phenomena to a man born in the fifteenth century?

There would be no possible way to prepare for such an onslaught of visual effects. Even the popcorn would be a miraculous surprise, and I wondered what a 15th century palate would make of Coca Cola. It would burp through Leonardo's nose and cause searing pain. I know this. I rarely drink soda and that's what happens to me. The experience is hostile. I always avoid pop for six months afterwards.

I cherished being on a blind date, alone in the dark with Leonardo, in a world where the miracles of technology were mine to offer. Imagining him in the seat next to me was easy. Watching him would be as breathtaking as the film itself. I take bizarre comfort from pretending to be his personal tour guide. I'm such a kid.

I opened the balcony doors and the windows… humidity has left the building, and the scent of awakened grass is delightful. The cats are ecstatic, rolling on the nearest thing to outside they're allowed. There's too many ticks and fleas and teeth hiding in the foliage to make feline life safe or comfortable. I especially don't relish an infestation of parasites, since my entire cat colony prefers my bed to the dozens of their own. ~𝒟ℒ

The storm suited us both. Neither Veronica nor I were working to task. I welcomed the thunder, hoping it would clear Veronica's head. She had harkened to my suggestion to write, but became side-tracked with the best of maternal intentions, in a weak project. It was dutiful, but dry.

I knew the better vehicle (mine) would encompass the same topics of autism with none of the tedium of clinical observation. Veronica's enthusiasm for writing was waning. I needed the mythological lightning bolt idea to part her from her dull essay.

I walked with Veronica and Peyton, my gown windswept as Nike's, along the deserted promenade that hugged the coastline of Vancouver Island. The collie closed her eyes, faced the bluster of wet wind, and stepped daintily forward into the sponge of wet grass. Peyton was a subservient creature, unlike Rinato – hesitant but obedient. She surrendered to Veronica's will the same way I'd wished Veronica would defer to me.

Veronica looked like a monk, huddled into a hood of dark wool. She held her umbrella in front of her like a shield, to displace the intensity of the wind, walking behind it rather than underneath.

Venus' portrait was an ironic choice of shelter. Her father Kronos, has disappeared from view; there had been no need for a mother. Kronos descended from Gaia the earth and Uranus the sky, which made Venus their granddaughter, and later, the half-sister to Zeus, who donated her to her husband in an arranged marriage against her wishes.

To complete her genealogical highlights: Venus/Aphrodite had an affair with Mars. She is the only goddess to be awarded a divorce. Going against Aphrodite's rules of love have serious consequences. - *Lisabetta*

One of the most mysterious
of semi-speculations
is, one would suppose,
that of one mind's
imagining into another"
~ John Keats

Medusa's Match

Victoria, B.C. – April 11, 2008

Medusa's hair had to go first. It bursts into purple flames when Veronica faces her in the mirror. The crackle and sizzle obscures the high-pitched squeals of snakes that twist into dead charcoal strings and crumble away. What will begin to grow is a golden fuzz of baby hair, pale and tender.

This is the silent promise that's missing from the label encircling a clear cylinder of yellow tranquility tablets. Veronica thinks it wouldn't hurt for pharmacists to be a little more poetic with their instructions than: 'take with food.'

She concentrates on her new meds. They're a gentler cocktail of anti-depressants to clear the muddle for renaissance pathways; the unplanned pregnancy of her re-birth, goddess style without a sperm donor, but scaled small and intimate. One life saving itself.

She cools her temples with a cotton ball soaked in witch hazel, pauses to drink in the scent of freshly-milled lemon soap, and dabs Chanel #5 on her throat and wrists. Her en-suite oasis is a cozy sauna where a thin vapor shimmers between herself and Medusa, who now looks relaxed.

Veronica winds a towel around the shadows of snakes charmed by the first pill, and smiles at her reflection – surprised it smiles back.

The house is electric. It's been that way for days. The scent of violets lingers in every room. Peyton can't be bothered, but the cats are hot-wired to each other. They twitch at sudden intervals and leap into the air to swat invisible plasma balls of St. Elmo's fire, no-doubt passing overhead. Veronica has noticed Pico and Nattie hissing more into the corners, and there is no obvious cause for their fur to be frizzed into body halos.

Outside, the spring rain is gentle enough to fill the heads of early tulips in perfect stillness; inside, a buzzing hurricane riffs against the pots and pans like a jazz drummer. Veronica likes it. The infra-violet wind grows small fists and breaks the silence.

The bathroom door pounds from Jupiter's six-year-old impatience. "Mom... Mom... Mom!"

Veronica opens the door and faces her son – her best friend. One word captivates him: "Pancakes?" she says.

He looks enraptured by the prospect and makes for the maple syrup. She hears his enthusiasm retreat as he tears down the stairs trailing the words *'syrup syrup syrup'* like a scarf. According to the brightness of Jupiter's eyes, he should be in bed with a fever. He is hyped on the merest promise of sugar.

Jupiter and Leo One, shadow the green mixing bowl filled with flour. Jupiter counts the plop of two eggs that slither down the powder mountain and puff a white cloud into the kitchen's sky. A pair of yellow eyes rest like the blobs of a cold lava lamp at the bottom of the bowl. He hands his mother a third egg. It cracks cleanly and avalanches into its companions. Sugar buries them. Milk drizzles them into a paste.

"Syrup," Jupiter shouts, hugging the flat bottle.

Veronica pours dollar pancakes and asks: "two, four or six?"

Jupiter grins back the number eight.

"Eight it is," she says.

He licks the batter from the edge of the jade glass, using his finger as a spatula.

Veronica arranges the golden discs into a grid. Piles of pancakes disturb the fabric of breakfast.

Three lion dolls watch them eat; the fourth has no eyes, nose, mouth, or ears. Jupiter explains again that Leo Four can feel the nearness of pancakes, and hamburgers, and rice pudding.

"They're all boy lions," he tells her.

Veronica knows better than to ask why. The answer will arrive, and it does.

"Cause' girl lions don't have this." He flicks the yarn mane of Leo One.

Pets, Nattie and Peyton, are Veronica's surrogate sisters. She doesn't count the presence that followed her from Paris, but she feels its femininity shimmer at her elbow. They've been home one week. Like a voice in a library, it speaks smaller than life, and Veronica's automatic reaction had been to stifle the intruder before it did any harm, but the entity had retreated to a respectable distance, and now it has become family. It observes Veronica and waits for the right moment.

Gradually, Veronica accepts its probing and senses a benign Italian greeting: "Buongiorno," it sends in a rush of electrons. Veronica drowns out its persistence with Andrea Bocelli played loud. She loves the anonymity of Italian lyrics. A foreign language is safe from meanings that trap a mind into story. She can soar with the swell of it and absorb it with her right-brain. Music floats her against the ceiling. Out-of-body cooking. When Andrea sings a line in English, Veronica crashes to the floor.

"She wants to talk," Jupiter says.

Veronica searches her son's eyes and asks 'who' with her eyebrows.

"The happy lady," Jupiter says.

He points to one of two empty wicker armchairs in the sun porch. "Her."

"Okay, you take the gang 'Jupiter's Pride,' she calls them off the table, and go brush your teeth."

"Syrup syrup syrup," he sings, and scoops them away.

Veronica takes her cup of Earl Grey to the other chair and sighs into it. It creaks like weary bones. The violet perfume is intense now.

"My name is Veronica," she says to the chintz cushion opposite her.

The DIARY of VERONICA LYONS

Rainbow's End

April 12, 2008

We're mostly settled in. Victoria suits us; perhaps because we are strangers here. Only a few more boxes left to unpack and some paintings to hang. As promised, an agency is sending over a housekeeper who will double as a baby-sitter three days a week. All on Niles' tab. There's that to be grateful for. Deadbeat dads with rich mothers have juicy side-benefits.

I set up my old easel, but poetry eclipses paint like the rock-paper-scissors game. I felt the quickening of a story in the National Gallery in London, and then much stronger in Paris, but I'm a poet not a writer – now it plays with me. It hovers half-evaporated, out of reach like rainbow gold. I hope it will reveal itself once I feel stable. Flying unhinges me. Jupe is picking up on my hallucinations. He sees what I hear. Change is not one of his favorite things yet he seemed calm in Paris, and so far, he has accepted our new lodgings as a natural progression. Highly unusual. He is as ever, a role model for me.

Jupe says the trees here smell safe. I know he loves the color green, so maybe living surrounded by the rain forests of Vancouver Island is a lucky break. We are barely ten minutes from Victoria, perched at the end of a developed cul-de-sac high up the left flank of Bear Mountain and far from street traffic, but I won't let the cats out. There are cougars. Pico and Nat will have to get used to being inside creatures. Peyton is thrilled. There are trails to walk her around several local lakes. This province is an enigma ... primeval aboriginal wilderness that surrounds an old-world pocket of Old-English, Victorian culture. I will explore its retreats and delicacies later. Right now, crowds and city streets unnerve me. I wonder if I am unwinding in a good way or just unraveling. My dreams are scattered and I wake up from sandalwood voices, displaced – nervous as a bag of cats. I'm hardly a rainbow.

I began my new meds yesterday. Anxiety is a fluttering of emotional indigestion – an inner boil of malevolent chemicals. The feeling is like the nausea of low bloodsugar, deep-seated and lingering. A tangible contraction of the vital organs like emotions forming a circle against joy. I shut down and breathe through the gag reflexes. Knees pulled up. Arms hugging myself. Breathing, clinging to the three words, 'I am fine,' until the wave subsides into something bearable. New meds – new doctors – new world – new beginning – new enemies... old battles. I experience jumpy spurts of indiscreet sleep – a vague, dozing off the horizon into innocence. Yesterday, I talked to an empty chair. Très philosophique n'est ce pas?... I am almost positive there's some French in there. ~𝒫ℒ

April 13 –

It's been 24 hours. A lot has gone through my mind. Mostly negative. The feast/famine connection unnerves me: I've had an amazing 'April in Paris' experience and now the month of May looms with all the horrors of moving to a new city. The joys of spring feel overrated. I'd rather have a steady flow of drip-feed care than an outpouring of suffocating 'do-good' rescue. I watched a DVD. I let the ghost choose. It guided my hand as I plucked it from the shelf, the way a jukebox arm tweezes selections from its vast innards. I have a year to get things right and the tease of a project that haunts my dreams. I must rally or Jupiter will suffer, and more power will be thrown to the bipolar phantoms I need to fight. ~𝒫ℒ

"I had been there all along.
Waiting.
Nine little letters
but she only read the first four: L-I-S-A"
~ Lisabetta

A Theme of Her Own

Victoria, British Columbia – April 15, 2008

*I*f it hadn't been for the umbrella, or the storm, or the wet dog, Lisabetta's story might still be a blank sheet of paper, but the moment Veronica gives up, she opens a door to energy. Giving-up clears the mind. Surrender is like wiping an old lesson from a blackboard. Words smear into a white swirl that once held meaning, and the ideas stick to the erasers, beaten together to be released in a cloud: wisdom to wisdom, dust to dust.

I can see the black and white photograph of my old home on Veronica's computer monitor. Little has changed. The old cottage is a rustic cube of crumbling masonry, plain and unlovely. The contrast of light on bricks and dark shrubs is the same, and the reach of wild countryside grasses still touch its threshold.

Veronica pours tea and allows the steam to rise in a lemon-scented facial. She breathes in her tea like perfume. A green electronic glow tints her paperwork as the dim light from the computer screen flickers with my impatience. She's close now.

Veronica's cup and saucer bear a classic Florentine pattern. She rests her elbows and peers into the windows of the cottage. Her artist's mind brushes past the long skirts of the heavyset women in the photograph and wanders through the door left ajar. Veronica is desperate to see inside. I want to wave hello, madly from behind a tree.

She's denied entry, scrolls down the text, and rests the pointer-device on a 'Mona Lisa' mouse-pad so that it covers my right eye. Veronica straightens it parallel to the laptop. For a while she allows the pleasure of tea to distract her. She sips idly and casts her eyes to the shelf where her lashes try to dust the objects there. So many clues collected unconsciously for years against the next moment. She hears the word 'clue' in her mind and pictures the word 'Cloux.'

Veronica surveys the ornaments: the winged lion of Venice, a prancing tin horse, and a Victorian butter-mould of a fork-tailed swallow in flight. Her mind swirls inside the core of a broken seashell and out again to a crystal prism with triangular facets, to glint off the apex of a small glass pyramid. To her right is a bookcase holding Leonardo's 'Treatise on Painting' and several volumes on sign language. She's made a collage of 'Mona Lisa' memorabilia: a postcard, two admission tickets to the Louvre, a novelty button, and three conjoined pieces from a large jigsaw puzzle that make up my smile. I love the irony of my smile being an actual puzzle, especially the irony of it broken into fragments.

To her left is the book she's currently reading – 'In Search of Om Seti.' I can see an orange bookmark poking from the top. I cause it to fall, and a fifty-dollar bill flutters from the pages like a pressed flower. It makes an imperceptible sound on the carpet, but she sees it go. She retrieves it and pokes the money back, marking the wrong page. I make a fuss and shout 'look at the screen,' but she cups her hands over her ears and closes her eyes. The money is a sign.

She looks at the screen again, and Mozart's peace is sabotaged with the clatter of her teacup crashing into its saucer. Veronica leans back and ogles the screen image of Campo Zeppi, circa 1908. It's an image captured one-hundred years to the day, in order for eternal synchronicity to register with sufficient poetic grace. Her eyes rest on the text below the photograph.

I am going crazy. Veronica speaks slowly and deliberately to herself, the room, the drying dog, the violets, and to me: "Omigod you... you're there!... you are... there." Her astonishment is contained, but a dog on high alert can feel the aftershock of human epiphany. Peyton experiences it as canine anticipation that arrives as a round sweet disc, covered in chocolate.

Classical music surges in a post-dramatic swell and simmers into profound silence to isolate and celebrate an historic revelation. Veronica pours and stares, and between sips she suppresses the muffled hysteria of a child awake too early on Christmas morning.

Veronica used to hear me, but now she listens. I give her the year of my birth as 1458 and our work begins. I tell her there are two Lisas. She reduces my birthplace to an icon box, and I watch her type excitedly. A deft move opens a blank document file that balloons into a white window. She saves it as 'novel-Lisabetta -doc.' I have the pleasure of reading her working title. I see it float, safely centered on a fresh electronic page: 'Seconda Gioconda' – a novel by V. Lyons.

Veronica toasts my poster at dawn with the champagne of teas and wipes the gritty surface of her 'Mona Lisa' mouse-pad for better traction. She waltzes on ozone, stands on her balcony, and gazes over the panoramic rain forest of British Columbia; she can smell a sense of purpose on the awakening grass mixed with the aroma of bergamot.

By April my anniversary year had already been ticking for three months. I know instinctively that I have till December to achieve my goal. The day in Paris when I followed Veronica, she became my surrogate mother. I had been awarded the prerequisite nine months to gestate, now she must write me to death in the remaining eight. I will need every moment to breach her resistance. My little poet must make my life rhyme in what appears to be ironic pentameter.

One thing is clear. Mrs. Bently has to go. ~ *Lisabetta*

The DIARY of VERONICA LYONS

Minotaur

April 15, 2008 – Victoria

I witness the spectacle of what used to be, by journey-ing through pages of text, highlighting with the frenzied glow of yellow ink as I go. I travel down side-word roads, and back-track to sniff out a warm trail, and pick up the labyrinth string trampled in the mud, missed from dizzy busy-ness.

The Minotaur is my guide. He is not stubborn… only persistent. I know he would surrender and turn his neck to Mithras for me, but I don't ask for sacrifice.

He is my consort to the sacred cow of Isis, and his lair is the crucible which burns away the chaff that surrounds me. All along I have been fearing his Apis form, never guessing he was tamed gentle from accepting he is the last of his kind. It is time to grab his horns, to spin and orbit a few far-distant world stars, before comet-ing myself back to the present day, reborn a Taurus baby-girl… priestess of the Serapeum.

I think our ghost really is 'Mona Lisa.' She is Jupiter's Lizzie. She told him that her name is Lisabetta, and the research confirms it. She is mentioned as an obscure throw-away in a government census. I will take steps to insure she is gone immediately. Right after Mrs. B... Religion mixed with a paranormal visitor is like a lit match and gasoline. ~*VL*

Daddy's Girl

Victoria, British Columbia – April 17, 2008
A dream of Campo Zeppi – April 17, 1463

Veronica watches a scene from the balcony seat of a flimsy pop-up theatre. A brown-faced peasant girl, five-years-old, waits center-stage on a cardboard floor. She kneels, surrounded by violets spread around her like a spell. She teases a ball of puppy-fluff with the stem of a flower. It barks ecstatically in a frenzy and rakes the violets into a small cloud behind it. The child's head lifts suddenly and her joyous expression evaporates. A man eclipses the sun. She squints up at his face.

Veronica feels the presence of cruelty. She reads defiance in the girl's eyes. The puppy chews at the flower unconcerned. Veronica sees the back of the man's grimy shirt. He lifts a dirt-encrusted boot towards the creature, and the child, anticipating the worst, throws herself in front of the dog.

The boot's trajectory collides mid-air with the girl's forehead. She is knocked off-balance – her neck whipped with pain. The man moves off snickering and the girl rearranges the disturbed violets as if they will keep her safe.

A vicious bruise spreads across the child's temple and blood trickles into her left eye; the puppy begins to lick it clean. The girl is too dizzy to stand. She leans on the puppy pulling it into the curve of her arms like a pillow and brings her knees up until she looks like a child ready to be born. It is the last image Veronica remembers: a dazed girl and a reprieved dog viewed from above, inside a witchy circle of purple blossoms, getting smaller as she floats higher into the sun.

"There's no way I'm getting involved with this." Veronica says. "I was wrong to agree."

"Think about it for a few days" Lisabetta pleads.

"Absolutely not... no... no way. I refuse to tempt crazy. I've changed my mind. I will not entertain collaboration with a phantom, so please go." The effect of Veronica's last three words lacks the forcefulness she had intended.

"No matter," Lisabetta says. "We will find someone you won't be able to dismiss."

NIGHT SCRIBBLE READS:

true — puppy — violets
5 — fear — bully

"I am her muse. She is my writer.
The story is ours."
~ Lisabetta

Wake-Up Call

Victoria, British Columbia – April 19, 2008

I watch Veronica's hand reach out and turn off the dark with a blind finger-tap on her bedside table. A sensitive magic lamp reveals the power of a human touch.

Pico lifts his feline head and blinks into the light. Nattie squirms. Veronica's hand fumbles for a pen and small coil notebook, and narrowly misses knocking over the owl-size statuette of 'Nike.' These are her staples of writing. As her muse, I dictate at any hour. Her home and car are littered with spiral pads of all sizes. I remind her that her name means 'veritas icona.'.. true face, and tell her once again how mine has lost its name.

Veronica captures a couple of dream words, and taps the table. A blind thump... and the silver table turns-on the dark. Your twenty-first century is a miracle. ~ *Lisabetta*

NIGHT SCRIBBLE READS:
amber — olive mill — autism
Lezza?

"This is how I get to her…
in waves of lucid dream fragments
or while she drives her car.
She believes she is writing fiction.
What else can she think?"
~ Lisabetta

Traces of Violet

Victoria May 2, 2008 / Manor House of Cloux
– France May 2, 1519

The hem of an emerald silk dress catches the light as it rustles across a carpet of Persian flowers towards a four-poster bed. The dress perches on a gilded armchair at the bedside. Graceful hands rest in the pose of the 'Mona Lisa' and wait.

Leonardo da Vinci, sixty-seven, hallucinates near death with his eyes closed. His long white hair splays out like a silver halo on a red velvet pillow bordered with rows of seed-pearls. The canopy sky above is blue velvet embroidered with gold stars. He opens his eyes and smiles. A green sleeve takes his hand. The scent of violets permeates Veronica's bedroom and follows her all day and into the business of controlled dreaming.

NIGHT SCRIBBLE READS:

four poster — emerald — hem
silk — fear – sleeve

'Diana: Queen of Heaven,
Mother of the animals,
Goddess of the hunt,
midwife, woman in the moon,
protector of the weak,
Daughter of Jupiter'
~ Anonymous

Art (emis) Victorious

Victoria, British Columbia – May 2, 2008

The latest rescue cat arrives as fortuitously as the others – a discriminating feline, this one culled from a house fire, via the SPCA. The cat had been on one of her hunts when the flames expelled her from captivity and for a while she evaded the traps and the domestic embrace of a charity shelter. She has one life left.

The tabby is picky. She will know home when she smells it. For weeks she surveys the cul-de-sac network of Bear Mountain and scopes out the boy on Electric Street. They chat often. He tells her his name is Jupiter; she tells him hers is Nadia.

Nadia's coat is dapple grey and it reminds Jupiter of a nursery rhyme.

Nadia basks in Jupiter's voice with her eyes closed and listens to him recite: *'I had a little pony. I called him Dapple-grey. I lent him to a lady, to ride a mile away. She whipped him, she slashed him, she rode him through the mire. I would not lend my pony now, for all the lady's hire.'* Nadia is hooked.

There are two women at odds in Jupiter's house; Nadia studies them. She has a plan, but the goddess of the forest lures her into a savory bowl of delightfully fishy paste, left as bait. It's one of her leaner nights, and hunger is persuasive.

Lisabetta sees the cage door swing shut, and she soothes the little creature. "Do not worry little one. Jupiter will help you." But when the van takes Nadia away she cries out while Lisabetta memorizes the number on the side of the vehicle.

Jupiter and Veronica formally adopt Nadia the next day.

Nadia tours the house, regal as you please, and claims her space. The tabby is starved for attention, but being a night huntress, she has managed to stay plump on the abundances of the wildwood.

Jupiter announces the cat's name is Nadia. Veronica looks up and to the right, and scans something invisible there. "That's a great name," she says. "It's an anagram. Both her names are."

By nightfall, Bear Mountain has weathered a freak snowfall, and Nadia has endured a bath and had her identity restored. Lisabetta is impressed and says so when she and Nadia share a moment under the moon. "It should be so easy, to have one's name respected," Lisabetta says, petting Nadia into a blur of soft tremors. "What's your secret?"

Nadia loves to chat. She tells Lisabetta why she's plump.

Nadia sharpens her claws on the nearest tree trunk. "Jupiter says this is your tree," she tells Lisabetta.

"He named it for me. Jupiter likes naming things," Lisabetta says.

Peyton accepts Nadia completely. Nattie will take time. Pico sniffs and plays possum. There's a feral scent about the new arrival which gives her authority, and alpha males aren't as dominant as their press. A familiar of Pan has presence enough to eclipse neutered power.

Nadia likes to play hide and seek. She's distracted by anything not tied down: a single Cheerio, Jupiter's triangle eraser, or a paper clip. Shiny things interrupt her cat thoughts. Batting them senseless under the furniture is a compelling career. Veronica indulges her; she knows that fire can make a girl crazy. Nadia deserves a second chance.

Trauma is everywhere for a cat with a cautious paw on the pulse of *humane* nature. Nadia is nocturnal as a ghost, compelled to sleep under the scent of a full moon. Captivity is a steep learning curve, but hunger wins out. Gift mice are laid at Veronica's bedroom door. The open air of the oak grove and the Lisa Tree calls, but the warm side of the cat flap is a world of pleasurable surrender. It's the place Nadia wants to birth her kittens. She knows they will be twins – a male and a female of Gemini power. Female cats learn early to submit to the males.

Nadia had spit at the old black tomcat before she surrendered, herself only a young girl, and becomes a mother at only eighteen and a half weeks-old.

<hr/>

The DIARY of VERONICA LYONS

The Spirit of Christmas: Past & Future

May 8, 2008

Christmas tried to repeat itself last week on the second of May, with its bells and baubles and an untimely gift. It was an out of season boon I ignored. The story arrived with complications. It scared me. Lisabetta's aura unnerves me. The last thing I need is to follow my mother down the slippery slope of mental illness. I decided to disregard the presence and paint... leave the writing thing be, but I have the feeling 'it / she' isn't going to leave me alone, and that my new life is only one out-of-control-event away. My poor son. I will call Uncle Oz if I don't feel stable soon.

My imagination is flying north and south at the same time. How I will ground myself remains a mystery and a must-ery. I had thought assembling thousands of words would do that. My must-story. I had been looking forward to a promise of literary stability – finally a peaceful writing nook. Seems I was wrong to wish for such an animal.

I will turn my Jupiter diaries into a sort of layman's guide to autism and polish my years of clinical observations with margins of emotional commentary. At least it will get me to the safer motion of an east-west keyboard and a left-to-right brain. Somehow, the ticking sound of the keys calms me. It's like a conversation with a trusted friend, and I think I am hooked on the fact I am in control of the text that comes. I can delete anything or change and rewrite. It's me talking into a neutral box, and after seeing my words spin out of my head onto a flat-screen I am free of a burdensome weight which has suppressed me.

There are different kinds of mates. Intellectual ones. Business ones. Teacher ones. So, is it greedy to expect an intellectual one to also fill the role of romantic lead? Having control is the only freedom a woman can have, apart from wealth. I want both. Then I can rule a subterranean world exactly how I want – lived apart from society, in luxurious reclusive freedom to purchase any environment I care to design. My own Mt. Olympus inhabited by goddess sisters and holy cats, and Jupiter and his trusty canine sidekick.

Zeus, Apollo and the rest of the toadies can be kept, boy toys – small action figures sealed in their original packaging on shelves in a dark room. ~*DL*

NIGHT SCRIBBLE READS:

Nadia = *Diana*
Diana = *Artemis*
Artemis = *art is me*

"My writer
is a modern renaissance woman;
she's a painter and a poet,
and she has a hunger
to know more about my brother.
Her name is Veronica.
Her name means true icon... true face.
I am drawn to her, and she is drawn to me.
We collide somewhere in the shadows
between thought and paper."
~ Lisabetta

Mistress Lisa

Victoria, British Columbia – May 17, 2008

"Jupe, is the happy lady here now?"

Jupiter scans the room, and knits his brows into 'of course not.'

"What does she look like?" Veronica asks. "I can't see her."

Jupiter looks through his mother's face. He never fakes interest.

"Hello? ... Jupe?" Veronica snaps her fingers in front of her son's eyes. "Just describe her for me, please and thank you." Jupiter responds to the pre-thank-you line of his own invention. It's efficient. It's short-hand for an impatient question in a hurry, disinclined to waste time. Fait accompli.

Jupiter selects Leo One and takes his mother's hand. He leads her to her studio like a lamb to slaughter and brakes in front of the 'Mona Lisa' print. "That's her." He drops Veronica's hand and leaves her, a shaken leaf wilting under the portrait's smile.

Veronica keeps her breaths steady and deep. "I told you I won't entertain this" she says to the woman in the painting. "I won't lose my mind." It's her mother, Cate, all over again; talking to walls and sliding off the reality track into dementia before her time. Refusing to go there is hardly an effective strategy. Some call it denial. Veronica calls it plan A.

Veronica's gaze drops to the floor where she steadies herself by examining the sculptured texture of the carpet. She raises her eyes to 'Mona Lisa' and absorbs her celebrity. The room is a confessional. What is said here, stays here.

Veronica and Jupiter explore Vancouver Island on cozy drives and keep to themselves, stopping to walk Peyton on every beach and in every park they find. New friends remain invisible until Veronica begins to feel she and her brood are three memories who tramp the moors of a previous life, roaming old paths in the fractious mists that separate the living from the nearly, almost wanna-be, dead.

"Lisabetta lives in a condo" Jupiter tells his mother. "Like that one," he says, as they pass a waterfront spill of cubic habitat. Jupiter's volunteered information haunts Veronica. Her son's custom is to unconsciously blurt casual remarks while he's engaged in remote viewing, as if he has to periodically empty his mind of junk mail. After the words leave his lips they're up for grabs and Veronica is left with his loose threads. This latest is a bizarre concept ... that the Mona Lisa resides in a high-end walk up overlooking the straits of Juan de Fuca, when all along Veronica has been persuaded to believe the woman wanders her own home.

Veronica has visions of Lisabetta poking into her bureau drawers and closets, with nothing much else to do. Why, seems rather a ridiculous question, but the ridiculous also borders the sublime, which is a continual source of inspiration for a right-brain processing the world. Wings and prayers are obscure entities one must still court from time-to-time, even though Veronica tries to avoid the possibility of life after death. The second is moot to an atheist, but she forces herself to remain as open-minded as possible. She continues to hear the Italian voice that trails after her. It has become a pleasant Mediterranean Tinnitus that shadows her like the hook of a song.

Veronica leaves Jupiter to his movie with Nadia's newborns, named Venus and Mars, and takes Peyton on a freedom run in order to experience the vicarious conversations of strangers, and to soak up the indifferent camaraderie of a population seemingly at odds with her visitation rights. Her elevator soundtrack fuses with the swell of wind and water that hugs the coast of Cordova Bay.

Today, mingling is suspended; the main path is deserted. She makes a beeline for a human dot in the distance and stalks it like a destination. Veronica designs a new Tai Chi move: *'walk dog to horizon.'* She glides in a walking-meditation, lassos her target, and reels it in, but he turns out to be a creep with a pair of jumpy Jack Russells. She lights a mental smudge stick and swings it ahead of her like a catholic priest. Pendulum power plus the cleansing effects of incense. From now on she will use a sharper dowsing rod.

For the rest of the walk, Peyton sidles up to a dozen panting acquaintances of canine small-talk, but their owners remain anonymous and they smile like imbeciles at their surrogate offspring, tug them away from olfactory heaven, and toddle off for toast and tea. Veronica misses plain adult conversation.

Why would 'Mona Lisa' haunt a condo? It's a slippery question that requires an autistic answer. Images that leap from Jupiter's audio-visual frequency bounce on rhythms displayed like kindergarten flash cards. Veronica has to hear them as a sound-bite in order to descramble. She projects his latest declaration on her mind's movie screen – displays Jupiter's personal tarot deck and makes a spread of three blank cards. She writes condo on each one for a possible match. Condo condo condo. Its meaning is invisible, but the cards de-cloak into three images: The 'Mona Lisa,' a square apartment building, and an assortment of geometric shapes – and there it is... a door opens with a mechanical hiss... geo condo.

Turns out what Lisabetta said was: "Tell your mother, I'm not Lisa Giocondo."

The door gently closes with a soft click.

The DIARY of VERONICA LYONS

Beyond Grief

May 17, 2008

This morning I woke from a nightmare. Now I know the meaning of the term bereft. Something so unbelievably devastating had occurred. The world was empty. I was determined to ask the entity to explain, because for sure, she is part of it. By the end of the day, I am in shock, and I still can't shake the terrible feelings of loss. ~*VL*

The DIARY of VERONICA LYONS

Slippery Slope

May 30, 2008

Maybe at the bottom of the slippery slope it's life rebirthing in the sludge and not the death we so often assume. Maybe death is a bright thing one ascends to, where one's host ushers us in with companions and white light. Maybe it's an instant release with no residue, or perhaps a faint memory of what was suffered in the name of entertaining a muse.

I digest 'other's triumphs. It's only my personal story that's too hard to accept. I feel like the supporting character, 'everywoman,' who lives and breathes achieving no large thing. Small roles are left off the credits to float like the background static of soundtrack ghosts. How many hundreds of generations, born-once, did we miscast to find ourselves on a planet spinning in crisis? How many more will continue to read their lines as written? How many will throw a curve into the production, and call for a new script?

The burning between my shoulder blades from sitting hunched over a keyboard, reminds me that I am blood and bone, and that all forms of pain act as gatekeepers to block success.

Like attracts like, so how does one dis-spell the bad fairy's curse? Beasts of burden can also carry a jubilant messiah into an Emerald city. Pollyannas can still skin their knees.

The merry month of May's semi-invisibility is over.

This is the world I have made. It has locks, and bolts, and alarms. It has guardians, and moats, and spells against intruders. Ghostly males are as welcome as the ones playing easy to get. ~𝒱𝒦

"Being invisible is cruel;
being insubstantial is hell."
~ Lisabetta

Time Pirates

When I sipped the hemlock of fame it spat me out. I was grit in its wild teeth – a bitter lovechild expecting sugar.

Those claiming to be authorities, label my century a cultural renaissance, which gives it the air of a romantic party; a poetic notion incongruous with the violent shufflings of power that took precedence over human life. I've learned that historians err on the side of naivety and that time is a dishonorable editor. Rebirths of civilizations are more painful than human birth and they take much longer.

I know what it's like to be ignored. History only ever recorded me squeezed between two commas in a population census, and after all my climbing and dedication and discipline, I was still not a vital enough statistic to warrant a footnote in the memoirs of art. The irony is, Leonardo's 'Mona Lisa,' the most famous portrait in the world, lost her identity while Lisa Giocondo, the spoiled 'principessa,' became a household name with the wrong face... my face.

If time or the hand of man has not destroyed her, the original Lisa sleeps in the shadows, perhaps catalogued under an assumed name by a confused translator. She waits in the recesses of a museum warehouse, or palace cubbyhole or a humble attic. She may be breathing underneath the facade of another skin in order to slip past covetous warlords, in which case, her disguise is a death mask. The world knows us too well without camouflage. It knows the slope of our shoulders and the curve of our folded hands, our long parted hair worn loose, the square of our neckline, our direct gaze, and our signature enigmatic smile.

For a time, in the year 1911, I was stored in a shabby box, locked in the dark hole of a closet. It was musty and hot. A stove belched dry heat beside me for two years. If my abductor had not been hungry enough to give me up, it's likely I would have rotted there until his death and been discarded in the smelly trunk with my companion newspapers, rags, and old boots. Rescue is an event which requires the grace of miraculous intervention, but my infamous vacation pushed me center stage; fate is more mysterious than a smile.

In my time, artists were forbidden to sign their works, and there were female artists in almost every studio of Florence. All of us were daughters, wives, nieces or siblings of our male counterparts. I was the half-sister of Andrea Verrocchio's star apprentice, Leonardo da Vinci.

I grew up as an invisible presence within the creative milieu of Florence and Milan, and Venice and Rome, which I suppose was only fitting because my beloved brother called me his little shadow. I was the silent updraft under his rising star so he could process his anguishes.

Leonardo was hardly the incandescent artist the world has decided to immortalize as a genius in amber. He lived and breathed quiet triumphs and weathered humiliating defeats. He lived a double life, riding a pendulum of erratic energy, equal parts outrageous exuberance and irrational despair.

While I had never managed to gain the Paris streets, I acquired an audio-visual understanding of the modern world that drifted through my 'still-life' every day, and I learned the English language, such as it could be gleaned from the limited conversations overheard within the sanctuary of museum hush. I referred to my visitors as the 'parade of forever' and thought of them as my consumers. A true visitor would stay longer than three minutes, but they offered a harvest of entertaining facts and speculation. I grabbed hold of a few likely hosts every day, but they brushed me aside, and most of the remaining clock-time of visiting hours, I retreated into the wall behind me to contemplate my folly. I am fortunate that meditation affords me glimpses of a healthy Leonardo who patiently awaits my return, but even in death he's never idle. I don't know if he can observe civilization's advances; whenever I see him he's wrapped in the serene embrace of our Tuscan hills with our dog, Rinato, too far away to hear me. Sometimes I think he is, as he usually was, too involved in an idea to respond to me... the selective hearing of the possessed genius.

I'm a masterpiece in situ. I would even suggest that I am an investment in the machine of commerce; I've heard I'm a lucrative million dollar industry and that my portrait is priceless. And so, the consciousness of the sixteenth century spins its course while I wander a parallel existence of half-death and wait for synchronicity to save me from the shadow-lands between centuries.

My brother was widely known in the art world. Hardly revered during our many lean years and barely honored by a scatter of loyalties at the end. It was twentieth century spin-doctors who elevated Leonardo to a veritable god. Leonardo's professional reputation lacked responsibility and we navigated our peasant legacy of poverty by floating on debt and never staying too long in one place. We lived sparingly on a bland diet of random success and I'm not being metaphorical when I say, we often starved in a famine of our own making.

Women artists were of little consequence outside the sweatshops of paint and marble, and counted for nothing at all on the general map of social topography. We were child laborers and domestic slaves, and faced intensive periods of serial mother-hood if we survived childbirth the first time. Yet, we were also the alchemists who made beautiful children from our husband's shame and a many of us had the audacity to help turn raw minerals into the golden age of art.

Most studio panels were painted by several hands, each assigned according to the rules of cre-ative worth. Senior artists painted the faces of the main figures: saints and the Christ-child, and the Madonna. Junior capabilities were calculated at a lower rate to placate the customers. We painted scenic backgrounds and the persistent swarms of hovering cherubs as well as draperies, hands, wings, and skies. This was how Leonardo began when he was twelve; he was given wings to paint and he couldn't have been happier.

Leonardo's childhood obsessions with flight caused his painted feathers to preen on the page... to flutter against the sticky surfaces of the wood panels and lift free of the paint. Leonardo studied live and dead flying creatures: birds, butterflies, bees, dragonflies, moths, flies, and bats. Each wing was a marvel. None were too insignificant to analyse.

Generally, customers believed what they were told, but in a demanding season, details were often executed by inferior hands. This was how Leonardo won his break. A sensitive rendering of a fish caused a stir in the hierarchy of Verrocchio's domain, and when asked to add a dog beside a sandaled figure, my brother painted our pet mongrel. He rendered Rinato's coat with the same delicacy as a wisp of escaped hair on the main figure. Both ruffle in the breeze of a summer day. From there he was promoted to higher service and sweetened the contours of the mural's faces even when the senior assistants were idle. Leonardo painted movement and texture and air... and most of all, the divine breath called spirito.

Arresting beauty and talent eclipse visual sightings of everyday sainthood; Leonardo had both. I was allowed to work beside him, grinding his colors and painting translucent clouds. My skills were quietly noted and even Sandro Botticelli asked for my help. As I said, skies were my specialty.

Only creative courage flaunts the rules of artistic order. My brother was one of these. Visual conventions were slight annoyances to be brushed aside, but Leonardo never did anything small; he swept away the canons of art and started fresh. He surprised himself. He allowed every feral idea to evolve into its own story and he lived between the rules.

My brother was a born explorer and if we had lived by the sea, no doubt he would have discovered the new world long before Captain Vespucci. As it was, Leonardo was surrounded by a different sea.

The grasses of Tuscany grew to the edge of our doorstep and the hills gifted him a place to hide and rest, and offered up their abundance of natural species: fauna, flora, and elemental. The countryside was a living entity – his home, his church, and his best friend. It was the safest place Leonardo could talk to me while I awaited physical rebirth.

To summarize: my father, Antonio, was a kiln worker and a part-time soldier, and when he was away fighting in some local skirmish or distant war zone, I sneaked into the city to be Leonardo's assistant. I needed no excuses. I was in love with art and my brother's colleague, Sandro Botticelli.

Sandro was a striking contrast of copper hair and blue eyes. He had the confidence of a nature god and indeed he was one to me. I was ten when he first tousled my hair and told me I had the face of a ripe little Madonna. He teased that he would paint me, and that I may even be the one woman to supplant his obsession for Florence's darling, Lady Simonetta. He left seductive hints for me to follow like breadcrumbs.

Sandro made every woman feel she was the only angel on his horizon. His horizons were always suffused with sexual honey, and I found intoxicating flashes of violet intimacy in his eyes. Leonardo was decidedly anti-Sandro for reasons

I didn't yet understand, but Sandro continued to hold a dear place in my memory, and then later, much more.

First love is second to no other; fantasies form a diamond within every young girl. Feminine potency polishes women into gems of cosmetic allure, but age dulls us into yesterday's jewels. We burn bright... zeniths of wild abandon and fall to earth spent like roman candles. We know our arc is complete when we become invisible to the least significant street courtesies; we see our decline in the reflection of common indifference. Such is the stretch of a woman's brief glory.

I knew Ginevra Benci well enough to be diplomatically civil the few times we met. We were not friends. Peasants and princesses do not mix; we were the oil and water of women, but more alike than either of us cared to admit.

Both of us were ambitious and extreme in our loyalties. I was loyal to Leonardo and Ginevra watched out for herself. Her biggest mistake was to underestimate me; she never understood that I could be a threat and she neglected to consider both high and lowborn women shared the same maternal instinct: that we are protective tigresses, and lionesses, and leopardesses... huntresses of transient beauty – cunning feline predators under our fated veneers of servitude.

Ginevra chose Sandro to paint her portrait, but he turned her down, and therein lies the crux of our collective problems. Leonardo was then chosen to paint her likeness by Master Andrea – a decision planted by Lorenzo. The contract came through Verrocchio's studio and it was my brother's first semi-independent work. The motto 'Virtutem

Forma Decorat' (virtue adorns beauty) was appropriated to purge Ginevra's soiled reputation using blatant techniques of iconic trickery and in case the message proved too subtle, in a fit of creative sarcasm, Leonardo emblazoned it in a formal crest, on the portrait's reverse side.

No painted likeness ever flattered the privileged as much as their own flowery self-descriptions; portraits rarely show a true face, and without truth, beauty and virtue are rather superficial qualities. It's more honest to admit that any virtue worth having was twinned to wealth. Ginevra's family were rich. Verrocchio would have painted her under a thousand lies for the sake of profit. The business of art was his driving force.

Later, the title 'La Gioconda' was a clever name that took innocent root. My brother played with words like a cat plays with a piece of string – agile and quick, twisting suddenly into grace. He loved the double meanings of a phrase or title – the second joke under a first jest... the riddle above the pun... the visual clue inside a puzzle with a gentle sting in its tail, but in the years that followed his death, I became a shadow turned to stone.

I know that I blunt fame's teeth with my persistence; the pursuit of recognition serves no purpose other than vanity, but I want a lot of things: I want to return to the serenity of my skies – their simplicities of lavender, and the blues of robin's eggs, and clouds suffused with light. I want to sit at the right hand of art and taste the fruits of eternity. I want to rest in peace.

Being ignored burns like acid, but the truth can expose the unfairness of history and remedy its indignities. Psychic varnish can leach off my skin. I'm tired. I want to have my real name whispered on Earth in the sanctuary of galleries and be written into the credits of Leonardo's life story.

My attachment to my portrait was not meant to last five-hundred years. I had thought I could join Leonardo any time. I was wrong. It's clear to me now that I created my present situation and that I was as trapped in the Louvre as I had felt in life. I have discovered that death is a continuation of purpose, so the anonymity I suffered in the fifteenth and sixteenth centuries, grew tenfold.

Being invisible is cruel; being insubstantial is hell. ~ *Lisabetta*

The DIARY of VERONICA LYONS

Territorial Claims

June 4, 2008

Lisabetta led me through Mona Lisa's landscape. It was a confusing country of opposites: looking east there are stark mountains like shards of crystal. Cathedral-like with wild stalagmite pillars, where bears are limber enough to inhabit high caves and the desert plain below is populated with lions that roam over their yellow grasses. The rolling hills ramble to an ocean where Lisabetta's heaven waits as a faint light on the horizon. The aurora borealis of judgment. Lisabetta goes there to stare at her destination – her anticipated alternate destiny that beckons with freedom.

The living world is on her right. It flashes quietly – a receding thunderstorm with the muted grumbles of a distant battle. The 'other side' divides the picture plane in two.

Looking west, a chalk cliff gleams under a green blanket peppered with violets – a gentle pasture that slopes to a clear drop-off for the ornithopter launched by a griffin or two. And once I dreamed her a dragon that puffed sfumato breath across the vista and made her sigh.

Looking out, into the territory of the near dead – there is lush greenery and a red-brick manse embraced in the dewy emerald embrace of the Loire Valley. On the night of Leonardo's passing it had been encompassed by a malevolent ball of weather. An electrical storm – a tempest in a large French teacup. I witnessed Leonardo's bedroom window glowing like a square of fire and the Leonardo Tree as it exhaled bursts of sparks; it too was ready for death. The gargoyles stretched their wings on the pinnacles of each gable and frightened the ever-present birds ready to guide their champion home.

Trickeries of light polish the sky with undulating stripes of colors like the searchlights of an aerial circus. The small bridge to her left is the demarcation line that straddles failure and success. A trickle of the River Styx slips under it teeming with effervescent fish. We spend hours on its banks rearranging her clouds and pruning them into a menagerie of topiary clouds.

One can study the surface of the 'Mona Lisa' and imagine the rest. What you can't see are the marvels she and Leonardo have conjured. To me it's heaven, but Lisabetta insists no, it is the art behind art. I described it to her as a whimsical hologram. She didn't argue.

At dusk, the sky ballet begins with the finest display of fireworks imaginable: crimson showers of falling stars and firebrands flashing from gold to violet, and horned comets with forever tails that lash the air with flames. The smell of the wild moon, big as the planet Jupiter, floats on an ozone of smoky wind. And in the daylight we visit her formal sculpture gardens of angels and winged beasts where Pegasus and the Lion of Venice preen their stone feathers.

Lisabetta says she has created her personal heaven, far more grand than this. ~ *VL*

PART FOUR
Second Childhood

"And so we beat on,
boats against the current,
borne back ceaselessly into the past."
~ F. Scott Fitzgerald

"I would sooner fail
than not be among the greatest."
~ John Keats

From First to Last

Campo Zeppi, Tuscany
April 29, 1452

A young peasant woman heaves her tired body to the next task. She sets a basket with her newborn, two weeks old, under a shade tree and turns from her son towards the whinny of a grey pony. "Come Lezza. I have something for you," she says, and pulls a rosy apple from the pocket of her apron.

She doesn't see a small kite land on the blanket of her sleeping boy and tap its tail on the baby's lips. Tap tap tap. *Are you awake?* the bird says, three times.

A chubby hand reaches for it and clutches empty air and the ghost of a dreamed feather. Rather than cry, the infant blinks curiously at the space, that seconds before had been a pair of wings and an impertinent tail.

The sky which recalled the bird is a fractured triangle of dazzling blue, floating between two overhead branches. The branches interlocking fingers form a pattern of shimmering green spangles. Soon the tossing waves of a leafy sea hypnotize the child. He smiles, closes his eyes, and continues to dream that he is Leonardo da Vinci.

The MANOR HOUSE of CLOUX,
Amboise, France – May 2, 1519

Leonardo da Vinci sits at his open window, his mind a flutter of birds as he awaits death. When he hears the call of thunder behind him, he hesitates. No matter. He calls softly over his shoulder into the deepening shadows.

"Lisa, is that you?"

NIGHT SCRIBBLE READS:

kite — tail – lips — birds

*"My arrival in the world
nearly killed my mother,
but she was part of the magic
that created my brother...
and the day of my birth
was the day that Leonardo
discovered his wings."*
~ Lisabetta

Running to Ground

Campo Zeppi – April 15, 1458 (Leonardo's Sixth Birthday)

There are birds inside the house. Only this can explain the chaotic screeching. Leonardo stares into the rafters and sees the undisturbed bundles of herbs drying there. The window is open – a square of morning sky. The birds must have escaped to the eaves outside. The noise is still close.

Aunt Fiore is busy attending to the bird screams that emanate from the bed. The birth is not going well. The face of Caterina hovers above the bedclothes. Her shift is pulled high, covered in sweat and clings to her body. She can't see her son.

Leonardo is no longer there, he's running.

The tall grasses crush underfoot and bend away from him. Rogue stalks scratch at his face and try to grab his hair. They close around him and pull him down. He curls into a ball and rolls around until he's made a clearing. He looks like an egg in a nest – a huddle of a child wound tight, humming like a beehive in a copse of lemon trees. His song increases. He is a drum. The terrible screams of his mother turn into the sound of friendly kites calling mid-swoop overhead. They let him take their song.

Leonardo rocks as they serenade the day into health. Until he feels safe. Bird-cries tell him to look up. They say "join us."

Leonardo opens like a flower and unfurls like petals in the wind. He lies in a curve on his right side in order to see a flurry of wings between himself and the sun. Their busy movements force his eyes closed. Wings make the sun flicker dangerously and he vomits his fear into the grass.

The birds laugh. Their grey fluttering departs with a noise like dry leaves as the sun falls on him like a blanket. He stretches his six-year-old body as far as he can to relieve the tremors in his legs and arms, and forms a triangle with his hands to view the black dots that circle the sun and spin clockwise. He can't turn away. He is drawn inside the centrifugal force, pinned like an insect to the earth. His arms flail sideways in the pose of crucifixion.

Leonardo holds his breath and closes his eyes. The birds sound far away. He lifts to join them, soaring higher into the tree canopy. A branch stops him and he looks down on his body. He sees a smiling boy embracing the wind, inviting down the sky. He loves the weight-lessness as he ascends, pulled upwards on invisible strings at his wrists and elbows and head. He streams higher, and the purified wind massages his sore temples, and the clouds turn into giant swans.

When Leonardo wakes, the sky is green. The birds have swarmed back to the house. He rises and the breeze cools his damp spine. It feels awkward to walk. He's clumsy and heavy... thrashing through the fields like a wild beast. The sky turns red with purple clouds. Gold threads sew them together. It looks like a pillow he has seen made of rich stuff in his father's house. He wants to pull it down or swim to it and lay his head upon it. His wings are tired, he feels them folded over his shoulders like a heavy white cape. He is grateful for the warmth they provide and imagines what it would be like to fold his head under one of them, the way he has seen the cranes do on the marshlands of Anchiano.

A yellow square of light lures in the darkness. Leonardo trudges towards it like the memory of a moth seeks the dream of a flame. He feels sleepy. The light is friendly. It means something. He is a sliver of light, and more than anything, he wants to disappear into the night like a waning moon.

The storm of birth is over. It has blown his cousins and sisters into a heap with their snoring grandmother. There are other piles of bedding with no children, or uncles, or stepfathers, under them. They glisten with sweat and specks of blood.

A helpless movement stirs the bedclothes. Leonardo sees his mother's mouth move... a tired face too spent to disapprove. She raises herself as if to beckon him, but she gives a shriek and the child flows into the room on a river of transparent blood. Fiore blocks his view too late. Antonia stirs and calls out to her daughter-in-law. "Is it a boy?" Fiore's answer is slow... "a girl."

Leonardo is frozen with conflicting emotions. He is horrified and curious. These two feelings will be forever fixed as motivations to discover, uncover, and understand women. There are more bird chirps, but this time they sound like a bleating lamb. It's an animal song, safe to explore. Leonardo is drawn to the voice of a newborn's language.

His aunt is brusque. "Take her. I need room. Go outside. Hurry," she says, shooing him away.

A bundle is pushed into Leonardo's arms. A small pink creature that mews like a cat, or is it a baby bird with wet feathers? It squirms inside its covering. The midnight sky mutes the sounds emanating from the window. He hears the wail of his mother and then silence.

Caterina is riding Lezza and the day is suffused with joy. She tells the pony she is beautiful. "Bella-Lezza," she says. The name is uttered within a lucid smile. "Lezza" she says to the animal, "my beautiful girl. Bella Lezza." She lets the pony take her away from the shabby room and the faces that stare down at her in fear.

Fiore hears Caterina call out: *"Lisa my beautiful girl."*

Leonardo looks down into the miracle of his new sister. "Your name is Lisa... Lisa-bella," he whispers. A pink rosebud searches for milk. Leonardo puts an index finger into the rose and feels the hard tug. His soul enters the rosebud through his finger and into the creature.

He is drenched with warm honey. The lamb surrenders. "Is it you?" Leonardo asks her.

The stars bend down to Campo Zeppi for a closer look. Leonardo pulls aside the cloth that has blown over his sister's face, and is captured by a pair of wise-dark eyes, bright as a bird's. "It is me," they say.

What can a newborn possibly retain from the hour of her birth? That the stars are in or out of alignment? That they trine favorably or fight in opposition? The zodiac does not care to answer.

The swaddled infant short-circuits Leonardo's six-year-old brain. His eyes move from the horse to the cow and up to a star he has chosen as theirs.' This thought fuses Leonardo and his 'Lisabella' into a mother and child icon. This birth is a miracle. Caterina rests in a compassionate swoon and sleeps. God has finally smiled on Campo Zeppi: Twins, born six years apart.

When Lisabetta is five, she thinks she can remember something of her birth – a face she will always know as mother. Leonardo can recall more. He sees the Christ-child in his arms, surrounded by a night sky, animals, a bed of straw, a manger filled with sweet hay... and stars. Perhaps one is brighter than the others. He had wanted to fly into the brightest of them, but they danced for his sister, he is sure of that, and her sacrifice is a long way off – too far away to disturb the night.

"Il sole non si muove"
"The sun does not move"
~ Leonardo Da Vinci – 1510

Mother & Child

April 16, Vinci – 1459

The marble font is to be the same one used for Leonardo's christening. Caterina is half-awake and makes her wishes clear: the child is to be taken to Vinci and not the parish church of Anchiano.

"You will take the child," Antonia commands her son. "…and Leonardo will hold her."

Fiore is adamant. "Lisabetta will die by nightfall," she says. "and… maybe Caterina as well."

Antonio is reluctant. "Why should I? We can bury the thing right here… or *them*" he adds, addressing his last comment to his sister-in-law.

Antonia crosses herself. If she can help it, Caterina di Marco di Buti's last conscious act will not add further cause to her son's suffering. "A dying mother's wish may turn into a curse," she replies. "I order you to go and go quickly."

There is a rush to get Leonardo and the baby into the cart. Her name is to be Lisabetta; Fiore had misheard Caterina. "Don't forget," Fiore reminds Leonardo. "It's what your mother wants," but Leonardo still calls her Lisa-Bella. "Antonio, be careful," she says.

Antonio shrugs off Fiore's order. "I should overturn the cart and be rid of two mouths to feed who do nothing but exhaust my patience."

Fiore looks appalled, and Antonio is delighted to see that his lack of compassion still has the power to shock her. "Perhaps I should load you and your daughters, and my other two as well" he says. "Have done with you all… my brother would be pleased, yes?… to be free of another wife who makes no sons. Both of you drain my wages with your brats."

Fiore watches the horse and cart pass through the gate and stares after the broad back of her brother-in-law and the small shape of her nephew. She takes a deep breath and turns towards the sound of children crying. Her next task is bringing Caterina back from another swoon into the world of sleep.

The bleeding is stopped and with infusions of herbals Caterina may live. The baby is a different matter. The child must be baptized today before she goes to God.

Inside the house, four toddlers watch the rise and fall of bedclothes to see if death has claimed their mother and aunt. They are too young to be horrified; too old to be indifferent. Fiore pushes them towards their grandmother. Fiore fans Caterina with the edge of her apron and waves the rind of a fresh cut lemon under her nose. Caterina turns away from the scent and dreams of lemon trees. She lies luxuriously beneath them, unfurling her toes, stretched on a blanket soaked with blood, and gazes up at the bright yellow fruit hanging above her. She smells the white blossoms that open and close like the mouths of birds. The baby is hungry. She must wake and feed it. She hears her name called and feels the sharp slap that accompanies it. Fiore's face smiles. Caterina can relax again. Her competent sister-in-law has fed the baby enough worms and she can sleep. Her name floats again.

"Caterina?"

"Yes, I am here"

"You must stay awake. I have something here for you. You must drink. Lisabetta is safe. Antonio has taken her to Vinci with Leonardo."

Caterina hears on a wave of lucidity. "Who is Lisabetta?" she asks.

Antonio drops off the two children near the church. "You have the day" he says to Leonardo. "Be here later or I will leave without you." The interior of the chapel chills Leonardo. The contrast after cooking his skull under the sun for three hours is a relief. The walls of stone sends waves of cold like a winter wind. It's not good for a newborn, near death.

If anyone can save Lisabetta Leonardo can. He only needs to get to the bargaining table below the crucifix and beg. He has seen it done often.

Leonardo's body heat comprises the entire boundaries of Lisabetta's world. She is warm but she feels trapped. She tries to make her mother understand: "Let me out." While everyone is sure Lisabetta is struggling to survive, she struggles to be free. Swaddling clothes are the first of many things that will try to control her. She protests with a scream: "I want to move" she howls, and Leonardo hushes her.

A pair of godparents are hastily borrowed from the street. The promise of wine and honey-cakes brings them inside, but they will only receive a short prayer for their time. There are no honey-cakes. Priests negotiate with honey cakes of power and the citizens of earth are charged to follow the cloying scent of nectar, spewed in a fury of servitude, the gift of God's bees, to its inevitable conclusion. Complicity is an easy bargain to make with fear. Soon enough, a message for their soul's salvation will make its way to heaven on candle-smoke and they can wonder at their good fortune, passing the parish church of Santa Croce at such an hour when they may serve God and his priest as well as themselves.

Leonardo wants the rites of baptism to be over so he can give his sister the comfort of dying under the sun. They are of one mind. Leonardo understands Lisabetta wants to lie on the grass and kick her legs. Wave her arms. Signal to the world she is animate. She is less than twenty-four-hours-old. She must feel the delights of fresh summer on her skin. She is a fragile baby bird, her wings still wet, but the hot Tuscan wind is ready to dry her feathers. Lisabetta tells him she is strong enough to survive outside her linen prison. She begs for the vastness of space outside the tomb of cloth that threatens to choke her.

Friar Piero di Bartolomeo echoes Leonardo's desire for a hasty performance. He intones and gestures appropriately in his theatre of lies, and it is done. Another soul saved with a dispatched formula of grace. He is eager to climb his stairs, to where a woman waits. She waits on his authority to intervene on an obscure matter of feminine conscience and is willing to loan him her body in exchange for his best advice.

Such paltry urgencies as a newborn's passage into Christianity with eternity waiting to steal her, is not as important as the carnal promise that shivers upstairs. In any case, the infant is a girl... a peasant girl, and here is the illegitimate brother – the only family interested enough to deliver her from purgatory. At this moment, brother Bartolomeo feels himself a powerful figure. This moment that looms over two children: one dying; one, a bastard; and a desperate woman waiting in deference to his smoldering power.

When the baptismal waters pour over Lisabetta's head, Leonardo hears the mention of the trinity and is rewarded with an image of Piero da Vinci, himself, and a Holy Ghost, walking in the clouds of heaven surrounded by angels. He hears the priest offer up the name Lisabetta, and Leonardo's reverie shatters quickly. The water is a shock. Lisabetta screams and now she needs her arms to release the full sound she wants to make. The effect is instant. Leonardo stops her mouth with his finger and Lisabetta pleads with him to liberate her from the blanket and dry her head.

Leonardo's first impulse is to remove screaming from the world, but he needs to be angry with someone for making his sister cry. It must be his mother's God who has the power to order his priests to upset babies. The building is oppressive. Outside there is room to think. He will return later to light a candle, but for now he wants space between himself and God's apprentice as much as Lisabetta desires the space to move. God's rules may be overruled for an escape, but Leonardo dares not change her name.

Leonardo wants his sister to live and if he's not swift about it, she will die in a fit of colicky despair. Aunt Fiore knows of these things and she says Baby Lisa will die before dark. Leonardo's maternal task had been clearly stated – it is to deliver his sister's sin to this font belonging to God, and bring back a purified baby whose body his stepfather can give to the earth of Campo Zeppi.

Leonardo ignores the jurisdiction of three fuming men. He counts his mother's God as a third angry father, another man who rules her with a hard fist. The creator of his own territory is a benevolent white-winged thought. If Leonardo runs into the hills without delay, he can lay Lisabetta in a manger of grass that stretches to the horizon and bargain for a sky miracle. Leonardo's own god can kiss her wings into life with divine light, but Lisabetta can't fly to heaven unless Leonardo performs this task for her.

Leonardo is in his church. He feels the green breath of the trees on his face. He listens to their sap, bubbling yellow under the bark and through the roots. He feels golden blood surge into his back as he leans against an oak pillar that supports the dome of his sky. Leonardo is the trees' priest who writes their contracts with humans for wood and paper, and amber and shade. He squints into the blue and watches his angels. They swarm as a colorful breeze and land like painted leaves. A butterfly's wing held up to the light is a miniature stained-glass window.

Leonardo and Lisabetta melt into the landscape outside the fortress walls and he unwinds her swaddling next to a small stream. The sun's zenith is blanket enough. He fetches a handful of water, wets Lisabetta's head, and invokes three potent symbols: the sun, the moon, and the stars. In a strong voice, Leonardo offers Lisabetta's name to the sky. This time she laughs at the gentle trickle of holy water that has warmed in her brother's hands.

Leonardo makes Lisabetta a bed of wild marigold. He sits hugging the curve of a budding fig tree and watches his sister commune with the sky. She has a lot to say. He looks up at the scorching disk and the yellow color hurts his eyes. He shields Lisabetta's twice-blessed head so that the shadows of the fig branches dance over her face. He can see she is beautifully formed. Her tiny hand wraps around one of his fingers like the tendrils of a plant. Her ear is a pink shell. He feels entrusted with her future. His path is clear: he must take her away and provide for her. His promise is a soft echo inside her head as she, in turn, vows to nurture and protect him.

The big why of everything is a large task for a six-year-old. Always,

Leonardo demands: show me, prove it... tell me. Now there's a 'where?' and an urgent responsibility to find a place of safety from the chaos of the world. He is no longer alone.

Leonardo recites the story of the labyrinth and the Minotaur to Lisabetta. In his perverse way, Leonardo changes the fable to suit his purpose. He tells his sister of two children who follow the thread into the maze rather than out. The monster is only a bull, after all, and he talks to horses and cows, and will know what to say. It will listen and somewhere, lost inside its lair of twisting tunnels, Antonio Buti, or Piero da Vinci, or his mother's God, will never find them.

Lisabetta gurgles and waves at bird shadows. Leonardo tells her "I am your brother" She blesses them: The Mother, the brother, and the Holy Ghosts.

"Take me home. I'm hungry," Lisabetta says.

"I've been waiting for you," Leonardo tells her. "I thought you would never come."

The Retrograde Moon

April 16, Vinci– 1459

The weathered stone font in the church of Santa Croce in Vinci, is the site of Leonardo's first holy bath. It makes a fine story. Caterina retells it on one of the days she is well. Leonardo is happy to see his mother smile, but reluctant to let her hold her daughter. Most of the time Caterina cries and stares at the wall.

Leonardo cuddles Lisabetta and listens to Caterina. This story links them together and it is important to ask questions. "At your christening," Caterina says to Leonardo, "there were nine godparents."

"Where are they now? Why do they not visit?" Leonardo asks. "Why does my father not want to see me?" Leonardo notes that all nine godparents have disappeared into their own histories and left his blank. His past is a cloudless sky. These missing well-wishers and relatives had been the birds meant to fill it. Leonardo decides that he will go to each one and ask if he may share them with his sister.

Caterina reminds Leonardo that he has met one or two of his godparents on the saint's days in Vinci. Leonardo vaguely remembers being presented and expected to speak rather than stare. He had tried to remember why these well-dressed strangers were of interest to his mother. Their manners towards him told him he was strange. Flawed and of no consequence.

There were rare times when Leonardo glimpsed his father in Vinci. Leonardo fixed on him like a cat after a mouse, but his father refused to look back. Piero da Vinci always makes sure he sees someone or something, behind his son. Once Piero noticed a pair of wide eyes staring at him from between two women and had been puzzled. When he recognized Caterina, he turned away.

It has been six months since Lisabetta's birth and Caterina still slips in and out of a private dream where she cries and curls into a ball. Antonio and his mother are furious, but Leonardo has occasion to thank his mother for her illness. When everyone in the family is busy, he is given Lisabetta.

Leonardo washes Lisabetta and fastens fabric around his waist in a knotted sling so she can travel wherever he goes. He takes her into his church of hills, and valleys, and trees, and together they count the bird-gods in the sky.

Caterina has days when she refuses to talk or eat. She acts as if Lisabetta is invisible. Nothing can persuade her to focus her eyes. Antonio says she's mad... her boy has always been loco. He rides to Vinci to petition Leonardo's grandfather. It's time for Leonardo to go; he is acting even more strangely. Leonardo is the cause of Caterina's disruption; he guards Lisabetta like a dog... sings and talks to her. Perhaps school?

Leonardo devises a canopy of branches and nails it above Lisabetta's cradle. He hangs shapes cut from leather: a star, a triangle, and a bird. He strings a feather and a blown egg, and hangs them as well. Lisabetta spends hours watching it while Leonardo watches her. When Antonio sees it, he tears it down and feeds it to the brazier. The egg rolls away and Antonio crushes it like a fragile skull. Leonardo grabs at the ornaments as they're tossed into the flames.

Leonardo's da Vinci grandfather agrees it's time Leonardo attends school. The da Vinci patriarch has the right to take him. Lisabetta is pried from her brother's arms and he's forced to mount his grandfather's great horse, bundled like kindling. He is returned to the da Vinci fold, carried as dead weight and deposited in a room of his own. Leonardo's mind twists into a resistant knot of cool defiance. A six-year-old boy, almost-seven, has no power. He rolls himself into the bedclothes like a swaddled baby. He thinks to himself, this is how life will stay if he remains passive. This is how Lisabetta felt. He wonders why he can see her face at odd hours of the day and night. The only roles he can play from this house are dutiful grandson and alienated brother.

But the first night away from Lisabetta, before he forgets, Leonardo draws what he remembers of her: a lock of her hair curled into a circle, a rosebud mouth, and the outline of a bird, an egg and a feather inside a triangle.

It is morning when Leonardo unclenches his fist. In his hand, is a crushed leather star.

During the first estranged months, on trips to Florence, Leonardo is fascinated by street faces – drawn to the deformed beggars of the city. When he sees them, he takes as close a look as he's allowed. In his mind, Leonardo records their twisted faces, warts, and rubbery lips. He is pulled away, but is determined to ask questions. Always Leonardo has questions. Later, when Leonardo is troubled, these are the deformed faces which appear in the blank spaces between designs for war machines. Demonic faces come to haunt his most violent creations. They spring from Leonardo's pen so often, he is unaware of their subliminal presence.

Leonardo decides he will surrender to the abacus school and do well. He will learn how he can gain back his sister. He will defy the rules. The da Vinci patriarch orders Leonardo to never return to Campo Zeppi, but grandfathers of his advanced age are a small matter. Death will take him and not soon enough.

In his dreams, Leonardo tells Lisabetta to wait. "I will be right back. Don't cry," he says. Lisabetta is a quiet baby. She is used to waiting.

> *"He who is fixed to a star*
> *does not change his mind."*
> ~ Leonardo da Vinci

Saturday's Child

~ Lisabetta ~

I was a determined child. I took my labors seriously. Each task was another step towards something I knew vaguely as the concept, destination. I followed my father's orders with numb obedience. These were the ways of the conscientious child-farmhand; work never ended, but the word destiny lingered inside this grand destination of mine and confirmed fate was tied to the stars.

I was fascinated by stars. They drew me upward from my bed. It was the stars that taught me how to count. Caterina had to drag me inside on clear nights, when I insisted I said goodnight to each one.

I spoke to the invisible stars that watched me during the day. They demanded dedication, and I decided to be worthy of their grace. Performance and attitude were relevant to stars; what mattered to me was leaving.

Born into servitude meant I was all the more precious to the stars, but complaining was dangerous. Work was a valuable thing. I learned how to comb the horses, and feed the chickens, and wash the clothes. I made the cheese curdle, and discovered the best way to bake bread and preserve olives. I proved myself invaluable, followed Leonardo's lessons in secret, recovered from the verbal cuffings and physical blows, and stood stronger for them. I was sure nothing of value could be accomplished without effort. My freedom was coming. I loved the feeling of earning every moment of it.

Leonardo did not spend much time with Albiera, the stepmother who loved him; Piero sent him to his grandmother, Lucia, in Pistoia. That was when a woman, other than me, encouraged him to paint. ~ *Lisabetta*

"Merely throwing a sponge
soaked in colors at a wall
will leave a stain
in which a beautiful landscape
can be seen."
~ Leonardo Da Vinci

New Beginnings

Amboise, France – 1519

Leonardo shared his life force with me the day I was born, refusing to let me die, and later, during his last days, when he lay close to death, I held his hand so he could feel the weight of my bones. Such was our close connection, that even as an apparition, I had density. I closed my fingers tightly over his, so that Leonardo knew beyond his failing senses, that he was not alone.

My brother's perceptions were like crystal. He always spoke as inspiration came – often too clear for others to hear. Leonardo taught me where illusion began and in 1519 it was my duty to show him where it ended.

In Leonardo's presence, I was more than a seventeen-year-old poplar-wood panel. I was greater than an animated thirty-by-twenty-one inch portrait coated with new varnish. I emerged from the flat window Leonardo created of me, and left his masterpiece where my young colors glowed under a glaze of light. I no longer cast a brittle sheen in the moonlight, but to Leonardo, I remained, the fleshed-out Lisabetta of his middle years. I took this form to ease his grief and to especially comfort his last years. I would have done anything to make him feel safe.

A portrait's voice is captured in the eyes. Only eyes may speak silently, most elegantly, in magnetic communion. My brother and I conversed this way for eleven years. After the fire, he called me through the art that was the best of us. Leonardo heard my eyes as a voice inside his head, inside a waking dream, inside a memory. I listened back in the ways open to me. He always knew I would tell him the truth. - *Lisabetta*

Lisabetta's earliest memory of Leonardo is not visual. It's a voice surrounded by stars. His beauty materializes later and dazzles. He keeps his bouts of hopelessness preserved, away from public nosiness. After Grandmother Lucia's, brief reign, Lisabetta is the only one close enough to help Leonardo through the debilitating episodes that dull his brightness. Without Leonardo's remarkable capacity to recover, Lisabetta's own career under the auspices of the painter's guild, would have decided her creative stillbirth.

Leonardo and Lisabetta share more than a country upbringing under a tyrannical father. Lisabetta first believes that Leonardo's skill as a teacher engages her own artistic capabilities, but it's not entirely so. There is a natural talent within both of them, separate yet the same, to observe and translate the treasures of the visible world into flat windows of illusion. Their minds are connected to each other as much as their hand-to-eye coordination. What they observe flows into the art they make. They isolate different aspects of design, but the procedure is identical, and it's because of this, Leonardo remains convinced only artists may truly understand each other.

That Leonardo and Lisabetta are kindred is documented. Caterina expels them from her womb and into the world six years apart. It's the weightier bond of paternity that separates them, but empathy and a strong priority for each other's survival, guarantees them mutual protection, and doubly-victorious fame.

Leonardo daydreams in loops of relentless pictures, endowed with the ability to hold them in his hand later and circle them under better light. Events so crystallized, wait for the right time to emerge fully-formed. Regardless of encapsulating joy or pain, Leonardo's thoughts remain alive to be recalled with startling lucidity. Images take root in his memory, imbedded with sounds and textures and the accompanying scents of life. It takes only a small trigger to release them unbidden into the present.

Lisabetta's formative years condition her to the hard labor of a subsistence farm. Living in Campo Zeppi comes with the certainty of hardship, but it bequeaths her the edge she needs later, to fend for herself and Leonardo, in a world that has no time for women or those afflicted with eccentricities not easily bent to conformity.

Between them, Leonardo and Lisabetta have enough skills to meet the harshness of the world without crumbling. Without each other, creative survival is impossible. Lisabetta knows Leonardo never truly sees a thing completely until he has drawn it from several angles, written down its messages and questions, and shown her. She is the complementary yin of Leonardo's experience.

Run-ins with Antonio's bad humor prompt Lisabetta to keep her head during the heat of confrontation. She becomes a proficient formulator of strategies: how best to process defeat into a subsequent victory, how to feign compliance, how to use humiliation to her advantage, and the subtle art of exacting comeuppance over revenge. Later, it is Piero da Vinci and Verrocchio who vicariously coach her on the intricacies of covert diplomacy and protocol.

Antonio teaches Lisabetta that lashing out at real or imagined enemies is futile and that the art of manipulation is the consistent victor, and most of all Lisabetta learns that her invisibility is an asset.

It is Lisabetta's persistence that compels her to air her opinions the way Leonardo has always recorded his on paper. Leonardo's studies, being more of an academic nature than hers, come infused with the glorious stamp of breakthrough engineering, and medicine, and scientific discovery. Lisabetta's musings out loud, are impressions of feminine economy – the specific reflections of a defiant woman at odds with her time.

Lisabetta hasn't the patience to disguise her observations with codes. What she writes is not so much secret as private, although in her century, a closely-guarded diary is regarded as suspect.

Long before Leonardo is hailed as a genius, he is considered delusional, according to the conventions of society. Poetry is the accepted repository for emotional pain, but challenging the church with science amounts to a personal revolution. Leonardo's compulsion to record his thoughts in clandestine journals begins early. From the age of seven he trusts no-one. He takes confidentiality to extremes, covering his innocent tracks as often as guilty ones.

Lisabetta notices what unexpected life lesson gems may sprout from trouble as much as the trials which emerge from success .

Leonardo composes music and lyrics embedded with word pictures. He paints images which border on heresy. He provokes authority. He loves to twist the meanings of words into eternal loops of disapproving commentary. His mind can never let go, but it's paper that captures Leonardo's dreams and Leonardo's papers that will eventually destroy Lisabetta.

Campo Zeppi – 1463
Leonardo, age eleven; Lisabetta, age five

The sky is promising. Lisabetta doesn't want to lose the rest of the day. The immediate crisis is over as far as she's concerned, but Leonardo hides inside the animal shelter. She can hear his tortured humming... his way of moving past brutality and chaos.

"Leonardo, come out. You can't stay in there," Lisabetta calls into his cave.

She hears Leonardo's muffled response. "Yes, I know. I'm coming out crazy girl. Wait there and be quiet. He will hear you and come back."

"Antonio's gone," she replies.

"He can return. I'm not supposed to be here."

For a five-year-old, Lisabetta considers the absolutes of life. "If he does I will kill him. How would that be?" Her father has beaten Leonardo and deserves to die for it. "Rinato says he will bite him and rip out his ugly throat." She hears Leonardo laugh and sniffle at the same time. "I have a triangle for you," she says. This last, is a peace offering that usually tweaks her brother's curiosity. Triangles calm Leonardo down.

"Where?" he replies.

Leonardo emerges – the sun covered in straw. "Where?"

Sometimes Lisabetta is surprised by the energy Leonardo brings into the world. She is reminded that she has struggled to survive in order for this moment to exist.

"Here." She forms her hands into a triangle-shaped window and peers through them at Leonardo's face. Her fingers frame a swollen eye that looks back, bruised into green, and brown, and yellow. "Dio! Your eye, let me see. I will call someone." But she stops. She knows Leonardo wants to remain invisible, even as his poor eye declares its dominance in the world. "I should write down the colors I see in your face" she says.

"Describe them to me."

"Leonardo, let me see."

"I have something for you," he says. "Give me your hands."

The power of curiosity distracts Lisabetta when Leonardo reforms her hands into a cup, stirs the palms with his finger and taps the center. "Right here," he says.

Lisabetta looks there, but no magic appears. "Where?"

Leonardo squeezes his fingers together to indicate something infinitely small. "I know where there are trees that can fit into your hands. Miniature hills and valleys as well."

Lisabetta is captivated. "Show me... *dimmi*... where? Can we go now?" Her impatience means she has accepted Leonardo's rainbow eye and the manner of its creation. The world spins too fast to miss one of Leonardo's treasures.

Leonardo always sees outside the ordinary world. He coaxes Lisabetta with his visions, and whenever he is away in Florence, she concentrates on the assignments he gives her. Sometimes she has to wait several weeks between visits, but Leonardo shares every glorious detail of his progress in Verrocchio's bottega with her, until Lisabetta craves the creative heat of the workshop as much as freedom.

Leonardo also shares his darker moods with Lisabetta. The frozen melancholia that pulls him out of time, when the world is too chaotic to bear. These are times Leonardo considers himself uneducated, when he dwells on the insurmountable challenges of inborn shame, and he despairs of Piero's acceptance. Lisabetta is the only one who sympathizes with a form of compassion that makes a difference. Leonardo has an inbred demon that clamors for attention, but he can call out golden visions to render it senseless when he chooses to.

There are times Leonardo gives permission for the ice to take hold of his mind and travel down to his feet. He had been freezing in this despondent state for an hour, seeking the warmth of the Buti's horses. Suffering can be an art. He's familiar with its self-serving shapes and colors and the length of its teeth, but even during the stressful times, Leonardo has a subconscious understanding, that Lisabetta fights his enemies with a power he calls forth from her, to the same degree her courage inspires his audacity to provoke them.

This is the day Leonardo leads her to the tiny trees that live in moss and bark, and the surface of stones stained with rain. They drop into them with Rinato, and run wild through the brilliant greens, and the blue-grey skies, and the muddy swamps. Lisabetta watches her brother capture them in his notebooks. He shows her his simple translations. She understands the language of the charcoal smudges and hatchings. She feels each movement of his concentration. For those peak moments, Lisabetta exists behind Leonardo's eyes and shares his dreams. Their visions are intoxicating.

Art is a better world to live in. An escape from not belonging – a space to live apart from the insignificant and commonplace. Art is proof of Leonardo's worthiness and defines his purpose. Art promises to downgrade one's father and family as inconsequential.

Lisabetta strives for Leonardo's approval much the same way Leonardo holds out for acknowledgement from the da Vinci clan; the Buti name carries an even greater burden of inadequacies to overcome.

With the art lessons comes philosophies still forming inside Leonardo's mind.

"Leonardo you are two people" Lisabetta says, after a day spent sketching plants. "You have artist days and the days when Antonio makes you small."

"Some people make you forget who you are."

"Fathers?"

"Some people make you feel small," he says, studying the sky.

"Then I hope you will be an artist all the time."

"Hope is unworthy of true artists," Leonardo tells her. He taps Lisabetta's temple. "Artists live up here behind the eyes." He gestures to the open fields. "Hope lives out there. It's like the wind. You cannot hold it, and it will not sustain you."

"Artists can hold the wind?"

"Artists can paint the movement of the wind, the world, and everything in it. We can capture what people think in their expressions. Art makes you think 'yes' all the time."

"To be an artist I must think 'yes' all the time?"

"As you observe. I have small days, when I think, no."

"I love you the same," Lisabetta says.

"You are an artist. Separate. You live in a different world than everyone else."

"As long as it is away from here," Lisabetta says.

Leonardo understands, Lisabetta must leave Campo Zeppi, just as Lisabetta knows Leonardo wants to take her away, and that for them, living small is out of the question. She knows Leonardo will always have his small days, but she is possessed of a practical nature. Cows do not milk themselves. Olives do not fall into baskets and turn into oil. Hard work on the farm is as necessary as imagining angels in the workshop of Verrocchio, and two small artists do not make a greater one.

This twin goal binds them together, and by the time Lisabetta reaches ten, a way opens that allows her a delicious glimpse of a future more tangible than hope.

Sometimes my portrait feels like a five-hundred-year-old mirror. My green dress has soured into brown homespun. My smile is deeper under layers of yellow grime. I see my skin fractured with age lines. My sky has a tear near the topmost edge of its gilt frame. I can see the faces who peer at me in wonder. I know what they see.

I still beam the love of my brother and Sandro Botticelli out into the world. It's captured whole and left burning like the candles lit around a bier. Those who understand the human heart can read me... as I said, the eyes speak more than all the scribbled manuscripts, frantic diaries and blots of historic propaganda. Five-hundred years is but a wing's beat of time to spend loving another with one's entire being. ~ *Lisabetta*

The DIARY of VERONICA LYONS

The Name Game

transcribed — age twelve

Halifax,
June 9, 1991

I met Baz again in a dream. He teased me for my latest name change. I've asked everyone to call me Nicky. Only Uncle Oz humored me. He showed me a photo of an ancient statue with no head and called me Nikey, instead. He says the name means victory and that I am victorious. Then he suggested the name Vicky. Its funny how words flow into the same things. Nicky to Nikey and Victory to Vicky. Nicky with a V sounds better. Then Uncle Oz made it Victoria, and hearing it gave me a funny feeling.

Basil called me Budinsky in the dream and I adopted it for a few days until everyone got impatient with me. Uncle Oz had often said that I was his 'little bud' and that name had grown into Daisy.

Last night Baz and I ran through a field of them and he made me a daisy-chain necklace. He has a puppy in his heaven – a mongrel terrier he calls Wren. He's a boy dog made of white smoke. His bark sounds miles away, muffled by a distant fog, even when he's right beside us. I saw the puppy float into the crown of a tree and disappear like the Cheshire Cat. – *Daisy, Bud, Nicky, me me me*

P.S. – It's not pronounced Nicky. Uncle Oz showed me: 'Nykee' – it's like the shoe, 'Nike' which is way cool.

PART FIVE
Second Generation

*"The dreams of art that survive the night
are more powerful than we can imagine."*
~ Lisabetta

"I now begin my book,
'De ludo geometric
(On Geometric Games)
in which I show further ways
to infinity."
~ Leonardo da Vinci, 1514

Lisabetta

*O*ne must take it on trust that a child may know more than her years should allow. By the time Lisabetta reaches the age of ten, she has become well-educated in spite of herself. She misses little, and on her visits to the city of Florence, she absorbs the conversational tones and mannerisms of her social betters like others breathe in air. She watches Verrocchio's painters, and studies the art while the apprentices sleep. She sketches in borrowed hours, during the days spent in the successful studio.

"You may stay here permanently and work here in two years if Verrocchio agrees," Leonardo tells her. "And, if you work hard at your drawings."

Lisabetta returns to the Buti homestead with bundles of drawing materials, her head filled with the shapes of saints and landscapes, and sketches Rinato, the scruffy little dog that Leonardo gave her on one of his visits, five years ago. They tramp enthusiastically through the grasses outside the boundaries of the farm, following the invisible scent of Leonardo. They imagine him at the edge of the tree line or beckoning from the low rise at the end of the rows of olive trees.

He has left an imprint of himself on their world. The golden brother – the benevolent master who charms with his brilliant madness. The dog and the girl wait for his return at the hours of dawn, and midday, and late at night under the stars... all the times that he had made larger.

They can never know how Leonardo shivers, eighty miles away, under thin blankets and holds tight to the thoughts of them, clinging precariously to a precipice, always alone.

Leonardo reaches for flesh and fur touchstones with outstretched phantom arms. All the while his real arms hug him into a safe embrace. He calls out to Lisabetta and Rinato in his waking dreams and hums them into his reality. He clings to a thread of belonging, where sister, and brother, and mongrel, escape from the clutches of expectation, and run freely into the long grasses of Campo Zeppi to evaporate under a scorching sky. They tumble into each other in paroxysms of joy, happy to be somewhere, anywhere, no longer separate. On the occasions of his monthly visits all three run mad with delight.

Leonardo teaches his sister to look beyond the colors she expects to see and to dive inside the miniature world where plants, and trees, and rivers, can be discerned in the textures of bark, and nestled into the hills and valleys of fresh moss. These are the fanciful land-escapes they share. Hours are spent pretending they have fallen through the roots of the olive trees into the tiny worlds, away from the larger one, oppressive and cold, choked with rules and rough treatment.

They collect stones, and osier stalks, and lizard skins, and rabbit bones picked clean by the sun. All of these are laid out carefully and precisely, to be copied into the small librero books of bound drawing paper. Leonardo shows Lisabetta how to flesh the outlines with life and to make notes of their colors. He instructs her to log the wind and weather that had rustled the leaves, or feathers, or flower petals. Nothing is insignificant.

Lisabetta's backyard is a panorama of natural wonder. Leonardo teaches her to observe the movements of things. He encourages her to notice wings, and the emotions of water, and a single drop of rain splashing onto dry dust. She is quick to see that everything life-size has its counterpart magic in the smallest of details. At night she dreams of the wild places that continue to hold them safely together.

Leonardo says Rinato is to be her new brother. She recalls the day Rinato is delivered, and how she had clung to the dog's trembling body when he whined after his disappearing master. She kept the pup close to her for days and was rebuked for taking such pains as tying a string between herself and the creature. It slowed down her chores and both were ridiculed, but in the end, all the fuss had been worth it. Rinato no longer pined for Leonardo and she could finally see the part of Leonardo that lived inside the dog's eyes.

Both girl and pet are content in each other's company. She tells the puppy stories when they run into the wild hills. His ears follow Lisabetta's voice even while he sleeps.

Leonardo had arrived one afternoon with Rinato as a tiny bundle inside his shirt. The feelings of another's abandonment pressed hard on Leonardo. He found the runt of a litter, near death, nurtured him back to life, and kept him out of sight till he was strong.

Leonardo takes the animal as a positive sign. Rinato brings their number to sacred three. The young dog cements Lisabetta and Leonardo together during the long weeks spent apart, when time moves slowly and Lisabetta dutifully captures the changing seasons on bits of paper. She records the world so Leonardo can sift through them, read her drawings, and ask her questions. He wants details: had she sketched after a rain? What was the light? Where would the shadows fall if she moved to another angle? What had been the time of day?

Leonardo teaches his sister to describe the colors in ways that read like poetry: greens washed with sunlight, stormy blues impregnated with thunder, the earth-tones shot with flecks of gold that smell of rain and wind, the reds ripe as dawn cherries, and the yellows charged with the happiness of divine breath. Leonardo points out the natural triangles that fascinate him and Lisabetta learns to give them back to him as the threes he craves. Trinities focus Leonardo, when his mind wanders into the dangerous everyday things that settle upon him and make him uneasy.

Lisabetta counts with Leonardo or paces silently beside him, understanding with some unconscious force, that this is a good thing for her beloved brother and therefore also a part of her own best experience of the world, and her need to be his strength. There are times only she can bring Leonardo back from the abyss that threatens to extinguish his light.

When Leonardo retreats into his shadows, Lisabetta stays close, ready with a shape to distract him, or a question only he can answer, and Rinato presents him with a new trick. Anything to erase the pain in Leonardo's eyes and make him look directly at them again, and smile.

Anyone who sees Lisabetta and Leonardo together notes the two look uncannily alike in spite of having different fathers, and for ten years, only three people are aware of their true lineage.

There is more – the siblings think along parallel lines and they know more than they should of the other's deepest trials. When Leonardo smiles, Lisabetta thinks the sun has come out; when Lisabetta smiles, Leonardo is content. Rinato cares only that his two gods send vibrations directly into his animated tail.

The DIARY of VERONICA LYONS

A Gargoyle High

February 7, 2006
Tantallon, Nova Scotia

Lisabetta presents the scenes of her past out of sequence for me to organize later. I end up with postcards and details.

The Harry Potter movies have infiltrated my daydreams.

I pretend I sleep with a ghost owl on my windowsill. It perches under an imagined pointed arch against diamond panes covered in frost. The tall ceilings make me feel small scale. I need magic to pull me out. I feel like an abandoned orphan about to embark on a new life. Being saved feels imminent and I hold high expectations of a knock at my castle's studded-oak door.

I will creak it open to reveal a rescuer with an enchanted car, or hippogryph, and a spell to cast on my enemies. A flying car. An escape. An adventure. The opening bars of Harry's theme music quicken my pulse. Fourteen magical notes.

I fell asleep to it and it embedded in my psyche as a lullaby. It engaged me.

Magic exists to remedy the wrongs and hurts of a world gone cruel. I dreamed gargoyle high, peering down the long drop to the crusty snow below.

This day is as warm as spring. New flies are born, buzzing out of season. Sultry breezes blow warmer outside than in. Some of the days' horrors recede and I begin to piece together some writings. Last night I got the bug and wrote several poems. I felt gifted with imaginary friends who appreciate the art of story.

Such is the power of a dreamed life coming true. ~𝒫ℒ

"Chiego merzade e sono alpestro tygre"
(I beg for mercy; I am a wild tiger)
~ Ginevra Benci

Wednesday's Child

~ Ginevra de Benci – 1466 ~

"No girls allowed," Ginevra's brother says in fun, when she tries to join him, but Giovanni's words are filled with truth. She feels it. She looks to her father to chastise her brother hoping for an invitation to stay, but Amergo de Benci laughs with his rambunctious son and fails to comply.

Ginevra Benci has one older and two younger brothers; she is their only sister. Their dismissal of her turns their play into years of invisible war. She becomes a spy for both sides, watches men for weaknesses, and becomes expert at playing inside their rules. Ginevra plays chess with human game pieces, not to defeat, but to conquer; she plays for total annihilation and to kill when she has to. Her clueless mother plays to win jewels; her aunts and cousins, to achieve small freedoms. Only Ginevra's nurse, Angelina, is afraid of her eight-year-old charge.

The stamping of Ginevra's foot will only cause further humility and likely land her another hour's detention inside the narrow closet of her father's office. She has three fears. One of them is being alone. The other two are being alone in a dark place, and being alone in a small space. Any form of confinement infuriates her. She believes in a God who favors the rich and privileged. She is entitled to *His* attention, if not her father's. At night Ginevra Benci's room requires open windows and extra candles to burn away hints of a stifling crypt or tomb or cavernous pit.

Ginevra is shrewd enough to play the roles of prim fakery of the woman she is expected to become. She saves her tantrum till she is out of earshot and flails out at Angelina, biting her arm.

In a practiced move, Angelina shoves Ginevra into her stepmother's chamber, but not before she places a sweetmeat on the girl's tongue to keep her quiet. Angelina keeps a pocket filled with crystallized fruit. Eyes above the sugar glare at her with hate. Mouth satisfied. Ginevra's soul is out for blood.

The evening nursery forbids lit candles to be left unattended. The children are a different matter. Ginevra's youngest male cousin, Tommaso, gives her a tender smile. She moves towards him smiling back and slaps him hard enough to shock even herself. For an eternity he stares without breathing. He looks as if he may die. His cherub face turns red, but he exhales in a shriek of tears interspersed with gasps for air.

Her own two brothers cry in support. She pinches them all the same. When their nurse, Rosa, hurries in, there are two angry marks on the arms of her charges. They are too young to explain. Ginevra acts as if she had answered the screams.

"These two have pinched each other. Michele fell and hit his head. Boys are such idiots."

Rosa nods in deference. It's best not to cross Ginevra, and it's true, most girl babies are less trouble. This is why they enjoy a separate room.

There is too much distress for one servant to handle, and the nursemaid scuttles off for help.

"Ginevra... watch they don't hurt themselves again. I will be back."

Ginevra sweeps her miniature skirts across the room in a rustle of blue silk. By tomorrow, the boys will have forgotten she has any power. Tomorrow will be a new time to play the maternal sister or cousin, with a vengeance. She will jostle them up and down like a mother and smother them with kisses. Cuddle them into complacency. Slaps on bottoms already red with rashes, hide signs of a thrashing... "*shush don't cry,*" she will croon softly.

Ginevra has a brooch with a sharp pin. Tomorrow, she will pull the boy's hair and pat them back into comfort. A sharp jab will leave a tiny sore dot. Ginevra will play up the little mother as she wipe their faces with feces.

"Boys do disgusting things," Ginevra says to Angelina, when they pass the bowls of brown water and dirty towels outside the nursery door. Angelina always agrees.

"Stupido," Ginevra whispers to the room, later. Then louder, till the boys begin to cry. "Quiet! Insignificante! Non importante!" The howling is unbearable. Angelina arrives with three frantic faces in tow, maids still drying their hands on soiled aprons.

"Ginevra, come with me," Angelina says. "I have some new dress velvet for you." But the girl stares her down.

"I don't want another dress. I want breeches," she shrieks.

The DIARY of VERONICA LYONS

Mission Out of Control

June 5, 2008

Why mess with perfection. I used to be strongly programmed for romantic companionship… apparently a g-host of the virus still remains. I have been deeply lulled into false security from the healing circles of friendship I created around myself. Then I moved, and for the hundredth time, loneliness found me. Prolonged suffering projects us forward, outwardly seeking DNA wholeness. Old commands from mission control still arrive unexpectedly and override my new orders for solitude.

So I sit here, deranged, writing a mentally dictated replay of devil's advocate-jeers, in order to confirm my worse-case-scenario suspicions. Only then may they be aired, addressed, faced, and wrestled to the ground. Resistance may be futile, but it's also a safety net against a tightrope high-wire act of human defiance, thumbing my nose in the face of Lady Luck, the goddess of chance.

Placing myself smack in the path of her erratic brother-gods is irreverent, gutsy and not a little foolhardy. ~*VL*

*"The painter
should withdraw apart,
the better to study the forms
of natural objects."*
~ Leonardo da Vinci

Singularity

At the age of thirteen, my brother supplanted all but a few of the senior artists in Verrocchio's studio. Within his first year of apprenticeship, at twelve, his forte for delicate rendering was a driving force behind the workshop's current success. Leonardo's work thrived, as Verrocchio's bottega rode a wave of an unprecedented number of commissions. It was this general affluence which transformed Leonardo from a talented boy to a professional artisan. There was no time for the master's art lessons, so Leonardo taught himself and was quickly absorbed into the frenzy of a busy production team.

There was a general atmosphere of prosperity in Florence. Palaces rose on several street corners as our noble families established headquarters and reclaimed the streets surrounding them, plowing them under as if they were virgin land. Our city was a bustle of creation. Every section of the city was blocked with scaffolds and workers and piles of bricks, and in the midst of such largesse, mundane art was promoted to the unprecedented status of 'art-on-a-pedestal.' Creating 'fine' art became the declared virtue of a few 'chosen ones.' Creative skill was learned; but great talent was labeled: divinely bestowed.

The church proclaimed art to be inspired, and so there was an influx of religious altarpieces as each parish church and great cathedral vied for God's approval. Leonardo was at the top of the almighty's special list. God smiled down on his Florentine painters, sculptors, and architects. Artists walked the streets a little taller, wore the latest fashions, and performed within a growing aura of respect. They were considered an extension of God-the-creator, and by doing God's work, artists gained a social voice. Creating was the latest sacred duty. Only a few stuffy diehards failed to embrace this new fascination for breakout art. No longer, were saints and holy families the only icons to worship. Art changed.

The rich and the beautiful decided to formalize their power with family portraits. The murals which lined the walls of prominent buildings, were more likely to depict members their patron's family tree, paraded out for subsequent generations to remember, and homes made spaces for paintings and sculptures of living men, women, children, animals, and landscape.

It's easy to see that portraiture was the precursor to modern photography, and as today, a blatant form of vanity: the beautiful-people of Veronica's magazines, paparazzi wars, and retouched offerings of plain-faced celebrities to compete in the ongoing pageantry of power. The power of beauty over brains and talent, and pedigree and genetics.

Suddenly it was competitive to hire the best painters to immortalize the mortal princes and princesses, the uncrowned kings and queens of Florence. The Romans had declared warts and all to be acceptable, but it soon became apparent that flattery was the better part of Renaissance portraiture. The art of patronizing took on a new potency.

Clay and bronze ornaments were one of the mainstays of the art business. Verrocchio's kilns and furnaces burned day and night, and when war loomed over us, it was the best artists who rallied to the calls of generals, and dukes, and princes, with new ideas for weaponry, and patterns for armor, and new designs for standard bearers.

But when Leonardo was thirteen, we were at peace, and Leonardo was busy designing entertainments. We Florentines loved the pomp of fine theatricals, so Verrocchio employed teams of workers, who churned out banners and costumes and sets, and on any given day, a tour of his studio could showcase a small child being painted gold and fitted with the latest design of mechanical wings. It was common to fit children with harnesses connected to a network of wires and pulleys, so that they might fly over the heads of the spectators as angels or putti.

Leonardo took the time to listen to his materials. I watched him stare down a color and weigh the heft of a brush until he was part of them. Until they were an extension of the image held ready in his mind. His arm was a bridge which connected his thoughts to a panel. He had a subtle touch and was the undisputed hero of sensual techniques only possible with the new medium of oils. What Leonardo managed to achieve with the slick wet-on-wet colors, astounded us all.

Verrocchio was so entirely taken over with palaces and cathedrals and other grand works, he deferred the painting of portraits to my brother. Lorenzo was not pleased.

Leonardo's career advanced far more quickly than his ability to handle the horrors of the social world. He created in seclusion and once a month he rode out to Campo Zeppi and taught me everything he could remember. I practiced during his days in the city and the time crawled by.

I rose early and completed my chores with an artist's eye. I noted the different shades of white as I poured the cream into buckets, and the pink and orange behind the clouds of sunset, and the folds of my mother's brown dress when she sat weaving baskets, and the golden edge of candlelight that softened the outline of her face.

I couldn't help but sketch my pony, Stella, or Rinato, or each plant that called out to me to capture the wonders of their design in the small notebooks Leonardo brought me. I hid the libricini in my apron, so as to avoid a confrontation with Antonio.

My father thought me a moody girl, but he could make no legitimate complaint of my work. I was a hard worker, and art improved the performance of all my duties. I worked with my hands, in time to the flow of images in my mind, and time evaporated. I worked to hold the spell of art. So I chopped more wood, or stirred the cream longer and with greater concentration. When I groomed our two horses, they emerged meticulous, and while my family slept, I worked at the table with my charcoal and paper, or etched on small lead-white panels with the new silverpoint stylus that Leonardo gave me.

I envied my brother's ability to paint the atmospheric haze of far distant landscape. He called it 'sfumato' – the lands that shimmered out of focus behind the transparent smoke of living air.

Leonardo disappeared into the countryside he painted – the keeper of wind and weather. He saw what other painters missed. He laid the results at our feet whole and clear. I knew, because he withheld no trade secrets from me. I tried to duplicate his tendresse with trees, and mountains, and waterfalls, and he taught me to capture the soul behind a sitter's eyes.

When I understood each new law of art, I was amazed. The translation appeared flawless under Leonardo's tutorship. I felt a happy surge of understanding – the 'ah, I see!' and the 'yes' moments of incredible bliss, and at these times our faces shared the beauty, and I saw myself mirrored in Leonardo's eyes, so I knew my face must also be suffused with joy. Our creative world was separate from the harsh realities of human squabbling.

Leonardo and I combined our specialties. I coaxed him out of his moodiness and he taught me to play with the ideas that danced in my head. We were one creature, made possible from two brains, four arms, and a singular purpose to master the art of art.

Leonardo's status meant that one day, he could open his own studio, and I would have to be ready. I glimpsed what we could achieve if we could slay the dragon headaches that lashed at his brightness. I was the only one who understood the enchantments of Leonardo's triangles, and the roses and lemons, and the number three. We dedicated ourselves to each other's best interests, but I knew that the harshness of Campo Zeppi would be magnified a hundredfold in the alleys of the city if we weren't careful.

The streets of Florence were a maze of pleasure-seeker's haunts as well as a cradle for artists. To live and work there, required the type of social ambition that my brother lacked. I was the wrong gender to succeed alone, but I had a masculine toughness and the energy needed to protect Leonardo. He held the receptive feminine spirit of the art we wanted to create. I grounded him and he offered me the freedom to fly. - *Lisabetta*

The DIARY of VERONICA LYONS

New Dogs

June 6, 2008

I found a play group for Jupiter. Our house can't handle another intruder. It bothers me that I failed to sense how Mrs. Bently, with her penchant for murder mysteries and bodice-rippers, was so wrong for us. I blame my erratic transition to Victoria. Jupiter is still asking if he can have a rosary. I took him into a church and he lit a candle, and afterwards I bought him a fake candle with a battery. He flips it on and talks to it. How can I protest when we both acknowledge that Lisabetta is real. Besides, if I make a fuss, Mrs. Bently's crazy religion will have won. It's best to keep recent events, low profile. Candles are innocent enough.

Sandro and I continue to enjoy a relatively flawless relationship.

When a boy and girl hold hands across the sea or make eyes across a dream, signs are released like nervous doves.

Casual, mixed-messages are sent: receive-perceive-deflect-reject-advance-retreat-hint-invite-flaunt. The cat and mouse event danced in slow motion is a diversion which leaves dignity intact. Good-sports with no faces lost at the end of the day. Game set and match.

Real-life lovers must willfully step freely on every crack; land on every eggshell landmine and dare to remain whole and not try to hold back the tsunami of rejections that will eventually come. The world is easily thrown off balance by a pair of lovers.

Toe-dipping conversations are frail gestures of promise. If ever a house of tears and bone can be persuaded to be perfect, the adage of old dogs and new tricks offers little encouragement. It feels so very awkward at this stage of life, to break through to the kinds of freedom required for successful mating. ~𝒫ℒ

"The eye
as soon as it opens
sees all the stars of the hemisphere.
The mind in an instant
leaps from east to west."
~ Leonardo da Vinci

Mercenary Gifts

Campo Zeppi – 1466 (Lisabetta, Age Eight)

Rinato skulks in the shadows with the rest of the family and keeps to the edges of the room. Even the promise of a meaty windfall is never enough to lure him nearer the dinner table. The poor creature announces visitors with a hesitant bark from wherever he's hidden; his canine nature unable to keep wholly silent. Table scraps thrown to the floor lie where they land until Antonio grunts away from the meal, and rides to Anchiano. Lisabetta has learned to toss morsels far enough into the corner where Rinato slavers. Waiting for Antonio to leave is a constant state of expectation for everyone.

Rinato and Lisabetta are inseparable. They escape to the open country whenever time permits. Lisabetta is permanently assigned to the livestock, such as it is: a single cow, a dozen chickens, and two horses.

First light on a limp September morning is routine until the squawking of hens and the jangle of bridles alerts Lisabetta, inside the animal shelter, that horses and riders have entered the Buti courtyard. She lifts her head from her chores. The air smells better when it brings the soldiers who gather Antonio into their posses and take him away.

Immediately the sound of Antonio chopping wood ceases. They have come for him again, and when Antonio sees his comrades appear through the windbreak of fig trees, he flashes a rare smile and greets them with an exuberant "Thank God! I am saved!"

"Lisa! Boots!" he commands, without bothering to look. "Saddle the grey."

"Wait, you can't take Stel... the mare. She's lame"

"No matter, she will get me to Anchiano."

"I will saddle the black."

Antonio takes a step towards his daughter and lifts his arm to clout, but she ducks, and his backhander misses and swipes air. The absence of impact throws him off balance and he fails to grab her neck, but one of the riders speaks:

"Leave her, Antonio. She makes good sense. Take the black. We're late. Hurry."

Antonio listens and looks past his daughter. "Thank you Lisabetta, my son" he says to the air above her head, but he knocks hard into her insolent shoulder as he strides past her towards his freedom.

Antonio wants away from his women and his brother's women, and his aging mother. There are nine of them: Antonia the matriarch, his wife Caterina, his brother's wife Fiore, four daughters: Piera, Maria, Sandra, Lisabetta, and his two nieces: Maria and Simona. Francesco, his long-awaited son, lies as yet inside Caterina, but even had his gender been known, this future son would never have been enough to keep Antonio home.

When Antonio barks orders, most of the family rushes to obey from their own eagerness for his departure. He pushes past Caterina, heavy with child. She does not exist. Antonio's only message for them is delivered laterally when his fervent thanks to God to be 'gone from this place' reaches their ears.

Antonia fusses. "Do you have enough to eat?" She pokes extra food and a blanket into the spaces between a sword and a bedroll. The men look away. They have no mothers to wish them well and it's embarrassing to watch Antonia Buti mollycoddle her grown son. The food is pushed out of sight but the blanket is pulled out and tossed back, aimed at her feet.

"Stop fussing Mama, I have enough," he says and swats her away.

Antonia dusts off the blanket, shuffles away to her outside kitchen, and makes a loud protest loading wood into the oven to drown her son's departure. She hates his soldiering and later her pots feel her displeasure as she scolds the uncooperative flames underneath them.

"Stupido," Antonia shouts at Lisabetta, dispersing the smoke with her apron.

"I'm sorry, Nonna" Lisabetta replies automatically. She had been the nearest granddaughter to blame for the fire. The logs had been too damp.

Lisabetta and Caterina offer the same prayer every night: that Antonio's absences may become permanent. When Antonio is 'gone from this place' they remember how to breathe.

Lisabetta smiles watching her father grow smaller as he rides away. That day, when the dust from his companion's horses hangs thick in the air, she watches his red jacket fade into a pink shape down the track. It's the brightest thing left to describe him and Lisabetta waits, frozen until it turns to the color of flesh and disappears. The men's muffled camaraderie can still be heard. She listens until the road takes him completely.

When Lisabetta's father vanishes into that autumn day when she is eight-years-old, her energy expands. The sun rises every morning, but on leaving days it's as if it shines on her alone. The emptiness of Campo Zeppi fills with light. Caterina and Fiore smile and bask in the warmth of silence.

Caterina rests on a millstone near the east door. She eases her pregnant weight down and stretches her brown toes to the first strong rays of the sun, making small circles in the air with her ankles. She beams at Rinato clowning in the tall grass. Rinato, the keeper of enthusiasm, materializes in a frenzy of joyous yelps and hops on hind legs making the younger children laugh.

Caterina rarely smiles; she becomes smaller as she's consumed by God. Lisabetta sees her mother retreat further from the world each day, but she's too young to know how to stop it or to realize that only Caterina has the power to stop it.

The prospect of her freedom to come, sustains Lisabetta. She will be an artist. She is the most stubborn of Caterina's daughters, but it's this optimism which enables Lisabetta to nourish a dream in blissful naiveté. Determination gathers as the momentum necessary for leaving home. Lisabetta has been ready since she was six.

The Buti carnival celebrates. Grandmother Antonia is the only one who preserves an expression of wretchedness. Bitterness has made a permanent home in her eyes. She's accustomed to the barren years spent scraping against starvation with a husband she can barely tolerate. Her purpose is married to the betterment of her eldest son, and now against her wishes, he's off to fight another small war for wages.

Antonia declares loudly that her younger son, Jacopo, is too soft for war, reducing him, along with his miserable father, to phantoms of men who cleave together as one entity rather than stand alone against her tongue. Between them the three men muster enough wit and muscle to scratch a bare living from the acidic soil of the Tuscan flatlands. This morning Lisabetta's Uncle Jacopo, wanders the distant hills with her grandfather on a happy assignment snaring rabbits. With any luck Antonio's ornery disposition will happily widow Caterina and orphan them all.

Lisabetta's ninth birthday draws near and the olives celebrate her survival by dancing a jig against the sky. A feeling of independence fills her. She feels the presence of a more permanent freedom. She had purposely lied about Stella. Lisabetta saddles the pony she has raised from a foal and rides at a leisurely pace towards Vinci in search of Leonardo, to tell him Campo Zeppi is safe for a while.

Lisabetta is well past the initial blush of eight and Leonardo is nearing fifteen, back from the city while the Florentines recoup from an outbreak of plague.

The chains of Florence seem sweet, but in the meantime Lisabetta perfects her talent in secret as much as Leonardo flaunts his own in public.

"A time to keep silent and a time to speak;
a time to love and a time to hate;
a time for war and a time for peace."
~ King Solomon

The Knot Eternal

Campo Zeppi – 1468 (Lisabetta, Age Ten)

The walls of the room glow with amber light from the hearth-fire and paint the inhabitant's faces gold. Lisabetta sits with her mother, trying to copy the fluid patterns Caterina weaves into the rim of her basket. Lisabetta is nearest the oil lamp. Her basket wants to be different, and Caterina corrects her.

"No, like this, Lisa. You're not pulling the reeds tight enough."

Weaving is tedious. Lisabetta's fingers are too wild. "I think baskets are not my calling," she says.

Caterina looks up amazed. Her favorite daughter has sprouted wings. "Women don't have callings," she says sharply.

"I do. I'm going to paint like Leonardo. There are women in Verrocchio's studio who grind the colors and..."

Caterina interrupts, her voice kinder. "I hope you won't be disappointed."

Lisabetta lets this solemn forecast sink in and forces it to shrivel. She can't allow disparaging thoughts to take root inside her mind, and though she constantly weeds out her mother's predictions of failure, she must be quick to replace them with an affirmation of an artist's, yes. Lisabetta wants to throw her stupid basket in the fire; she wants to shout that she's different. In her imagination she visualizes another Lisabetta who waves her arms and dances, but these are not the revolutions one reveals to Buti women by their fire. Secrets shared in the dark are thirsty knives in the daylight. Lisabetta is like Leonardo, she prefers to glow like a banked fire and keep her best thoughts to herself, or share them with Rinato. She's not even sure if it's safe to confide in her mother anymore. There are times when Caterina is a stranger and Lisabetta fears her.

"Why did you give up?" Lisabetta asks her mother.

Caterina is silent long enough for Lisabetta to resume her first announcement: "It's easier to design the knots on paper. Leonardo showed me how" she says.

Caterina nods approval at this. "You must go from here. Leonardo must leave Florence" she agrees, in a hushed voice. It's the sentiment that Caterina used to spin often, when Leonardo visited against da Vinci orders.

Lisabetta is surprised to hear Caterina express herself the way she used to – as if she needed to hear her proposal out loud in order to test it for strength against the prevailing future. It's the same plan that Lisabetta carries like a torch against the inconceivable darkness of its failure.

Aunt Fiore is dead. Her uncle's new wife, Maria, shows her sister, Piera, a new stitch. Both seem entranced with the possibility of yet another way to push thread into cloth, but Lisabetta only feels this way when Leonardo shows her his drawings and how to smudge a soft line of charcoal into a contour of sublime form.

The orange light defines a tribe of priestesses in front of a campfire, where Rinato is free to sprawl amongst them, undisturbed now that the small children are sleep and the men are away. For this, Lisabetta blesses the storm that rages across the marshlands and keeps them huddled together.

Lisabetta's two older sisters nestle with her cousins and Aunt Maria to chatter of marriage. The womenfolk speak freely of old dreams and current aspirations, but Lisabetta is only ten; she has only one dream, and Caterina has been silent about hers for a few years now.

"Why do they care so much about love?" Lisabetta asks her mother.

"They think it will take them away from a life of hard work."

Lisabetta knows it isn't true from Caterina's expression, but she demands confirmation. "And can it do that?"

"Love is the hardest work of all," Caterina says.

Lisabetta wonders what could be so difficult about caring for another. It's easy to love Rinato and Leonardo. "It's not hard to love *you*," she says. Caterina smiles and pats her daughter's cheek, and Lisabetta feels sorrier for her than usual. There's no light around her mother even when she expresses affection.

Caterina hears Lisabetta, thanks her daughter, and goes on weaving a perfect loop. Complicated and elegant. A snake eating its own tail.

A recent month spent helping Leonardo in Master Verrocchio's studio has Lisabetta more determined. "I won't marry," she announces. "I will be an artist like Leonardo."

Caterina explains: "Lisa, I don't understand your brother's world, but it can't be too different from the rest of Florence. Women shine at love and motherhood and even then, not for long. I hope you receive what you wish for. Being stubborn helps." Caterina makes sure the others aren't listening. "You have to lie to fool them... to fool men, and be ready to compromise."

Lisabetta's eyes are wild. "But art *is* different. Art isn't a trade. Leonardo has seen many women painters and he says I am better. He says I am good."

"Of course he does. Leonardo loves you."

The possibility of this explanation rises like bile in Lisabetta's throat. She remembers an even greater truth: Her brother is incapable of lying.

"Mama, Leonardo can't lie. That's why he needs me to help him ... to lie for him."

"Then be very good at it," she says.

Caterina knows that although she encourages her teenage daughters and nieces to speak of dreams, her own have ceased to flicker with life. They've been dead for years, fading further from a sanctuary even she no longer cares to reach. Instead she's built a shrine in her mind and submits to the religious icon of a woman's face that never ages and her divine child who can make promises that continually bless.

Maria's twin boys sleep in the same bed with Lisabetta's youngest sister, Sandra, and their baby brother, Francesco. The comforting drone of wise-women lulls them to sleep. The hearth is a warm cave of domesticity. A blaze of green logs function as an altar, and the women crouch before it calling down the sacred energy of feminine power and spin it into songs and stories and baskets. Lisabetta strokes little Rinato softly with her toes as he twitches beside her chasing dream rabbits.

A barrel of osier reeds soak in a tub away from the fire. Piera splits the stalks with her teeth and lays them in neat rows according to length. Caterina selects one and weaves it into a knot pattern that looks like the braids of hair. The wet stalks smell of fields after a rain.

Maria has set tomorrow's soup to simmer on the kitchen brazier and Lisabetta continues to weave into the lateness of the night even though her eyes water from the smoke. She sees her straw creation in the patches of flickering light. The rain softens and falls in a wet song. Her hands stay awake and work while she drifts into sleep. She startles with a snap of firewood to find her basket appears to have turned into a bird's nest.

In the Buti household baskets are another rule of conformity. The designs have been the same for a hundred years. Lisabetta is considered a failure. The fire wants to eat her basket. She finds its heat oppressive. She wants to run into the storm and scream. Lisabetta craves the fury outside to shake her whole again. She wants wild rain to purge her from the drab plague of hopelessness that permanently cloaks Campo Zeppi.

Caterina's hands are swollen with calluses and twisted into ropes that still work their magic with the baskets. Lisabetta knows she's old. "Thirty-three," she says, when her daughter asks. Her head is bowed from her responsibility as the family's new matriarch and her eyes need to be closer to her work. Lisabetta is grateful the sour smell of her grandparents is gone.

In this light Caterina's face is beautiful; her hair glows like copper in the flames. The kindness of evening defines the contours of her face with tenderness. In the sun she will not fare as well. Her mother has ceased to care for appearances; her vanity is replaced with a desire for inner beauty and God's forgiveness. But Lisabetta has only just reached her tenth birthday and doesn't know how to save her mother from disappearing into the shadows of the church like a bitter prayer.

Piero da Vinci had ceased to be a possibility when he married Francesca di Giuliano Lanfredini after the death of Albiera. For a brief while Caterina had waited for a message. She frequented the mill cairn and left word – several messages, but the only answer that came was the announcement that a new bride of fifteen was to grace Piero's new house on the Via delle Prestanze, in Florence.

Piero's second wife dies with her stillborn child, and not long after, Ser Piero's third wife, Margharetta, forces Leonardo into the workshop of Piero's friend and client, Andrea Verrocchio. Piero had concluded it was bad luck to keep a reminder of illegitimacy in the house. It's easier for Piero to believe that Leonardo is responsible for his lack of heirs. Leonardo had been eager to go. He moved out of his father's office and into the art studio down the street the same day. Everyone seemed happy with the arrangement, but six-year-old Lisabetta, heard the news with dismay until Leonardo had explained this is what she needed as well – a trained brother who can employ her when the time comes.

Piero's mother, Lucia, had been the only one of the da Vinci family to visit Caterina and bring words of comfort after Lisabetta was born. Caterina had been twenty-three then and still counted her days as stepping stones towards the da Vinci fold. But Antonio Buti did not die at war... Piero's love for Caterina did, and she devotes her time to the Madonna's son now.

The talk is of nothing special. Maria wants only to discuss her babies. Caterina's nieces and daughters giggle together about nonsense. Caterina muses of angels and saints and how she will join Fiore in heaven, perhaps to talk and laugh as they had never managed to for very long on earth.

The room is empty of her mother-in-law, Antonia, who died along with her husband last year. Fiore had gone that year as well. Another girl child finished her time. If Caterina could lay down her head and die this night she would go willingly to bed with her rosary and pull the covers over her face. She's had enough of suffering.

Leonardo thrives... Caterina hears of his shining progress and sees him once a month when he comes to teach Lisabetta. The two of them need no others, she can see that. This thought, excludes her, but she is pleased by it nonetheless. She has brought two love-children into the world, strong enough to conquer a country-life, if they persevere.

Caterina had been thirty-one at her third son's birth. The eyes of the men at his christening had told her she looked old, and later the doctor informed her that there would be no more children. He knows from pressing his fingers on Caterina's abdomen, that her womb is collapsed with tumors. The news had made her happy. A rare emotion… at last there was no need to hope, and her sadness could be placed at the feet of the virgin and her son, who surely understood the terrors of mother-hood and sacrifice.

Caterina's other three girls can see no further than their sunburned noses. She can't summon the emotion to feel sorry for them. They are who they are, with no chance for better. Her chance is gone and it is Lisabetta's turn to wait for a destiny that may not come. She has told Lisabetta to listen and watch for signs.

The light from an oil lamp emits a trail of black smoke. Perhaps a soul with a message. The eternity knots Caterina weaves remind her she is somewhere riding into herself… a heavenly life that will take over this one without a break. She wonders when. She hopes it will be soon.

The DIARY of VERONICA LYONS

Midnight Pancakes

June 7, 2008

Lisabetta accuses me of being routine. She says I'm in danger of becoming predictable. That soon she won't be able to tell me from a typical sleepwalker. I can't let her think such a zombie exists under my skin. I tell her it's the work ethic kicking in and that it erases all other urges to create. She says to stop and refresh the page. She is learning computer-speak, and it made me laugh as well as making a lot of sense.

She gave me a pep-talk like a soccer coach. She commented the house is in need of a duster and mop. In spite of her enthusiasm, I finished my chapter before I attempted to score a goal in her game of search and reveal. She expects me to come out of hiding with her, but she's right. I need to play and paint and dream regular dreams.

Two hours later I challenged Lisabetta. I walked Peyton into a moonless country road with Jupiter. We ate midnight pancakes in the dining room off the best china. I decanted apple juice from a cardboard container into a glass Art Deco pitcher, and Jupiter was seriously impressed drinking from a wineglass.

The next day I said hello to a stranger. I watered my parched house plants and cleaned out their dead dreams. I wore a peasant skirt and shook out the rugs, and I washed the bedroom floor as if I was under military orders. ∿𝒱ℒ

"Avoid loud and aggressive persons;
they are vexations to the spirit."
~ Max Ehrmann C. 1820 (The Desiderata)

Nobody's Child

~ Lorenzo ~

Lorenzo di Credi is a human pet. He visits the studio of Andrea Verrocchio as a seven-year-old innocent and stays permanently, as the master's latest plaything. By the time he turns eight, Lorenzo is irrevocably lost between a greedy mother who sells him into lechery and a man the age of his grandfather.

One year later Lorenzo is still being groomed for intimacy – a novice lover with no rights, no humane parent, and no home other than the studio where he sleeps like a pampered dog. He is disillusioned with the iconic Mother Mary who reigns in profusion around the studio walls. She taunts her maternal smile from dozens of paintings and statues. Lorenzo's experience is different. He knows mothers to be dangerous and selfish.

He learns to adore simple luxuries, and to address the priests in the cathedral as father, even though they are only apprentices like himself. They are human sons of God, but in Lorenzo's domestic prison, Andrea Verrocchio's word is god – a continuously dysfunctional presentation of second-hand fatherhood.

Biblical lust is easily re-configured for maximum profit. In the end, immediate gratification overrules affection and affection usurps love. What begins as an innocent ticket to prosperity becomes a permanent lifestyle – the known over the bleak past and the dangers in the streets.

Feminine power is too mercurial to trust. It's better to pursue the physical opposed to the emotional. A homeless boy should align himself to the might of cold brute-strength; mothers tend to disappear early and fathers count their heirs in descending order. It's only practical to have a surrogate male to champion one's chances of survival.

Leonardo da Vinci arrives unexpectedly one morning as a breath of fresh talent and immediately bursts into creative flame. It's apparent after the first flush of beginner's success that the thirteen-year-old Leonardo is the latest rising star of Verrocchio & Company.

This latest addition is also its most eager recruit. The younger Lorenzo feels demoted overnight. He's confused, unsure if he's an acquired sin, an adopted son, an apprentice, a surrogate child-bride, or all four like the apocalyptic horsemen he hears about in church. He feels apologetic for his audacity to have been born. For now, Lorenzo may best be described as a jealous *'brother'* who prays hard for the destruction of a rival, studio-sibling.

Leonardo ignites a terrible disturbance to Lorenzo's already fragile concept of world.

Lorenzo prays to plaster statues hoping they are divine receptacles for messages to God. He asks that Leonardo, the intruder and the object of his loathing, should experience his own feelings of being eclipsed and left bereft of an identity with a status borrowed tentatively, at best.

At nine, Lorenzo is quick to rally multiple agents to serve the remainder of his boyhood years. He can do or say no wrong in the eyes of his smitten master, but *'Papa Verrocchio'* shows off his newly acquired *'son,'* Leonardo, at every opportunity.

Lorenzo is the only one who cares; he's the only one who has anything to lose by Leonardo's gain – even if only in his imagination.

Lorenzo di Credi hates Leonardo like a brother. He makes no pretence to disguise it.

PART SIX

Second Start

THE DESIDERATA
(Desired Things)
"Speak your truth quietly and clearly, and listen to others,
even to the dull and ignorant; they too have their story"
~ Max Ehrmann C. 1820

*"Do you not see
how necessary a world of pains
and troubles is,
to school an intelligence,
and make it a soul?"*
~ John Keats

The Summer of 72

~ Halifax ~

The year 1972 is spiritually high and politically low. Jonathan Livingston Seagull soars over the Watergate break-in, a dozen eggs cost fifty-two cents, the hit song 'Nights in White Satin' caresses New-Age ears with romantic sentiments hinting of obscured truths, and Albert Einstein's 'Theory of Relativity' is validated.

While fans of 'Star Trek' lobby for a rebirth from the ashes of its second 1966 pilot, an unsuspecting Elizabeth Lyons, wonders why her three-year-old daughter, Beatrice, doesn't respond to toys and cuddles, but coos incessantly to cats.

Of course – it's the family curse. Elizabeth had wanted to pretend otherwise. The shadow had come again and fallen on little Bea.

Thirteen-year-old Cate plays with her baby sister. Their seagull book needs no words. Pictures fly and soar and reach into Bea's eyes. She searches the sky for shapes.

When Cate reads to Bea from her Alice book, she shows her the face of the Cheshire Cat hanging in a tree and is rewarded with a smile. From then on, Bea looks into treetops and waves at the floating smiles she sees there.

A smile is more mysterious than the fate of a seagull with an extraordinary wish.

"Wisdom
is the science of other sciences"
~ Plato

Uncle Oz

Oxford, England – 1975

"Cowardly Lion," Cate calls her brother, with affection.

"Dotty Girl," he calls back.

Cate and Perry Lyons are inseparable. Cate dubs Perry, Oz and he calls her, Dodo.

Autism stalks the Lyons family. Every second generation one of their line presents a neurological anomaly within the spectrum. Its presence ignites Perry's compassion late. At the zenith of his Fine-Art's degree, Perry sets aside a love affair with painting in favor of bio-chemistry, and downgrades his freelance venture restoring paintings, to an obsessive hobby. He is comforted that both disciplines live side-by-side under the same microscopes of revelation.

In whimsical moments, Cate and Perry refer to their genetic predisposition as creative programming. "Remember, Lyons live in prides" Perry says in the moments they rally against the odds.

The Lyon siblings: Peregrine Arthur (Perry), Dorothy Catherine (Cate), and Beatrice Alice (Bea) were meant to be wealthy from the start. The family art collection guaranteed it. Their mother, Elizabeth, shows signs of Alzheimer's, but little Beatrice, who lives contentedly in the necessary embrace of a fine institution is the recipient of the Lyons' rogue gene.

Perry is a free spirit, and while riding-high towards his doctorate, he meets and forms a lifelong friendship with fellow geneticist, Alistair MacKay. They meet the Canadian, Charles Duke in their last year, and on a summer break, Perry introduces Alistair and Charles to Cate.

By Christmas, Elizabeth's condition deteriorates from sporadic episodes of memory loss to being completely oblivious of her children's identities. She passes in her sleep, and the true financial standing of the Lyons' estate is revealed. Trusted legal counsel has bled their investments into the red. Perry is away at school when the family's art collection is auctioned. It's the beginning of a long financial winter that threatens to last for years.

Cate had been expected to marry well, and fate decreed that the Houses of Lyons and MacKay should blend into one perfect family, but Alistair, is determined to remain a bachelor. The two friends mirror each other's sentiments regarding intimacy vs. career and the hesitancy to produce offspring, as much as they share a great affection for Cate.

Cate is the love of Alistair's life and it's with guilt that he adores and beds her, and she is delivered of a stillborn girl, Carola. Three years later, still unwed, they produce healthy twins, but there's no way to reconcile Alistair's passion for Cate with the joy of his growing success.

A male provider outweighs the prospect of single parenthood and twins, and Cate was shaken with the inevitable acceptance of a situation in which she had been a willing participant, but even in her greyest hours, Cate had believed that Alistair would one day, be her husband. After all, wasn't love the great transformer? She was mistaken. Alan Laird, a suitor from Cate's past, was brought up to speed, and bribed sufficiently with the promise of gaining his first love, as well as the guarantee of financial support for his step-children's education. Cate's practical side, begrudgingly said, yes.

Cate's second pregnancy had been spent in tears laced with reasons to die: no proper husband, a dead-end service job, one girl-child stillborn, twins on the way, permanently unwed, and persistent attentions from an ex-boyfriend who now repulses her.

By 1979, the only thing left of Lizbet's estate is the family Rolls Royce, kept mint, in hibernation, waiting for a miracle. Then it too, faces the block. It's Perry's last touchstone with a past affluence he took for granted; a reminder of trips to the continent, tennis parties, and milling with the country-club set. It sleeps safely like a prince under a spell, covered in soft tarps, polished and sleek. A child's picture book waits on the backseat, but cars and toys have no concept of yester-day's sorrows or today's fears. An auctioneer's bloody gavel is to be the method of execution, the same year as Veronica and Basil's birth.

The first month after Veronica and Basil are born, Cate refuses to have anything to do with them. She lies in a postnatal funk, still a teenager.

Alan is hopeful. He's willing to take on Cate and her newborn twins, providing they emigrate to Canada. He visits every day until Cate says a weak yes to his proposal. What does it matter? Life has to be endured rather than enjoyed.

Cate refuses to trade in the name Lyons when she marries Alan. "No" she insists, "my name is the part of me that I won't give up." It is the last time Cate fights to be real, and she surrenders to a fate worse than invisibility. The Atlantic shore of Halifax is achieved, but after only a year, Alan feels the same. Indifference is a contagious disease.

Perry fancies himself an art detective. Following cold trails of art into the void of anonymity inspires his love of all things forensic. Scopic-cameras become his latest toy. Mathematics, Physics, and tin-kering with machines is love-work. High-tech machines are the bridges which connect his twin career.

Inspired by smoke and mirrors and technology, Perry dreams solu-tions which manifest several hybrid inventions from the discarded par-aphernalia of outdated lab equipment. He sifts through camera shops and flea markets for lenses, and raids junk shops and charity stores. His electronic creations allow a more invasive analysis of pigments and fingerprints. To relax, Perry burrows beneath dried varnish and time, leaving the amber fog behind, and heads for the past. A color meets him halfway. "Hello beautiful" he says. Close proximity to great art causes Perry's nerves to flat-line into peace.

Perry's artist half is committed to the family's passion for fine art; his scientist half is dedicated to the family crisis. Political power backs any urgency which extends the lucid stage of old age. Senile dementia and gerontology draws the grant funds and the code word genetics is a magnet for official largesse, but autism fails to register on their financial radar. Down the road, token philanthropy will hopefully cover the rest.

Wanton cells and genetic minutiae call Perry away from gallery time. He tunes them out. Invasive squeals from electrons choke camera time. An exchange of microscopes is painful. Perry's appetite for paintings to dissect is aggressive. Medical research is a distraction, but one discipline balances the other. He divides his time into shapes of joy and guilt.

Synchronicity plays equal hands as the matchmaker-tease and the destroyer. It presides over the collisions of human continents, and the forming of intellectual mountain ranges. It cements karmic deals.

Charles Duke's mother, Millicent, is an avid art collector with the finances to frequent prestigious auction houses, but she prefers to troll small antique shops and pounce on hidden treasures. She vets and acquires Perry, for her genetics institute while he's an Oxford student with her eldest son.

It was easy for the three fates to throw the uber-rich, Charles Duke, Perry Lyons, and Alistair MacKay, into the same corner of an Oxford University dorm. Millicent sniffs out the gold in her son's friendships and discovers how easy it is to charm an underdog and make him salivate at the sound of money. She will hire one of them.

Alistair is passed over in favor of Perry; the deciding factor is Perry's uncanny ability to appraise, authenticate, and restore old paintings. Having an expert on staff to interpret the sign language of art is convenient. Medical funding is a write-off, but turning a thousand percent profit from an authentic masterpiece is pure income. The clincher is Perry's past. He is easier to manipulate than Alistair, considering he has two unstable women as dependents. Millicent obtains Perry as a shrewd investment.

Millicent, hooks Perry with a triple invitation: funding for research, a chance to work on the Duke art collection, and a state of the art institution for Beatrice, and when Perry tells her his decision rests on Alan agreeing to bring his new family to Canada, a small cheque makes its way into Alan's pocket.

Cate worries that close proximity to Bea's institution and her old love may destabilize her already shaky disposition, but thoughts of living near Perry tip her decision. Cate, Alan, and the twins, settle in Nova Scotia, while Perry works to save the next generation of Lyons from mental discrimination, and sister, Beatrice is housed in a facility near him in Antigonish.

The science of art is unchartered territory. Millicent likes that. Her lawyer seals her pact with Perry in a tight contract and her skewed philanthropy opens the Lyons Institute for Genetic Research. Perry feels he's pulled off a coup; Millicent knows she's pulled off a takeover. Perry has been overthrown. He feels he owes Millicent. Millicent feels she owns Perry.

Halifax 1982 – 1987

No, Cate decides... Veronica must be suppressed for her highest good. Which 'her' remains ambiguous. Boys are different; they can inherit... they can join 'old boys clubs' sponsored by a more robust gender. There can be no exotic feathers in nests of sparrow dreams built one prayer at a time. One hears of strange eggs hatching in wrong-time baskets, and her children had arrived with violet eyes which scared the midwife. At four they declared themselves artists. It was all too disconcerting, Cate thought, to want above one's station with quite so much vigor. It wouldn't do to encourage children to expect much from a world that responds so contrarily to best intentions. She is proved right when self-fulfilling tragedy strikes. The twins are separated at six with Basil's accidental death.

Blame remains: had Cate allowed Veronica to go camping with Basil, he might still be alive. Veronica reminds Cate often enough, that she would have saved her twin or died with him, and that either fate was a fair trade for being the daughter of a madwoman. The day after Basil's death, Veronica cultivates a new stepfather/daughter bond calculated to aggravate her lowercase-mom. Hate can do that. This stance gave Cate a reputation she didn't wholly deserve, but whenever do children truly understand the complexities and variables which push their parents one way or another? Mothers and fathers arrive whole and flawed. A smart child endures them.

When Veronica turns nine, she becomes a latch-key kid five days a week. Her job is to peel potatoes after school. She is only free after six raw potatoes rest cold and white and round, in a saucepan, by six o-clock. Other freedoms aren't that easy. Saturdays are hard. Basil died on a Saturday. Veronica always talks to him on Sundays.

Halifax 1991

Millicent shmoozes Perry into a luncheon date with Cate – the weakest pulse in Perry's energy. Millicent's spies tell her Cate has good days. Lucid days. And every time Perry is reminded of his duty to protect her, he is likely to perform on marionette strings because when a dedicated man feels his responsibility acutely, he is malleable – less likely to test his independence.

Both women have highly individual radars: Millicent's automatically scans for flaws; Cate's is finely tuned for threats. They are experts, and the scents of guilt and betrayal are always the same. Cate thinks Millicent's chic turban the height of sophistication, but she senses the snakes underneath it.

Perry is a troubled man – the classic professor who dithers at life outside his laboratory, and there have been rumors of rival interests keen on sweeping him off to better funding. Perry keeps a brittle secret and Cate is the keeper of its truth. Control is everything.

Table talk is innocent enough until Perry is called away during the first course and the real meal begins. Cate is raw meat to a jackal.

Perry returns to find Cate looking flustered."I need an aspirin," Cate says to the empty chair next to her brother." Code for more serious medication.

Later in Perry's apartment, Cate twists a scarf around her head and faces her brother calmly before delivering a serious warning. "Your Millie is a nasty piece of work. Watch out. I felt strange. Like I'd been stared down by a cobra. Anyway she gave me indigestion and a headache. Do you think I look good in a turban?"

Cate is not strong. She takes several secretarial positions and eventually allows herself to unravel, and willingly follows her mother into a twilight of murky regret where she can hide as insubstantial and invisible as her sister, Baby Bea. Loves missed like a last bus will have to wait for another lifetime. Life is tough and after forgiveness, finding true love is the toughest work of all.

The Lyons Institute is, as ever, subject to at least one of Millicent's siphon companies. The Duke Empire has been cultivated to placate a ravenous team of investors too greedy to wait for their meals to die. Perry's autism project' waits patiently underneath the promise of research grants, and Millicent is a dangerous surgeon, forever hacking at the edges of Perry's guilt, turning his skills into something she can fit into her wallet. Charles younger brother, Niles, is placed in control as part of his continuing education.

The teenage Veronica can understand why her mother teases her Uncle Oz. He's too sweet for business, but they love him as he is – a brilliant man who seeks refuge in the anonymity of his work.

Perry can't know that one day his niece, Veronica, and Millicent's son, Niles, will connect in chemical steam. He has enough to contend with, including the debilitating effects of processing seven years of guilt, rehashing the death of his nephew and his own part in it.

The DIARY of VERONICA LYONS

I wish I may

June 8, 2008

> There's nothing for it. I don't believe in God, but I beg any energy with chutzpah, to release me from the earth. My time is over. I have no interest in a long life. All I want is a clean death as soon as Jupiter has a hands-on father. It's all I think about, but I can't go until I know my son is in safe hands. ~*VL*

*"Some dreams
are too small to keep;
no life is too big to dream."*
~ Veronica Lyons

The Covenant

Halifax – 1995

ranny Lizbet's book 'The Ghostly Lover' begins with a blast
of poetic nonsense. Veronica reads with glazed eyes: *'There's
a restless serendipity that arrives as a warm shiver. It drifts, sighing over
miles of tear-stained deserts. It hums over barren sands that shift their
course from the weight of a single human prayer.'*

Ethel Elizabeth Howard-Lyons bequeaths her seventeen-year-old
granddaughter, a literary collection of romantic exotic, including
a dozen Marie Corelli novels, and it takes two years for Veronica to
force-read her way through them in homage to her thickest bloodline.
It's a choking marathon of pulp melodrama, but every page has been
navigated by her beloved grandmother, and reading her books brings
Granny Lizbet into the room. It's as if Veronica holds the books open
and turns the pages for her, and together they share the stories.

Veronica and Lizbet are more like psychic sisters who talk in whispers beneath the covers. Lizbet is the inspiring force which enables
Veronica to jumpstart her confidence, misplaced during childhood.

It would be more accurate, to report it was misappropriated by an
over-zealous mother with no pizzazz of her own. What finally emerges
is an authentic nature continually recuperating from being nipped by a
woman already jealous of a daughter's panache at age six. Flamboyance
skips a generation, and Veronica's ancestral beeline leads like an umbilical cord straight from her maternal grandmother, who renamed herself

to counter the effects of her mother giving her the name Ethel. For some reason, Veronica's great grandmother, Catherine, had thought the name wildly exotic.

Veronica romanticizes Elizabeth Howard into a woman of poetic substance, bypassing Cate's doleful influence. She feels obliged to carry the torch of female energy like a relay runner to honor the Howard-Lyons clan.

In the eighteenth century, Marie Corelli's stories were a mainstream hit. Her theories of paranormal love served the Victorian appetite for gothic melodrama that swept immature academics and bubble-headed women (including the Queen) into the same pile of rapturous exhaustion. It could hardly be called the 'age of wisdom.' Hysteria had been the upper class' malady of choice.

In 1885 Marie re-birthed herself. She borrowed the name Corelli and hid the name of MacKay beneath it like a coat of old paint. Marie was propelled into second fame and her name still crops up in the bibliographies of the trendy self-help books that Veronica consumes like spiritual candy. Marie's constant referral to twin-flame love still cuts Veronica with gut-wrenching significance.

Reading Marie's fantasies is a much-appreciated distraction, and Veronica's imaginative hopes stockpile against divine timing. She honors the other memorabilia she has inherited from Lizbet: an amber brooch, a smooth lump of bloodstone Lizbet used as a large worry bead, a few candid and posed sepia photographs, a copy of Virginia Woolf's 'Flush' from the original Hogarth Press, and especially, a first edition of Marie Corelli's 'The Life Everlasting,' signed by the author.

Veronica has obsessed over romantic love all her life, which is why she has never experienced it first hand – that is, consciously on a surge of left-brain chemicals. It has been enough to pretend such time-sensitive anomalies exist. Marie's Gothic reunions of ill-fated lovers, pick up their fractured destinies with sudden clarity when awarded timely second chances. She suspects they're the delusions of a spinster, but Veronica reads them for a different reason: to please her dead grandmother and upset Cate.

Veronica dubs the novels *'hystorical follies'* in the grand genre of the Victorian bodice-ripper, by authors possessing uncommonly-blessed passports to realms of cosmic coincidence. So far she has only been able to visit there on the tail of her grandmother's favorite literary comet. Illogic spills an intoxicating trail of promises: if her grandmother believed, there may be a seed, a stalk, maybe even a flower of truth. Veronica can only daydream it so.

One thing is true: recipients of grace are less likely to speak of it. Silence is a powerful connection to non-local mind. Veronica calls such events, renaissance moments. Peak experiences where time stands still – explosive births of butterflies expelled from cocoons in blasts of psychic sparks rather than emerging slowly on fragile wings.

Veronica thinks that miracles only happen to other people, and that thought puts her in a temper. The nature of serendipity is uncanny. She knows that, but for all her sceptical bravado, she is a respecter of the wild occasions when raw desire triumphs over wishful thinking.

Marie believed contracts existed between artist and a divine source. Her explanation was that the gods of imagination translated dreams into fanciful language. "They played with dreamers" she had premised, and one day Veronica hopes to know what Marie professes to know, but not quite yet, although she is beginning to hear the laughter of fanciful creatures – the ones that children say they can see, running in the wild grass at the edge of their parent's cultivated gardens.

Serendipity-doo-da

June 9, 2008

Serendipity is an electric promise from the universe. It's a charged opportunity delivering a payload of grace. It's a karmic pardon. It is rare. Pregnant entities such as these are all too often trampled in the dust that gathers after expected disasters, or become ensnared in leg-traps of undetermined fears. It's easy to trip over a gift left at your feet. One learns awareness after many mistakes.

Wouldn't it be grand, if beyond love there was a creator residing at the back of the north wind, breathing life into puny human scripts with loopholes like French lace?

With an omnipotent presence directing magnetic attraction, people could turn into stars, and wouldn't biographies be all the more magnificent for it? I would pray for such a sentient father, willing to forge diamonds from his creation's soft flesh, but for being a devout atheist.

I can only continue to celebrate the times when passion wins. I admire the naiveté of man, who says that time heals or that it passes. I am amused by the moxie of the pyramids that embody the elegance of divine math, and know the sacred movements of vortex energy, and the life-spans of engineers and slaves, when they reply that it is man who passes. I especially love it when the cosmos whispers that art is eternal and that love endures longer than art. ~*VL*

*"Synchronicity
is macro-managing taken to extremes;
the divine marriage of events
for better or worse,
but I still wish I had a save key
for my dreams."*
~ Veronica Lyons

A Dream of Air

Halifax – April 15, 1995

The bird is in trouble. It's too heavy for the wind. It's tossed backwards into a rolling pitch and tumbles towards the earth. Cate has the disconcerting sensation of spinning widdershins against a blue sky, but even inside her altered state, she is aware she's in a falling dream. The image of white wings and the sound of renting cloth is strong, but Cate is willing to stay lucid to see what happens.

Gravity shifts, birds morph into helicopters, and Cate feels herself lift vertically from her body. She lets go of her resistance to things dimly registered as paranormal and endures floating like a kite above the world of shadows. Cate parachutes back to earth under a tent buffeted by severe updrafts... a hapless woman strapped to a silk pyramid, descending to the olive groves below.

A Tuscan sunbeam catches on the capstone and melts into a dodecahedron lit from within like a paper lantern. Cate forgets she's in a dream and experiences the terror of dropping uncontrollably, but the vertigo is mercifully brief and her plummet is interrupted by a timely pull on puppet strings, which jolt her away to a theatre where she waits in the wings, about to go on.

Cate watches a Shakespeare play from backstage, waiting for her cue, but she's trapped behind a diaphanous cloth wall. She hears the sound of a script being torn in half. Shards of paper flutter to the floor from the rafters like tiles of snow. She grabs at the propaganda pages filling the air. The plane which dropped them drones away like a satisfied bee. She is frantic to make her debut, but a solid shower-curtain blocks her entrance. The scent of grease paint and turpentine fills her nose like smelling salts. Cate paws helplessly at the plastic drape until she hears her name called sharply. CAT!

Cate wakes in the icy waters of the Atlantic desperately flailing. The scream for help echoes around her. She sinks into the dark cold and resurfaces through warmer water into a sparkling morning, in spite of her wish to stay in the moving picture where she is both star and audience. Leaving the dreamtime with her is the familiar imprint of a woman's face, framed inside a box office display case under the banner 'Now Playing.' She thinks it's her own, but it's her son on a missing person's poster. 'Loves Labors Lost – Grand Opening.' Someone very dear has disappeared. A beat later, her brain reminds her she no longer has a son.

She is a born follower who requires a placid routine, but some delusions are fine things to have as friends. She is a slave to thoughts of lack, and a rogue gene culls her from a carefully manicured safety zone. Now someone is screaming *'cat'* and she has to go. It's time to go. Now! Timing is everything to an actor.

"The cat has a bird!… Mom! Help!" Cate defaults to three little letters which changed her identity forever. Hearing her second and third names, cuts into the turbulent dream. She wakes already out of bed. There's no time to put the dream away properly; her seventeen-year-old daughter's dilemma is urgent, and Cate's true north is anxiety.

"Help me! He's got a bird... Mom… help!"

Veronica's cat, Mo, rampages through the house after a successful hunt, having returned through the triumphal arch of the cat door and laid his bounty at the feet of his mistress. The 'bounty,' once released, flaps upward into folds of drapery, gains its bearings and tries to penetrate the window glass. A second later it hits the floor where it's reclaimed by the relentless Mo. The present commotion is Cat-Mo, streaking down the hall leaving a trail of feathers with Veronica in pursuit shouting for assistance. Cate skids into the kitchen almost fully-conscious and catches up to the fuss.

Veronica corners her black cat, now making internal growls of feline protest with his mouth full of sparrow. The rejected sacrifice is now his alone and the blood trickling down his throat tastes sublime. The bird is dead; its head separated from its body. Feathers drift lazily down and swirl about the floor like low lying fog. All Cate can think, is that fog is a dangerous condition for flying. She opens the drapes with a theatrical sweep and experiences a wave of stage fright that buckles her energy. The show must go on without her. Cate's final cue reaches a sleepy understudy, while Cate shakes her head into making coffee. It's better to trade polite applause for the immediate acceptance of a dustpan and brush. Domestic safety wins; she can be a success at home. She lacks star quality.

Cate had needed no urging to cancel her recently booked flight to Toronto. Ever since she had swiped her credit card, Cate had wanted to undo the reservation. She had been cooperative with the travel agent, distracted by a poster behind his head of Michelangelo's David, promoting Florence as a prime holiday destination. The day had been full of déjà vu feelings that alternately tantalized and terrorized her.

Knowing she has contracted to leave the ground aggravates Cate's uneasy view of life. She had slipped out of her reverie in time to hear the agent say, "you're in luck, all the *air lions* are having seat sales."

There was no holiday on Cate's bleak calendar. She must jump from Halifax to a compulsory training seminar: *Women, the Art of Management,* as a condition of her recent promotion to executive assistant. She complies with the faces that own her, accepting congratulations and smiles and handshakes. She had won a contest she didn't enter.

Cate recovers with the alarming realization that her new position puts an entire typing pool under her authority. Having worked among them, she knows how spitefully thumbs-down they are. Her secretary companions have the habit of resenting a female boss while pledging a general allegiance to the corporate advancement of their gender. It's a tricky ladder to climb and Cate is afraid of heights. She prefers her former position of anonymous servitude which allows her emotions to evaporate at the end of each shift. The eyes of the pool count mistakes.

"Cara?", the travel agent had said, and Cate had shuddered into focus.

"Pardon?"

"I was asking if you required a car," he repeated. "I can make the arrangements now if..."

"No, thank you, I won't need a car," she had said.

Perry would have stated that Cate experienced random bytes of overlapping subliminal imagery that flashed with inappropriate speeds and stimulated corresponding receptor patches under her skin. He would have explained that optic nerves translated light pulses into pockets of awareness. Cate simply said, that her brain liked to send her stories. Precognitive intuition is too complex a term. Nevertheless, Cate's memory searches for anchors.

She phones in her resignation and sidesteps Toronto. The rest of the day Cate feels deliciously released, but is consumed by the idea she has been given a warning and feels vaguely alarmed at curtains and birds... missing the son she once had.

Flight terrifies Cate. Perhaps the dream is a sign. No-one calls her Cat except Alistair. Now she will miss him all day and probably call him later and undo the distance so carefully plotted between them. He is her Romeo impervious to poison, and she, his Juliet, too squeamish to handle a dagger.

"But I don't want to
go among mad people,' said Alice.
'Oh, you can't help that,' said the cat.
'We're all mad here."
~ Lewis Carroll

White Shoes

Halifax – Shady Rest Retirement Home – 1996

Cate stares at the word 'love' until she feels herself slip through the 'O' like a wisp of smoke. She evaporates from the fresh sheet of white paper, but love remains as a crisp black line, curved into language that stands for something larger than grief. She floats free from the horror of middle-earth, trapped between the past and the future where she has learned to expect pain. She blinks into the brightness of a cramped waiting room on the edge of a dream. Her thoughts incubate and are born deformed. They flap, screeching into the walls, echoing and doing harm in the room of shivers where she abandons the love that abandoned her. In the darkest hour little matters and the abyss seems sweet.

Cate is alert enough to hear Nurse Sally's white shoes approach with her pills. They tread purposefully through halls, where soft souls stir inside their dreams a moment longer in order to remain young and tender, and supple, and toothed and vital, and loved – where inmates Sunday-Best shoes are dreamed red with bows or shiny black with silver buckles.

Cate sees in flash cards: shapely ankles, smooth legs, slim calves, straight toes, and cool feet.

"Cold feet," she shouts out loud and startles the succubus at the end of her bed. She watches it scuttle away. She was once a woman who denied the quick steps of life – the toe-dipping, ride-anticipating, time-marching desert boots. She had hung back from the life-plunging walks and paced any angel who turned up, matching them prayer-for-prayer. Now, Cate has to be careful and avert her eyes from the peripheral demons who slink in the gutters beside her bed. She has to count them to be safe.

Cate's neighbors are old; she has joined them far too early – a crone at thirty-seven. Every afternoon, Cate's feet shuffle inside her plush old-lady mules. She concentrates on keeping up with her unfaltering starched-white companion. Cate keeps her eyes down so she can step on *all* the cracks. *Whose feet are these? Whose hands?* She dares not risk meeting her wild-haired reflection in the glass doors to the terrace, so she closes her eyes and once again her feet are tanned, graceful, sweet things in white sandals.

The beach that runs alongside the boardwalk absorbs the haste of pushing on. Cate strides boldly towards a banquet. Cork meets wood and pounds a friendly beat of espadrilles on an easy-glide trip. She loves softly draping summer skirts, loosely swinging, keeping time to holiday legs.

The maiden Cate is out for a stroll on a blind thunderbolt path where the crossings of strangers and planets find enemies, and teachers, and lovers, and affairs, and magic fish daring them to accept three wishes. Orthopaedic life hangs in the balance. Cate listens carefully to a pair of ankle-strap messengers with wings and shushes their bad news.

She should have worn her *'there's no place like home'* shoes – enchanted, clicking, red Mary Janes, disguised from their true nature of cursed dancing pumps. A young woman can sail through her finest years of glass slipper midnights without a boat or water or shoes or a prince or rubies.

The folds of Cate's linen skirt billow into the wind. Into the fine deep weather for living barefoot through broken glass, but there are days where Cate finds a pocket of fresh sand – the fearless treading zones of all that crazy earth jazz.

A woman must surrender to feet that take her past the teeth of a storm, into it's mouth to make it sing. Every night Cate swims in a safe domestic harbor where the world gently laps at the edge of a teenage summer. Beyond this place, there be dragon ladies with ward shoes, and clipboards with clickety pens, and brisk questions.

The white uniforms pass by and move on to other sterile-white rooms to perform clinical administrations, and leave Cate alone with rain streaming down her windows. She watches a roof ballet where a rusty fan vent, shudders sixteen revolutions per minute: *turn turn turn*, there had been a season. A cycle of wet weather and a dry spell or two, and more ice. The years go. Cate's rusty conscience blows hot. It calls, rarely cheering... mostly jeering: 'go... leave... come back.' Her shoes command *'on the double... quick march... left right left'* It's all the same: the now or nevers or the always,' or might have beens,' and especially the *till death do us parts.*

Emotional pain is Cate's elevator music. She keeps rocking in her cradle with birth and death spinning. She craves windswept gauzy white sheers on attic windows of glass lace, white peonies and white summer dresses, and spritz's of Chanel-scented evenings. She asks for rosewater every morning. She must learn to tiptoe with confidence and let the hired white shoes do the work for a change, but Cate feels trapped in endless white-sheet days with hospital corners that swaddle her too tight.

Carpal pain reminds Cate of a near-distant future. Her thoughts struggle inside the amber of endless old-folk whiteout, where she shape-shifts as a daydream night-stalker competing for the best heaven. Golden amnesia spreads like honey. Cate keeps to the edges of her dreams, and wakes covered in snow, to white nurses with practical shoes that squeak like reassuring Cinderella mice.

On lucid days, Cate realizes she must give herself up to the white army of hospice and the one who calls her Granny with such contempt, until sentience 'twinks' out like a light bulb. Fizzing and flickering... burnt out lives, the electric sputterings of hopeful candlepower. One retreats from the memories of bold light, and the spotlights and flash bulbs, and sun lamps and moon-glow, and the glimmer of shooting stars. The end of life is a psychic revue of highlights in low-lit rooms.

Cate tries to finish her love poem each morning. It's the word love that catches her pen, sure as a hook and sends her mind spinning: It had rained for three days. She and Alistair had stayed holed up in his apartment on Haro Street. She's there again, watching a parade of colorful umbrellas from their third floor love nest – a sweet ballet, dancing to the music of courtship. Cate decides each umbrella has a story beneath it, moving toward or away from a lover.

She is hypnotized by a rooftop fan on the building next door. Slowly it pulls her in – spinning her dreams of marital promise into a blanket of impossibility. Its arms rotate like a slow-motion Catharine wheel. Named for her. It's easy to cast her hopes into it, throwing a spell the way a potter manifests a vase from a lump of clay. Cate spends hours staring into it from the window.

Stolen weekends of Halifax rain, splash playfully and the power of romantic love seems flawlessly choreographed. Cate watches the shallow silver puddles fill and merge into a sea while Alistair sleeps.

The roof is a skrying bowl. Cate throws her last dream into its mystery and the splash it makes pushes a regal, slow-motion crown, into the air. Queen Cate wonders where to go next. She wants to stay in the grove of lemons or the rose garden, but she's pulled into leaving. Her pony waits. Her daughter, Mona Lisa, holds the bridle. They ride a million miles past the human chemicals of adoration. Cinderella dutifully extends her toe towards a glass slipper presented by a toady prince. Cate blinks and the clear crystal leather turns red, then white. Then, happy-ever-after. Alistair had called her, his principessa.

Alice Liddel, dressed in a blue dress with a white pinafore, is a sprite of a child who visits with all the others who intrude daily, but memories of childhood stories are only another way to focus and hold on to the nothingness quality of regret. As Cate falls down the rabbit hole, she hears a cat laughing and Alice muttering: *"it gets curiouser and curiouser"* and Cate knows she's extremely late. Timing has always been her downfall.

"In my world,
the books
would be nothing but pictures."
~ Lewis Carroll

The Haunted Library

Wolfeville, Nova Scotia – February 7, 1997

*V*eronica's creative lifeline is a nervous companion now that she believes its teenage sanity to be finite. She scans the library for sympathy. Her neighbors are page-logged, out of reach. They are strangers in a familiar landscape. She watches their eyes move like REM sleep over their open books. How could a layman understand the terrors of art? There are invisible traps everywhere.

She looks up from the cover of the oversize reference book in front of her and rubs at the pain in her eyes too deep to reach. It lodges behind eyes grown red from staring at pixels and the strangle of annotated text. Here, on a rainy Sunday, in the Art History stacks of Acadia University, the world is safe. She wishes she could live here, where the abject mumblety-peg of business is kept at bay by ferocious crone librarians too old to be afraid of the law.

An employee wearing a pink sweater-set and pearls, drops a heavy pile of papers with a satisfying thud in the adjacent carrel. It reverberates off the leather bindings, and green velvet armchairs, and the polished wood. Veronica loves the aftershock from the manuscript; it's the sound of research. Time spent here is kind. The downcast focus of her neighbors separates them into cerebral islands. The kindness issues from the building, and the shelves, and the smell of lemon polish, and the orderliness of things.

The pink matriarch continues on, deftly navigating her trolley loaded down with literary detritus, and steers it back into the narrow canyons between the walls of books. Her spectacles sway precariously from a seed-pearl chain, her expression, ever ready to admonish any takers who challenge her authority in this hallowed space.

The library expresses itself in quiet order. Veronica loves the muted sounds of careful soft-soled shoes, and the gentle punch of the hydraulic stapler, and the passive shuffling of files that rifle like the rippling of a paper fan. She loves the smooth yield of the narrow metal drawers that glide on oiled runners. She loves the muffled coughs and the tentative whispers. She loves the reassuring rustle of turning pages that insist upon intensive study. She defers to the accumulation of human curiosity indexed in a mosaic grid of deposit boxes – the bank of known things.

Last Sunday she loved the round clock with Roman numerals. Now it hangs ominously like a full moon over Science-Fiction. It's an ironic reminder that time is her enemy. She once savored the comfort of its dull metronome tick. Now its gloomy face mocks her. The library shifts on its axis of peace and feels like a mercenary taking back its illusion of sanctuary. She survives as best she can… as only one can, who resides on countdown row.

A large volume lies on her table like a slab of meat on a butcher's block. The light from the green banker's lamp falters. It's sheen off the glossy printer's ink obscures the eyes of the portrait on the dust jacket. Veronica adjusts the angle of the glass shade until the eyes engage her. She sniffs the rarefied air for the ambience of academia. It comes to her like a puff of sedative. She relaxes and lays her fevered cheek on the cool book, sucking up its contents. The two women, literally face-to-face. Connected. The spine of the book reads: *'Mona Lisa – a retrospective.'*

"Veronica Lyons?" The disembodied voice startles her. "You're wanted on the phone, you can take it in the office." The library witch points with an arthritic finger wearing a fake pearl ring the size of a walnut. "It's through that door."

Veronica scrapes back her chair with the minimum of disturbance, shoulders a canvas tote silkscreened with an image of 'Vitruvian Man,' and passes under the clock. The squeak of crepe soles on the hardwood floor is the last sound the library will know of her.

There's symmetrical irony present within the elegance of an eleventh-hour miracle. The phone call had pronounced Cate, dead. She has been released. Holding opposing thoughts of defiance and surrender up to the light had been exhausting work.

Veronica enters a surreal space of grief. She feels mentally kicked out of season. A stream of consciousness can drown an artist out of her depth.

'Mona Lisa' had thrown Veronica a lifeline... snuck a message into a mental pocket – the image of a library slip with an ISBN number.

The clock is timing Veronica with ancient hands. For the time being, her 'Mona Lisa' thesis is resigned to obscurity. An historic autopsy of the world's most famous painting must begin so the portrait can rest in peace.

The enquiry into Cate's death freezes her body for four months before it's released for burial, and 'Mona Lisa's' true identity is in jeopardy, as the world teeters from violations made with the best of intentions. Even a library is unsafe, but a new chapter of past-perfect complexity will dawn after the fair face of Thursday's sun settles into wild waters of St. Margaret's Bay.

Epitaph for Cate

Halifax – June 9, 1997

The roses are plastic. They sit heavy on the oak casket. Raindrops bounce off their hard surface with small explosions of water. The mourners are thankful for any distraction offering escape from the words of a bored priest droned by rote.

The strangers huddle together like siege warriors, standing shoulder-to-shoulder; their umbrella shields overlapping in solidarity against the violent shower. From above, a perched crow sees clusters of dark shapes trembling from the dry-eyed emotion collected underneath. Death from dementia is free of sentimental remorse. Any tangible tremors are of the mourners' own fears of being next.

Thunderstorms offer a nice touch to funerals. This one has used up its melodramatic lightning effects and eases off to a steady grey drizzle, but from time-to-time, the sky sends a renewed effort of fresh rain-power which stands in nicely for the absent tears. The long ceremony continues to unfold under a canopy of black discs slick with June rain. Only the crow can see a far-off sunflower weaving through the grave-stones, making its way towards the sombre theatre.

The approaching yellow sphere promises to scatter the others like billiard balls. One of the clusters parts and the sunflower is absorbed as well as a brightly colored upturned bowl can be, but it has breached the circle. A purple umbrella notices the newcomer with interest. The other, eleven standard black umbrellas, continue to stare at the red petals and waxy green leaves, too bright to be tasteful. They count the seconds which tick in time to the latest drops, noticing the way each one leaps off the ghastly wreath in different directions. It seems even the droplets can't get away from the coffin fast enough.

The sunflower keeps her eyes averted. Her hair itches under an unfamiliar wool beret. Uncle Oz is absent, convalescing in traction from a broken hip, unable to attend, and Veronica focuses on the tip of a lone walking stick that accompanies a pair of shiny galoshes. Aluminum walkers encompass the other pairs of shoes like metallic parentheses. Veronica notices a pattern; all the toes point towards the grave like an accusation. The eyes under the purple umbrella, singles out the estranged daughter mingling in the crowd.

Eighteen-year-old, Veronica holds the stem of the sunflower while her brain analyzes the shoes. She carries a small bouquet of marigolds like a reluctant bride. She is determined not to cry at the sensible old-people shoes. Only one pair of brogues has decided to wear a rubber guard against the inclement weather. Veronica's shiny yellow Wellingtons make the others look dull. She can't see the shoes on the other side of the coffin, but they're no more revealing than the others. There are twelve pairs of black mourning shoes. Eleven of them are elderly comrades from Cate's institution. All of them have theories for Veronica's late arrival.

'This is all we are,' Veronica muses, *'shoes will be left after we're gone. Rows of worn out empty shoes, wasting away in dark closets.'* She envisions hell as the great maw of a dumpster filled with decrepit ex-shoes and recalls the image of a terrible pile of shoes seen in a documentary about Auschwitz. Its museum displayed thousands of disembodied shoes, discarded, separated from their mates and owners, stacked in a grim mountain, kept as a permanent reminder of selective victimization. Someone had recognized their humanity, and a great effort had been made to create a statement with them. Nothing could have been more poignant. They were the perfect commentary of extinguished life – more than any formal monument could and more than the expensive stone angel lurking here in the graveyard, looking suitably sorrowful, wings at half-mast.

Veronica looks up at the marble face and allows a few drops of rain to revive her. The angel is looking down at her yellow boots with disdain. Veronica shuffles her feet. The gravel makes a comforting crunch that confirms life above ground and reminds her she is free to leave anytime, but guilt roots her to the macabre daydream of burying her mother.

The coffin is lowered on saturated ropes. Finally, it's time to file past the grave. Each person mouths a farewell they hope resembles poetry. The crow watches greedily. The bereaved, carelessly drop their orchestrated tributes: one artificial blossom after another tossed on top of the varnished wood below. Each flower lands with a dull thud. One is thrown nervously, misses its target, hits the edge of the pit, and casually rolls away from the gaping earth. Another retrieves it and tosses it to join its hapless friends in one fluid motion. It's done imperceptibly; the line pauses for a heartbeat, shuffles on as one entity, and the thrower blends into place before anyone registers the gesture for what it is... indifference.

Nurse Sally Caulfield, from Cate's extended-care wing, has helped Glynnis Connelly make the arrangements. Veronica can't think of a more fitting send-off than ersatz flowers that will make their way back to the Shady Rest's store room by nightfall. Glynnis, manager of the establishment, knows no better than to purchase an arrangement that can be reused for years if need be. Funerals are frequent events as residents escape to their various heavens.

There is an awkward moment when a dozen fresh red roses fall softly on the coffin, but no-one sees the shadow of uncertainty pass over Veronica's face. Some of the witches hats have veils which mask their curiosity. A huddle of small black bows and flowers bob together in geriatric sisterhood. The stranger makes no eye contact, but they will pin him down at the reception. One of them will be sent over as ambassador to glean details, while the others wait like a colony of spiders. Each in turn will offer the stranger their bony hands to shake in mock sincerity. Afterwards, their false teeth will clatter like skeletons and pick apart imagined grievances.

Veronica lowers the marigolds until they point to the earth, touching the rim of her rain boots. The mourners need permission to leave. No one wants to be the first to break formation. A period of confused mingling ensues. A week-long minute snails by. A woman speaks with shrill authority, and the sound of her voice startles the crow. The marigolds drop into the grave as the distant thunder returns, growling like a threatened dog.

"Anyone need help to the cars?" Stony pause, and then … "No? Well, see you all there then." A collective murmur disperses the crowd. This ordeal has another mission to fulfill. The solemn funeral director continues to direct his show and urges the senior citizens to be careful of the slick mud and grass. They've already been instructed to keep to the gravel paths. Glynnis wishes her charges were linked together with a rope like a kindergarten class on a field trip. They will make slow progress going it alone.

The hungry crow waits for them to leave. Perhaps they've left some pickings. He flaps to the ground and tries to picks up a shiny button, but it's too slippery and he abandons it to the shallow pool. It flashes there like a guilty beacon and the image of an eye inside a pyramid winks slyly from the greasy puddle to stare up at the sky like a tiny gold island. He will try again until he wins the prize.

In the distance the humans look like ants. The button's owner climbs into a polished limousine that slips away from the city of the dead. Less glamorous transportation will deliver their cargos of low spirits to the living world of hot coffee and sandwiches with no crusts, and dry pound cake. A straggle of old folk from Shady Manor are helped into their waiting bus. The memory of their friend, Cate, is already eclipsed by the promise of refreshments. The empty hearse has already slunk away like a beaten dog.

The distributed single-stem plastic roses are irretrievable if Glynnis is to maintain a semblance of dignity. The ersatz flowers will remain small pockets of incorruptible landfill. The wreath, however; is swiftly removed in a rehearsed move behind the retreating mourners.

The ladies of Shady Rest take no prisoners. Most of them have learned to dislike people; it's easier to label everyone as flawed – an old lady's privilege. They're a coven of ancient vampires, hungry for gossip to offset the sugar they consume in vast quantities for comfort. Their care-givers medicate their sour-tempered, sweet-toothed charges, with efficient regularity, from cinnamon bun breakfasts and afternoon cream teas, to hot-chocolate nightcaps.

Glynnis is fishing. "Nice service," she says.

Veronica anticipates her next thought. "Yes, the roses almost looked real," she glares.

Glynnis beams, accepting the remark as a compliment. "Yes, they sure did." She glances at her watch, detaches from further comment, and rushes off clutching the offending flowers. The plastic roses still hold vestiges of rainwater like small bowls. The preserved storm is tipped out casually into a planter when Glynnis spins sharply, heading for the kitchen.

The folding trestle table covered in a dollar store plastic cloth, displays a huge catering urn flanked by a container of coffee whitener, an open box of sugar cubes, red plastic stir-sticks, and a stack of paper plates. Veronica meets the gaze of the interesting stranger over a stack of clean white mugs while the coven of gossip watches from the wings like stakeout police.

Veronica bridges the gap with words raised in a hesitant gesture of resignation. Small talk is inevitable… and here it comes: "Very practical… the… uh…" he tries to say.

"Spartan lack of fine dining," Veronica interrupts.

Alistair McKay understands. He shifts on his feet uncomfortably. "Economical" he says. "Hello, I'm Alistair." The proffered hand is manicured and smooth of wrinkles. This man is approaching fifty, clearly not one of the inmates. Veronica checks his shoes. He brandishes a cane more like an accessory than from necessity.

"The cups, I mean mugs, are real china, they could have been styrofoam, and the forks are actual metal, so that's almost fabulous." Veronica waves her arm in the general direction of the reception. "It's appropriate though. Rather like my relationship with Cate."

"You called your mother by her first name? That's unusual."

"We were more like strangers. Anyway this sad little effort is a tad wheeled out. They probably do it at least once a week. You can see they've spared no expense. Sorry I didn't introduce myself. Veronica Lyons, daughter of the deceased, nice to meet you. I've always thought funerals were a waste of resources, but then, I'm a dyed in the wool atheist. So, no afterlife for me."

Alistair absorbs Veronica's declaration. He can see Cate shining through her.

"Cate didn't believe in one either," Veronica continues: "this sham isn't for her. The Shady Rest tenants expect tea and cakes laid on at regular intervals. I would have to guess that the frequency of deaths obliges a considerable amount of social mourning. A complimentary wake is probably written into their living-will retirement package."

Veronica stops, waiting for a comment, but Alistair is speechless and she continues with more social filler. "Well, my mother wasn't actually retired. She lived at the Shady Rest because of her failing mental capacities, so my stepdad was able to take *care* of her... literally, as it turned out. They had an apartment suite. It was practical. There's that word again."

Alistair's awkward smile gives Veronica permission to keep talking. Her need for disclosure is a volcanic bubbling of lava and Alistair is happy to stand out of its way. He prefers the role of listener, and is, for the moment, content to wait for the inevitable break when he may offer his personal touch of bold serendipity. He can wait. He has already waited years.

"Our family has been estranged by miles and attitude since the year dot, but I credit Alan, that's my stepfather, with holding down the fort for as long as he did. He couldn't take it anymore. It was a murder-suicide you see. One may as well be honest about it. The truth always comes out eventually. He was buried yesterday. He didn't have much affection in his life and ended up an alcoholic. He and Cate were married by default. She needed a breadwinner and he was willing. He had a crush on her since grade school and padded after her like a puppy until she said yes out of desperation. She was pregnant with me and my brother at the time. My biological father hadn't been so keen."

Alistair's eyebrows are in shock. "That must have felt good to get out."

"Yes."

"Are you all right?"

"My real father sent me a present once – a fifty-dollar bill with a note attached. It wasn't a special occasion. The card said: buy something incredibly silly and nice."

"and... what did you buy?"

Veronica opens her purse, retrieves a dog-eared paperback, *'Pilgrimage to the Rebirth,'* and produces a pristine banknote sealed in a clear archive sleeve. "I was going to frame it."

"You kept it?"

"I read a lot. It makes an interesting bookmark."

"You see it every day then."

"Yes, Sorry. I talk too much. Do you have the time?" she asks.

"Pardon?"

"My 'Mona Lisa' watch is apparently not waterproof," Veronica says, tapping its glass crystal.

Alistair points to his empty wrist. "Sorry, I never wear one. I have a need to be separate from knowing what time it is or isn't, but there's a clock over there. It's half-past something. I need my glasses to see that far. Events live or die on half-past-somethings. There's no need to worry about Cate you know."

It's Veronica's turn to appear mystified. "Well of course... No. I... wasn't. She and I didn't see eye to eye, but with Alzheimer's... she was clearly not of this world at the end. She had an unhappy life too. Strangely though, I couldn't care."

The candid admission requires a response, but Alistair wants fresh air and to be pummeled senseless by rain. He wants to stamp his feet through deep puddles of guilt and release the tension between polite diplomacy and what he's come to say, but courtesy demands his ears follow Veronica to the end. The end as she decides it.

The shiver of the old ladies attention changes from Alistair and Veronica to the arrival of a slab cake, presented late on a large foil platter. The flavor of the confection underneath the pink icing is mystery enough to divert them.

"Cate didn't like me either," Veronica confides. "She was from the 'don't do anything in case it goes wrong' school of parenting. It must have sunk in. I was her star pupil."

"She was over-compensating," Alistair offers. "Guilt has a long shelf life. No expiry date even after death." Alistair reconsiders the benefits of remaining anonymous. He has no edge inside the conversation. No sense of stability. He will do well to ride the present wave and float unknown, out to sea and disappear, father unknown.

"For what? I mean, did you know Cate well? Sorry, how long did you know her?"

"Ages," he says. "For the death of your brother."

Veronica is stunned by the sudden memory of Basil. "You knew my brother too?"

"Of him," Alistair replies, "I was… I *am* a friend of your uncle." He changes the subject. "Cate's guilt will pass now."

"Are you saying my mother is going to haunt me?"

"No. Oh no, the words guilt and haunt are interchangeable I think. Never mind, you can make it up to her another time."

"Time, yes, well, I'm late. I've got to go. Pleasure to meet you, Alistair. You're an interesting man. I enjoyed the way we passed right over the small talk for a real conversation. Lucky we didn't have time to slug out the life after death thing though. A parting of the ways there I think."

"Before you… please don't go because of… of my remark. I'm a scientist. A mad one by all accounts. Crazy goes with the territory. Crazy helps one survive. Anyway, eccentricity is an occupational hazard of quantum physics I'm afraid."

"I envy you; I wish I believed what you believe, but there's no proof."

"Well, actually there is… and if you read books like the one you just showed me, you may be interested in the possibility. Think of it this way. Do you believe there's death after life?"

"Considering the present circumstances, I'd say yes, but that isn't a belief, it's a fact."

"So keep the premise going… death after life, after death, after life, and so on. It's a logical transition. The flow of life to an *afterlife*. Do you see?"

Alistair escapes into the night with a last hasty message of condolence for Perry, and Veronica is too scrambled to enquire how he knows her uncle.

The unhappy front legs of the Masonic hall's chairs creak with the weight of the guests inching forward in anticipation of departure. The Seniors are restless for the familiarity of their cells. Funerals are disconcerting social obligations which spike small fears into deeper anxieties. All of them smell the nearness of death. Polite conversation is performed in careful voices. A knot of gossip at the tea urn stirs the Shady sisterhood into forced small-talk. Much is said of the weather and the stale sandwiches are praised beyond reason. The tea fortifies the trip back to lives of twilight expectation. The cake had been chocolate.

Nurse Sally hovers beside a box of the collected table decorations: a dozen milk-glass bud vases, each with a plastic flower. She is wearing an amber brooch. Veronica ignores Sally and approaches the jewel. "My mother had one exactly like that" she says into Sally's eyes.

"Oh, yes... I... found this in your mother's room. I wore it today to give it to you. Sorry, with all the fuss I forgot" she says, unpinning the brooch with embarrassed fingers.

Veronica accepts it with a dirty look and drops it into her purse.

Sally blushes. "It's raining hard again" she offers meekly, and retreats with the box.

The brooch makes a decided closure to the whole tawdry affair. Typical. Trust disintegrates on all sides. The usual. Look the other way and count the silverware. If the little bee inside it could speak what more could it tell of behind-doors compassion?

Mrs. Connelly claps her hands for attention' "It's time to depart" she starts to say, and stops, mid-announcement. Her faux pas is missed. "Time to leave" she says, and the exodus begins with a groan of energy. Like a true intrepid leader, Glynnis's umbrella emerges first and explodes in the night air like a military order. "Follow me. This way, mind your step... over here. Sally? Where's Sally?"

"Is it raining?" One old dear enquires. Nurse Sally doesn't reply, but welcomes the cool rain on her flushed face, and chides herself for wearing Cate's brooch.

A woman looking out her upstairs window across the street, is treated to a stream of similarly deployed contraptions from the swarm escaping the hall. The patterns they make look choreographed. Hasty goodbyes ricochet off the moon and fall onto the street, unheard. Seniors shuffle into the warm bus and forget their recent worries in the ensuing traffic jam of wet umbrellas, canes, and walkers.

Outside, the black umbrella known as Alistair, pushes higher over the others, holding its position beside a chauffeured car bearing vanity plates that read 'GEN 0ME. Veronica fails to appear, and when Alistair tries the door, he finds it locked.

The sunflower holds back and helps clear the tables – anything to delay joining the world where she is abandoned. When Veronica leaves by the side door, she is met with a fresh torrent of rain on a deserted street and Alistair waiting beside a Rolls Royce *'Silver Ghost.'*

Alistair approaches Veronica. "Can I give you a lift. I waited for you... I thought you seemed a bit unwell in there. Delayed shock can be a strange thing."

Veronica connects the car to her recent acquaintance. "Nice ride Mr....?"

"McKay," he says.

She notes he pronounces it correctly, the Scottish way: 'mah kye.' Veronica shivers unconsciously as his name resonates like a distant bell. To save herself, Veronica's mind latches onto the silver Art Nouveau hood ornament. It causes words to form. Rain splashes over the long glossy hood of the car, the same way it did on her mother's coffin. They are the same color and shape. It unnerves her, but a brain synapse reacts to the familiar form of a miniature woman embracing the wind like a figure at the prow of a ship.

Veronica dips the tip of her umbrella towards the statuette. "She was inspired by my favorite statue" she says. Her voice is too high and breathless. She consciously slows it ... "the 'Nike of Samothrace' ... and your grille there, is based on the architectural façade of the Parthenon. Sorry, ex-Art-History major. I can't help myself."

Veronica's attention comes to rest on Alistair's cane with its lion head flanked by wings. She points to it with relief.

"And, the winged lion of Venice, mascot of St. Mark, but in reality just another bit of treasure looted from the Assyrians." She grins. "I'm showing off."

"Actually, no," he says, listening for a sign. "This particular lion represents the family crest of the da Vinci. Now, the hood ornament is an interesting story… an homage to a secret love affair. The usual oil and water rubbish. A woman of low social standing and a blueblood, too well-born to marry or openly acknowledge her, but not well-bred enough to challenge his family's authority... but you're right, the sculptor was originally inspired by the image of Nike. He called this little lady the 'spirit of ecstasy' after a woman named Eleanor. Can I give you a lift?"

Veronica is overcome by the unexpected discourse. "I stand corrected" she says "but thank you, I have my own car. Bye again. I'll tell my uncle that Alistair MacKay said hello. He's laid up with a broken hip or he would have been here. I'll bet that's some interesting story… about the ornament."

Any mission of further discourse and an invitation remains futuristic. Perfect timing is a rare bird, but Veronica pronounced his name right. It's almost a sign, and Alistair follows an inner prompt to collect a handful of rain and hold it out to Veronica.

"Perfect example of life after death right here", he says. "This rain is tomorrow's snow and yesterday's ocean, but we don't think of recycled clouds as *dead* water. Nice to meet you again, Veronica. Well, goodbye and best of luck."

The door of the car closes with a rich thump. Barely audible. The automobile reaches the end of the cul-de-sac and makes a wide lazy turn in a silent wash of water. Veronica rifles in her purse for her impudent car keys, now hiding under quantities of small triangles of ham and cheese wrapped in cellophane. Her pockets are similarly filled with booted cake and fruit. Her fingers meet the smooth warmth of amber and the cool dampness of grapes. She pops a purple grape into her mouth and lets the juice wake up her mind. The sunflower bursts open. The posh car returns and glides past on floating tires, its chauffeured elegance swallowed by a curtain of rain. Had she dreamed it? The car seemed more unlikely than its owner's theory.

Veronica heads north on Mason Street towards her gold Mini. She walks slowly under a downpour, as if strolling a sunny beach with an umbrella for shade. She loves the drum of the jungle rain on the printed silk and the sharp taste of the grape. She can't remember Cate's face, and her uncle lies in traction in a state of semi-conscious grief. She will visit him within the hour.

In various rooms, relieved ex-mourners peel off of their dark sodden coats and step out of soaking shoes. Veronica flings a never-before-worn hat into a corner. Alistair heads straight for his hotel liquor cabinet with his shoes still on to pour himself a stiff drink, dripping puddles on an innocent rug.

Some head for the blessings of a hot shower. Soapy water splashes in a half-dozen sanctuaries of gleaming porcelain in frenzies of absolution. The freshly-baptized emerge and wrap themselves in protective robes. Some seek other comforts of herbal tea and strong coffee, and join their companions in a disguised toast to the years they have left.

Residents of the Shady Rest listen expectantly for the dinner bell. A dozen half-closed umbrellas drip in twelve doorways. Another, makes a cheery addition to a bouquet of companions in an oak stand. One umbrella knows the mourning will never truly be over.

Alan Laird had known his wife was dead years before he euthanized her. He envied her. He had tried to tell Veronica this, but she had busied herself with his supper tray, making overly sure his tea wasn't too hot. He liked to drink that first. In the spirit of long-term matrimony and after he was absolutely sure Cate was gone, he swallowed his own lethal cocktail from the remaining pills in the medicine cabinet. There had been so many.

Four weeks later, Uncle Oz, his leg in a cast, Veronica, and her amber brooch, face the same patch of Mount Pleasant turf. Cate and Alan lie, as they did in their cold marriage bed, far enough apart, two departed souls, side-by-side. The plastic bouquet that once anchored

Cate, had been immediately confiscated by the economy of Glynnis, and squeezed into the trunk of her car to be transported like a cold pilgrim to its next station of the cross. That was two lifetimes ago. It had been replaced with an anonymous wreath of fresh yellow roses that had waited until the last car in the funeral train had filed out of the parking lot, and the grave was filled.

The card read: 'as ever,' in peacock blue ink, written boldly in large script, slanted to the left. Four weeks of dry weather has turned them into a dried circlet like the wreathes trapped between a pharaoh's double sarcophagus. which makes the long rectangle of grave dirt look like a horizontal door to the underworld. In due course, a flow of annual flowers will arrive with the same inscription.

Veronica sprinkles the new sod with marigold heads. Perry lays a spray of red roses. The ground looks garish, even with fresh flowers: yellow and red blobs on a green blanket. The struggling grass looks like it's covered in dandelions, but there is a feeling of relief lingering about the grave, like the white TV static at the end of a broadcast day. The last episode of a tedious drama has dragged on to fulfill the prerequisite number of shows. Veronica thinks the season is over. In a perverse way, longing to die just got easier.

The DIARY of VERONICA LYONS

Plastic Sorrow

June 9, 1997

> The funeral was today. I almost didn't go. Rain seemed like a good enough excuse. But, I inherited some of Cate's guilt... and I didn't attend Alan's ceremony. His family has never been interested in me and he did murder my mother. Doesn't that look strange on the page! Plastic roses. Plastic grief. Plastic shame.
>
> One of the mourners was a mystery. We had a strange

conversation about life after death, so he was a bit of a nutter, I suppose. He seemed familiar. Nice car. I feel numb. I barely endured Cate. Uncle Oz has gone off the charts with grief. I can't be around him for long. I am depressed enough, and I don't share his sadness. I must be an awful creature. Not that I care. ~𝒫ℒ

"Especially do not feign affection.
Neither be cynical about love;
for in the face of all aridity
and disenchantment,
it is as perennial as the grass"
~ Max Ehrmann c. – 1820

Professor Corelli

Dalhousie University, Halifax – August 22, 1997

Professor Luca Corelli points to a figure within the projected image of women dancing on a carpet of wildflowers that flutters over his extended arm like the ghost of a tapestry. Botticelli's masterpiece dissipates into a misty collection of wallpaper pixels. His fifteenth century painting of spring maidens shimmers in a twenty foot arc, spread across a hanging screen pulled down over a blackboard the size of a wall.

From their glazed expressions, several students have been absorbed into its fabric. This is the desired effect. It happens on the University of Dalhousie campus every Thursday morning from 10 a.m. to noon in the old wing of the Rutherford Library. Professor Corelli's Art History classes are always filled to capacity.

From the back row of the lecture hall, Veronica hears a fuzzy snowstorm of white sound in a delightfully sonorous blur of intellect, as Luca describes the painting, 'La Primavera.' It's one of Veronica's favorites, but she finds it hard to listen. Two of her senses are out of alignment with her century. She averts her gaze from the painting and concentrates on the impassioned poet in front of it. Luca's voice is pure music.

There's no finer way to hear descriptions of Italian Renaissance art than from Luca Corelli. He gives the impression of an eye-witness reporter of the Italian Quattrocento by punctuating empty facts with as many human scenarios he can imagine. His lectures soar. Luca is a believer in the value of historic entertainment – his style of instruction holds and inspires beyond academic rote. Luca sees his students more as an audience for his performances.

It's every teacher's dream: to captivate a crowded auditorium of indifferent sponges into a hush of impassioned scholars. Luca is aware that he transports several of his female students to the heights of infatuation; he receives fan mail, but he believes there's no reason to subscribe to a past devoid of flesh-and-blood life.

If Veronica wasn't already invested in the emotional atmosphere of the Italian Renaissance, Professor Corelli would have won her over. He makes heady stuff of Art History 101. He could hardly do otherwise – Veronica had been immediately hooked by the name Corelli in the university prospectus. It's a name she knows well. She had circled it like the date on a calendar.

A buzzer breaks the spell and releases Luca's devotees like a hypnotized stream of salmon. Veronica joins the shoulder-to-shoulder hustle of students flowing late on strict timetables. Due to the hour, most blink into the sunlight of lunchtime and regain consciousness, but Veronica chooses to remain spellbound between classes, a prisoner of art.

The world outside the darkened theatre is unfair. There are no sculpture gardens and red domed cathedrals, no Tuscan sun. After an hour of confined bliss, Veronica needs a decompression chamber to bridge the gap between the past and present. What history buff would choose to live in 1997 when they could roam the fifteenth century?

Veronica's conscious brain remains tangled from weaving fact and fiction into reality. That they're so jostled together is proof of Veronica's ardent relationship with art, literature and the desire for historical truth.

Luca rejects the leftover semantics of the sixties idealistic romance with alternate cultures. He feels its implausible histrionics are a waste of spirit. He is an archaeologist – an explorer of old-world documents. His colorful take on the past is based on facts sieved from bursting folios in the Italian archives. His second homes are musty backrooms, where lost human minutia await rediscovery. Luca separates political propaganda, back story, and superstitious melodrama, from miscalculated dates and lost identities – assumptions must be drawn in context in order to reconstruct an authentic landscape. Guessing is too unscientific, but speculating must be intuitive.

Leonardo da Vinci's times are a five-hundred-year-old puzzle with only a handful of pieces. Logic plays a part, but reconstructing a faithful observation of Leonardo's world, is in itself an imaginative renaissance. Veronica chooses to live between Luca's timelines and absorb his interpretations. She senses close proximity to her professor has relevance to the quality of her future.

Luca's patriotic sensitivities to Italy leaves him no choice but to raise his academic performance to more than a cold read. He must be a tour guide and express the genuine passion he feels for his country's heritage. Some days he isn't sure if he lives in the fifteenth century and sleepwalks in the twentieth.

Luca discovers his forte for teaching, as a grad student of the Accademia D'arte, in his hometown of Florence. Years as a research assistant and curator in the city's museums and galleries kindles a desire to humanize the day-to-day truths of the old master artists who have become more like friends and family than cold legends. His intention is to portray his ancestor's lost realities that have become foggy over time: their childhoods, romances, fears, and losses. He likes to tell his students that the anthropology of art is essential for an honest historic record and to consider art as a spectator sport.

Luca injects a few personal snapshots into his travelogue of Florence: a series of small neat black and white squares with pinked borders show Giotto's Campanile, a piazza blanketed with pigeons, and a majestic statue of a pig. A student questions the picture where Luca pets a large bronze boar with a gold nose.

Luca smiles indulgently. "This is one of my favorite spots on earth.

You see here, a faithful replica of the 'Porcellino Pig,'" he says. "A fountain designed by Pietro Tacca, circa 1620 to replace an ancient Greek statue of stone, now lost. In one incarnation or another, it has been the mascot of the Mercato Vecchio, the main market piazza in Florence, for hundreds of years. Tradition still considers this replacement copy a lucky charm. In its era, a nose rub was sufficient to ask a favor.

Coins would never have survived the day, and in any case, the stone version had never been a fountain. It was situated next to a small spout of water, more like a trickling birdbath.

So many tourists rubbed the original's nose to make a wish, the bronze patina was burnished to a brassy color. The pig was removed to a museum for safe-keeping after being designated an art treasure. There's a rare copy here in Canada. If you get a chance, visit the Butchart Gardens in Victoria."

Veronica daydreams she is strolling the Florentine market with Sandro Botticelli. He wears an apricot colored cloak and the market transforms into acres of flowers. The stone pig is no longer in evidence. Sandro leans on Pietro's bronze statue and his face changes to Luca and back again. Veronica makes a wish – places a gold coin in the boar's mouth and the water gushes into the pool below. She wishes she could be transported to the sixteenth century and never come back. She sits perfectly still. Imagining. Breathing Italian sunshine. Somewhere twenty-year-olds were taking risks and frisky teenagers relied upon living forever. Veronica's life consists of breathing in and out – nothing more. Old age can begin at six if you let it. When Luca refers to several Botticelli works burned on Savonarola's bonfire, Veronica recovers with a start; fires and burning are anathemas. Sandro had been about to kiss her.

Veronica's perfect world is a microcosm of art gallery, ashram, and library, where she can transform into a butterfly, but when your wings are still wet and folded small, and when your horizon shrieks with red thunder, it's best to scooch down tight and stay asleep.

Karmic brownie points are tricksters; human desires can shrivel from the heat of too much attention. "Fate likes to play with its best friend synchronicity" Veronica tells a fellow student as they unravel over coffee. "Expecting a miracle is presumptuous." Poetic greed is still greed. Focusing on the horizon is supposed to ensure the safe delivery of life's gifts, but they often arrive as dark packages that tick. Opening them is a gamble.

The DIARY of VERONICA LYONS

To Dream or Not to Dream

June 10, 2008

      With fanciful expectations of mating on some divine level, I enter the delusion from the boldest and most naïve parts of myself. I am either poked by an invisible dare-devil's trident, or prompted by a whisper from an angelic crusader… maybe both. How long I am prepared to endure the unpleasant 'humiliation by dissociation' depends on my emotional stamina. Remaining anonymous would certainly help. ~𝒱ℒ

"Contrariwise,
if it was so, it might be;
and if it were so, it would be;
but as it isn't, it ain't. That's logic."
~ Lewis Carroll

Relative Theory

Halifax – 1997

Veronica may have seen her biological father for the first time at her mother's funeral, but his secret identity will remain safe for twelve more years. The name Alistair MacKay had stirred a ghostly echo over the surface of Veronica's memory and scored a faint hit, but she had become disenchanted with her ancestry and social circles in general, and had already drifted towards a reclusive life. Her Uncle Oz tactfully referred to it as a 'basement life,' and encourages his niece to complete her Fine Arts degree by including her on his quests for lost paintings.

Veronica and Alistair had shaken hands and parted as strangers. Mumbling abstract formalities over lukewarm cups of tea at a reception hardly represented a full disclosure. Veronica had excused herself from his ring of power and engaged her time with abject busyness. It was out of character for her to participate so enthusiastically with her mother's memorial tea, but instinct dictated she purposely evade the stranger whenever he seemed about to approach.

Alistair had remained in a quandary of escape or advance, relieved that Veronica's distance released him. It was a relief to have an excuse for prolonging his secret identity and accusations which would surely follow. He had hesitated. Waited too long for a perfect opening, and ignored the ones that had come. He decided to wait for a braver window of time.

Alistair's intense scrutiny had made Veronica nervous even though she had been charmed by him. His presence triggered an automatic threat from close proximity of the rich and powerful; two attributes he radiated like a pulsar. She had mingled conscientiously until she saw him leave.

Alistair had remained suitably incognito and Veronica had thought to never see him again, but later, watching his black Rolls glide away, she had been reminded of a dream she once savored as her future.

Alan Laird had reason to blame himself for Basil's death. Alcohol and guilt unraveled his mind for twelve years, and Cate had embraced the Alzheimer's she believed stalked her like an old friend. Twelve years of demon-driven matrimony proved long enough to unhinge Cate's cuckold husband. Alan had fed his wife quantities of barbiturates to tranquilize her for eternity and swallowed enough to join her.

After Cate's memorial, Veronica returned to the Shady Rest retirement home to sift through the leftovers of her parent's belongings like an archaeologist. She sorts clothes, jewelry, ornaments and papers: donations to the left, and a row of hungry garbage bags to the right. She has no desire to keep anything which descends from star-crossed dysfunction. A huge bonfire of her parent's residual flotsam seems practical, but Veronica can't bring herself to burn her student paintings they had stored for her.

The childhood photos of Basil upset her; cremating them would be like a re-enactment of his death. Veronica had heard that packing the leftovers of the deceased into boxes would bring closure, but fresh beginnings are someone else's reality. She wants something big to set her free from the aftertaste of her parent's failed relationship.

Uncle Oz had been Veronica's science teacher from childhood and taught her fire only destroys form. She had thought of that often after

Basil's death, especially on the occasions he visited her in a form she could touch as well as see.

"Basil are you here? I need to talk," she says.

"Fire can't cleanse a guilty conscience, crazy girl," Basil answers, from behind her.

"It's supposed to be a sacrificial purge"

"It will only release a finite amount of emotional drag," he says. "Don't kid yourself."

Veronica enquires about Cate and Alan. "So, are *they*... with you?"

"No."

"I met a guy named Alistair."

"I know. You should listen to him."

"He was a bit... nuts."

"Just crazy enough to be right... listen to him okay?"

"Look at all this junk."

"It's okay to be selfish for a while," Basil says. "Just don't get stuck in it."

"What good would that do?" Veronica asks, deliberately preoccupied.

Basil's voice gets louder. "Can you stop that for a while and look at me? Selfishness happens to be the shortest path to inner peace. Its not self-indulgent to meet a true emotion face-to-face. It's smart."

"Why do I feel so awful? It's not like I loved either of them. I didn't even *like* her."

"You're stuck in tunnel vision. That will always separate you from awareness."

"What is there? A Death University or something? How did you get to be so wise? You used to be a smart-aleck kid, and now what? Solomon?"

"Only the chemicals of love can blast away chronic sadness and the negativity of indifference."

"Stop talking like a guru. Can't you just be you."

"Guru means teacher."

"Like I don't know that. I actually *lived* through the sixties, remember?... sorry, that was out of order."

"Where I am it's always profound... and in order."

"Then tell me where this stuff is supposed to go."

"I can tell you where you're supposed to go."

"So, there's fate then?"

"But, I'm going to let Alistair tell you."

⁓

Veronica hates the measure of a life expressed in metric weight. Possessions have been her nemesis ever since she was been bitten by the 'lack bug' at age six. She collects things to compensate for the unworthiness she feels so keenly. Each object is a reward to offset the pain of failure. She carries the heavy load of emotional baggage, but the physical mass of material storage has already become a more cumbersome accumulation. No-one had forewarned her that the joy of abundance carried a curse.

Five weeks after the funeral, Veronica still can't process the shock of Cate's death. Murder is the sort of thing that happens in movies or to other people. Now her family has experienced three headline deaths.

As executor of her parents' estate, Veronica remains bound to the building which housed them, long enough to be stunned by the ugly reality of human disintegration, and generally depressed from the business of aging & dying. For the last year she has witnessed a generation withering in antiseptic hallways, suffering various states of mental confusion and organic decomposition.

The pastel walls are haphazardly broken by glossy posters of puppies and kittens too high for wheelchair level, and arrows meant to be followed like breadcrumbs to private suites of despair. No interior design service had been contracted to create environmental sanctuary. And the excuse for the lack of living plants is a feeble myth that they compete for the finite supply of interior oxygen.

A wave of cheap soup-kitchen smells accost the visitors who exit the elevator on the third floor where it always seems to be mealtime or the immediate aftermath of one, where the diners are parked in the corridors wearing stained bibs. The ward offers basic institutional hospice for the working classes. A death row with catered medication. It takes every ounce of biological fight left in the inmates to survive their 'compassionate care.' Windows open the designated inch, are slammed shut if one person complains of cold, so their neighbors must endure the trapped smells of collective human suffering. The staff looks haggard. It's a system designed for processing the elderly into the next world – a way-station for lost identities with no dignity in sight. It would depress the most enthusiastic of Pollyannas.

Cate's and Alan's deaths short-circuit Veronica's hopes. She had tried to return to the library where she got 'the call,' tried to resume her 'Mona Lisa' research... but it had proved impossible to face the ticking of the once-benign clock. She transfers from Acadia to Dalhousie, frequents new libraries, and concentrates instead, on the portrait of Ginevra Benci, a different 'Leonardo.' 'Mona Lisa' is banished to a higher shelf. A lady-in-waiting, for more tranquil times. For now, a thesis is required for her Fine Art's degree, and 'Lisa' can be saved for the future.

Uncle Oz comes through as Veronica's champion and she finds it therapeutic to continue her degree under a regime of anti-depressants while under his care. The two of them become more like brother and sister, visit Aunt 'Bee' most weekends, and keep the social world away in favor of academic research. Veronica's confidence rises and falls on a quiet calendar, and Perry invites her on his trap-line of auctions and estate sales following cold trails of lost art.

*"One does not ache
for mediocre things."*
~ Veronica Lyons

Cabin Fever

Dalhousie University, Halifax – December, 1999

Professor Luca Corelli's Art History 301 podium waits alone in a darkened gallery like a column without its statue, thwarted by innocent snow after an expected maritime blizzard pre-empts the one class Veronica treasures.

It seems impossibly decadent for Veronica to lie in bed past nine o'clock on a week day, but it gives her time to enjoy the space she has created. Her joy of decorating shines through the once boring rooms, turned into apartments from the great house it once was.

A small window hangs like an abstract painting on Veronica's bedroom wall. It frames a scene of bare winter trees, traced against the cold sky in a pattern of drunken black lace. Under the window is an oval writing desk covered in an array of cosmetic bottles and a clear glass vase of baby's breath that looks like a giant dandelion head gone to seed. On the inner sill, the shapes of the assorted bottles push their shadows into a silhouette that emulates the skyline of a miniature city.

Plodding slowly across an art deco mantelpiece is an elephant statue, cut in half to make a pair of whimsical bookends. It's painted to match the rest of the eclectic furnishings in a palette which evokes the colors of seaside shells and gull's feathers. To the right of the elephant is a framed photograph of the 'Winged lion of Venice' – a twin shape for the window holding the lace. It shows a pale cloudless sky in the same proportion. The image of the famous statue high atop its column in San Marco Square, is captured by a tourist who got lucky with the light.

The lion in profile, crouches, ready to spring. It has shifted its weight to its hind legs. Its wings are open, set to carry out unholy orders, after all its masters are Mesopotamian kings and animal-headed gods.

Being shut in can cause cabin fever, but the first snow is always a blanket of peace. Veronica's mind runs a continuous program of critique. A lazy assessment. Decor is vital. Light reflects every object and is read by her artist brain. Images are exchanged down miles of circuitry to be color-corrected and edited by Veronica's, ever-vigilant, internal art director with demanding tastes. New designs are sent to her muscles. On energy days Veronica responds accordingly; on lazy days she makes mental notes which are re-routed to a perpetual memo pad with revolving doors. Her rooms hug her. She has never been to Italy.

Veronica's eyes video-cam every surface and register the contours and textures of every 'thing' as well as the negative spaces between them. Draped over the mantel is a long garland of fake green holly. Its spiky plastic leaves manage to soften the corners. The panoramic tour hooks onto the Christmas boa and fasts forward to a framed reproduction of Leonardo's portrait of 'Ginevra Benci,' a woman who's head is surrounded by needle-sharp Juniper boughs.

A message travels imperceptibly… one shape superimposes another causing a mental 'click' – an overlap match. A 'hit. A 'yes,' and a mental storage faculty files them together under the label 'spikes.' Another function collates it and sends the young woman it serves, a thought: Veronica is reminded of the due date of her term paper analyzing the portrait of Ginevra Benci. The thesis remains unfinished. It haunts her as an image as well as a time-sensitive assignment.

Veronica studies the floating square of art – a scrap of fifteenth century that clings to a twentieth century wall. Her research tells her it should be larger and rectangular. Some cretin in the past sliced off a strip from the left-hand-side and removed at least a third of its overall height. The resulting shape is awkward. Leonardo's use of sacred proportion is destroyed.

The altered format torments Veronica. Ginevra's head and shoulders indicate a great deal, but the hands are lost. The balance is precarious, and the integrity of the composition is badly compromised.

The portrait begs a compelling story. The questions of who, why, and when, are the reasons Veronica has pursued the work so aggressively. Ginevra is the left bookend which culminates in the 'Mona Lisa.' Between them is a timeline of masterpieces. Leonardo's executor, Francesco Melzi, had been the librarian who sorted their secret identities, but all his secrets died with him.

Veronica devours the textbooks that attempt to piece together Leonardo's life. Francesco had been twenty-seven the year Leonardo died, barely five years older than Veronica is now, but he had done so much more, and had been entrusted with preserving the works of his master.

The generation which followed Francesco, began destructively, with little to excuse their crimes. Francesco's own heir, ignored his father's archive, or perhaps intentionally sabotaged it as an act of defiance, and as the years passed, half of Leonardo's work and paintings went missing.

Carelessness and forgetfulness hardly cover the atrocities of ripping, tearing, retouching, editing, misplacing, erasing, and over-cleaning that have persisted till modern times. Even now, the rare surfacing of a Leonardesque work is more controversial than a cause for celebration. With the thousands of items unaccounted for, the experts seem decidedly sure there is nothing 'Leonardo' left to find. Veronica remarks in class, that some scientists give greater odds for alien life than the discovery of an undisputed Leonardo.

Finds are chewed over in factions of divisive debate, that mostly end in legal battles over value and ownership than pure authentication. "For financial prestige", Professor Corelli pointed out to his students, "the art world prefers its collections to remain lean." He had gone on to speculate and invite his students to examine the possibilities of a major discovery which would rock the foundations of art. "What if", he asked, "a second 'Mona Lisa' was to emerge? or new, undeniable provenance that trumped the biggest calling cards of museums? Would information be suppressed?" The bizarre sums of money involved indicated a distinct possibility. "Corruption eclipses the truth every day" he lectured.

Ginevra's skin is sickly pale. The luminosity of the eyes is missing. Veronica assumes it was once there. She has a sense of apricot blush-tones and an emerald flash in the eyes. Both are gone, along with the flowers she may have held. Leonardo painted the reverse of the portrait with an heraldic device, now off-centre due to the destruction. It reads: 'Virtuem forma decorat' which expresses the Platonic sentiment that chastity adorns physical beauty. Veronica imagines Leonardo inscribing it tongue-in-cheek. She searches her imagination for the missing hands of Ginevra... stares into the past, but willpower alone can't materialize what she wants to know. It's impossible to cat scan a phantom limb.

A free day offers an opportunity to finish her assignment, but Veronica's eyes resume their survey and track the residual room candy. Balance levels record a thousand subliminal hits. Veronica unconsciously spins every image into a coherent web more tightly each day. Her devotion to visual harmony polishes her environment; interior design basics are also pure sculpture.

Visions intrude for nanoseconds too fleeting to register consciously. The mass of sharp holly leaves had flashed the same impression as the cloud of juniper needles behind Ginevra's head. A short-circuit game of 'snap' had overridden daydreaming. An artist runs additional screens for chasing shapes, clashing colors, and misaligned angles. More programs note conflicting negative space, compositional integrity, the ratio of mass to weight, and the refractions of indirect light. Creative brains teem with neurotic detail: over-calculating, reshuffling, resolving, tweaking, combing – ever mindful of the elusive 'yes.' They stalk slippery perfection for the joy of it.

Veronica's visual radar is micro-tuned for symmetry. Bright reflections off chrome surfaces make her nauseous. The twist of an ornament against its best angle jars her senses. Her nature compels her to scan for defective shapes. Veronica can't help but scan her life as well.

Her waking fingers are devoted to ongoing correction. Under the widest possible autism spectrum she would be classified as eccentric. She is an artist. Her brain is skewed to visionary math. Geometry is law. She detects visual anomalies the way a musician locates a sour note above a satisfied audience.

Veronica can feel the irritation of a misplaced color or shape. Her sensitivities are linked to genetic reflexes: audio-visual-tactile-poetic-psychic details of exquisite significance shatters the garishness of sordid chaos. The renovations of sloppy civilization is a work in progress. The artists of the world are keepers of the creative flame. Society labels her artistic... perhaps a *tad* obsessive-compulsive, while her Aunt Bea is called autistic. Left brains always confuse obsession with passion. Lives that run on random awareness miss the divinity in most things. Artists are born with high-strung metabolisms in order to survive actual starvation.

An artist's eye is more complex than a fly's bombarded by a thousand refracted images. The fly reacts to survive; the inspired eye responds to create. A true artist ventures behind the vanishing point to resolve depths of field and fore-shortened bodies and to feel the thick intaglio of hot and cold colors. It takes a critical eye to care for the density of shadows and symmetrical harmonics, or to examine a singular dust particle that deflects surface light. Luminosity matters as much as a million dots of iconographic intel.

Overstimulation accounts for the classic moodiness of painters and sculptors, and extends to designers of every discipline as the pervading force that rules their time on earth... an internal 'feng shui' that lectures in endless code. These are the humans who shape the visual world.

Veronica lacks the confidence to believe there's a genetic link from her quiet calling to the renaissance masters she reveres, but she honors her connection to them through the acute awareness of organic listening. Every nuance of vision has a binomial response of yes or no. The no's call for physical adjustment; the yes's release a jab of rewarding endorphins. Stress levels drop in a room with a seventy-five percent or higher yes-count. Artistic habitats score in the ninety's... pastoral landscapes deliver peak experiences. Every trim and accessory, fold or wrinkle, scent and temperate ambiance must string together in a rosary of peace. Binary Y's and N's form the default blueprint of an artist's internal map. Creativity is an exhausting practice.

Fifteenth century masters had no word for burnout, but retreated into melancholia, able to slide under claims of emotional moodiness. Physical collapse was rarely equated to a creative mind.

While Veronica makes morning tea, the white cup reflects the delicate fragrance of bergamot. Its rim is a pure ellipse which widens or flattens with every shift of perspective. The dark liquid meets the snowy porcelain – light plays in the swirling steam. The poised spoon gleams – its long handle echoes the edge of the table, leaning from the saucer at a precise angle of forty-two degrees. The deep engraving of its surface pattern throws the Art Deco design into sharp relief. Veronica has chosen the right spoon… a 'yes' spoon… a spoon that will tickle the inside of the china with a pleasing delicate chime.

The art of tea is a real phenomenon. Veronica's breakfast ritual is only one aspect of the hundreds of synapses reading jam and toast, crystals of blue-tinged sugar, snow-beams on the unmade bed, and a flash of dust-bunny caught in peripheral movement. She scoops it up, removes this 'no' thing and the checks and balances continue. One of a six-spoon set is missing. Where is number six? This domestic mystery must not go unsolved, and five spoons is an affront to order. Loss is inexcusable. The lost spoon assaults stability. Her kitchen has wrong vibes. Mathematics rule. Five is a fractious number.

She is lucky to see trees from her windows. Veronica's room is on the 'fortunate' side of a century home now converted to sardine accommodation for students. Her view backs on to neighbors who have resisted the trend to replace gardens with parking lots. The house next door remains a single family residence with crab apple, birch, and maple, shade trees. The 'sinister' side of her building presents a wall of red brick from a new high-rise. To see the sky from there requires flexibility and willpower.

Veronica lives with a mob of university lab rats at the mercy of a greedy landlord. Judging from the cooking smells and music drifting through the modern partition walls they're all home. The dog next door barks her awake at first light and Veronica climbs into cold clothes abandoned beside the bed. She crosses the chilly hardwood and flicks on the electric fire. In the half-light it's easy to believe the fake flames licking the fibreglass logs are real. She can't afford to use it as a heat source, but the appearance of red-hot fire tricks her brain. Flames that can't burn read as warmth to neurons permanently connected to man's primal desire for tamed power. Real fire is an old enemy.

Veronica is attired in an absurdly long navy-blue pullover and a pair of bleached jeans shredded at the knees. It rests on faded blue legs stretched out, crossed at the ankles, and culminates in snug, tan calf-length mukluks. A fringed paisley scarf twists around her shoulders. She is the student gypsy – a centerfold of Bohemian fashion sporting the latest peasant-look fad. Veronica has not yet donned her rings: enormous extravagances of jet and moonstone big enough to hide behind. They are the signature of a creative young woman who holds no stock with dainty embellishment. Jewelry comes before groceries and art supplies. Fresh flowers before jewelry. Eating is incidental. Fashion is essential.

Veronica has settled into a contrived 'niche.' She polishes her look while she dares to emerge, like a debutante turtle who builds trust slowly. This way she tests her reception and is able to dart back into the sanctuary of her dark incubation chamber where she's sure she still isn't good enough.

Veronica pretends to believe in karmic rewards... that there is honor within the art of sacrifice, and still second chances for bliss-infused fate. That supernatural nudges from Olympus may reanimate a body forward into the light where one's personal story can be the recipient of a fresh chapter. Where the fizzle of a drab life meets the horizon in a blue flash of grace. In 1999, Veronica is the twenty-year-old who once displayed little flair, no zest for life and wanted to join her brother on the *'other side'* "where death is greener" she had said. Today she rejoices over knitted striped slippers and the benefits of cabin fever.

Ginevra Benci beckons from the wall, her face an alabaster moon that peers out from behind a gathering storm. The black sky has sapped her energy. Her auburn hair is brassy. Sadness permeates the woman's posture. Her shoulders droop. There is no engagement of spiritual health here. It's a portrait of vacancy, but money spent to visit her museum had been worth it. Veronica had felt so much more being in the same room; psychic space revealed a partial story.

Veronica's room is full of revealed secrets. It has to be; it's a sanctuary – built to comfort and picked apart to perfection. The domain of a bipolar mind is never finished. Never at peace. An autistic mind is fraught with traps. Hazardous shapes are polished daily into softer challenges. Veronica imagines inviting Professor Corelli and his girlfriend here for a Saturday afternoon cream tea. She visualizes the Blue Denmark tea set she would use, the precise arrangement of scones and éclairs on a white plate, the bowl of clotted cream, the square impression glass plate piled with red strawberries and their green stems ... and the remaining silver spoons.

Veronica plans to wow her teacher with her essay on 'La Bencina' – sufficiently sprinkled with historical fiction and fanciful first-hand observation. Veronica will give Ginevra a voice and motivation. She will allow Ginevra to speak outside the vault. Outside the bland flavors of desiccated documents. For a brief reading, Ginevra will breathe and project her emotions on the present world, and if Veronica's intuition is correct, there's going to be a meltdown. An angry woman bursting with spit and vinegar. Even Veronica has no idea what Ginevra will confess, but she is determined to listen. Cognitive psychotherapy for a woman in a painting who has been silent for five-hundred years.

Luca Corelli's specific assignment had been to write a description of a master's work, 'beyond the data or lack of data' and create a plausible iconographic interpretation. His express words were an invitation: "knock my socks off" he'd said, with his devastating lopsided smile.

All day Veronica keeps paper lanterns lit against the winter's dark. White globes and a nautilus shell break the shadows into glowing shapes of thin paper walls with wire skeletons. Two cats purr Christmas peace on hospital-white sheets, next to empty saucers that recently held oyster pate.

Not so long ago, Veronica had been eighteen, newly abandoned with life crumbling on the other side of her door, but she had breached it daily because it also led to a saner library. Today's storm disturbs the fabric of academic routine and Veronica still worries she might not endure past it. Not without Luca. Not without his history of art. Not without her imagination.

Veronica imagines Ginevra's eyes lifting to meet her own. She feels the contact in her solar plexus. There is a plea for help. Modern cameras fail to capture such frozen moments of psychic grief. Clearly this creature suffers from depression. Veronica decides she knows why.

If Veronica has to miss someone, she thinks it better be someone she doesn't know. Not a brother or a mother or a professor, but someone anonymous. She savors the possibilities of the befores, and the healing echoes of the afters – the hesitant moments: After the plastic funeral and the crude tea party that followed. After she's orphaned. Before the lion of Venice beats his burning wings into the sun, before the lace melts in the windows, before death, before she unleashes the rebirth of a tortured woman – before the sixth spoon went missing.

"I knew Ginevra Benci well.
We were not friends.
Portraits rarely show a true face,
because without truth,
beauty and virtue
are rather superficial qualities."
~ Lisabetta

Hotel Ginevra

National Gallery of Art – Washington D.C. – August, 1999

There's something amiss with the symmetry. Veronica stands before the portrait of Ginevra Benci and adjusts her eyes to the florescent lighting. Veronica is underwater, looking through glass. The painting is a thin aquarium suspended on a wire; the reverse inscription too precious to be lost facing a wall. The art of encryption is Leonardo's signature within a signature and the reason Veronica is here.

The perverse epitaph *'Virtuem forma decorat'* – chastity adorns beauty, confirms the painting's original proportions. Leonardo would never have placed the motto anywhere but the center point of a sacred square. The portrait has been lopped. Ginevra's hands severed like a thief's. She floats unanchored. A painted bust without its pedestal.

Veronica perches on a bench on the far wall waiting for closing time. A cool fifty buys twenty-five minutes alone, afterhours. Meditation with a work of art can only be achieved one-on-one when the vibes of the room have been cleared. She notices the disappointed faces of the visitors. 'She's not the 'Mona Lisa' they say, as if surprised.

When Veronica and La Bencina are alone, they are bathed in aquatic half-light that shivers life into the portrait's eyes. Ginevra, an Atlantean priestess working overtime, gives audience to a mortal unworthy of eye contact. Here in the subterranean world of the sea gallery there are messages to be received. Over the doorways are boxes that flash red lights in the semi-gloom. They turn to steady red security dots like the eyes of wild things in the darkness of a jungle.

It is worth the two-dollar-a-minute fee.

The DIARY of VERONICA LYONS

Life is a Wendy House

June 11, 2008

In Act Two of my life, the wind picks up and throws needle rain into the window alcove where Pico sleeps on one of his pillows. He stretches, breathes huskily, and smiles. The flies trapped between the sheets of window glass buzz a summer lullaby. It's an about-to-rain June day... perfect time for a tea tray and to sit high in the house with clouds forming and shadows of cool wet rain whipped into a whispering drone... easy to fall asleep or under a spell and such a good dwelling place for writers... reaching into the fantasy that we all pay to visit in theatres.

I can believe anything and spin a yarn that entertains the child in me. I want to Peter Pan myself into endless salad days and make them stay. Life is not a workhouse. Life is a Wendy house. Life is a playground. When I skin my knee I cover the scar with a cartoon band-aid, treat myself to chocolate and smile at the next thing. Glasses of milk with warm cookies resolve every last growing-up pain. And when I am crone-old, living deep in Act Three, I will still continue to hold out for sweet success and conquer the dragons that take dry women on rides of flame. ~*VL*

*"Perspective is to painting
what the bridle is to a horse,
and the rudder to a ship."*
~ Leonardo da Vinci

Second-hand Prose

– Jupiter Trines with Earth -
Halifax – 2000

*T*he day after graduation. Veronica's creative confidence sails into the Bermuda Triangle of career choices and is swallowed up by cynicism. Poetic ambition is a smokescreen to describe the paintings Veronica will never paint. Cold left-lobe calculations inform her she will always be a failure without her brother. He was the brains to her creativity, and right without the left spells instability. It defines the half-life.

After university is buried, Veronica gravitates naturally to the solitary work of inner sanctums. She comes close to throwing her diploma into the fire, but she hears Basil whisper no, and his imagination is enough to save it.

Veronica remains on general alert against small-talk. She keeps to herself: working, reading, and writing a thesis in her spare time that begs out of her in a stream of therapeutic consciousness. She defaults to rubbing elbows with other devoted introverts – happy to reacquaint herself with the sanctuaries of libraries and museums. The art of research is underrated.

Becoming a recluse is an occupational hazard. Veronica grows morbidly jaded on a diet of menial jobs, waiting on tables and moonlighting as a gallery cleaner. She juggles shifts of dull labor and supplements her income selling the occasional poem to a hacked-out snooty magazine at twenty dollars a pop. The fact that she looks forward to nightly debates with a ghostly brother feels normal. Baz suggests she write a book…"about separated twins" he says. "Write about us and what you feel. If nothing else it will be cathartic." Basil's vocabulary has grown up with him in his heaven.

Basil's proposal has merit. He will help: "I will be your ghostwriter" he jokes and they laugh in their dream. Veronica has other projects in mind. Old ideas that resurface from time-to-time and Uncle Oz has a fortuitous solution: Perry offers his niece a more tangible role in his art restoration sideline. One that comes with a salary. It's an ideal arrangement. Perry's laboratory cameras have advanced his creative hobby into the profitable zone and Veronica can double as his lab assistant.

Uncle and niece work compatibly, each supporting the other's talent. A surrogate twin-ship, she realizes later. Haggling with Basil makes Veronica a formidable negotiator. Perry refers to Veronica's tasks as the 'Lyons share' of the work, and she dubs him, Lyon tamer. Veronica knows that her life hovers over an abyss. She wants to join Baz, but he has the power to lock her out. Basil tells her: "We are still together. In different rooms is all. It's not the end of the world."

The edge of Veronica's revised plan requires her uncle's intervention. The best maps spin like a planet where no ships can fall, and old paintings are worthy of scholarly attention. Luca Corelli would be proud of her.

Veronica views her underground writer's den as a noble sanctuary and her hiatus from greater society an ethical stand. She no longer cowers in a hidey-hole like a scared rabbit, and much later, with her newborn responsibility, she learns that one's inner wild-child can thrive extremely well in captivity.

Veronica feels incompatible with the greater world and shelters herself from shallow entertainments skewed to popularity and beauty. She blanks out news of the day by refusing to own a television set or read newspapers. The headlines which sneak under her radar, enter by way of automatic computer windows, scanned peripherally to flag major catastrophes, and deleted immediately after reading like top-secret messages.

Supermarkets upset her jealousy threshold. Tabloid celebrity successes rubbed in her face evoke resentment. Ostrich fantasies serve no-one, and Basil chides her: "your life is a sand castle in the kitty litter'" he says trying to make her smile. She suffers from isolation sicknesses – too alienated to foster new acquaintance; too healthy to die; not confident enough to compete for independent prime-time employment, and not feeling attractive enough to comfortably schmooze with those who can.

Veronica is a world-weary, unfulfilled painter, stifled poet... the bitter unsung heroine of a life even a dead person regards as reduced. She feels shunned by an outside world – banished to an inner world by envious default where she is denied big rewards. The few small victories she owns seem unworthy of a soul that had once celebrated its share of unlimited duality.

Veronica writes in her diary, on her twenty-first birthday: "It seems like Baz has been gone five-hundred years."

*"I don't believe
in random acts of creation."*
~ Veronica Lyons

Second Date

Halifax – 2001

*V*eroncia and Niles Duke's first date lasts two months – the time it takes for polite exchanges of interested chemicals to decide it isn't the real thing. Veronica's emotions respond hopefully, a heartbeat before they shut down in defense. Underneath her indifference is the tainted fantasy of a lover's eyes, and lips, and kiss. A vision she holds as a golden memory, but she lets the dark take that dream along with the rest.

Their second date is the follow-up of stage-two flirtation which continues to be courteous from the diplomatic necessity of employer to employee.

Tangible Mr. Rights are a non-starter. Veronica is fixated on a love-story of escape: from 'lack of' to 'more than,' and from being alone, to a life of adventure with a devoted companion. Things a mere man is incapable of providing. The compassionate blindness of dating a dream compensates for the organic lies of love, and promises which end in betrayal.

Ghostly lovers may leave before the morning, but they're unselfish masters of intimacy who leave a girl feeling cherished. Worthy enough to make it through a day of routine slavery with the anticipation of a night of sweet comfort.

Jupiter is conceived on a night of celebration.

The Duke's Company Christmas party is a swarm of perfunctory fellowship. Veronica puts in the token appearance, kisses her uncle on the cheek, and whispers: "Are you having fun yet?"

"Any day now," he replies.

Veronica grabs a bottle of champagne and leaves quickly for a sane space and Niles watches her go.

Behind the solid doors of the boardroom it's another planet of empty chairs and a long table like a barren landscape. It's hardly domestic cheer, but more authentic than the force-fed merriment of seasonal decor down the corridor, trying to blast an aura of goodwill into the chilly corporate offices of business as usual.

Medication with a champagne chaser sends Veronica into a comfortable retreat. She stretches long, autopsy-flat on the boardroom's sofa, no different than the countless times she has flopped there after-hours. The blur of yuletide music recedes into cool snow.

Veronica awakens too weak to protest with any conviction. She claws at her phantom attacker with rubber arms. Niles takes Veronica's moans for pleasure and finishes quickly. Veronica swoons into a fever-dream where she is an embryo swimming in the effervescence of champagne.

Niles allows the hot water of his shower to explain what happened. Someone who looks a lot like him is responsible. He dials the water pressure to massage and leaves his face in the direct stream for a million years. The recent incident becomes smaller like his bar of soap. He turns, and the back of his head receives the same luxury of therapeutic forgetfulness. He feels safe in a glass room, blissfully separate from business and women and family politics.

The confines of Niles' shower make a perfect booth of confession where his crimes slink away as lazy suds. He shouts everything with brazen confidentiality while his brain is gently pummeled into amnesia.

Each lie drizzles down his body and drains between his feet. He watches them disappear in a comforting whirlpool of white foam.

He emerges clean and guilty, wraps his certainty in a thick robe, and sleeps like a baby.

While Niles showers, Veronica's still wanders inside a fractious nightmare. She burns three candles. Surely her brother will see the flames and head for home. One candle is for him. One is for a fluttering new life. The third is for her ghostly lover. Hadn't Prince Charming just visited and kissed her into this hundred year sleep? He's her answered prayer, but before she drops into beta, Veronica remembers that she's an atheist.

Niles wakes from his own nightmare with an alarming headache. In his dream, he was being baptized. A bottle of champagne had been smashed over his head while a crowd cheered. He had dived under the water where a predator circled him, and a net captured them both. He remembers the feeling of being hauled into harsh sunlight – exposed and still in danger of being eaten alive.

His day begins shakily, but after strong coffee, Niles feels reborn, and sends Veronica a dozen undercover roses to mask his shame. The roses are yellow; the attached unsigned card reads: sorry.

The day after Veronica discloses her pregnancy, Niles feigns disinterest.

"I am no longer in the picture. The child could be anybody's," he says.

"Do you really want to claim that, when you run a business based on genetic research? A DNA test is, like, ten yards from this room! It isn't a picture. It's a situation, and you *are* in it."

"My bank account is temporarily dry. You'll have to be on your own for a while," he says, "but because of the esteem in which this company holds your uncle, you can keep your job. If, however; there is any reprisals such as a claim of any kind for financial compensation, I'm afraid his funding will not be renewed. Is that clear?"

"You are afraid? Of me?"

"I am protecting my company."

"From an unwed mother?"

"From a... slut." Niles had rehearsed the word, but his hesitation fails to deliver it with conviction.

The blank expression on Veronica's face makes Niles ashamed. She is a great girl, and he is fond of her. She has never revealed his drunken behavior nor kicked up a fuss when he ignored her afterwards. She had even thanked him for the flowers.

"They are my favorite color," she had said, and he had made a lie of saying he had remembered it from one of their conversations. That was when she had smiled and looked at her feet. When she looked up he had gone. She had given him that time. They had formally dumped each other on Boxing Day.

She had never accused him of sexual assault. Their week of corporate civility had made the holidays more chilly than usual, but there were no recriminations. She had gone about her duties, unmoved until the bombshell of expecting a child blindsided them equally.

"I apologize. You're not a slut. Anything but, and I'm grateful that you've been so..."

"Discreet?"

"Understanding."

"Millicent may not be," she says.

"An understatement," he replies, and disappears into the woodwork.

Niles meets a maternal wall of accusation. Millicent takes over and settles Niles' matrimonial options quickly on a wealth-to-wealth society merger. Moira Salt and Niles will make a lovely power-to-power couple. Niles slouches off to compose an alibi to cover the past twenty-three years.

Veronica's pregnancy starts to show after three months.

Niles' reaction is predictable. He makes a gallant speech – a stream of apologies with interjections of child support and best wishes. He delivers it like an actor testing the wind – an emotionless voice-rehearsal just to get the words out.

If Niles is going to placate Millicent, he's going to need a killer excuse or a miracle.

He gets both.

Halifax 2002

Mr. French's second-hand store, 'Buried Treasures,' is cat-friendly, precisely because he is never there. His manager, Pamela Saddler, runs the shop and is quick to bargain, barely glancing at the selections through her thick glasses. Pam has to squint at the price tags she ignores. Disinclined to play bargaining games, she has devised her own system, an inexact science of accepting any reasonable offer if the cats respond favorably. The good stuff is sold in the main location, uptown by Mr. French, himself. The merchandise in 'Buried Treasures' has already been skimmed like cream: it's the repository of remnants, passed-over scraps, bargains, and seconds, controlled by a team of feline appraisers. Pamela's only instructions are to move inventory, fast.

Cats perch on shelves and rub against the legs of customers. Some sit in sunbeams refusing to budge. They're her employee-children, and any customer who offers them a kind word is awarded an intuitive discount.

Mr. Perry is not only a regular, he is a 'cat person,' and so it seems, are his niece, Veronica, and her son, Jupiter. Veronica drifts through the aisles with twelve-month-old Jupiter, cuddled into a navy-blue corduroy, baby sling.

The cats have brought Veronica's solemn child to life, and it seems as if Jupiter magnetizes the cats to come closer. Pamela remarks how they don't usually respond so positively to children, and Perry makes such a fuss of Princess, that Pamela is prepared to markdown even more generously.

It is generally accepted as an urban myth, that miracles of science periodically slam into existence from lateral mistakes. The times when left-field discovery is drawn to right-brain activity. Like the breakthroughs of genetics before them, Veronica and Perry stumble upon a 'Botticelli' when their minds are open.

The small painted panel is warped and scarred... an image of the goddess Diana, whose face is familiar. Veronica had been sifting through loose sheets and panels while Perry concentrated on framed works, and recognizes the startling countenance of a teenage 'Mona Lisa' staring through a fog of ancient varnish and grime.

"Uncle Oz," Veronica calls, "I think you should see this."

"What have you got there?" Perry starts to say, and stops, momentarily stunned at the painting in his niece's hand. When his eyes lock with Veronica's above the painting, Perry's expression is of a man deranged. All he can say is "Bloody Hell."

"This one could be good," Veronica mouths softly.

"I know this painting," Perry replies. "It's better than good. Do you believe in coincidence?"

"I used to believe in everything, until I grew up."

"I think you mean cynical," he says.

"You don't look well. Maybe you should sit down."

"You had better go buy this, I can barely stand up."

Perry drops into a creaky roman chair and reaches down to pat Princess but she leaps into his lap. Pamela is impressed. Princess Barometer, Perry calls the little cat, later.

Pamela is eager to fair-trade with Mr. Perry, and Princess shows Pamela where a desirable price-cut is appropriate. Princess says the price is fifty dollars. Skip the tax.

Veronica clutches the purchase trying not to look excited. She stifles the urge to run into the street, where the painting would seem more officially owned. Instead, Veronica looks casually at a blur of junk and searches around for a cat to ground her emotions.

When Veronica visits a preening 'Russian Blue' on the other side of the room, Perry is still reeling from shock. Disoriented. He hears a female voice over his shoulder. Lisabetta is dreaming, somewhere between Electric Street and the Louvre. She shares the thrill of discovery with Perry and sighs an invitation: "I want to show you the Vanity fire" she whispers, all the way from Paris.

Back in 1987, within Cate's need for sympathetic woman talk, Cate had unwittingly handed Millicent the keys to all her subsequent victories with Perry. Cate told Millicent that Veronica had been a half-child since the death of her twin brother when she was six. A strange waif with eccentric tics and airs. Mention the word 'fire' and Veronica pales into submission, Cate had said.

Millicent had commented: "Veronica dotes on her uncle."

"Yes," Cate had replied, smiling. "And he dotes on her. They're quite inseparable."

Veronica surrenders to the painting. Her Fine Art degree and a short stint as an art teacher gives her the stamina for scanning paperwork and graphic design. She identifies each plant and flower in the surrounding landscape of the 'Diana,' and correlates them to the flora of sixteenth-century Italy.

Veronica is divided between instinct, love and responsibility... drawn to what promises to be a five-hundred-year-old masterpiece, her son, and the money to be earned from successfully uncovering a lost masterpiece.

Art grounds her as much as it frustrates: the vulnerable provenance of works swirl in the disturbing anonymity of an artist's mislaid signature. Veronica and Perry have the torn half of a map or an underexposed roll of film. Conclusive evidence meets the grit of detective work where the educated guess is emotional speculation at best. "*Attributed to*, is an academic opinion with a revolving door," Veronica tells Perry.

The inner spiral of 'Diana's trial by fire; her DNA (Diana's Nebulous Adventure, Veronica calls it) transports Veronica to another world, and affords her a low research profile underneath reality. The work before her may or may not be a Botticelli, but it had definitely been executed by a hand long-dead, and that in itself carried a mystery within it. Someone had allowed it to be charred. Someone had cared enough to keep it. Someone had saved it from a fire.

Wherever it had travelled it had not been discarded, but conserved in its damaged state and eventually found its way to a shipment of eclectic antiques: aka. abandoned junk from estate sales and auction houses.

Perry and Veronica successfully clean and authenticate the beleaguered work known as 'Diana,' as a missing Botticelli.

Millicent stands to make a cool profit with six zeros. Perry and Veronica are offended by a pat on the back for their efforts. The compensation game becomes legal and nasty.

Millicent hates that the worth of her painting is dependent upon Perry's report and legal stranglehold, and his niece's claims of child support in perpetuity, and decides it is time to kill two birds with one threat.

Perry's inventory had cataloged the 'Diana' honestly, expecting fair play, but their instincts are crushed by Millicent's conscience. As soon as 'Diana' is authenticated Perry loses it to Millicent's vault where it languishes in dispute – a frozen asset awaiting trial. Perry blames himself for using his company expense account to purchase the painting.

It had taken twenty-one years after meeting Millicent, for Perry to realize that Millicent had declared war the first time they shook hands. A war that left him festering under the auspices of royal servitude. Millicent's soured sponsorship had come swiftly enough after Charles' kid brother, Niles, stepped in. Perry gained an eager young ally the same year he lost Cate. The same year that he became a surrogate father to Veronica. The same year Millicent decided it was time to name Niles, her heir.

Halifax – 2003

After the birth of his son, Niles had found himself weakening. He is rebuked by three women: his mother, his wife and his mother-in-law, but eighteen months later, Millicent has an excuse to act more indignant: Jupiter is not quite 'right.'

Niles' marriage had lasted less than that. Now, he has alimony payments.

Jupiter's condition is irreversible. "Autism runs in your family not mine," Niles says. There's no counter to his declarations. It's true. It's an accusation. "Contrary to our recent renewal of friendship, you are..."

"Out of the big picture?" Veronica finishes.

"Well, I want to be friends," he says.

"Really. You can pretend whatever you want as long as I'm not out of the 'Diana' picture. I found her. I don't need my boss to be my best friend. I work here. And I'm due a bonus from that painting. If you want to play footsy with 'Diana,' you can expect a lawsuit."

"Well, technically we bought her, so..."

"Technically, you're an asshole."

"Jupiter will be taken care of, but mother thinks he should be in a mental institution."

"This place is a mental institution. I wouldn't leave my son alone here for a second. I don't need your money. I earn mine fairly. My instincts recognized that painting. Not yours, and not your mother's."

Veronica believes she needs a father figure to support baby Jupiter. She will settle for any breadwinner – anyone kind will do.

Halifax – 2004

While Perry defends his right to the 'Diana' painting, Veronica acts as his paralegal assistant and Jupiter receives the necessary care he needs from specialists. Perry has even more incentive to study his infant nephew. Veronica is in the no-win of financial dependence, and surrenders. She uses work as an additional sedative and sieves the internet like an archaeologist. One day it's to dissect the provenance of art and another it's to shake down the genetic data from the Lyons' computer base into graphic charts. Veronica welcomes the long hours, and gradually the humiliation of Niles' abandonment recedes, but over-thinking her lack of options and Jupiter's future, seethes into a slow fuse of depression, and while her uncle's counterclaim reaches a breakthrough, Veronica heads for a breakdown. Alzheimer's-in-waiting shadows her – a mother/daughter relationship taken to extremes, in death after life – or is it a karmic glitch necessary to clear a pathway of higher healing? Perry thinks so. He's seen it before. Denying the truth of non-local medical remissions requires an open mind, and he is a scientist who is living a miracle.

Jupiter's challenges are as great as the painting struggling for identity, and if it hadn't been for the Botticelli, and because of the Botticelli, Veronica feels she might have joined Cate.

Humility has a bitter aftertaste. Hate, the collective cruelties of the legal system, and fate, eventually burst Veronica's reigned-in life, and Perry has a more immediate problem to contend with. Millicent and Niles call a meeting to discuss a solution, and Perry first hears the deal to send Veronica and Jupiter to the far side of the country.

Out of options, Perry negotiates a European vacation for Veronica and Jupiter to spare them the agonies of moving. He proposes their effects are shipped west and unloaded in a property of his approval... not in the hot valley of the Okanagan or the grey cement slide of Vancouver, but near the fresh open sea. He chooses the core of Vancouver Island's, Victoria.

Millicent reminds Perry the house in Victoria could be purchased later, and is worth more than the commission he and Veronica claim, but Perry has the accumulation of lawyer's fees to pay. The Dukes will make the legal bills disappear if Perry extends his niece's stay to five years. They also agree to continue to pay for Beatrice Lyons expenses as well as Jupiter's care in institutions of his choice, providing Niles connection to Jupiter is erased.

Veronica and Jupiter must stay three-thousand-miles distant, on the other side of Canada, and Perry gives up all claims to 'Diana.' Halifax and Victoria are the bookends which hold the deal together. Under litigation, 'Diana' is a prisoner, barred from sale.

"It isn't enough," Perry says. "It will never be enough."

Halifax – 2008

Veronica plays no for days, holding out for more, until she strikes the bigger deal in her uncle's favor. Millicent gets to play puppeteer a little longer. Three full years of guaranteed funding for Perry's life's-work will continue. Niles will survive his nuptial demotion, and Veronica's pride is diffused with fake grace. Oz says he will join Veronica and Jupiter when he takes an early retirement. "In three years," he says.

"And Aunt Bea?" Veronica asks. "Aunt Bea will come too," he says. "No-one gets left behind."

Veronica had shutdown six years ago, one hope at a time. Sacrifices of sleep, and laughter, and trust, had been lost in the fog of motherhood. She had come to believe her choices were made without her. Basic needs were all she had left, but lately Veronica realizes the beauty of this statement. Her possessions are neatly boxed and on the road. She has all she needs without them. Her pets are safe. Jupiter is excited, and she owns two sets of plane tickets in a flight bag for three horizons: London, Paris and Victoria.

There's an art to leaving home. The mixed message of see-you-later, lodges in the language of goodbye. Veronica wants something fine to take away. Basil will know what to do. His gravesite during an electrical storm seems contrived, but Veronica is familiar with surreal moments. Her sunflower umbrella has been replaced by a design of Vincent's, 'Starry Night.'

Veronica addresses the name Basil etched into the flat granite marker.

"So, I guess I'm leaving."

"Not without me," Basil replies.

"Of course not... I have to fly," she says.

"You'll be fine, crazy girl."

"This storm is a tad Gothic," Veronica comments.

"There has to be a reason for that, don't you think?"

"I have the impression something strange will happen in Paris," Veronica says.

"Well, it is the home of impressionism. The impressionists were strange. You can see your new umbrella in its original state."

"But London and Stonehenge first... then the Louvre.

"The best for last."

"Race you to the car."

Back at the apartment, thunder cracks the dry sky into grey shards. Weather pours down. The elemental battle of heaven and earth is a thing that's deliciously out of Veronica's control. She joins it outside. Dares it to zap her to smithereens. Her laughter feels good. The drench of a noon-dark storm soaks her black T-shirt emblazoned with the words: 'I'm Outta Here' printed in white, her khaki cargo pants, and her gold pixie hair streaked with brown stripes. A tigress in the rain.

Water catches in Veronica's eyelashes and polishes her upturned face. She captures some drops on her tongue and tastes minerals and clouds and birds. She rubs it into her hands. Turns slowly. Clockwise arms embrace the last downpour. The trees of Phoenix Street swim behind a curtain of needle rain. The gutters flow. Rivers of homely tears channel down the parched tarmac and over the toes of her new running shoes. Nikes wrapped in guilt – a parting extravagance from Niles that arrived with another Spartan message that read: Thanks.

Veronica surrenders to the puddles. She splashes and whoops – the facsimile of play she remembers as a carefree child of five. She lies back on the sponge of grass, spread-eagled, and makes rain-angels that evade capture. The rain covers her like a blanket.

The 'going away gift' storm, is upgraded to hurricane urgency. Back in her hotel room, Veronica stays in character and sits in a bathtub of tepid water, fully clothed, eyes closed. She dims the red heat lamps, adjusts the whirlpool jets to gentle, and pretends she is listening to a tape of thunder sound effects. This is what she will carry with her; a raw Maritime tempest with flashes of karmic whiplash, entrail-deep, although where she's going is rain-forest-wet nine months of the year. One could carry a pregnancy full term and never be dry on Vancouver Island.

PART SEVEN
Second Choices

'All the world's a stage,
And all the men and women merely players:
They have their exits and their entrances;
And one man in his time plays many parts…'
~ William Shakespeare

> *"Alice tried to fancy*
> *what the flame of a candle is like*
> *after the candle is blown out,*
> *for she could not remember*
> *ever having seen such a thing."*
> ~ Lewis Carroll

Farewell to Nova Scotia

~ Halifax – March 25, 2008 ~

*V*eronica calls out: "After I get there I will get some quality sleep."

Perry looks away from his niece with love and concern. He has looked at her this way for eleven years. He holds an empty envelope against his cheek and taps it against his lips before he answers.

"Goodnight little Toto," he says.

The upper left hand corner of the Monday envelope reads: the Duke Institute of Gerontology. The right hand bears a fresh stamp. Inter-departmental communication is too fast. The letter had been posted after the close of business week. Its contents seal the deal. A certified cheque now lies, crisply folded, behind the row of pens in his lab coat pocket. Its illegible signature is a power-scrawl, the indelible statement of a miser. The letters M and D, are worked into a malefic knot of black ink that hates to release money. Millicent Duke chooses to misunderstand the finer nuances of the term 'silent' in silent partner.

The white lab coat Perry wears is blue in the shadows. He looks across the room at his niece framed in the arch of a doorway. The right side of her hair and cheek are traced in a violet line. The dark hall-way pushes her forward into the light. It defines her. She looks like a Flemish masterpiece.

"I will miss you and Jupe," he says.

Perry has been waiting to air his regrets one last time. "Missing was always too small a word to convey the heartbreak of my sister's death," he says.

"Yes," she says. "I know."

"And your father's," he adds.

Veronica corrects him: "Stepfather's."

Perry turns away and looks through his own reflection in the dark window. "I can't get the 'Diana' out of my mind," he says.

"Sometimes I can't either," Veronica says, "but I don't want to be given a reason to stay. I'm chicken enough to be persuaded. The logic of going is perfect. Give me this one thing... to look courageous even though I'm a coward. I'm not equipped to withstand feeling scared all the time. Over there, in Victoria, I'm free; I'm safe. You know I want to do something brave. Something symbolic and sacrificial."

Veronica steps back into the protection of the hall where her uncle can't see her eyes. The purple corona disappears now that she's a shape in the dark. She wants no more debating, but he deserves some time. Out of character, Perry chooses discussion over solitude.

"It's a completely inadequate expression to cover the tragedy of losing the rest of my family. Lost is a pathetic human cry to throw against such calamity. I will miss you both. Missing implies the loss of casual things. You and Jupiter are not casual things," he says. "I promised your mother ... *and* your father."

The word father implies Alistair. Perry offers it as an anonymous hook, but Veronica is too keyed-up to notice.

"Three years isn't so long," Veronica says, "you can visit."

"I disagree."

"Consider Friday as just another work day. I will be away on a little business retreat. 'Pushing the boat out' is the next logical step. It's about time. It's my lifeboat... Jupe's and mine," she says. "And yours, Captain Oz."

"I'm supposed to be your guardian, Toto."

"British Columbia is a new world. As I see it, Victoria will be a finely-tuned space. Jupe won't be continually rejected by his father; I

366   SECOND LISA *One*   V KNOX

won't be suffocated with bills for a year, and maybe I can catch them up. Your work continues, so you can get closer to reversing this shitty curse. It takes big money to finish what you started. Jupiter and I need you... and you have our backs, which, as I recall, is the essence of guardianship."

Veronica's hands are on the door. The thought: "I need my pills," keeps her focused.

"I've got to get Jupiter from his art class" she says, talking into the door. "Duke money funds the autism. You can't give that up." She turns away from her escape route and lifts her eyes to Perry's face. "I thought you mathematicians loved that. A little elegance in a universe of suffering. Besides, your life work gets erased in bankruptcy court if you don't deposit that cheque. How will that help Jupiter? How will that make things right?"

Perry reverts to Uncle Oz. "Niles is bluffing," he says. "His mother put him up to it. Millicent wants my cooperation as well as my credentials. They need me."

"Millicent wants control. She won't allow herself to need you. She can't blink first. That would kill her. Screw what it *feels* like. Take her money. Use it to control the work. If you don't, she'll destroy what's left of us after the lawyers are done."

Perry removes the cheque, unfolds it slowly and holds it towards her. It makes a papery snap when he flexes its length several times.

"I can tear this up right now."

"Now *you're* bluffing" Veronica says. When her uncle resorts to even the mildest of threats, he is out of his comfort zone. He can't play poker. He can't act tough. If he could negotiate fair deals they wouldn't be in financial crisis living hand-to-mouth in a lousy walk-up. She needs to pick up Jupiter and drive home before she can take some meds against the spinning night. Her brain is on fire.

Veronica speaks across the emotional static between them. "Don't worry."

Conversations rarely end the other side of a closed door. What Perry should have said whispers wiser comebacks and a stronger case. What Veronica could have said loops like a tape. Her thoughts feel like a row of prayer flags flapping in Nepal, buffeted by high-altitude winds, torn, tattered, bright triangles. The heat of the car feels oppressive. She opens a window to take in cold air laced with road fumes. It hits her face like a blessing and cuts the impression of altitude sickness in a quick brutal slap.

"I just need my pills," she says, to her eyes in the rear-view mirror.

Perry's missed opportunities lie anaesthetized in plain brown wrappers, left somewhere he can't quite place. When Veronica goes, things will be different. He will squeeze the Dukes like a sponge. He will play dirty. Hide his ace card. He will trickle his finds to his benefactress and hire the best lawyer… again.

Perry's anxiety and subsequent rush of enthusiasm, leaves him shaking. When he can leave with composure, he drives methodically, eyes straight ahead like a waxwork chauffeur. There are no emotions left. He loiters in Point Royal Park and feeds the ducks, watching them flap at each other over the crumbs. They all want more.

The nun sitting on the park bench gives Perry a sympathetic smile. Perry makes a wish and tosses a toonie into the pond. The ducks converge on the splash and flap their wings to scold him.

Later, a brandy jumpstarts Perry as surely as God's touch on the Sistine ceiling animates Adam. Mad scientists can do pretty much anything under the cover of eccentricity. His expertise and naivety will net potential millions for Millicent. The time for being transparent is over.

The new ugliness within himself cheers him. Perry knows Veronica and Jupiter are better off where they can drop out of immediate cruelty. When the mind surrenders, hindsight is beautiful. Veronica has been the parent lately. Sometimes a child leads. Jupiter leads Veronica. Veronica leads him. It seems about right.

Work is Perry's way of coping with guilt. He welcomes the fatigue. A religious man would call it penance. He silently endures the faces of his colleagues with performances of corporate dignity. Accountability to work is nothing to the confrontations of conscience, but he worships at the feet of science, and in fifty-five years he has never properly apologized for a single one of his professional sins.

Dark circles of insomnia underscore eyes red from forensic squinting. Perry's microscope takes him away from big life... life that asks too much and gives back contaminated love. It reveals the future of medicine and the past lives of art: hidden complexities of cobalt blue and the organic ochres of earth's minerals, trapped particles, and ancient fingerprints. The purple lives of crushed shellfish and insect wings were not sacrificed in vain. Sleeping cells give up their secrets without blame. The underworld of a painting's private life is a landscape of fossilized peace. Perry can dwell there in right-brain time and let the surface of business agendas somewhere above him, unfold as they will. This time he 'has' Millicent where he wants her. It's time to call Alistair.

"What do *you* want?" Veronica asks Perry, over the phone.

"Let's see where it goes. What else is there to do?" he answers.

"Let the Duchess have 'Diana' I am weary of her... of both of them," Veronica says.

"I wanted 'Diana' for you and Jupiter," he says. "For your future."

"Please no more guilt. This family has had enough for two lifetimes. I hate to burst your view of my selfless sacrifice, but I actually prefer the thought of living solitaire. For me it's an escape more than anything else. I don't want a life under financial pressure. I don't want Jupiter to grow up in a world that runs over people like us with tanks. I am excited to be a prisoner on house-arrest. Really... I want out. I want Jupiter out. I wish you could come with us and cut the strings to everything. Restoring paintings is profitable enough."

"That's not such a bad idea," he says.

"Well maybe it *can* still work out like that. You can follow us," Veronica suggests. "Just abandon that ghastly company after my first year is up."

Double-malt Glenfiddich begins to assuage remorse. Microscopic furies swim into focus. Perry soaks up the stagnant electricity in the room, and displaces his anger with an offensive line of attack. Thoughts of revenge turn a pleasant shade of optimism, but the ice in his glass tells him his hands are still shaking.

He calls Veronica, misdialing several times in haste before he connects. It rings forever.

"Okay, to hell with them. I will join you out there in one year. I love you. Enjoy Paris," he says into the answering machine. The message makes his niece cry.

Veronica and Perry are family bookends, and between them lies Jupiter. Perry will miss them both. He will make the sacrifices count. There's an art to missing. Perry Lyons-Uncle Oz, the wizard of genetics, art, and playing possum, can taste it between the waves of discovery. It feels a lot like courage mixed with revenge.

~

The DIARY of VERONICA LYONS

The Vanishing Point

March 25, 2008

I dreamed that Jupiter and I belonged to a primitive tribe of humans, huddled in a corner of jungle defending the right to peace from a race of territorial blunderers still intent on fighting over hilltops. But we are fortunate; our community is one of multiple mothers and fathers who share their maternal instincts and paternal protection under the umbrella of universal family. The attackers evaporate from the collective power of compassion.

I wish I could have stayed dreaming... but there's real life. The Duke's chess board looks stable. The cuckold King is impotent. Queen Millicent is always on guard. She and her knights of the boardroom table can indulge their secret couplings. Millicent controls the board. Her bishops can resume their clandestine bargaining with the devil. Compromises lie rotting where they fall. It was always going to be a fixed game, and Niles makes any wolf at the door look like a marshmallow puppy.

I have been to the back of beyond and experienced the invisible drowsiness of limbo sleep. My calling is clear. I see from an artist's perspective... a vanishing point on the horizon and the singularity of a blue flash where the Aten hisses into the water. Ra is content at the anointed hour that marks the end of each solar day. Sol Invictus is hitched to every spin of the spiral clock of animated time. I see the tail of a disappearing dragon. I glimpse the return portal; an ever-revolving gateway for the divine art of subliminal thought to enter the world of shadows.

I hear Hydrogen's computer purring with infinitesimal calculations of fourth-dimension mathematics ... the almighty 'I am = 1 to the power of eternity.' Jupiter and I surrender to the gods of bon-voyage. The rest will find its natural level. It's too crazy to fight or align to anything less miraculous. ~$\mathcal{VL}$

The DIARY of VERONICA LYONS

Renaissance Games

June 13, 2008

This morning I was back to fear and feeling unwell in body and spirit... all sick nerves and uncertainty. Feeling too alone and out on a limb. Some rogue thought snapped a last nerve. I called time out. Enough was enough, and I had the presence of mind to cry and surrender to its power. Waterworks are a wise way to release tension.

I am breathing a little easier for it, but one butterfly remains to keep me on my toes. Ironically, the feeling of desperate heaviness comes because so much is up in the air. How I wish I had the optimist gene. ~*VL*

Looking back I can say this: the rich are well aware of money's multilingual reach, but the fabulously wealthy are not cash-wise... they're hoarders of treasure, addicted to loot, and unabashedly consumer-predators with elastic bankrolls to prove it. They shop in a collector's paradise that defies description, where spending limits are left at the door. These were Millicent's people... the funders of crazy... the outrageously solvent, who know that money is nine-tenths of the law of possession.

Rejecting love had been part of Niles' agenda – he volunteered the offer of a long-distance retreat for a couple of candy-coated promises, trying to comply with Millicent's orders in a desperate need for her attention.

Veronica had been limp from holding together the hallucination of a perfect life.

Niles had been in a funk, and when a newly anointed king is offline, the wallflowers hold their breath; his business associates gave their champion a wide berth and huddled in carrion mode. One must wait for the wind to blow before taking a stand; declaring too early spells disaster on the gravy chain.

Veronica had run on brain chemicals with attitude that spiked through her façade of high-octane chutzpah. Of course the Valium helped. In her mother's day it had been gin. They called it Dutch courage. Veronica had reserve courage in several languages. What she needed was a flash flood of serotonin, and a good night's sleep. She has fooled Perry, Niles and Millicent, but not herself, not Jupiter... and not me.

A few years back, the tiny yellow pills of temporary amnesia once helped Veronica rock Jupiter to sleep while she wept uncontrollably into the crocheted squares of his security blanket. The wool had absorbed her anxiety. Then tiny blue pills helped when Niles started to pull rank with his latest blackmails. Tiny white pills helped calm her in the face of cruel bombshell destruction both real and imagined. Now, she has progressed to green and black capsules. I see her at night – a voodoo doll, arms outstretched in a gesture of mock surrender, invaded by pins tipped with adrenalin. ~ *Lisabetta*

The DIARY of VERONICA LYONS

M and M Monster

June 14, 2008

I must say, after last night I'm starting to like surprises. But last night was nothing compared to my dawn frolic with Sandro Botticelli.

I don't actually want to write it down. I'm savoring it on so many organic levels, that describing it on paper seems a tad crude. Maybe later.

Suffice to say, my news will more than surprise Lisabetta. I will explain all tomorrow. I have a place in mind that I think she will find interesting. All I'm hoping for is a distraction.

Completely off-topic: Jupiter offered me all his orange M&M's, separated from an enormous bag, and it reminded me of Nile's shrill of a mother. I can't bear the thought of Uncle Oz facing her alone. I wish he could be free of all the mess. Millicent still holds 'Diana' and the family's finances taut as harp strings. Staff called her 'Militant' behind her back.

The spiteful harridan had an expensive paperweight of porcelain roses on her desk, and I told my uncle that 'old Militant' must have looked at some fresh flowers and turned them to stone. After that I referred to her as 'M&M,' short for 'Mother Medusa,' but everyone else thought it was because of the jar of color-coated chocolate buttons she always kept hostage on her desk.

I was too excited to cook breakfast this morning, which meant the M&Ms came in handy. ~𝒱ℒ

*"They make poetry
out of their love triangles"*
~ Lisabetta

Immortal Romance

June 14 – 2008

*V*eronica's surprise has to wait. Lisabetta speaks first, and claims the day by admitting her weaknesses. Her contrition does nothing to alleviate the pressure of Veronica's hot date with Sandro.

"I lost control yesterday," Lisabetta explains. "I was twelve again, and I wanted it all back. Can you understand? Can you forgive me?"

"I can understand, and you were right, I was being melodramatic and not on task. I can imagine being six again, saying goodbye to my brother for the last time. If I had to witness a replay of Baz leaving for that camping trip without being able to change the outcome, I would come unglued. I guess we have something in common; we both want to change the past."

"No no no, I didn't want to *change* anything. I just wanted the same madness of first love to start over, when I was young and Sandro wanted my help with his skies."

"And I want the madness to end," Veronica says.

Lisabetta looks determined. "What I ask of you will not be easy. I want you to spend today alone, and tomorrow I will take you somewhere special we will make a party of it and celebrate a woman who actually deserves my anger."

"But I was planning to show you something special tomorrow," Veronica says.

"No, please Caro, mine is time-sensitive. An anniversary. Dreaming on anniversaries carries more power. I think that it will be better if I go with you another day. Yes? And I promise, no more emotional outbursts... our excursion will inspire you." Lisabetta winks. "Then, if you don't want me to stay, I will return to Paris, and you will have to make two more flights."

"But I have something important to tell you, and it really can't wait," Veronica says.

"It must. It has been ten weeks since we met and we are nowhere. One more day won't make a difference. I want to inspire you into a proper commitment. Jupiter needs a champion; I need a writer, and you need..."

Veronica interrupts. "I know what I need, and one of those things is to tell you something that may change everything."

"Thank God! Lisabetta exclaims, "because unless you and I change, you can be sure that both our prisons will win. A painting is as much a prison as a mental institution; if what we are doing now is crazy, then so what? Who cares?"

Lisabetta senses breakthrough or utter failure; Veronica senses commitment or being committed, but her loyalties are mixed, and miraculously, she has a plan B.

Only the 'Mona Lisa' appears calm. The eyes of the most famous painting in the world gaze inward, the true portrait of a lady-in-waiting. Some variant memory of an old saying replays itself in Veronica's mind: 'Patience is a virtue; have it and *death* will never hurt you,' it sings.

The DIARY of VERONICA LYONS

The Morning-after Pill

June 14, 2008
evening

So, I guess I've been invited to a party. It's a 'come as you are' thing which means a 'come as you were' in Lisabetta's case. One more day can't hurt my big admission-statement. Can it?

I shall find a moment to come clean. I was hoping the classic spot for 'true confessions' could stay in this diary. It's what they were invented for. Still, I imagine that confession is good for the souls of the dead as much as anyone.

I may sound glib on paper, but my intestines have tied themselves in a Vinci knot. A ghostly lover changes everything, especially when the ghost-man in question is Sandro, but surely possession is nine-tenths of the dream.

There's one of my least favorite words again. Being obsessed is one thing, but being possessed twice?... no thanks. ~𝒱𝓛

End
of
book
one

Time Travails

Veronica Knox

Subconscious is definitely the only way to travel.   1
I listen between the lines of my odyssey and ecstasy
scribbling back story in travailogue-speak
jet lag and duty free
back-trekking and back-peddling destiny for old time's sake

where wandering diamonds   2
fill the night sky with shining questions
in an endless why of juicy suggestions
thrown out by brave voices
once silenced by death and feeble choices,
caught by me, in bold quotation marks
out of the mouths of history.
Earth's heroes reveal their incandescence
as human comets of sentient luminescence
who leave 'a wake' of animated sparks.

I wonder...   3
Are the vapors of events too preposterous to reveal
or too ridiculously obvious to conceal?
Are the best clones given second chances?
Is it ever too late
to expose the times and shapes of fame's betrayals
and the weak protesting trysts of love's denials
that edge hand-over-hand at glacier speed
racing the worms?

Sleep, the great movie romance,   4
has front row beds in a soft theatre

where I play inside a whorl of moonlit chances,
spinning adrift within a vortex of emotion as a visitor shadow.
I reside fretfully on daydreams and nightmares
hanging on the angel-hair thread of a moonbeam
within an omnipotent blue nebula
that, breathing out of control, sends spiraling memories
to lure clusters of dreamers.
Wonder-driven and ghostly, I fly high, working the updrafts,
wind-taken, buffeted and invisible,
toe-dipping into once-upon-a-time
– an extra in the crowd scenes,
rubbing shoulders with box-office honey,
a fan, schmoozing with the brightest stars.

Gravity-soaked, I descend, a happy vampire of truth   5
heavily drawn to the warmth of living blood,
floating low as a curious passer-by
grasping at random perfumes of the past,
tasting its mystery fruit,
intoxicated from a gallery of true-faces,
to land knee-deep in the poison of a confessional.
Where sins are recorded for old time's sake in a dark box,
and the stinking lies of verbal blight
are bland contritions in search of sunlight.

I freefall slowly through particles of what-was,   6
to be caught on the spires of an ancient temple.
Now-and-then awake,
I dropped from the clear turquoise of an upturned scrying bowl
– one Tuscan sky in early April,
where a copper pearl perched on the fingertip of God
pointed to the dome-home of a heaven so tranquil
to inspire a seeker suspended above the fumes of rebirth.
Neither there nor here
– a non-believer balancing on a spinning sphere.

New rain falls on ancient streets   7
and slips down grimy windows of greased paper
yellowed with the forgotten weathers
of anonymous wisdom and dusty rage.
Primeval tricks of archaic light,
– the enchantments cast by eons of eternal faeries,
baptize the chosen mortals,
glamour-sprinkled behind the veils beyond time's portals,
who huddle next to hearth fires
stirring endless pots of soup and salted porridge.
They arise in answer to the church bells
and make their way to shrines,
automatons gasping and praying and bowing their bones
to replicas of reliquaries encrusted with sugar gemstones,
housed under-glass in gingerbread cathedrals
where the finger-bones of saints are dipped in chocolate,
and pawned to the lowest bidder.

Altruistic, and all true-phobic, and from being none too stoic   8
and faced with unrelenting, unfolding, and unalterable fate,
or something untoward I ate
I trot back to Zeno School with a new backpack
filled with scented magic-markers and remorse.
My back against a tsunami of tainted data,
I highlight my way through faded documents and crumbling arguments,
with acid yellow trails of pungent ink –
blazing a neon road to Oz – where the tall wizard of Vinci
forges new games under the shade of a giant horse.

I'm there   9
when Leonardo conjures a mechanical lion with a tin heart,
to wind-up a childish monarch.
But that royal fool, distracted by new flavors,
betrays art's patriarch,
and allows his toy to fall down the rabbit hole of history

– so a priceless lion-king roars down the slippery slope of mystery.
Far below,
the fallout of an archaeologist's best golden mirage
awaits in a deep cache of cheap thrills
and noble art buried by regret and lead apologies,
polished and sharpened into new enigmas and mythologies.

Samothrace's white Victory   10
– a statuesque goddess once dressed in gaudy bling
for the Hellenistic naval ball,
stands defeated at the top of the stairs, passing the time.
The toppled lighthouse queen's retrograde destiny
hovers, frozen in the space of eternity.
'Nike,' a cryogenic lady-in-waiting,
held captive within the stasis of a hermetically sealed museum,
anticipates the technologies of two thousand years
to restore her broken limbs.
An archaeological donor's card of marble body parts:
to transplant an injured wing
and heal the massive head wounds of ancient color-blindness
and the shattered windblown draperies of hindsight.

In the shady past,   11
when a greased palm covered the sun with backsheesh antidotes,
it unleashed the science-friction of dark and tall back-door anecdotes.
Tell-alls stained with power.
Leonardo was sideswiped by a brief notation
from the brotherhood of platonic accusation
scribbled in the wild by a devious malcontent.
A spasm of soapbox time, archived in amber
that spread dirty rhymes, and paroxysms of jealousy and lust
unscrupulous convulsions of raw spite on spare shards of paper,
posted without hesitation or compunction
to the ballot box of harm where truth turns on a dime
whenever a lawyer stirs the pot.

The music of Leonardo's lute, spills from its jawbone frame,   12
singing his praises of posthumous fame and his silent shame
Lyrics sighing over trembling horsehair strings and bats wings,
and pegs of ivory and silver tuned to a master's perfect pitch.
And when Leonardo was angry or I heard him laugh,
time gifted me the timbre of his voice
resonating with feminine stamina and masculine grace.

Only literary rebirth and relentless re-search   13
could free Lisabetta's caged bird-soul
or credit Leonardo another true iconic gold star.
I separate the persuasive fakes from the sheep
Balancing the genuine attempts
left in the dark by his students and copyists.
Menageries of honest forgeries all in a row
– an elite sisterhood of immaculate deception.
On the face of it, compliments to a beloved master,
but under all, the perpetual Leonardo boy
teased by family, colleagues, and the heartless sons
who had imprisoned him with the look-hooks of love.
Leonardo unplugged, is a warrior teenager of family dysfunction
and a later self-esteem junkie burning out his salad years,
both workaholic and erratic,
a weaver of disenchanted magic
compelled by law to wear the masks of love.
Leonardo, the consummate escape artist
who had lived dangerously
– vulnerable behind the abject busyness of addictive discovery.

I have stood enchanted beside Leonardo, the alchemist,   14
and watched an incubus spring from the flames of sulphur.
And awed by the pious, Leonardo,
dreaming a holy painting onto stretched paper with rust-colored chalk.
I have sat at his side as he scribbled in code beside midnight candles.
Watched him lean weary elbows upon a tallow-dripped table

piled with tattered manuscripts and the wings of dead birds,
and room temperature ideas left to boil.
Checked the Petrie dishes of his fresh thoughts,
brain-simmered and juicy, ready to spawn.

I have daydreamed on the banks, where   15
renaissance stories collide gently on the mudflats of the Arno
laundered over the rocks of make-believe, delivered to the ears of a
beach.
Tales immortalized by the ink of a passing teacher
who volunteered to reach into the future.
I visited a civic sculpture garden – a sunlit petting zoo of stone lions
and the rearing white meat of Carara's marble-fleshed horses,
and rubbed a bronze pig's nose for luck.
Seen it turn to fools gold from too many potent wishes.

I have tarried in the throng of a brutal piazza   16
guarded by the claws of Marzocco,
choking on the befouled air of its vanity fire
and the gathering stink of martyrdoms and heretics
and executions of vengeance and comeuppance
that dangled from the windows of a violent city hall.
And I turned to observe a young Leonardo in the bustle,
casually sketching the limp body of a traitor
as it swung heavily on political ropes from a makeshift gallows.
A common or garden window sill where we plant flowers
and the fifteenth century displayed frightening consequences
of involuntary justice.

I remember my 'First Supper' with Leonardo.   17
A table for two, set under a wild moon,
sampling thin-slicings of life presented on a golden platter.
We passed tidbits back and forth of a personal matter
which involved a second-seating of dainty dishes,
porcelain finger-bowls, and a boat of gravy wishes.

He and I dined on information bytes
– light snacks of vicarious fame served with a side order of lies
and the high-fat intimate content of newly spilled beans.
I was determined to make a meal of it
and Lisabetta was hungry for publicity.
Other meals were a dog's breakfast of false information,
but the tastiest was an honest buffet
spread on a table as long as the food chain of history
– an 'all-you-can-digest' feast of surprises
with a third course of just desserts and birthday cakes.
Leonardo and Lisabetta fared alternate repasts
of gluttony and seasonal starvation;
they told me so as we sipped tea and sympathy in the afternoons.
There were lengthy meals of tasteless rumors and the lowest calories,
but I wanted fast-food ordered to-go.
Stimulants for the road
– my short time-sensitive windows in a personal tour of deadlines.
It takes ages to read a mystery menu written in foreign magic.
I wake with portable morsels to digest later
– tragic leftovers carried home in a tinfoil swan.

Daybreaks and sunsets remind me   18
that Leonardo and I share the same planet.
His rain and mine were equally wet.
We both puddle-splashed barefoot through mud and water.
My century's snow is as crystal white and chill as his.
Our winds blow hot and cold
in-time to the same rhythms of the moon's pull.
The spectrum of landscape greens and sky-blues refresh our vision.
Roses and lemons and damp earth deliver the subtleties
of heaven-scent grace.
Our collective need for beauty spans generations.
The pursuits of pleasure and the anguishes of pain rack our nervous
sensibilities to bliss or shreds.
As always, we are slave to the chatter of an incessant monkey overlord,

prey to our own propaganda of self doubt.
By varying degree, we know the same appetites of love and fear.
Loneliness and sadness and remorse remain our diseases of default.
Hate and jealousy rear the same ugly heads.
The grape intoxicates as ever.
Science is where the first cracks begin to show;
religion is where it ends in the great divide of intellect or superstition.

But now, un-faith in deity is safe,   19
up for clean atheistic grabs...
G on the table, biopsied with intellect –
the ultimate social and moral dissection without prejudice.
The dire consequences of mother church's tortures and executions
are circumvented with human rights and reasonable protections.
The color spectrum is as constant as a rainbow.
And math, the one eternal truth, is a treasure of sacred gold
underneath creation.
Even now, modern art fights old wolves at new doors.
Artists in hand-to-teeth combat, up against walls of financial substance
not significantly different from Leonardo's.
Altruistic patrons notwithstanding
A good commission, man, or woman is still hard to find.
Technology sets us apart; art unites us,
but our wishes are still governed by the whims of flying pigs.

I have heard the breath catch in Leonardo's throat   20
with a fervent wish as he dared to cope
and seen his knuckles whiten with hope
as his ornithopter approached the edge of the void
heaving itself like an arthritic dragon into the sky
to greet the pale swan-shaped clouds of daybreak that cling
to Mt. Ceceri.

Faces have deliberately turned towards me   21
to reveal the colors of their eyes

and the depth of their need to be remembered
While I stood unobserved and alone
noting the fabric of their cloaks and the profiles of genteel bones.
I have studied the Sistine masterpiece
before the soot of a thousand desperate candles
turned it sallow from too many prayers.
I breathed in the scents of art and the violet shadows of the setting sun,
leaning against the campanile
soaking up the language of their excitements and grievances
– bereft from loss and disturbances
of abandonment and argument
or delirious from lusting and craving
unsweetened consummated love.

I have stalked the guilty footsteps of the little devil, Salai,   22
who remembered only the creative truth
as he glided towards depravity.
His boots of calf leather inches below the old paving stones
of yesterday's Via Ghibellina, feet desperate with evasion
– his fear flying ahead like a bat from a midnight clock-tower
whenever he sensed the authorities closing in.
And many times I ducked into a shallow mauve doorway
to avoid Botticelli, shuffling and old,
his eyes wide with the terrors of religion.

I am a literary sponge, there to absorb the first rays of light   23
which filter through the heavy scent of lemons
that wafts down to Florence from the slopes of Fiesole.
I stroll the inner sanctum of the city's heart
running my fingers over the polished toes of art
and the coarse stones of the Medici Palace
and saunter through the wide open doors of the studios
both Leonardo's and Verrochio's.
Carefully walking between the great tables
groaning with the weight of sculpture,

mindful to preserve the sacred dust of culture
that settles from the ashes of cold kilns
and the dry summer streets of Firenze.
I thirst for more, the way sunlight drinks from a fountain,　　　24
travelling in the armchair of my own room
to gather the August olives of Campo Zeppi
and weave green wicker baskets in September
that dry to domestic bliss by November.
And trimmed the wicks of midnight candles
on the frosty feast of Mithras.
I have journeyed far, and landed fly-on-the-wall obscure,
to watch a mechanical lion slowly inch forward towards a king...
majestically creaking toward its stately exit.
But I already know a toy species can suffer velveteen extinction
from the shortness of a regal attention span.
So I followed the blasphemous Leonardo, and the scapegoats of yellow dogs,
and the Templars with their sacrificial women,
down into the chilly catacombs of Rome
where cults and seers divined my future
and, insight be damned, I could at least put them right.

Lisabetta and I fast-forwarded past the girly small-talk.　　　25
I spent quality time reading her childhood palms,
calculating her years ahead of lifeline sin.
And listened to a mature icon wagering on heaven,
who had studied charts of astrological tendencies
to avoid the perils of earthly hell.
She was Giocondo-phobic.
Wary of her second-hand friend, yet trusting me.
And after a few visits with animated twin portraits,
I learned how a pair of oil and water women –
double Lisas, side-by-side,
deferred to the master's quicksilver vision.
Inspiring the same Leonardo
to different effect.

As Lisabetta's custodian   26
I filled a pharaoh's tomb with her yearnings
and downloaded her fallen stars into a ticking time-capsule.
Her thousand dreams (the macrocosm and the miniscule)
were crushed together with wishes and occult confidences
from the illogical to the phenomenal,
having been traced through the houses of the astrological.
From horizon to horizon
I met the cusps and the meridians of Lisabetta's successes.
Plumbing her inheritance of homespun failures and distresses.
Noting each delicate astronomy and hard-pressed economy
– the celestial and the bestial,
I bore witness to her zeniths and eclipses,
and held her hand during her oppositions and trines.

We shared worlds: I gifted Leonardo the miracles   27
of Polaroid and DVD.
I offered him stereophonic Mozart on a yellow walkman
– the same dimensions as the pocket-sized notebooks
kept strung at his waist.
The pure child of him revealed a man delighted
by all manner of workings –
from the swoosh of a deployed umbrella
to the stunning click of a ballpoint pen.
He bequeathed me his learning-curve diagrams and proofs
– a 'Vitruvian' display of sacred proportion.
I saw a human moth pinned by a lepidopterist
– the self-portrait of an alchemist spread-eagled in a witchy circle.
The art of anthropology arrived like a snake eating its tail, full-cycle
– the measure of a man's two dimensional ideals
contained in a bursting folio of sketches and in-situ jots,
and a leather diary which contained a blizzard of prophecies
and yearnings in code.
Inside, were lists of Leonardo's debacles of fate
and the lushness of his heart's secret poetry

– memories torn to confetti and tossed in a snowstorm of pixels.
They fluttered from his sky to my earth.
I have accompanied the extent of Lisabetta's fatigue   28
A renaissance woman,
lost in the surrounding ooze of da Vinci intrigue.
The mirror image of Leonardo's discriminating powers of observation,
silent as the grave's muted conversation
as she shifted her weight in a hard-back chair
while Leonardo laboured over a single rosy fingernail and a tendril of
hair.
Describing a perfect, delicate cuticle while calculating
a degree of ellipse that was never there,
foreshortened, as it was, in the perspective of creative license.

I have witnessed the citizens of Milan as they wept over love,   29
and rejoiced over the deaths of their enemies,
and survived the hungers of red plague and human pestilence.
I recorded a thousand fragments of organic imagination...
history and her story. The feminine and masculine dynamic
of plain folk, dazzled and besotted by saints,
but afraid of their own angels.

And while reinventing the dance of Hydrogen   39
with familiar strangers
I shared time with phantoms in a singularity of hours
hearing echoes of passing juxtapositions and conversations
floating down wine-soaked streets
drifting aimlessly from palaces and hovels,
and the love-stained sheets of the brothels.
I stalked art that sneaked past the guardian, Janus,
measuring irrefutable miles of provenance,
mapping the truest longitude and latitude of overgrown land escapes
and the intimate territories of a portrait's shining countenance
for me to discover copious copies of copies of copies.

I dined with Leonardo at his Last Supper   31
of minestrone and bread.
Watched a silver spoon fall from his grasp in slow motion;
heard it clatter upon an oak table
as he reached for a grail of spiced wine.
The air, violet-scented and electric,
mixed with leftover April sunbeams
twisted into an evening maelstrom
when thunder and lightning approached the Loire Valley
to play silhouette tricks around the walls of Clos de Luce.
Leonardo had received death alone as Cecco slept.
I was the intruder as Lisabetta helped his spirit to the window
where, to his delight... he flew.
The aftermath of the next morning revealed fallen trees,
unfinished soup, and the 'Mona Lisa's empty pedestal.
Abandoned art at the end of the rainbow.
It has been my quest to restore the missing credits   32
and the shattered business of art,
and paste together the pages torn from burned diaries,
and take mental snapshots of lost paintings.
Privy to her casual messages of contrapposto,
I have translated every gesture of the Mona Lisa's hips
and traced the secret language of her lips.
And the obscure nuances of her invisible eyebrows
told me everything I needed to know.
And once, Lisabetta saw me shimmering in a mirage,
leaning over Leonardo's shoulder as he painted her,
and she sent me an impassioned plea:
"write it for him as well as me,"
and I understood she meant Sandro.
So how could I ever forget the radiant thanks she sent me
when I told her that I would, of course I would?
And so, I took my leave and left her dreaming   33
in a French prison
where she awoke, smiling.

Glossary

Apoplexy:	*a stroke*
Aslan:	*the magic lion from C.S. Lewis' Narnia series*
Bargello:	*the Florentine prison with fortified walls*
Bottega:	*studio*
Buchi Della Verita:	*a ballot box called the 'holes of truth'*
Buongiorno:	*good morning*
Che cosa:	*what!*
Catamite:	*a boy kept by a man for sexual intercourse*
Campanile:	*bell tower*
Caro mia:	*my dear one*
Cecero:	*a swan*
Chiaroscuro:	*an object or figure in a painting emerging from deep shadow into subdued light*
Ciao:	*hello or goodbye*
Dimmi:	*tell me*
Ghirlandaio:	*an ornament worn in a woman's hair*
Gonfalonier:	*mayor*
Hypericum:	*St. John's Wort, a plant used in the treatment of hysteria and depression*
Ka:	*Egyptian term for the aspect of human consciousness which remains on earth as a replica of a deceased's body.*
La Vacca:	*the cow, nickname for the campanile bell which had a mournful, bovine sound*
Libricini:	*small books*
Loggia:	*veranda or terrace*

Melancholia:	*depression*
Niente:	*nothing*
Ornithopter:	*Leonardo's flying machine*
Piazza:	*a public square*
Predella:	*the decorated base of an altarpiece*
Putti:	*depictions of small boys with wings, who assist Eros/cupid and Erato, the muse of lyric and love poetry, in matters of profane love. * Cherubs are their counterparts who assist in divine love*
Quattrocento:	*the fifteenth century of the Italian renaissance.*
Runcible:	*a nonsense word invented by Edward Lear*
Sfumato:	*literally smoke; the soft hazy effect from the blended edges of oil paint*
Signoria:	*city council*
Stinche (the):	*the main prison in Florence. derivative of the word, stench*
Tempera:	*water-based pigments mixed with egg yolk*
Tronie:	*a portrait of no individual in particular*
Via:	*a street*
Virtuem Forma Decorat:	*chastity adorns beauty*

Art Themes
in Leonardo's World

Adorations: *the birth of Jesus*

Annunciations: *the virgin Mary's visitation from an angel, informing her she is with child.*

Ascensions: *an image of the risen Christ*

Battles: *political commentaries*

Davids: *images of the biblical boy warrior, King David*

Holy Families: *groupings of any combinations of Jesus' relations*

Last Judgments: *souls being judged to heaven or hell*

Last Suppers: *Christ's last meal with his disciples*

Ledas: *Leda is a Spartan princess who is seduced by the god Jupiter, after he takes the form of a swan*

Martyrdoms: *depictions of the deaths of saints*

Mother & Child: *Mary with the infant Jesus*

Pietas: *the Virgin Mary mourning over the dead body of crucified Jesus*

St. Johns: *John the Baptist, cousin of Jesus*

Transfigurations: *a vision of the risen Jesus inside radiant light*

> *"To sleep, perchance to dream...*
> *for in that sleep of death*
> *what dreams may come?"*
> ~ William Shakespeare

Author's Comments

It is curious, that the definitive snapshot of Leonardo da Vinci, is generally the magus with a long white beard, when what I find more compelling, is reaching back for the earlier Leonardo who was once a babe-in-arms crying for milk, a toddler who played in dangerous grasses without the protection of a playpen, and a mischievous boy with a pet dog.

Leonardo was also: a sensitive teenager with adolescent challenges, a confused youth with an identity crisis, and a handsome young prodigy, grappling with a relentless curiosity to understand the entire world as if it were a direct command from God. That he survived all of these stages amongst plague and violence, is astonishing, but without these experiences, our default Leonardo could not have been.

Yet, 'Second Lisa' must begin with the elderly Leonardo, because it is the moment of his death, when Lisabetta becomes ensnared and her story unfolds.

The end of creative lives are summarized by calendar highlights, but artists' works live on as random 'reincarnations.' It was the theft of the 'Mona Lisa' in 1911, which launched her to stardom. Until that time, the 'Mona Lisa' had been demoted to a relatively nondescript position within the art world. 'Mona Lisa's' celebrity revival (after her dramatic return) gave Leonardo's academic manuscripts their own rebirth. All eyes became focused on the 'miracle painting' and its creator. The population was bombarded with all things Leonardo: exotica and trivia. His achievements were harvested from scholarly documentation and reborn to the common man. Society loves its cultural heroes.

The vast 'Royal Collection' of Leonardo's folios, were once set aside, and overlooked in a trunk for a hundred years. The universal 'Renaissance Man' image, formed into larger legend after the media triggered (and milked) the 'Mona Lisa' frenzy. For a while, the portrait of a Florentine lady was the kite, and Leonardo, its tail. The tale that grew into the modern Leonardo myth – a giant among giants.

The works of the master painter, Sandro Botticelli, were similarly obscure outside Italy, unsung for centuries until the Pre-Raphaelites heralded his style in the late eighteen-hundreds. It is these random acts of posthumous celebrity which change the biographical face of fame. For an artist, life after death, can be infinitely more rewarding than the hand-to-mouth careers they once lived.

Leonardo's sisters never figured in Giorgio Vasari's biography of Leonardo, and his mother, Caterina, was a speculative first-name-only, byline. Vasari's 'Lives of the Artists' was published a mere thirty years after Leonardo's death. It would have been easy to trace Leonardo's family from contemporary sources, but references to women disappear first and fast, unimportant enough to document or research. Without old census records, Leonardo's half-brother and sisters, would be entirely erased from the life of a great man, whose life was no doubt interwoven with theirs.

Leonardo glossed over his family too, unless he wrote about them in his missing papers. Leonardo trained as an artist and moved on, leaving his peasant years to memory. Alas, Caterina left no diary to celebrate her existence and her son's childhood.

For me, it is infinitely more rewarding, to imagine how the impressionable, young Leonardo, first harnessed his creative talents, rather than after he had become the benevolent, elderly master. Yes, Leonardo had survived the upheavals of his time, and likely, never 'lolled about' in the French countryside during his retirement, but the main energy of Leonardo's extraordinary legacy, are his early years of transformation, which modeled him into a force of science and art. A force which eventually earned him the honorary title: 'Renaissance Man extraordinaire.'

The romantic version of Leonardo da Vinci, is a 'human bee,' engineered against impossible odds to defy the laws of gravity. He was seemingly born with a mission to sample knowledge, constantly lured from theory to theory before the nectar was gone, happily diverted by an insatiable appetite to document the world. To complete the metaphor: Leonardo's brain was a multitasking hive for distilling, processing, and filing organic quests - a slave to abstraction and distraction. Busy busy busy. He made art, but it was the sciences that were his academic honey.

I can still envisage the relentless sixty-seven-year-old Leonardo, an uncompromising charismatic genius, never quite tired enough to rest on his laurels.

I think Leonardo would have loved to have lived forever, and of course he does, by way of his fame, but wouldn't it be amazing to show Leonardo the evolutions of flight and photography, or the umbrella and the fountain pen? In my historical fantasy, 'Second Lisa,' we can imagine these things and more, through the posthumous insight of his sister, Lisabetta.

For the first six years of his life, Leonardo was subjected to a rough peasant life surrounded by half-sisters and female cousins. His stepfather, Antonio Buti, a kiln worker and mercenary soldier, was known as the local tough guy. One may surmise the relationship with a stepson, forced on him in a business deal, would be less than nurturing. Antonio's marriage to Leonardo's mother, while she was pregnant with Piero da Vinci's child, was a purely financial arrangement. It appears that the ruling patriarch of the da Vinci clan, paid Antonio to take Caterina off their hands in order that his heir, Piero, was clear to marry another girl.

An indifferent grandfather, father, and stepfather, were the primary male role models who influenced Leonardo, and it seems, instilled within him a sense of the unworthiness that he struggled with all his life.

I have speculated, that Leonardo's intense work ethic may have been, in part, a form of compensation, trying to engage the love of the father who abandoned him.

Certainly, it's fair to assume that Leonardo experienced an ongoing drive to perform above the low expectations his biological father placed on him. Leonardo was kept on the periphery of the da Vinci compound as insurance; an heir by default should no other appear. None did for twenty-four years. The birth of Francesco da Vinci, Piero's first legitimate son, impacted dramatically on Leonardo's social position, and no doubt, his emotional health.

This is the point where Piero turned his back on his firstborn son. Leonardo is rejected, ignored, and left to process his anguish and altered circumstances, alone. The push-pull years of early rejection and acceptance is a dynamic which could destabilize a vulnerable growing boy. A boy, perhaps already challenged, as the surviving records suggest that Leonardo may have suffered from the bipolar highs and lows of self-esteem, and possibly, the highest-functioning autism.

I also premise, that Leonardo was more than sensitive, and that he presented a rare form of autism I dub 'artism' being as he was, a creative-obsessive with a penchant for multi-level thinking and eccentric behavior. Leonardo's erratic work habits suggest he possessed a finite attention span. His projects were experimental breakthroughs, but Leonardo's temperament dictated that most of his major works of art would disintegrate or disappear.

I put forward, that Leonardo was not alone, and that his younger sister, Lisabetta (Lisa) was strong enough to compensate for his weaknesses. Female artists during Leonardo's time worked in the art studios alongside their male relatives as unpaid assistants. They were an invisible workforce on the surface, but I theorize that they would still have possessed a formidable energy, natural to their own gender, more powerful perhaps, because they were overlooked and suppressed. There must have been individual women with equal, if not greater talent, than their male counterparts.

Leonardo, 'farmed out' to an artist friend of his father's at the age of twelve, was a star apprentice by the time he was thirteen. Andrea Verrocchio, his master teacher, ran one of the most successful art studios in Florence.

Verrocchio's busy studio would best be described as a factory, and it would be natural for Leonardo to sponsor an artistic sister into his world when she grew old enough to be of assistance. I have presupposed that Leonardo would have trained her on his visits to the homestead, and that by the time he was eighteen (and a veteran apprentice for six years) that Lisabetta would be a proficient enough an artist at twelve-years-old. The most common age for a foster/apprenticeship to begin.

I have never accepted that Leonardo's mother, Caterina, was a peasant, but that she and Piero were contemporaries of the same notary class. In my novel, I write them as childhood sweethearts, separated by the legalities of the day. The children of such families were betrothed, often from birth, and it is highly-credible that a mate chosen by a formality could clash later from a conflicting emotional attachment.

Antonio Buti was away for months at a time. Liaisons between young lovers living in close proximity would be tempting and relatively easy to arrange. Therefore I have given Leonardo a full-sister in addition to the daughters and one son, sired by Antonio.

Historical facts are glimpses of shadows. Here today; gone yesterday, but the historic record reveals that Leonardo had four half-sisters and one was named, Lisabetta. She was younger than Leonardo by six years. I have claimed Lisabetta to be the only sibling with the same parentage as Leonardo, and that they shared a natural bond greater than the rest of Leonardo's foster family.

Some make it out of the cocoon. But a cocoon is a womb or tomb according to levels of self-esteem after the praise and criticism of others take it upon themselves to support the wing-less or the crashed and burned, or provoke an agitated spirit to self-destruct. For celebrities, then and now, fame or infamy is more mysterious than a curse or a smile; which explains the term: there's no such thing as bad publicity. History is, as history does.

Here now, is my declaimer for using the name 'Veronica' in 'Second Lisa.' I would have preferred to name Lisabetta's companion/poet, something other than my own first name, but in the end, iconography prevailed. A book about true faces, an iconic image, lost identities, and false names, demanded it.

The name Veronica is an anagram from the Latin translation: veritas (truth) and icon (image). Also, historically, St. Veronica is the traditional bearer of a mystical cloth imprinted with the face of Jesus. My use of the name Veronica is purely a literary device. No other woman's name would serve the story of the true identity of the 'Mona Lisa,' so well.

The face of the 'Mona Lisa' has the quality of a true portrait, and not a 'tronie' of an ideal woman-composite. Her likeness is the most famous iconic mystery to be trapped in the history of art.

'Mona Lisa' is in good company; the provenance of paintings is literally, a lost art. Even the attributed paintings, are often group efforts of master artists, senior assistants, and junior apprentices. Copies of paintings were made on a regular basis, with varying success. Admirers and followers mimicked a master's style. As Veronica says in the story, an attributed work is like a revolving door.

It is an extremely conservative estimate that two thirds of Leonardo's manuscripts are presumed destroyed, but it is possible that a lost episode of Leonardo's extraordinary life, may emerge from the darkness like an artist's technique of chiaroscuro. Revelations are serendipitous by nature: time still hides some Leonardo surprises. An obscure margin note or dry official document, or a diary of a credible source, still hold wonders waiting to be revealed.

Leonardo is known to have kept the 'Mona Lisa' by his side until his death. I premise, that during the last eleven years of Leonardo's life: grief, denial, and declining physical and mental states, that the portrait of his beloved sister, Lisabetta, had become as real to Leonardo as she had been in life.

In 'Second Lisa,' (a work of fiction) a newly discovered cache of libricini (the small notebooks Leonardo carried) changes the art world.

Veronica Lyons' altered states represent the artistic awareness's of the broadest autism spectrum. Are they presentations of imagination, reincarnation or insanity? You decide. What-if Veronica Lyons isn't crazy, but madly inspired?

Art is a form of reincarnation: styles and themes progress similarly to a genealogical map, and no-one knows the flesh-and-blood or emotional dynamics of another's life. As for little Lisabetta? Couldn't she have grown up as a sister in need of escape from the drudgery of farm life to become one of the invisible female workers in Verrocchio's studio? Perhaps encouraged and trained by a talented big brother? A genius brother who needed to be grounded with committed support in order to shine as brightly as he did?

~ V. Knox   May 2, 2012*

---

* these comments were penned on the four-hundred-and ninety-third anniversary of Leonardo's death

> *"When you want to confirm your personal power.*
> *Tell a lie and watch it come true."*
> ~ Veronica Lyons

Second Thoughts

Now Lost

The sfumato-like years between Leonardo's paintings become impossible to navigate. Francesco Giocondo likely bought (or was given) an original portrait of his wife, Lisa (Giocondo) which she took her with her to the Convent of San Orsolo when she retired.

Both of Lisa's daughter-nuns would probably have taken a different view (from their father's) regarding collecting and possessing art for personal gain. Secular art and religious subjects were at odds. By contrast, a portrait of their smiling mother would defile the solemn iconic Holy Virgins and their sacrificial sons. Lisa's portrait would have had to be displayed in a private room until after her death, after which, it would be sold, given away, stored, or destroyed (possibly even all four of the above) and once a painting goes underground, it leaves a cold trail.

Lisa's portrait may have been, at best, a frozen window of time, but at worst, a mirror – a vanity to be concealed before God, in a religious house where brides of Christ wandered on impressionable tiptoes. It would hardly have been considered true art within the confines of an institution dedicated to the sacred. Sacred art depicts the like of annunciations and resurrections and martyrdoms; portraiture was profane.

At Lisa Giocondo's death, her property was dispersed into the community (secular and social) where the practical functions of under-valued panel paintings were often reduced to table tops and doors, and manuscripts were left to attic mice and fungus in damp outbuildings. There is an historic sub-note-afterthought (hardly an excuse) that some of Leonardo's folios were used to repair a roof by Francesco Melzi's descendents.

There may have been no-one in the Giocondo line who cherished Lisa's portrait enough to keep it 'above ground,' or who bothered to claim the 'laughing Gioconda' after Lisa's death. It is a 'now lost.' If it is still 'alive,' then somewhere it illuminates a dark cupboard, abandoned, confiscated, and un-catalogued. If it lingers in a private collection, it's a clandestine one.

The pose will be the same as Lisabetta's 'Mona Lisa.' Easily recognizable. It will have the sublime touch of the master, of course, and the dress will almost surely be the same (but perhaps without the delicate embroidering of Vinci knots on the gown's neckline, and of a brighter hue) The pose will be a match because the second 'Lisa' was modeled on the first (painted side-by-side) – a variation in theme, as Leonardo perfected his new theories about the human expression. To our benefit; he was easily side-tracked.

Lisa Giocondo lived to the age of seventy-one, and her two daughters were cloistered inside nunneries, living apart from the world of art. Lisa may have lost her portrait, but she 'saved-face,' by gaining celebrity; Lisabetta lost her identity and gained immortality.

While Lisabetta's face captivated the King of France, Lisa's face hung on a private wall, safe from Salai and out of Melzi's protection. It was commissioned, temporarily held to ransom... and then it was purchased. It once belonged to Francesco Giocondo and his heirs.

Now it belongs to time.

Historical Footnotes

- **Leonardo da Vinci** had four half-sisters.
- **Lisabetta Buti** was born sometime between 1458 and 1460. Leonardo was six in 1458. He lived with his mother, sisters, and stepfather, enduring a rough peasant lifestyle until the age of seven. He revered cats and horses and birds.
- Historical evidence points to a separate version of the 'Mona Lisa,' the painting Leonardo dubbed 'La Gioconda.' She will be recognized from the pillars of a loggia which frame her, and a pair of reportedly stunning eyebrows. **Raphael** went on to use Leonardo's revolutionary pose in several of his own works.
- The portrait of **Ginevra Benci** has, in the distant past, been cropped. The lower third of the painting, containing her hands and what she holds, is lost. The painting surfaced in the 20th century, after being 'mislaid' under another mistaken identity for four hundred years. In 1480, four years after Leonardo painted her, the once celebrated Ginevra (Benci) Niccolini, age 23, retired to the country. She was abandoned by her lover, Bernardo Bembo, who commissioned her portrait. Documents suggest she died alone, at the age of sixty-three, a childless, hypochondriac, widow, after living forty years in relative seclusion.
- Leonardo left his signature on the first version of the 'Madonna of the Rocks' His collaborator artist, **Ambrogio di Predis,** had a deaf brother, **Cristoforo,** also an artist. From top to bottom, Mary, the angel and one of the babies sign the letters, L – D – V. Intentionally, either child can represent Christ or John the Baptist. Leonardo favored the underground cult of John the Baptist.

- The 'bucha della verita,' the **'holes of truth,'** were ballot boxes placed throughout Florence. Anyone could post an anonymous accusation against a fellow citizen.

- In 1796, French troops used the Santa Maria delle Grazie, in Milan, as an armory, and later a prison. The soldiers thought it amusing to throw rocks at the **'Last Supper.'** They climbed ladders and scratched out the apostles eyes. In 1943, during World War II, the church was severely damaged during a bombing raid. Several consequent restorations cover Leonardo's original work. What you see is what you get: an abused and befuddled, ersatz version of a da Vinci masterpiece.

- In 1802, during the demolition of the church of St. Florentin, at Amboise, France, Leonardo's mortal remains were dug up and discarded.

- **Lisa Giocondo** (1479-1551) was the mother of five children. Her two daughters, Camilla and Marietta, took holy orders and changed their names respectively to: Sister Beatrice and Sister Ludovico. Lisa's mortal remains fared a similar fate to Leonardo's. Her bones were raked from her grave in the foundations of the Sant' Orsola Convent when the building was renovated as an underground parkade for the local police station. In 1980, the rubble was dumped in a landfill outside Florence.

- **Salai** had a violent end; he was killed in a street duel at the age of forty-four, in 1524, five years after Leonardo's death. Salai peddled his own copies of Leonardo's work as originals for the rest of his life. An inventory at his death lists a painting called the 'Mona Lisa.'

- **Lorenzo di Credi** joined the followers of the fanatic monk Savonarola, called 'The Weepers,' along with his colleague, Sandro Botticelli. Both burned works of art in 1497, during the 'Bonfires of the Vanities' and descended into lives of religious penitence. Lorenzo later inherited his lover Verrocchio's, studio.

- **Sandro Botticelli** was reduced to wandering the streets of Florence peddling paintings of Madonnas, in his last years. He was buried at the feet of Simonetta (Cattaneo de Candia) Vespucci.

- Leonardo's manuscripts, in the present Windsor Collection, were forgotten in a trunk for two hundred years and rediscovered in 1760, at Kensington palace.

- There are at least nine known copies of the 'Mona Lisa' painted with the assistance of the master, by his apprentices... including the 'Nude Gioconda' (the 'Mona Vanna'), painted by Giangiacomo Caprotti, the spoiled child, gold-digger, thief, pimp, spy, and despot known as, Salai ('little devil'). He lived the life of a parasite, living off Leonardo, his gentle benefactor, for twenty nine years.

- Although Leonardo only knew **Francesco Melzi** for the last twelve years of his life, he made him sole executor of his estate, and left his entire body of work to his care. Francesco (Cecco) was a diligent and loyal conservationist of Leonardo's legacy... or what was left of it after it was ransacked by Salai at the master's death. 'Cecco' recovered several of Leonardo's works from Salai's estate. Melzi's descendents treated Leonardo's estate with considerably less respect, and the collection was dispersed for profit or destroyed due to negligence. Two thirds of Leonardo's manuscripts are now lost. *Two lost volumes of bound sketches were found in 1967, misplaced in the stacks of a Spanish library.

- **Marie Corelli,** 1855-1924, was an eccentric Victorian novelist – the illegitimate daughter of a doctor and a servant girl, and author of bodice-ripper/paranormal romances whose stories achieved a renaissance during the peak of occult New-Age soul-mate literature, in the sixties. Marie changed her name from MacKay to Corelli, and made a pretense of speaking Italian, borrowing the glamorous persona of an Italian aristocrat. Her desire for fame knew no bounds. Her novels were favored by **Queen Victoria**. Marie was a contemporary of the author **Lewis Carroll**.

- **'La Principessa'** (the Princess) and the **'Salvator Mundi'** (Saviour of the world) are two portraits which have been authenticated since the year 2008.

What Other Works of Leonardo May Yet Be Found?

- **'The Leda and the Swan'** last witnessed in 1519, in Amboise, France.

- The fresco, **'The Battle of Anghiari's'** lost location on one of the eight walls of the council hall of the Palazzo Vecchio, painted over, in 1560.

- A finished **portrait** in oils of Isabella d'Este.

- Hundreds of stolen drawings cut from **manuscripts**. The missing two-thirds of Leonardo's **notebooks** and countless **libricini**.

- A single fragment of the giant **clay horse,** twenty-seven feet high, which lay abandoned to the elements, scavengers, and vandals in the streets of Milan in 1493.

- The **mechanical lion** made for the King of France, Francis I, in 1515

- The **portrait** of a certain Florentine silk merchant's lady: The Monna Lisa del Francesco Giocondo, titled **'La Gioconda,'** last documented sighting in the year, 1533.

- And **notations** within contemporary documents: new facts, facts, facts.

Acknowledgments

This story has been a long season's hike over snow and water. Life come true in wilder ways than we can dream. I must not forget to thank my lucky stars:

My intrepid editor, Linda Clement, whose red hurricane of quirky margin notes – a fury of necessary cruelties, helped shape this book into a better place to read.

And Lisabetta Buti – the historic footnote to her illustrious brother, Leonardo da Vinci.

And the thousands of anonymous women who drove the arts forward during times that were less than nurturing.

And thank you, Leonardo. I wish I'd known you ... and maybe I do a little.

And for all the times I neglected to thank my parents graciously, or enough – a posthumous hug to my mother and father for their gift of time.

Referenced Works of Art

LEONARDO DA VINCI:
The 'Mona Lisa'
Portrait of Ginevra Benci (front and back)
'The Last Supper'
'Madonna of the Rocks' (London version)
'Madonna of the Rocks' (Louvre version)
'St. John'
Madonna and the Cat (drawing)
Leonardo's parachute (drawing)
Vitruvian Man (drawing)
the 'Battle of Anghiari' mural is lost
the 'Leda and the Swan' is lost
the portrait of Lisa Giocondo is lost

GIANGIACOMO CAPROTTI (SALAI):
The 'Monna Vanna' (nude Gioconda)

The STUDIO of ANDREA VERROCCHIO:
The 'Tobias and the Angel'
The Pistoia altarpiece
The orb for the Santa Maria del Fiore

SANDRO BOTTICELLI:
'Mars and Venus'
'La Primavera'
'The Birth of Venus'
* *the Diana is lost*

SCULPTURES & MODELS:

Verrochio's 'David'

Michelangelo's 'David'

Verrochio's 'Woman with the Flowers'

Leonardo's 'Angel of Gennaro'

Leonardo's Giant Horse is lost

Leonardo's Ornithopters are lost

Leonardo's Mechanical Lion is lost, but there are modern reconstructions

The 'Nike of Samothrace' the head, arms, and one wing are lost

Pietro Tacca's 'Il Porcellina' (The Market Boar)

The original Hellenistic Antiquity 'Market Pig' is lost

About the Author

*V*eronica Knox has a Fine Arts Degree from the University of Alberta, where she studied Art History, Classical Studies, and Painting. In her career as a graphic designer, illustrator, private art teacher, and 'fine artist,' she has also worked with the brain-injured and autistic, developing new theories of hand-to-eye-to-mind connection.

Veronica lives on the west coast of Canada, supporting local animal rescue shelters, painting, writing, editing other author's novels, and championing the conservation of tigers and elephants, and their habitats.

Her artwork and visuals to support 'Second Lisa' may be viewed on her websites and links:

www.veronicaknox.com